Heaven Official's Blessing
TIAN GUAN CI FU

5

WRITTEN BY
Mo Xiang Tong Xiu

TRANSLATED BY
Suika & Pengie (EDITOR)

INTERIOR ILLUSTRATIONS BY
ZeldaCW

Seven Seas Entertainment

HEAVEN OFFICIAL'S BLESSING: TIAN GUAN CI FU (DELUXE HARDCOVER) VOL. 5

Published originally under the title of 《天官賜福》
(Heaven Official's Blessing)
Author © 墨香铜臭(Mo Xiang Tong Xiu)
US English edition rights under license granted by 北京晋江原创网络科技有限公司
(Beijing Jinjiang Original Network Technology Co., Ltd.)
English edition copyright © 2025 Seven Seas Entertainment, Inc.
Arranged through JS Agency Co., Ltd.
All rights reserved

《天官賜福》(Heaven Official's Blessing) Volume 5
All rights reserved
Interior Color Illustrations by 日出的小太陽 (tai3_3)
Illustrations granted under license granted by 2021 Reve Books Co., Ltd. (Pinsin Publishing)
US English translation copyright @ 2025 Seven Seas Entertainment, Inc.
US English edition arranged through JS Agency Co., Ltd.

Dust Jacket Illustration by Arisk_k
Hardcover & Printed Edge Illustrations by Za Nian
Interior Illustrations by ZeldaCW
Endpaper Illustration by HuaEpiphany

No portion of this book may be reproduced or transmitted in any form without written permission from the copyright holders. This is a work of fiction. Names, characters, places, and incidents are the products of the author's imagination or are used fictitiously. Any resemblance to actual events, locales, or persons, living or dead, is entirely coincidental. Any information or opinions expressed by the creators of this book belong to those individual creators and do not necessarily reflect the views of Seven Seas Entertainment or its employees.

Seven Seas press and purchase enquiries can be sent to Marketing Manager Lauren Hill at press@gomanga.com. Information regarding the distribution and purchase of digital editions is available from Digital Manager Kristine Johnson at digital@gomanga.com.

Seven Seas and the Seven Seas logo are trademarks of
Seven Seas Entertainment. All rights reserved.

Follow Seven Seas Entertainment online at sevenseasentertainment.com.

TRANSLATION: Suika
EDITOR: Pengie
COVER DESIGN: M. A. Lewife
INTERIOR DESIGN: Clay Gardner
INTERIOR LAYOUT: Karis Page
COPY EDITOR: Jade Gardner
PROOFREADER: Meg van Huygen
IN-HOUSE EDITOR: Lexy Lee
PREPRESS TECHNICIAN: Salvador Chan Jr., April Malig, Jules Valera
MANAGING EDITOR: Alyssa Scavetta
EDITOR-IN-CHIEF: Julie Davis
PUBLISHER: Lianne Sentar
VICE PRESIDENT: Adam Arnold
PRESIDENT: Jason DeAngelis

ISBN: 979-8-89373-140-8
Printed in China
First Printing: July 2025
10 9 8 7 6 5 4 3 2 1

HEAVEN OFFICIAL'S BLESSING
CONTENTS

CHAPTER 73: My Puqi Shrine Will Collapse Supremely (Part Two) — 11
(CONTAINS WEB SERIALIZATION CHAPTER 136)

CHAPTER 74: Out in the Wilds, Rioting at the Shady Inn — 21
(CONTAINS WEB SERIALIZATION CHAPTERS 137-139)

CHAPTER 75: Sharp-Tongued with Pointed Teeth, Winds Devoured and Arrow Shredded — 53
(CONTAINS WEB SERIALIZATION CHAPTER 140)

CHAPTER 76: I Decide the Path I Walk — 67
(CONTAINS WEB SERIALIZATION CHAPTERS 141-142)

CHAPTER 77: Gates Open to Mount Tonglu, the Mass Gathering of Ghosts — 89
(CONTAINS WEB SERIALIZATION CHAPTERS 143-145)

CHAPTER 78: Ambivalent Regrets, the Clear-Sighted General Snaps the Hateful Sword — 119
(CONTAINS WEB SERIALIZATION CHAPTERS 146-148)

CHAPTER 79: Panic Left and Right, East or West Road Undecided — 153
(CONTAINS WEB SERIALIZATION CHAPTERS 149-151)

CHAPTER 80: Four Heavenly Kings Hidden on Darkened Walls — 179
(CONTAINS WEB SERIALIZATION CHAPTER 152)

CHAPTER 81: Why Not Xuli, Why Not Jing Wen — 189
(CONTAINS WEB SERIALIZATION CHAPTERS 153-154)

CHAPTER 82:	A Long Way to Travel, Blocked on Narrow Road (CONTAINS WEB SERIALIZATION CHAPTERS 155-157)	213
CHAPTER 83:	Same Grave in Life, No Resting in Peace in the Earth (CONTAINS WEB SERIALIZATION CHAPTER 158)	241
CHAPTER 84:	This Jade Refuses to Be a Thrown-Away Brick (CONTAINS WEB SERIALIZATION CHAPTERS 159-162)	253
CHAPTER 85:	Riddle of the Mysterious State Preceptor Confounds Minds (CONTAINS WEB SERIALIZATION CHAPTERS 163-164)	303
CHAPTER 86:	Saint Born Under the Ominous Star (CONTAINS WEB SERIALIZATION CHAPTERS 165-166)	325
CHAPTER 87:	Jealous Ghost King, Three Questions on Where the Friendship Lies (CONTAINS WEB SERIALIZATION CHAPTER 167)	343
CHAPTER 88:	Ghost Fire Top, the Unlocking Incantation (CONTAINS WEB SERIALIZATION CHAPTERS 168-169)	353
CHAPTER 89:	Resentful Female Ghost, Flames of Jealousy Burn the Affection (CONTAINS WEB SERIALIZATION CHAPTER 170)	375

CHAPTER 90:	The Last Princess, Throat Slit Before the Palace Gates (CONTAINS WEB SERIALIZATION CHAPTER 171)	387
CHAPTER 91:	Ride the Black Ox, Flying Hooves on Mount Tonglu (CONTAINS WEB SERIALIZATION CHAPTER 172)	403
APPENDIX:	Character & Name Guide	417
	Glossary	445

Contents based on the Pinsin Publishing print edition originally released 2021

73

My Puqi Shrine Will Collapse Supremely (Part Two)

NO ONE IN THE SPIRITUAL communication array paid any attention to Xie Lian's urgent announcement. The chatter in the general array was deafening—it seemed something huge had happened.

"Your Highness? Did you say something?" Feng Xin shouted to him. "It's really chaotic in here right now…"

Xie Lian raised his voice to reply. "Feng Xin! I said, Ling Wen is the original creator of the Brocade Immortal! She ran away wearing it; watch out for her!"

"What?!" Feng Xin shouted. "That's what happened?!"

Xie Lian was about to expand on the details when the noise by his ear abruptly stopped and nothing more could be heard. Confused, he tried calling again.

"Everyone? Is everyone still there?"

He attempted to reconnect a few times, but still, no one answered.

"It's no use," Hua Cheng spoke up. "Ling Wen created the Upper Court's spiritual communication array, and she must've just destroyed it. It'll need to be entirely rebuilt."

"What should we do, then?"

If he wasn't contacting Ling Wen or the Wind Master directly, he primarily communicated with the Upper Court through the general spiritual communication array. He didn't know the verbal passwords of any other heavenly officials. Now that the general communication array was destroyed and he could no longer depend on Ling Wen or the Wind Master, what should he do?

Hua Cheng seemed to sense his concerns. "Don't worry. Didn't gege already make the key issue clear? Not all the heavenly officials of the Upper Court are idiots, and Jun Wu is present in the heavens right now. As long as you've done your due diligence in reporting, it'll be fine."

Xie Lian had been thinking the same thing, and he nodded in agreement as he brought his mad dash to a stop. They had already crossed several mountaintops and left the pursuing religious masters far behind, though it seemed they wouldn't be able to catch up with the Brocade Immortal and Quan Yizhen.

"If gege still wants to investigate the Brocade Immortal, you'll have to hurry," Hua Cheng added.

However, Xie Lian shook his head. "That was before. Now that Qi Ying is chasing Ling Wen, we've got more important matters on our hands. San Lang..." He stared at Hua Cheng in his arms, his gaze intent. "Your form...seems to have changed again."

When Hua Cheng was disguised as Lang Ying earlier, he had the appearance of a fifteen- or sixteen-year-old boy, and it wasn't easy for Xie Lian to carry him—even if he could, it wouldn't look good. But Hua Cheng seemed to have shrunk, and he now looked to be at most eleven or twelve. Xie Lian could carry him with one arm, or even have him perch on his shoulder. However, Hua Cheng's air of composed ease had never wavered.

"No need to worry, gege; it's a non-issue. The mountain will open its gates soon. Changing form is only a temporary tactic, and my old self will return after this situation is over."

He unwrapped the bandages on his head as he spoke. A pair of deep black eyes gazed at Xie Lian from that snow-white face;

the shadow of that handsome young man was still there upon his brow. Although he wore the face of a child, he still had that familiar laid-back, unhurried air and expression.

Xie Lian watched him in a daze, not speaking a word.

Hua Cheng frowned slightly. "Your Highness, you…"

Suddenly, Xie Lian's free hand reached out and pinched Hua Cheng's cheek. Hua Cheng's eyes widened as his face changed shape from the entirely unexpected squishing.

"…Gege!"

Xie Lian laughed. "Ha ha ha ha ha ha…sorry, San Lang, but you're too cute; I can't help myself. Ha ha ha ha…"

Hua Cheng was speechless.

Xie Lian continued to tenderly squish him. "Then, San Lang, are you going to keep changing?" he asked gently. "Are you going to turn into a child of five or six? Or even better, a little baby?"

Hearing the hope in his voice, Hua Cheng could only reply helplessly, "I'm afraid I will have to disappoint gege."

Xie Lian dropped his hand and grinned. "Nonsense. San Lang has never disappointed me. I'm really happy to have this chance to protect you."

However, Hua Cheng muttered glumly, "I'm not happy."

"Why is that?" Xie Lian asked.

Hua Cheng's tone turned cold. "I…hate looking like this!"

Xie Lian could actually detect a trace of loathing in his voice and was slightly taken aback. Hua Cheng lowered his head.

"I don't want you to see me in such a useless form, much less be forced to protect me!"

His emotions seemed unsettled—perhaps it was because his physical age had regressed. Xie Lian felt his heart stir, and he quickly gathered the boy into his arms and gently patted his back.

"By that logic, I might as well just die; you've seen me in messes so many times." He chuckled. "Besides, it's not like you're actually useless right now. You're just temporarily conserving your strength, that's all."

Hua Cheng buried his face in his shoulder. "...It's not the same," he grumbled, voice muffled. "Your Highness, I have to be the strongest. I have to become stronger than anyone else. Only then can I..."

Although his voice was young and tender at the moment, a trace of fatigue lingered in his tone.

"You've always been the strongest. But you don't need to be strong every waking moment of every day," Xie Lian soothed him. "Just... think of this as giving me some face. Let me protect you this once. Please? Okay?"

It was a long time before Hua Cheng lifted his head. He placed his hands on Xie Lian's shoulders and gazed at him.

"Your Highness, wait for me."

"All right, I'll wait for you," Xie Lian promised.

Hua Cheng vowed to him, very seriously, "Give me a little time; I'll be back very soon."

Xie Lian smiled. "No rush. Go at your own pace."

The next day, the two came to a small town.

Xie Lian was holding Hua Cheng's hand, and the two chatted leisurely as they strolled along the streets together.

"Ghost kings of earlier generations are affected by Mount Tonglu's opening tremors. Does that also apply to Black Water?" Xie Lian asked.

Hua Cheng stood with one arm folded behind his back and held Xie Lian's hand with the other. "Yes," he replied. "But our situations are different, as are our training methods. Naturally, our ways of responding to stimulation are different as well."

"For example?" Xie Lian prompted him. "How does he respond to the aggravation?"

"Hibernation, probably," Hua Cheng replied.

A phrase written in large letters surfaced in Xie Lian's mind. *Eat when hungry, sleep when full.*

"When Black Water was mortal, he suffered the torment of jail. With only one meal every three days, he had to swallow it down even if he was given swill," Hua Cheng continued. "Hunger ruined his stomach. Sometimes he'll feed nonstop, sometimes he'll refuse to eat anything at all."

"No wonder he was always so impressive when it came to swallowing things," Xie Lian mused.

Given He Xuan's situation, he could have focused on devouring hungry ghosts—he possessed the same attribute, so they should have better suited his palate. However, of the five-hundred-some ghosts devoured by Black Water Demon Xuan, the majority were water ghosts. He must have chosen them because he remembered the face of Shi Wudu and would intentionally pick such meals to break his water magic.

At the end of these feeding frenzies, he would need to slumber and digest.

"Indeed," Hua Cheng said. "I might as well mention that Qi Rong was trying to imitate He Xuan by feasting on human flesh."

Xie Lian was briefly speechless. *How could anyone consider eating humans the same as eating ghosts?* After pondering for a moment, he asked, "The forest of upside-down corpses... Was he trying to imitate *you* with that?"

"Correct," Hua Cheng replied. "He wanted to copy my blood rain aesthetic, but he didn't know how I did it. So he just crudely strung up rows of dead bodies."

"..."

Today, Xie Lian finally understood why no one knew what to say whenever Qi Rong was mentioned. He had all the appearance but none of the class.

Xie Lian sighed. *Qi Rong took Guzi away; who knows whether the poor child has been abandoned or eaten. And Wind Master...who knows whether it was Black Water who took him away. I pray they're both safe.*

Then he asked, "What about your Ghost City? Won't anyone stir up trouble there in the meantime?"

"I locked up Ghost City when I left and leaked false information regarding my whereabouts," Hua Cheng replied. "Even if anyone tries to start trouble, they won't be too hard on that rabble when they don't find me there. But I'm sure there are plenty of eyes watching that place right now."

Hua Cheng couldn't return to Ghost City, and Xie Lian couldn't take him to the heavens lest they be exposed by a heavenly official. This was why the two were frolicking aimlessly in the Mortal Realm's crowds without a destination in mind.

Xie Lian knitted his brows. "You leaked false information, but Ling Wen leaked *real* information. I still don't understand how she managed to see through your Lang Ying disguise."

"What I don't understand is something else," Hua Cheng said.

"What?" Xie Lian asked.

"It's regarding that foul cultivator, Heaven's Eye. I've toyed with him a couple times; his skills aren't bad," Hua Cheng said.

"Yes. That's true," Xie Lian agreed. "He's got talent and puts in the effort."

"Right. So why would he say that gege's lips are covered in ghost qi?" Hua Cheng questioned.

"…"

Xie Lian's hands clenched, but he quickly loosened his grip when he remembered he was still holding hands with Hua Cheng.

Hua Cheng pressed him on the subject, his voice grim. "Gege, don't blow me off with words you'd use to placate those idiots. Tell me what I did to you that night."

"…"

It's not what you did to me. It's more like what I did to you… Xie Lian thought. Just then, his eyes lit up. "Wait, San Lang, look over there."

"Gege?" Hua Cheng questioned.

However, Xie Lian had already pulled him into a large and rather luxurious store. The store's owner stood at the counter and looked the two of them up and down—a cultivator and a layman made for a curious combination.

"What can I do for you, Daozhang?" the owner asked.

Xie Lian lifted Hua Cheng for the owner to see and smiled. "It's not for me. It's for him."

Hua Cheng tilted his head.

An incense time later, Hua Cheng emerged from the back of the store.

Lang Ying's clothes were suited to a fifteen- or sixteen-year-old and no longer fit the current Hua Cheng, so Xie Lian picked out a new outfit especially for him. Xie Lian's eyes lit up the moment he came into view.

What a dear little young master, with skin as white as snow!

Dressed in a robe as red as maple and fire and a pair of deer-leather boots decorated with silver chains, Hua Cheng looked both handsome and spirited. His raven locks were loose; he'd previously only had a single thin braid next to his right cheek, but Xie Lian couldn't help braiding another one on his left to match. It made him look even more sprightly. What was really too much, however, was his expression—his eyes were vivacious and bright, his air calm and steady; he truly looked like a little grown-up and nothing like a child! Such a contrast made it hard to look away. The ladies shopping in the store were all stunned, and they gathered around and clutched their hearts as they cried *"oh my, oh my"* nonstop in appreciation.

Hua Cheng languidly strolled over to Xie Lian, who clapped lightly.

"Just as I thought. Red suits San Lang best."

Hua Cheng helplessly tugged at the little braid on his left. "As long as gege is happy," he grumbled.

Xie Lian lowered his hand to put an arm around Hua Cheng's shoulders and smiled as they went to the front to pay. Hua Cheng's outfit wasn't cheap; Xie Lian normally didn't have much money to spare, so he usually wouldn't have entered such a fancy store. However, he had saved up a small fortune for renovating the shrine, and now that there was nothing left to renovate, he could buy Hua Cheng some new clothes before worrying about anything else.

As he was counting out his coins one by one, Hua Cheng squeezed in and slapped a piece of gold foil on the counter with a resounding *wham*!

Xie Lian commented, "..."

Likewise, the owner commented, "..."

Furthermore, the ladies also commented, "..."

"Keep the change," Hua Cheng said. "Gege, come on, let's go."

He tugged at the corner of Xie Lian's sleeve and strolled outside the store with his hands clasped behind him. Xie Lian smiled and started to walk after him, but was surprised when Hua Cheng backtracked right into his arms as he came back inside.

Xie Lian held him steady by the shoulders. "What's wrong?"

He looked up and saw a familiar figure in the flowing crowd outside, and his heart lurched as well.

Coincidentally, the store owner asked, "Would you two like to purchase anything else?"

Xie Lian raised his hand. "Yes. Please bring me that robe!"

74

Out in the Wilds, Rioting at the Shady Inn

THE STORE OWNER was taken aback.

"Huh? *That* one? Daozhang, are you sure that's what you want?"

"Yes, that one!" Xie Lian definitively confirmed.

With that, he simply rushed up and grabbed the robe himself. He then picked up Hua Cheng, dashed to the back of the store, and slipped behind a set of curtains. This clothing store was a daring one, and innovative at that—there was a small stall inside for fitting, so those who came to purchase clothes could try them on right there.

The crowd was bewildered at the ruckus. Moments later, a magnificently dressed cultivator walked past the clothing store, grumbling as he rubbed at his forehead. Behind him followed a mob of strange and fierce-looking monks and cultivators.

When he saw the large crowd gathered at the clothing store, he barked, displeased, "What are you lookin' at?!"

"*Sigh*. Forget it, let's hurry. I need to go to the toilet again!"

"Wait, Heaven's Eye-xiong, there are plenty of people here. Why not ask if they saw *them*?"

"My lady benefactors, have you seen a white-clad cultivator pass by, accompanied by a small child covered in bandages?"

The crowd of customers said nothing, but there were some who unconsciously glanced at the back of the store. The chasing mob grew cautious, and they made silent gestures at each other indicating that they should go inside to investigate.

Heaven's Eye strode inside and slowly approached the curtains, holding his breath. A moment later, he yanked them open, which prompted a shriek from inside.

Behind the curtains, there sat a woman. Her long, raven-black hair was twisted up in a loose bun, and her slender white neck was decorated by a black choker and a thin silver chain. She had pulled down a small part of her shirt, which revealed her snow-white shoulder and nearly half of her back. It looked as if the robe was about to fall, and the sight made one's face burn and heart race.

After Heaven's Eye yanked back the curtains, the woman trembled and covered her face with her sleeves while whimpering softly, as if she was shocked and terrified by such a sudden, brutish act.

Heaven's Eye instantly dropped the curtains. *"I-I-I-I-I-I-I'm sorry!"*

The band of monks and cultivators trailing behind Heaven's Eye screamed as well.

"What a sin, *what a sin!*"

They all covered their eyes. Using this chance, the "woman" whirled around—who else could it be but Xie Lian? Hua Cheng was sitting in his arms and had been blocked from view by Xie Lian's body. While Xie Lian was a man and his shoulders were wider than the average woman's, he had achieved the perfect effect by only pulling down half of his clothing to expose the best angle.

With one hand full of Hua Cheng, Xie Lian lifted his skirt with the other and dashed like the wind past those screaming monks and cultivators once they'd covered their eyes. The store owner and lady customers were dumbfounded. Seeing him flee, the store owner initially wanted to stop him, but as he opened his mouth, he spotted that gold foil—it more than paid for two sets of clothing. And so he shut his mouth, shrugged, and stopped caring.

Carrying Hua Cheng in his arms, Xie Lian dashed madly away, leaving nothing but dust behind him. Passersby on the streets stared with unbelieving eyes, but they only saw the blurred afterimage of a "woman" holding a child, racing as lithe and ferocious as a jaguar. The clouds of suffocating dust stirred up in his wake left the crowds choking and coughing. A small food stall on the side of the road got covered in the stuff, and the owner started cussing.

"What's wrong with you?!"

Xie Lian spared the time to turn his head and shout, "Everything's wrong! I'm sorry! I'm sorry!"

He heard wild hollering from behind him. "Stop right there—!"

When he looked back, he saw the mob charging out of the clothing store.

I have to wonder what's going through the heads of people who yell "stop right there." It's obvious the one they're yelling at won't stop. They'll just hold their breath and run faster! Xie Lian thought, and he put those very thoughts into action, dashing away all the quicker.

With such a large, roaring mob running down the street, more dust flew and choked the air. The food stall owner couldn't even curse anymore, and he flipped his own wok in anger.

"Why the fuck do I even bother?!"

After keeping up the chase for four hours, the ceaselessly hollering monks and cultivators finally ran out of breath, and their steps slowed. Xie Lian was experienced in the art of escape, and he quietly persevered to the very end. Once they had completely lost their pursuers, Xie Lian set Hua Cheng down and stood on the side of the road gasping for breath.

Hua Cheng held his shoulders and said glumly, "Don't breathe too harshly, careful not to hurt yourself."

Xie Lian looked up and saw Hua Cheng's tiny frown, but since his companion was still wearing the face of a child, he couldn't help but laugh out loud.

"Ha ha, ha ha ha...*ah!*"

He had laughed too abruptly; a sharp pain shot through his ribs, and he clutched his chest to seek relief. Seeing Hua Cheng's dismayed expression, he waved dismissively.

"It's nothing... Hmm? Is that an inn over there?"

Sure enough, there was an inn not far ahead, its warm yellow glow peeping through the steadfast blues of the evening. It almost seemed like it was beckoning travelers.

Xie Lian straightened up. "Let's go in and rest."

"All right," Hua Cheng replied.

Xie Lian grasped Hua Cheng's hand, and the two strolled toward the small building. When they arrived at the entrance, Xie Lian realized that this inn had two levels; it was much more lavish than it appeared from afar. The doors were closed, and Xie Lian raised his hand to give a light knock.

"Anyone there? We'd like to stay the night."

Soon enough, someone called from the inside, "Coming, coming!"

A moment later, the door opened. Several attendants came forward to greet them, their faces full of smiles.

"Good si—"

They initially meant to say "good sir," but the person before them was wearing women's robes. They amended their statement.

"Mis—"

Before the word left their mouths, Xie Lian fully emerged from the darkness with Hua Cheng in hand. This wasn't an unmarried lady if there was a child, so they amended themselves again.

"Mada—"

"Madam" was still half on their lips when Xie Lian's face became illuminated by the light within the inn. This guest was dressed in women's robes, but if they had to be honest... While his face was gentle in appearance, it was a man's face no matter how they looked. The attendants fell mute at once, and it was a good moment before they simply went back to their original greeting.

"Good sir, please come inside."

Xie Lian smiled as he nodded. He'd worn pretty much every type of clothing at some point, and he felt not a drop of mental or physical discomfort. With Hua Cheng in hand, he crossed the extremely low threshold and sat down at a table in the corner of the lobby. Other than the attendants, there was no one else at the inn. The moment they entered, the attendants had immediately closed the door and gathered around their table, smiles plastered on their faces—smiles that were now making Xie Lian rather uncomfortable.

He took the menu card. "It's not easy to find an inn like this in the middle of nowhere. Amazing!"

"Isn't that the truth? It's not easy to attract customers like you in the middle of nowhere either!" the attendants responded.

For some reason, while they were all smiling, those smiles looked painted on—quite fake indeed. Xie Lian didn't let his thoughts show. He looked over the menu and ordered a few dishes, and the attendants merrily left to convey those orders to the kitchen.

Hua Cheng toyed with his chopsticks. "Gege, we're at a shady establishment run by ghosts."

"Mmm," Xie Lian acknowledged.

Out here in the middle of nowhere, even finding a small, one-level inn with a few attendants would have been quite amazing. Why would there be such a lavish establishment with so many attendants if there wasn't something suspicious afoot?

Of course, this wasn't strong evidence on its own. The real indicator was the fact that Xie Lian had smelled the thick, fresh stench of blood from the moment he entered the inn.

Ordinary folks probably wouldn't notice the smell, but to someone with his sharp senses and considerable experience, it was so heavy, it couldn't be ignored.

"There are more people on the second floor. I hear their footsteps," Xie Lian said. "I wonder if they're also travelers staying the night."

If they were, then they must be rescued. The two sat across from each other and brought their faces close, talking in whispers for a long while.

The attendants finally brought over their dishes. "Coming!"

Xie Lian was about to speak, but he sensed a slight movement from the outside and rose to his feet.

"We're going to go rest in our rooms. Can I trouble you to bring our food upstairs?"

"No problem, no problem!"

Xie Lian took Hua Cheng's hand and lifted his skirt with his other hand with practiced ease as they went upstairs. He looked back.

"Oh, by the way—if anyone asks, please tell them you've never seen us."

"No problem, no problem!"

Xie Lian hurried up the stairs. It wasn't long before they heard someone banging brashly on the front doors and a gruff voice calling out.

"Open up!"

The attendants opened the door with smiles on their faces. The crowd that poured in was the relentless mob of monks and cultivators led by Heaven's Eye!

By then, Xie Lian and Hua Cheng had already entered their room on the second floor. As they shut the doors behind them, they could hear the people who had just entered yelling "Toilet, toilet, toilet!" and running for the outhouse while others demanded, "Boss! You got water?!"

The attendants were overjoyed at the sight of so many people coming in at the same time.

"We do, we do, please wait, it's coming!"

"*Haaah*. I'm so bloated!" Heaven's Eye complained. "Unbelievable. Those whatchamacallits—those Incorruptible Chastity Pellets really are tenacious poison. I've only gotten through twenty-something cups; how long will it take before I reach eighty-one?"

Xie Lian was speechless; he hadn't imagined that those monks and cultivators would be so gullible. He'd told them to drink eighty-one cups of water, and so they really planned on drinking exactly eighty-one cups of water.

"Amitabha Buddha. I have already imbibed twenty-five cups of water, and I must say it has been very effective as an antidote," one of the monks declared. "I am feeling much better already."

Hearing this, Xie Lian didn't know whether to laugh or cry. He fumbled around the room to see if there were any cracks he could peek through until he heard Hua Cheng calling to him. The boy was half crouched on the floor along the wall.

"Gege, look over here."

Xie Lian crouched as well and looked where he was pointing on the floor, but he didn't see anything unusual. "What am I looking at?"

Hua Cheng suddenly poked the floor, and a small hole instantly appeared. A thin ray of light shone through. "Here. Now we can see."

"..."

Xie Lian leaned down and peeked through the hole. The mob was gathered at a long table in the middle of the lobby, and Heaven's Eye slapped its wooden surface.

"Hmph! We were too careless this time. Next time we see that evil cultivator, we won't give him any chance to take advantage of us! We must take down Hua...Hua...Hua-chengzhu and eradicate evil in the name of heaven!"

"San Lang, just how did you offend them?" Xie Lian whispered.

Before Hua Cheng could answer, someone else had already asked in Xie Lian's place.

"That's right, I never asked, but what brings all of you here to catch that ghost king? What's the story?"

With that, their condemnation meeting began.

"Just talking about it brings fury to my heart! Twenty years ago, there was a pig spirit who went crazy and uprooted the village master's household. The building collapsed and the whole family was killed, and the pig fled to Ghost City. I'd only just entered the trade at the time. I chased after the creature, but I was beaten to a pulp by a bunch of ghosts. What humiliation! *He* also sent one of his lackeys to tell me that if you eat a whole family of pigs, it's only fair for a pig to slaughter *your* whole family in revenge. It's your lucky day if the pig doesn't seek revenge; if it does, then you deserved it. Now tell me, what is that rotten logic?!"

"What a coincidence! Our sect experienced something similar, but it was in regards to a rooster spirit!"

"Our story's simple. The heavenly official we worshipped in our sect had his name on *his* hit list, so no matter how many temples we built, he'd always burn them down. What an outrage! Absolutely unreasonable!"

"Hear, hear. You all know of my shixiong, right? He was talented and had an infinite future! He only had one tiny vice: he loved to dally with women. Decades ago, a prostitute ghost seduced my shixiong and sucked him dry—turned him into human jerky. That Hua...Hua...that ghost king dared shelter her."

The criticism was flaming down below, but above it, Hua Cheng looked bored out of his mind, not even bothering to give a taunting smirk.

"I think I've heard of your shixiong before," Heaven's Eye said. "Wasn't he the guy who would force himself on married women under the pretense of conducting rituals and ceremonies? The one who got locked up for three months?"

"Ahem, ahem, ahem!"

The attendants brought their food over just then, and the crowd's attention was diverted.

"Food's here, food's here. Come, come, come, let's say no more, Heaven's Eye-xiong. Let's eat."

Xie Lian straightened up and squinted at the dishes the inn attendants brought over.

"Don't bother looking. They'll keel over the moment they eat that stuff," Hua Cheng said.

"This is going to be troublesome," Xie Lian murmured.

While the mob of monks and cultivators was relentless and extremely annoying, Xie Lian couldn't just let them croak in this strange, shady establishment. But it would also be rather awkward for them to raise the alarm.

Suddenly, Heaven's Eye spoke up. "Hold it!"

He stared at the dishes and blocked the others from digging in, his eyes sharp and flashing.

He does have some skill! Xie Lian praised mentally.

"Heaven's Eye-xiong, what's wrong?" the others wondered.

Heaven's Eye reached out with one finger and wiped around the edge of a plate, then raised that finger high in the air. "So much grease from just one wipe of a finger!" he yelled in rage. "These plates aren't clean; what kind of business are you guys running here?!"

"..."

Xie Lian thought the man had noticed that something was off, but he hadn't imagined it was a different sort of *off*. He was rather surprised, but still, the result was the same. The moment Heaven's Eye complained, the others began to gripe as well.

"My gosh, it's true! What is this, it's all sticky like spit... Wait! There's hair in this dish!"

Someone reached out with their chopsticks and stirred out a few strands of long black hair.

"Holy shit, what's going on with your kitchen?! Who the hell's working in the back?"

The smiling attendants nervously rubbed their hands together. "Um... We recently butchered a few pigs, so those are probably pig hairs!"

But when the chopsticks plucked at those hairs to pull them from the dish, the hairs only seemed to grow longer and longer the more they pulled.

"What kind of pigs have hair this long?! Is your boss lady washing her hair in the kitchen?!"

"Take all of this away and redo it!"

"Yessir, yessir!" the attendants hurriedly acquiesced. "We'll redo everything right away! My Lords, please drink water, drink water."

They shouldn't drink the water either, Xie Lian thought. *There must be something in the cups as well!*

Just before the cups reached the mob's lips, and before the attendants could get away, Heaven's Eye called out again.

"Get back here!"

One of the attendants returned, smiling apologetically. "Does My Lord Daozhang need anything else?"

"Let me ask you something. Have you seen a very strange woman lurking around, accompanied by a small child?" Heaven's Eye asked.

So he did inquire after all. *Thank goodness I instructed them not to tell,* Xie Lian thought.

But as he was thinking this, the attendant responded without missing a beat. "Oh, yes!"

"…?!" Xie Lian was stunned.

The mob was shocked, and they put down their water and hushed their voices. "Where are they?"

The attendant also hushed his voice. "Upstairs!"

The mob went on high alert, their gazes flicking upward. Xie Lian swiftly blocked the hole Hua Cheng had poked out with his finger. A moment later, they heard the sound of a group of people creeping upstairs. Xie Lian skulked to the door, listening to the footsteps; it seemed that the attendant had led the mob to the second floor, and they were sneaking toward them. His left arm held Hua Cheng, and he clutched his sword in his right. Ruoye stood next to them to serve as a shield. All weapons were at the ready, and Xie Lian was tense and wholly prepared to launch an attack.

However, the footsteps passed by their room and continued down the long hallway. Puzzled, Xie Lian pressed against the door and looked out through the crack. The mob had passed them by and surrounded the entrance to another room.

There seemed to be someone in that suite. Faint light filtered through the paper windows and reflected the silhouette of a woman sitting at the table.

He never would've imagined that the attendants would actually stick to their word and keep their presence under wraps, but the attendant had been referring to another guest. It seemed there was *another* "very strange woman" accompanied by a small child who had come to this inn to lodge for the night.

Heaven's Eye and his group shared a look. After miming a series of hand gestures to each other, the group prepared to kick the door down.

Suddenly, the light inside the room was extinguished, and the silhouette disappeared. Following right after was a series of hurried footsteps. *Thud, thud, thud.*

A woman yanked the door open, cussing. "What are ya stinkin' men doing, lurking outside my door in the middle of the night?! Yer grandmama wants to take a bath, so what are y'all planning? Huh?!"

The lady's figure was slender and sensual, and her face was unpainted. Although she had the air of a fighting cock, she was nonetheless wholly a woman. She clicked her tongue, rolled up her sleeves, and continued to curse.

"And it's a bunch of monks and cultivators, to boot! Aren't y'all men of the cloth? What happened to all yer chastity vows?!"

A few of the monks mumbled, "It's a misunderstanding, a misunderstanding..."

The woman raised her brows impossibly high, then lifted her hand as if ready to strike. "I don't care if it's a *misunderstanding* or a *meeting*! Leave now or this grandmama will grant y'all a nice tub of bathwater!"

"Hey, hey, hey, lady benefactor, how can you be like this?! Consider your virtue!"

"Let's get outta here…"

While Xie Lian didn't recognize the woman's face, her voice and the air about her was extremely familiar. A moment later, he gasped in shock. "Lan Chang?"

"That's right. It's her," Hua Cheng confirmed.

Seeing the crowd disperse, Lan Chang seemed to let out a sigh of relief. She glanced around, then hurried back to her room, shutting the door behind her. She wasn't covered in heavy makeup for once and showed the world a plain face. While there were quite a number of wrinkles around her eyes that made her age apparent, unexpectedly, she was rather elegantly beautiful. Xie Lian almost didn't recognize her. If she had presented herself like this on that day at the Palace of Divine Might, Pei Ming's claim to innocence might not have been as convincing.

During the first wave of tremors from Mount Tonglu's reopening, a significant number of ghosts and monsters used the chaos to escape imprisonment. Lan Chang and the fetus spirit were among them. If the "very strange woman" the attendant referred to was Lan Chang, then that meant the "child" was…

"The fetus spirit must be with her," Xie Lian whispered to Hua Cheng. "That creature is too dangerous; we can't let them run loose like this."

But the inn where they were staying was already seedy, and on top of that, there was that band of mortal religious masters in pursuit of Hua Cheng. It wasn't going to be easy for Xie Lian and Hua Cheng to capture Lan Chang under these circumstances.

The crowd of monks and cultivators made it to the staircase, and the attendant asked, "How did it go? Was that not the person My Lords were searching for?"

"It was not!" Heaven's Eye replied, then sighed heavily. "Let me ask you this, then. Have you seen a cultivator with a small child?"

The attendant gave it some thought. "There's no child, but there is a cultivator who is here by himself!"

Hearing this, the mob grew spirited again. "Where is he?" they asked in hushed voices.

The attendant replied in a hushed voice as well. "Over here."

This time, he pointed to a different room. The crowd exchanged glances once more and yet again tiptoed after the attendant to where he indicated.

When they were still a stone's throw away from the room's entrance, a sharp sound snapped through the air. A yellow talisman shot through the crack of the door, brushing past Heaven's Eye's cheek before nailing itself into the wall behind him. Stunned, the crowd went to take a look and found the talisman halfway embedded in the wall. The wood had been split, like that sheet of paper was made of iron. The group was deeply shaken.

Several of the mob's members were about to charge into the room, but Heaven's Eye stopped them.

"It's not him! But it's still someone formidable. Don't be rash and start something." Then he gestured politely with an arm tucked behind him and called out to the guest. "Sorry to have disturbed you, skilled master. This is simply a misunderstanding."

The one inside the room declined to respond—as expected of a skilled master.

As the crowd backed away, someone asked, "Dao-xiong, why did you say it's not him inside the room? Wasn't that scrap cultivator's hand just as powerful when he threw those hidden weapons?"

Scrap cultivator... Xie Lian had to really think about it before he realized the "hidden weapons" they referenced were his Incorruptible Chastity Pellets. *Well, all right...*

"Of course it's not him," Heaven's Eye replied in a low voice. "They both throw hidden weapons, but the one inside the room is slightly weaker in strength and skill than that scrap cultivator..."

He hadn't yet finished his sentence before another seven or eight yellow talismans came shooting from behind them, nailing into the nearby doors and walls like a volley of arrows. The crowd fled downstairs in terror, and at great speed, without another word.

Seeing that everyone had left, Xie Lian stealthily opened the door, tugged a yellow talisman from the wall, and returned to his room. Hua Cheng pinched the yellow talisman with two fingers, then lightly tossed it away after taking only a cursory glance.

"Heaven's Eye's *eye* really isn't too bad."

A layer of spiritual qi was plated on the yellow talisman's surface, which was why it was as sharp as a knife and strong as iron when it shot out and nailed itself deeply into the wall.

When Xie Lian hurled those meatballs, they flew forth with such terrifying might that it was like they were a barrage of iron pellets. But they were not enhanced by any sort of spiritual powers—it was by his own strength alone. After all, he had spent centuries without any spiritual power, and he had long since gotten accustomed to depending on only himself and his own skill in all matters. The reliance on spiritual powers—that was how Heaven's Eye judged their difference in strength.

Just how many different kinds of people are gathered here? Xie Lian couldn't help but wonder. *Why is there even a cultivator like that lodging here? Could he also be here to exorcise evil? It's understandable that those mortal monks and cultivators didn't notice anything, but it* would be impossible for someone of his skill level not to sense anything weird about this place. Either way, now *I* absolutely *can't let that mob discover that San Lang is here. If they raise their voices and that cultivator overhears, we might gain another pursuer. And he might not be as easy to deal with as the rest of them.*

The mob went back downstairs and returned to the lobby, sitting back down at the long table. Xie Lian peeked through the hole Hua Cheng had created.

"I'll go have the kitchens redo your orders right away," the attendant said. "Please wait just a bit longer, My Lords, hee hee hee."

"Wait! Take the waters away too. Wash your cups properly before serving us."

"Of course, of course. Hee hee hee."

The attendant left with a face full of smiles; he was probably headed for the kitchen. When they were still outside, Xie Lian had noticed that the kitchen was located behind the building, so he picked up Hua Cheng and flipped out of the window to land outside the inn. As he circled to the back, he grabbed a few small pebbles and clutched them in his hand in case he needed to use them later.

He skulked to a spot outside the kitchen. Hua Cheng poked again, and a small hole silently materialized, as if the wall were made of tofu. Xie Lian pressed close, peering inside to see just what kind of person ran this shady establishment.

The light from the kitchen was dim. Only a few dying lamps were lit, and there was no one in sight. But if he listened carefully, he could hear the sound of crunching coming from one corner.

Xie Lian changed his viewing angle a few times, until he finally discovered that the sound was coming from below the stove. His vision was blocked by the stove itself, but there was a human leg flung atop the brick stovetop. Its owner was obviously already dead, but the limb was still twitching in time to the sounds of someone munching and savoring their meal.

Several attendants entered the kitchen. "My king…"

A disheveled, grimy man abruptly raised his head from behind the stovetops.

"What?!" he replied blearily, his voice muffled by what he was chewing.

The man's lips were covered with fresh blood, and his eyes gleamed with a greedy glow. A human hand dangled from his mouth as if it were a chicken foot. His expression and appearance were as horrifying as his identity was obvious—it was the man Qi Rong was currently possessing!

He slurped the hand's uneaten fingers into his stuffed cheeks. A moment later, he spat out a few bones right at the attendants' faces.

"You useless trash! Born from a pile of shit!" he cussed. "Coming in here to cry like you're at a funeral! And here I thought you were bringing this ancestor food. Well? Where are the humans? Where's the meat? DIDN'T I ALREADY GIVE YOU THAT POISON?! WHY ARE THEY STILL STANDING?!"

The person lying dead on the ground—and currently being munched on—was likely either the original owner of this establishment or some other traveler who had passed by.

The attendants were aggrieved. "My king, it's not that we're useless! Those monks and cultivators are all picky sons of bitches; they're making everything difficult. First they complained that the plates were too greasy, then they complained that there was hair in the dishes… They refuse to eat anything we're serving."

Qi Rong chewed, crunched, and then sucked on the remains of the blood from those ten fingers. "What?! What the fuck?! This ancestor will personally cook them an execution meal! They should already be crying tears of joy for not being forced to kneel and lick their food off the ground! Who gave those fuckfaces the right to complain about anything?! They should try eating what Cousin Crown Prince makes; that shit's worse than shit! THOSE FUCKERS SHOULD KNOW TO GROVEL BEFORE THIS ANCESTOR IN GRATITUDE!"

"..." Xie Lian was speechless.

"...Gege, don't pay any mind to what such useless trash says," Hua Cheng comforted.

"...Yeah."

Qi Rong leapt to his feet and erupted into a string of curses as he beat the attendants.

"It's 'cause you're all useless trash! Can't even wash a plate right!"

His anger satisfied, Qi Rong rolled up his sleeves and wiped his blood-covered lips clean with one hand. Cursing and griping all the while, he took up a spatula and impatiently beat it against an iron wok, producing a noisy riot of clinking and clanking.

"One more time! Open your shitty eyes—I'll let you witness this ancestor's skills! We'll see if any of you have any more crap to say after this!"

Flames roared to the skies, and he swiftly remade a full spread of dishes and ordered the attendants to carry them out.

And what a spread indeed! The meat was abundant and the vegetables fresh; the dishes were aromatic and alluring. Xie Lian returned to their guest room on the second floor and peeked below.

The monks and cultivators were in awe.

"This looks good!"

"Yeah! This is so well done. Especially these salt-and-pepper chicken feet. So fat and tender...though perhaps a little too fat and tender? I've never seen chicken feet with such long digits..."

"Oh! This is our house specialty. They're not your typical chicken feet. They're the finest specially selected feet sourced exclusively from the rare white phoenix chicken," the attendants explained. "With their claws removed, don't they look tempting? Just like the soft, delicate hands of a young woman?"

"You're right. But I'm most excited for this fried pig skin; it looks lightly crispy and tender, and the fire was controlled just right... Wait, why does the pork have tattoos?"

"Oh! It's because our chef wanted to demonstrate his godly carving skills," the attendants explained. "He intentionally etched that on to show off a bit, that's all."

"The sweet-and-sour ribs don't seem cooked through, and the sauce is too thick. You're not trying to cover up anything funny with the flavor, are you?"

"Oh! Nothing of the sort," the attendants explained. "Everything in this establishment is butchered on the day of and sold fresh. It's just that our chef has a taste for stronger flavors, that's all."

"..."

Seeing how they were endlessly praising the dishes and were ready to dig in, Xie Lian really couldn't continue to stand by. He flung one of the pebbles he'd picked up earlier out of the small hole. His shot hit the hand Heaven's Eye was using to raise his cup, which was filled with water for his continued pursual of "detoxing." His arm shuddered, causing water to spill from the cup and splash right onto a smiling attendant's face.

While the liquid wasn't hot, it was like he'd poured boiling water on the attendant. The attendant covered his face, wailing.

"*Aaaah!*"

Everyone at the table brandished their weapons in shock.

"What's going on?!"

Heaven's Eye seized the attendant's hand and yanked it aside, and the crowd gasped. The attendant's facial features were half melted, as if water had spilled onto a sheet of paper and blotted the ink. Blurry, hazy trails of ink spread along his cheeks and rolled down.

The attendant's facial features and ever-present smile had been drawn on with a brush!

"..."

Without missing a beat, the mob flipped the table and started a brawl. The attendants hugged their heads in defense as they were beaten.

"My Lords! Please stop!" they howled. "Um—that—um, that very strange woman with a small child you're looking for—that strange cultivator! He's upstairs! They're right upstairs! Go find them! Let us go! We're only part-timers!"

"Bah! Part-timers? Who are you kidding?!"

"Tryin' to deceive us? Think we're that easy to fool?! It's too late now!"

"We're not lying! It's true!" the attendants cried miserably.

The brawl downstairs was getting wild, and, seeing that the masters had an overwhelming upper hand, Xie Lian shook his head and left them to it. He was about to make his move to capture Lan Chang and the fetus spirit amidst this chaos, but before he could even open the door to his guest room, an unexpected shriek came from the hallway.

The terrified voice of Lan Chang rang out. "No... I beg you, I don't want to go! Please, I beg you, let us go! I'll kneel and kowtow!"

"Who cares about your prostrating?" said the angry voice of a young man. "If you leave, then what can I—what can my general do? Fuck, you two really did him in this time! Enough useless talk; you're coming with me!"

Upon hearing that voice, Xie Lian flung the door open.

"It's you?!"

A black-clad youth stood in the long hallway blocking Lan Chang's path, his expression dark. He looked up the moment Xie Lian emerged, clearly flabbergasted.

"It's *you*?!"

Xie Lian walked outside his room. "Fu Yao? Why are you here?"

Lan Chang saw him and widened her eyes. "The Crown Prince...?"

"..." Fu Yao looked him up and down. His lips twitched, but at least his eyes didn't roll. "Why are *you* here?"

Xie Lian glanced down at himself, then hurriedly stripped off the women's clothing he was wearing. "It's a long story."

Just then, Fu Yao noticed Hua Cheng standing by Xie Lian's side, and his pupils shrank.

"...You?!" he cried in spite of himself.

Hua Cheng sneered and ignored him. As for Lan Chang, she turned to bolt the moment she saw him. Fu Yao noticed and whirled around.

"Stop right there!"

He hadn't taken a single step before a long, white silk band shot out and wrapped around her ankle. Lan Chang tumbled to the ground, but she immediately flipped onto her back, hugging her belly. It would seem that the fetus spirit was hidden in her stomach again.

"If you wanted her to stop, you should've done this... Just shouting about it is pointless," Xie Lian said as he reeled Ruoye in. "By the way, you were talking about your general earlier. What happened to him?"

Fu Yao didn't respond; he simply humphed and stormed over to seize Lan Chang's arm. He seemed truly furious. Not only did he forcefully grab a woman with a hard, unforgiving hand, but he had even uttered a profanity earlier. This was not at all the Fu Yao they knew. Unexpectedly, before he managed to pull Lan Chang up, her belly swelled up like a balloon. A white figure shot out and lunged at Fu Yao's face, shrieking.

It was the fetus spirit!

Every time it returned to its mother's womb, it recovered enough energy for another round of mayhem. Thus, its strike was ferocious and treacherous, and Fu Yao had to focus to beat it back. With a swift smack of his hand, the fetus spirit was slapped away like a ball. It hit a nearby wall with a bang, then ricocheted off and shot toward Xie Lian.

"Catch it! Don't let it run away!" Fu Yao shouted.

Before Xie Lian had even moved, Hua Cheng was already there in front of him to act as a shield. The fetus ball abruptly halted in front of him, then changed trajectory to charge at Fu Yao once again.

As the ghost ball ricocheted and rampaged about the upstairs corridor, complete chaos also reigned down below. From the first floor, they could hear the cries of the "attendants" begging for mercy.

"My Lord cultivators, please be magnanimous! We lowly ones were only doing this for a bite to eat!"

"Yeah, we won't do it again! Truth be told, normally we only steal chickens at most to eat! We only did this because that green… green lord forced us to be his underlings! He's in the kitchen right now!"

Seeing that the situation had fallen into complete chaos, Xie Lian suddenly remembered something and leapt out the second-floor window.

Qi Rong sat in the kitchen with his legs crossed, picking at his teeth as he cheerfully waited for his "meal" to serve itself.

A loud rumbling sound shook the room, then someone kicked down the wall and leapt into the kitchen.

"Qi Rong! Where's Guzi?"

This classic martial god entrance shocked Qi Rong to his feet. "You?! Why are *you* here?! CAN'T YOU KNOCK LIKE A NORMAL PERSON?!"

Without missing a beat, Xie Lian went over and smacked Qi Rong's head onto the chopping board, then pinned him down hard like he was a duck to be butchered.

"Cut the nonsense! What did you do to the child?"

Qi Rong grinned a smile full of teeth. "Hee hee hee, look—isn't he right here, all over the ground?"

What was the ground littered with? Human bones!

Fury blazed in Xie Lian, and he squeezed harder. Qi Rong started wailing and howling.

"Ow, ow, ow, *ow*! Arm! My arm's broken! BROKEN, BROKEN! COUSIN CROWN PRINCE, WAIT! Okay, okay, okay, I'll be honest, I lied, I didn't eat him! I didn't! I was gonna, but I haven't yet!"

"Where is he now?" Xie Lian demanded.

"STOP CRUSHING ME, STOP CRUSHING! I'll tell you! The excess baggage is locked up in the firewood shed right there! Just take a look and you'll see!"

Xie Lian ordered Ruoye to bind Qi Rong, then he opened a small door on the side of the kitchen. Sure enough, Guzi was curled up inside. Xie Lian reached out under his nose to check his breathing; it was steady, and his little face was red and flushed. He looked like he was sound asleep. However, when Xie Lian lifted the boy, he could feel that the small child was feverishly hot to the touch. *Oh no,* Xie Lian thought.

By that point, the monks and cultivators had poured into the kitchen as well. The moment they entered, they nearly tripped on the piles of human bones on the floor. It was a shocking sight, and they cried out in alarm.

"Huh?! What a shady establishment!"

"So all those dishes… They were all…made of human flesh?!"

"I told you that I've never seen chicken feet that long!"

There was another loud rumbling noise, and a new hole was punched through the ceiling. A white ball came crashing down.

"What's that?!" the mob cried.

Soon after, Fu Yao jumped down through the hole as well, hurling out over a dozen yellow talismans with one swing of his hand. "Get lost! Don't get in the way of my work!" he yelled.

"Ah! It's the skilled master!" the mob cried.

Lan Chang dragged herself over and rolled down through the hole too. "Stop hitting him!"

"Wha—! A woman!" the mob cried again.

Yellow talismans shot everywhere like iron needles, like flying blades. While Xie Lian dodged by just slightly shifting his body, Qi Rong couldn't get away, and all of the talismans thudded squarely into his back.

"GHOST MURDER!" he wailed pathetically.

The mob swarmed over and gathered around him to examine the talismans, gasping in awe.

"Wow, what incredible aim…"

The once perfectly serviceable kitchen was suddenly horribly crowded, cramped, and clamorous. Fu Yao was chasing the leaping and dodging fetus spirit, and Lan Chang was chasing Fu Yao as if she'd gone mad. Half of Qi Rong's face had been crushed out of shape by Xie Lian pressing him to the chopping board, and his back had turned into a target for the talismans Fu Yao had hurled while the crowd watched. Lan Chang would even occasionally step on Qi Rong in the heat of her chase.

"Why? Why are there so many people?!" Qi Rong lamented. "Who are you? And who are *you*? Is no one gonna let me fucking eat?! WHY IS IT ALWAYS LIKE THIS NO MATTER WHERE I GO?! WHAT DO Y'ALL HAVE AGAINST ME?!"

As he wailed, his eyes spun, and he saw through the collapsed wall of the kitchen to the yard outside. Hua Cheng was out there, looking like he hadn't noticed the mayhem inside; he sat calmly under a tree, relaxed and idle enough that he'd built a gold foil palace. Who knew how long he'd been playing around, bored out of his mind? He had already constructed a sumptuous little mansion from over a dozen sheets of gold foil.

Qi Rong instantly changed his tune. "Everyone, look outside, quick! Crimson Rain Sought Flower turned into a ghost brat!" he yelled at the top of his lungs. "If you hold a grudge against him, go now! Don't miss this chance! If you pass this up, you won't get another shot...!"

Before he could finish, a cold, glistening, bloody butcher knife was thrust between his teeth. Xie Lian's hand was gripping the knife's handle.

Xie Lian smiled. "Hmm? What are you yelling about?"

Qi Rong did not see how Xie Lian had managed to thrust the knife into his mouth so swiftly; he had only felt a sudden chill on his lips before realizing there was a new and extremely sharp object present on the tip of his tongue. Although he was unharmed as of yet, blood would flood his mouth if he tried moving the slightest bit. His voice died in his throat.

However, the crowd had already seen Hua Cheng stacking the gold foil palace in the yard outside the inn.

"Is that him?!"

"Probably!"

With Guzi in one arm and pulling Ruoye with the other, Xie Lian dashed outside to get there before the rest of them. Qi Rong was still bound by Ruoye, and he shrieked as he was dragged along the ground.

"DOG-FUCKED XIE LIAN, YOU MUST BE DOING THIS ON PURPOSE! I've never seen anyone as evil as you! You fake white lotus, AAAAAAAAAH—"

The mob gathered around.

"Do we...charge?"

"Watch out for traps. How about we observe first?"

In the meantime, Hua Cheng had finished building the little gold palace and had risen to his feet. He arched an eyebrow as he looked condescendingly down at the building he'd constructed, and then he gave a gentle kick.

Flop, flop, flop. The gold palace collapsed.

And the inn crumbled as well, rumbling as it did.

The spell was broken. Xie Lian turned back and looked. Behind him was no inn but rather a collapsed little cottage—the type of building that was a normal sight in barren hills like these. The inn was only an illusion.

The crowd of monks and cultivators hadn't yet decided whether to charge outside, so they were crushed by the collapsing roof and knocked unconscious by rotten logs and ragged straw. Xie Lian jogged to Hua Cheng's side.

"San Lang, won't using your power like this affect you?"

Hua Cheng gave an effortless wave, and the gold foil disappeared into thin air. "Don't worry, gege, something small like this is no bother."

A piece of the broken roof moved, and Fu Yao's head poked out. He shoved a pile of hay away, exclaiming angrily, "You're not bothered, but *I* am!"

Just moments before, he had finally captured the fetus spirit—but his vision suddenly went dark. When he looked up, the dilapidated roof was splitting and caving in, crumbling right on top of him. What a disaster! Fu Yao plucked a bunch of straw from his hair and stomped over to Xie Lian and Hua Cheng. He glared at Hua Cheng, who was shorter than him at present.

"You… You did this on purpose!" he raged.

Hua Cheng blinked. He neither rebuffed nor taunted him; he only raised his inky black eyes to look at Xie Lian. Xie Lian immediately grasped Hua Cheng's shoulder to push him behind his own body.

"No, no, surely not. Kids don't know how to control their strength… Sorry about that, Fu Yao."

Fu Yao's hair was a frightful mess. He stared at Xie Lian in disbelief. "Kids…? Your Highness, do you really think I'm blind enough to not recognize who *that* is?"

"What are you talking about?" Xie Lian replied, sounding puzzled. "This is just a very normal little boy."

"…"

Fu Yao stared at Hua Cheng and narrowed his eyes. Behind them came faint creaking sounds—Lan Chang had also pushed away a chunk of roof and crawled out, and Fu Yao turned to walk over. Xie Lian sighed a breath of relief. He settled Guzi on the ground, but a somewhat hesitant voice sounded by his ear as he was doing so.

"Your Highness…?"

Xie Lian straightened up at once. "…Feng Xin?"

It was indeed Feng Xin on the other end, and it sounded like he was sighing in relief.

"Thank goodness! You haven't changed your verbal password."

Xie Lian gave a dry, soundless laugh. Eight hundred years ago when he activated his verbal password for the first time, it was "just recite the *Dao De Jing* a thousand times." He'd never changed it, even centuries later, and Feng Xin actually remembered what it was. Xie Lian recalled the way Feng Xin had laughed until he was hoarse when he first heard that verbal password all those years back, and he couldn't help but feel nostalgic—even though it was hardly the right time.

"Yes, it hasn't changed. How are things in the Upper Court? Has the Heavenly Emperor been informed of the matter with Ling Wen?"

Hua Cheng could tell that he was talking to an Upper Court official and conscientiously stepped away, placing his hand on Guzi's forehead to check for a fever.

Feng Xin's voice grew serious. "Things aren't good. And yes, he knows. The entire Upper Court is in chaos right now."

Xie Lian sighed. "Ling Wen has always handled coordination and management of Upper Court affairs, so there's no helping that. Can't any other civil gods take her place?"

"They've tried, but they're not effective," Feng Xin said. "Usually they're the first to scorn the Palace of Ling Wen—like they could do the job ten times better if they had the chance. But now that we actually need them to take up the task, not a single one can do even half of what she does. Just organizing news and information completely overwhelmed them; a number of civil gods have already dropped out and refuse to help any further."

Xie Lian shook his head.

"And it's not just Ling Wen," Feng Xin continued. "Something happened with Mu Qing too. He was detained at first, but he attacked and injured the official who was guarding him and escaped."

"What?!"

On hearing this, Xie Lian jolted, then immediately looked at Fu Yao on impulse. The black-clad youth was saying something to Lan Chang, and while there was displeasure on his face, the disquiet was more obvious. Xie Lian walked farther away and hushed his voice.

"What happened to Mu Qing? How did it come to that?!"

"It isn't just that he was locked up. The entire Palace of Xuan Zhen has been suspended pending investigation," Feng Xin replied. "It's all because of the fetus spirit."

Xie Lian suppressed his voice further. "What happened with the fetus spirit? Is he really involved in that case?"

"Yes," Feng Xin said. "Mu Qing was responsible for apprehending the female ghost Lan Chang and that fetus spirit, as they were among the nefarious creatures that escaped. But he didn't manage to capture them; he let them get away. During the pursuit, the fetus spirit recognized Mu Qing. It said Mu Qing was the one who carved it from its mother's womb and molded it into a little ghost."

"That's impossible!" Xie Lian blurted. "No way! Even though Mu Qing is someone who's...well...well, surely he had no reason to do something like that?"

"Who knows," Feng Xin said. "But apparently there's an evil cultivation method to accelerate ascension which involves the use of dead babies. Now many of us are suspicious of the legitimacy of his ascension, so they detained him so that they could take their time in thoroughly investigating all his past actions. Who knew he couldn't keep cool, or that he'd bolt like this? Now everyone believes he's guilty and went on the run because of it."

"Wait, wait, wait, wait, wait," Xie Lian said. "This really isn't right. If Mu Qing was the perpetrator, then why didn't the fetus spirit and Lan Chang recognize him at the Palace of Divine Might?

Why did they only accuse him while trying to avoid capture? It's very obviously slander, is it not?"

"By the time I found out, things had already gotten bad, so I'm not sure what really happened," Feng Xin said. "It seems Lan Chang and the fetus spirit didn't know the identity of the one who performed the evil ritual, but the fetus spirit had a random moment of clarity while it was being molded. In that instant, it broke free of the spellcaster's control and bit their arm. When the fetus spirit was fighting with Mu Qing, it happened to see that there was also a bite scar on his arm—and it was centuries old."

"...Did the bite mark match the fetus spirit's teeth?" Xie Lian asked.

"It was an exact match," Feng Xin replied.

"And how did Mu Qing explain this?" Xie Lian asked, brow furrowed in contemplation.

"He admitted that he'd seen the fetus spirit before," Feng Xin said. "But he doesn't admit to being the perpetrator; he says that he saved the fetus spirit out of benevolence, and it bit him in the process. He might as well not have tried to explain anything with a 'confession' like that."

That was quite true—as far as everyone else was concerned, Mu Qing would never do anything of the sort. He was hardly considered the type to help another out of the kindness of his heart, protect and cherish children, or perform anonymous good deeds. Mu Qing had always been a loner; he never showed any kindness that wasn't strictly required of him and didn't have any intimate friends in the heavens. Now that something like this had happened, no one would believe him even if he tried to argue, and naturally there was no one to speak on his behalf. This was probably why he chose to run away and investigate the truth himself.

"In any case, things are still out of control up here, Your Highness," Feng Xin said. "Where are you right now? The Heavenly Emperor said the gathering of ghosts probably can't be stopped at this point. Hurry back to join the emergency assembly!"

"I'm currently—" Xie Lian started.

Before he could continue, Fu Yao's cold voice sounded from behind him.

"Who are you talking to?"

75

Sharp-Tongued with Pointed Teeth, Winds Devoured and Arrow Shredded

XIE LIAN HEAVED A SIGH and turned around.

"Alas, I *would* like to talk to someone if I could, but I can't get a word through now that the spiritual communication array of the Upper Court is in shambles, and I don't know any heavenly official's verbal password. Fu Yao, do you have anyone's password information? Just so I can send news back and let them know I'm here, and request some assistance."

He looked at ease and natural, and the overall effect was extremely persuasive. The gloomy clouds shrouding Fu Yao's face dispersed.

"I don't," he said dismissively. "The heavens are a mess right now; everyone's busy. Take care of things on your own."

Just then, Hua Cheng spoke up. "Gege, this child hasn't eaten in two days. And he's burning up."

Xie Lian walked over to check, and sure enough, Guzi's forehead was so hot an egg could be fried on it. He immediately yanked Qi Rong up and demanded, "How on earth have you been caring for him?"

Qi Rong's face was covered in blood. "It's not like this ancestor is his real dad!" he spat. "It's already incredibly compassionate that I haven't eaten him! Mark me down for merits, quick!"

"That's only because he wouldn't taste good while feverish, isn't it?" Xie Lian commented.

Lan Chang hesitated for a moment before speaking up. "Is that child sick? Why don't I take a look?"

She was black and blue from the collapsed beams of that dilapidated cottage, but she felt sorry for the child and crawled over. She cradled Guzi in her arms and placed her palm over his head, using her body's ghostly chill to cool his fever. Fu Yao walked over with the fetus spirit in hand, squashed and tied into a ball with a talisman.

"Time to go."

Lan Chang obviously didn't want to leave, but her son was in his hands, so she was helpless.

Xie Lian spoke up. "Wait, don't leave yet. Fu Yao, are you able to communicate with your general right now?"

Fu Yao looked at him. "What do you want?"

Xie Lian chewed on his words. "Actually..."

Before he fully said the word, his hand darted out as fast as lightning. He restrained Fu Yao's arms behind his back, locking him in an unbreakable grip before he continued.

"Actually, I already know he's in trouble!"

Fu Yao had been careless and had allowed himself to be caught, and he was as shocked as he was furious. "You! You sly—!"

"No, no. I caught you by my strength alone. You're welcome to try ambushing me in the same way and seeing if you can hold me down."

Hua Cheng clapped politely. "I agree."

Fu Yao's eyes were about to roll from sheer anger. "Then why don't you let me go so I *can* try, huh?!"

Xie Lian straightened his expression. "Next time, if you get a chance. But right now, we've got more important things to worry about. Fu Yao, will you help me urge your general to return to the Upper Court?"

"Return...?" Fu Yao forcefully suppressed his anger and hissed out a reply. "That's easy for you to say! If *you* were the one stuck in this situation, would you go back? What would *you* say if others urged you to return? Would you return only to be wronged and wait for an equally wrongful conviction? Would you go back and wait for death?!"

"Don't get riled up, I'm being serious," Xie Lian said. "I'm not being sarcastic. Your general and I are different. His situation isn't so serious that it's unsalvageable; the real issue was him running away. That was the worst possible reaction. If you can manage to contact him, tell him I can help him investigate."

Fu Yao was stunned. "You...help him investigate?"

"Yeah. I've done a lot of investigations, so I'm fairly experienced. More experienced than he is, anyway," Xie Lian said.

"Your Highness, need I remind you? Since you returned to the heavens, how many heavenly officials have you investigated?" Fu Yao said. "And how many of those heavenly officials have survived those investigations?"

Xie Lian softly cleared his throat. "That's different. The problem doesn't lie with me here. If he really didn't commit a crime, I can prove his innocence."

Fu Yao puffed an exasperated laugh and cut him off. "That's enough! It's not like no one knows of the grudge between you two. 'Help him investigate.' Would he even have the chance to turn this around if you did? If you want to use this chance to drag him down and mock him, just say so outright instead of being fake."

Hua Cheng's face turned dark when he heard this. He smiled soon after. "Never mind, gege. This guy doesn't know how to recognize goodness when he sees it. Why waste your breath? Some people are simply born ungrateful; their wretched, selfish minds are fundamentally incapable of recognizing an honest man's integrity and heart. Who knows—after investigating, you might uncover that he really did commit the crime. He doesn't trust you, and *I* don't have the time to care about his issues. Let him struggle and figure things out for himself."

Fu Yao eyed him and taunted, "'Kid'?"

Hua Cheng returned his respects and mocked back, "'Junior Official'?"

Fu Yao's face dropped slightly.

Xie Lian tightened his hold. "Well, these are two completely different matters. Personal affairs and business shouldn't mix," he said gently. "It's one thing if there is a grudge between us, but whether he committed a crime is another matter entirely. Someone like Mu Qing... Even though he's petty, narrow-minded, overly sensitive, paranoid, has a bad personality, is prone to fixating on the little things, never says anything pleasant, likes to nag, is always offending others and has garnered a lot of dislike on that account, has no friends, and remembers small, unimportant offenses for far too long..."

"..."

Xie Lian went on and on with a straight face, all in a single breath. He concluded with "...I've known him since we were young. He's still got principles."

"..."

"He might spit in the cup of someone he doesn't like, but he would never poison the water," Xie Lian continued.

"..."

"Really? That's still gross, though," Hua Cheng commented indifferently.

Veins were popping on Fu Yao's forehead. "*No!* He would never spit either!"

"Laxatives, then," Xie Lian said.

Fu Yao seemed as though he was holding something back as he gritted out a response. "You... Must you describe him that way? Are you speaking for him or against him?"

"Sorry, I just couldn't think of any better examples at the moment," Xie Lian apologized.

Fu Yao tried struggling, but he couldn't get out of Xie Lian's hold. "Were you just snitching to someone in the Upper Court?" he demanded in alarm.

"Not yet. I was just chatting. Don't worry, I won't hurt your general," Xie Lian replied in a heartfelt tone. "If he really doesn't want to go back, then why not join me? We can work together. That way, there's a witness for anything he does. He won't be able to clear himself otherwise, and things will only get worse..."

Just then, there was a roar of crude laughter from behind them. Qi Rong had been staring at Lan Chang's face and suddenly lost his mind.

"HA HA HA HA HA HA HA, I wondered who this was! You—aren't you my lady Jian Lan?"

Lan Chang was holding Guzi in her arms to cool his temperature, but when she heard Qi Rong, she shuddered and her eyes widened.

"Who are you? How do you also—"

Qi Rong snickered. "How do I know? Please! You almost wound up having to call me your little cousin! What, did *everyone* from the past turn into a ghost? I've been fucking around all over the place, and all I see are familiar faces! This world is so small and lively, hee hee!"

Xie Lian frowned. "Qi Rong, have you gone mad again? Who's Jian Lan?"

"Heh, Cousin Crown Prince. Are you blind or are you just playing dumb?" Qi Rong taunted. "Look closely at who this is—it's the number one eligible maiden of our Xianle, the 'young' Lady Jian Lan! Her family was full of politicians and merchants, indescribably grand and glorious. Her looks were only so-so, but her name was always on the list every time there was a Xianle beauty appraisal. She was so proud that her eyes grew on the top of her head; she saw and cared for no one. She almost entered the harem to be elected as your consort!"

"What?"

Xie Lian's eyes flew to Lan Chang's face. Back then, the king and the queen did indeed intend to select a consort for him. They summoned a number of carefully selected, exquisitely beautiful girls to the palace for a banquet to let him see if there was anyone in particular that he might fancy. However, young Xie Lian had his heart wholly focused on cultivation, and he left the banquet after making only a single round of the room. He never even bothered to remember the faces or names of those girls, so he could recall nothing of Lan Chang.

Lan Chang glanced at Fu Yao, but Fu Yao only humphed. "My general mentioned nothing of this. This woman is also a surviving citizen of Xianle, so she must've seen you at some point in the past."

Xie Lian looked at Hua Cheng, who didn't appear surprised; he probably hadn't only just learned of this. He then turned to Lan Chang and mumbled, "Were you really…"

However, Lan Chang hurriedly covered her ears. "Don't say it! Don't say it out loud! Don't use that name to address me! I… changed my name a long time ago."

Xie Lian was taken aback at first, but he soon dropped his arm and sighed.

The daughter of a noble family from bygone years was now a prostitute in the Ghost Realm. She probably changed her name because she was afraid of bringing shame to her dead family, and she didn't want to admit that the woman she was now was still that same girl.

This woman was once his devotee, one of his people. How could he not sigh?

Just then, he felt warmth wrap around his hand. When he looked down, it was Hua Cheng; he didn't look at him, but his hand was clasped around Xie Lian's. He was currently in the form of a child, and his body temperature was as cool as ever. But he felt warmth when that small, cool hand held his own.

Qi Rong didn't possess any such sympathies and clicked his tongue. "Who would've thought that Lady Jian Lan, previously so out of reach, would turn into such an old, ugly hag! I never thought you were all that beautiful, and now—well, my eyes were certainly sharp back then; you really don't look like anything amazing! I might as well ask this question too—who's the dad of the mutt you gave birth to?"

His words were extremely crass, and Jian Lan's face grew pale.

"Could it be Cousin Crown Prince?" Qi Rong theorized. "No, no, that cousin of mine probably can't even get it up. That's why he's always pretended to be so chaste with no mind for women; what a faker. How could he sire a son? Oh, oh! How could I forget? After Xianle fell, wasn't my lady sold to *that* kind of place? It must be the seed of some Yong'an pleb!"

Xie Lian couldn't stand this anymore. He was about to make him shut up, but Jian Lan exploded faster than he did and gave Qi Rong a resounding slap to the face.

"What garbage are you spewing?!"

Qi Rong glared as his nose bled heavily from her strike. "You're nothing more than a fierce or a malice! How dare a nobody like you hit me! Me, who's an Almost-Supreme!"

Jian Lan spat on his face, then smacked him a couple times more after seizing him by the neck. "What's a shitty 'Almost-Supreme'?! You sure know how to talk yourself up! Who do you think you are? You seriously think you're worthy to be considered equal to the other three supremes?! Is there anything you're good at, aside from having such thick skin?! Of course I dare hit you!"

Her words stabbed Qi Rong where it hurt. Qi Rong grew frustrated and began to yell, spittle flying everywhere.

"FOUL WENCH, LET GO WITH YOUR CHICKEN CLAWS! THIS ANCESTOR THINKS YOU'RE DIRTY! BLEH, BLEH, BLEH!"

The two began to tussle, but it was a very one-sided fight. Jian Lan was free to throttle Qi Rong at will, as he was bound by Ruoye and couldn't move a muscle.

"Xie Lian!" he howled. "How come you won't stop the fight?! Where's your saintly heart?!"

Xie Lian kept his unbreakable hold on Fu Yao with a single hand and had his head lowered to talk to Hua Cheng. He paid no mind to Qi Rong's shrieks.

Jian Lan kicked at Qi Rong, her eyes flashing red. "Even if I've been wasted on plebs, I don't want a worm like you touching a single one of my fingers!" she spat angrily. "*Nobody* wants you, you despicable creature! *Trash!* Think you're good enough to look down on others?! Who are you to turn your nose up at me?!"

Qi Rong was livid. "Nobody wants *me*? Trash?! Does a rotted hussy like you have the right to call me that?! Who else but a pleb would appreciate looks like yours?! ...Wait! PUT DOWN THAT BOULDER!!"

As they brawled, a crash of thunder rumbled from the skies. Everyone looked up at the same time.

"Didn't you say you didn't snitch and were only chatting?" Fu Yao demanded.

Hua Cheng frowned slightly, then humphed. "Showing up uninvited."

A crackle of lightning exploded in the night sky, and everyone shielded their eyes from the sudden flash. When they blinked their eyes open, a tall, black-clad heavenly official with a longbow strapped to his back was approaching them in long strides.

"Your Highness!"

Xie Lian dropped his sleeve and surreptitiously pushed Hua Cheng behind him. "Feng Xin! Why have you come?"

Feng Xin quickly walked over to him. "You suddenly stopped responding, so I asked around and traced your location by following the ripples of spiritual energy." Then he knitted his brows. "What's going on here? What a mess. Did you run into something?"

Xie Lian was about to answer when Feng Xin noticed that he had Fu Yao seized in his grip and Hua Cheng standing behind him. It was a picture completely outside his imagination, and he seemed not to know which of the two should surprise him more.

"What..." Finally, he settled on pointing at Hua Cheng. "...What's with this child?"

Xie Lian laughed dryly. "Cute, right?"

Feng Xin glared as he observed Hua Cheng, whose expression didn't match Xie Lian's comment in the least. "...Cute?" He sounded doubtful. "Why do I think he looks a lot like..."

"Like my son, right?" Xie Lian easily replied.

Feng Xin was shocked. "...When did you have a son?!"

Xie Lian smiled. "I haven't had one yet. I'm just saying that if I do have a son, he'll surely be just as cute, right?"

Hua Cheng held Xie Lian's hand and smiled. "Right."

"..." said Feng Xin.

"..." said Fu Yao.

"Ha ha ha ha…huh? Miss Lan Chang, don't run!" Xie Lian called.

Feng Xin whipped around and saw a woman's shadow leap away from Qi Rong and start wildly dashing away. Without a moment of hesitation, he aimed an arrow and locked on to her legs.

Perhaps because it sensed its mother was in danger, the fetus spirit in Fu Yao's hand, still bound into a ball by yellow talismans, started quivering. It then burst out of its chains and shrieked as it lunged at Feng Xin. Jian Lan seemed like she'd just bolted due to panic; only when she heard the fetus spirit's screeching did she remember that her son was still in another's clutches.

She whirled around and cried, "Cuocuo!"

This was the first time Xie Lian had heard the fetus spirit's name—so it was called Cuocuo. Feng Xin changed his intended target and shot at that snow-white fetus spirit. There was a sudden loud *crunch*, and the fetus spirit flipped in the air a few times before hopping into a nearby tree. It had snapped the arrow between its teeth, and everyone finally had the chance to see its appearance clearly.

It could hardly be considered a human fetus—it more resembled a diminutive, deformed monster. Its skin was blanched, so starkly white it was like it had been coated in a layer of powder. Its eyes were abnormally large and shone with a peculiar light. Atop its head there sprouted a few sparse, yellowing strands of hair. Two rows of razor-sharp fangs gnawed at Feng Xin's arrow; when it noticed him looking its way, it rapidly reduced the arrow to splinters and then spat out the shimmering arrowhead to nail it into the ground next to Feng Xin's boots. A long, thin, dark-red snakelike tongue slithered out of its mouth, as if it was taunting him.

Without another word, Feng Xin reached for a new arrow and locked on to the creature. The fetus spirit crawled up and down the tree like a lizard, exceedingly agile—no wonder Fu Yao had trouble catching it.

"Don't fight him, *run!*" Jian Lan cried anxiously.

Only a blood parent could love such a disgusting, horrifying monster. Feng Xin locked on, loosed his bowstring, and let an arrow fly. One of the fetus spirit's little legs was pierced through, and it shrieked, unable to crawl around any longer. Jian Lan dashed back over, hand extended to yank out the arrow—but her level of power was too low, and when she touched the fletching, she was hurled away by the rebound, trailing sparks. She stumbled back a few steps but soon flung herself forward again, relentlessly attempting to remove the arrow and provoking splashes of sparks as she did.

Feng Xin put away his bow and approached. "All right, time to go back. Don't add any more work to our pile... Jian Lan?!"

Jian Lan had just been thrown back again, and she shuddered when she heard his voice. She stopped moving and quickly turned away.

However, Feng Xin pulled her back around to face him. "Jian Lan?" he repeated.

"..." Xie Lian could sense trouble and asked, puzzled, "What's going on?"

Jian Lan kept her head down and mumbled vaguely. "You've got the wrong person."

"What are you talking about? How could I mistake you for anyone else?" Feng Xin exclaimed. "You look very different now, but I still would not..."

But the words got stuck in his throat, because he really *hadn't* recognized her when Jian Lan was Lan Chang, caked in heavy makeup and done up like a harlot.

It couldn't be helped. Feng Xin still looked exactly the same as he did once upon a time, but Jian Lan's transformation was truly too great. Her looks, makeup, manners, speech, class… Even if her own parents stood before her, they might not recognize their precious daughter.

Feng Xin was astonished. "It's you… It really is you. It has to be you! I thought…you had gotten married and lived well. How did you… How did you become like this…?"

At that question, Jian Lan suddenly turned and shoved him, cussing. "You *motherfucker*!"

Feng Xin was forced back a few steps with her shove and couldn't reply. Jian Lan continued to aggressively shove at his chest while she screamed.

"I already said that I'm not that hag! Do you not understand human words?! Is your head totally empty?! What the hell was that—a triple attack of 'You, it's you, it's really you!' Can't you pretend to not know me? Can't you pretend to not recognize me?! Oh My Lord, please, I beg you—leave me some dignity, okay? All right?!"

Her behavior made her look no different from a shrew on the streets. This was probably too different from the Jian Lan in Feng Xin's memories, so he simply stared at her dumbly, unable to speak. Xie Lian was the same. Qi Rong was the most delighted of the bunch, rolling on the ground as he laughed.

"HA HA HA HA HA HA HA, OH MY FUCKING GOD! Cousin Crown Prince! Do you see what's happening? You got cucked by your most loyal dog!"

Jian Lan violently stomped on Qi Rong a few times. "Dog! A dog! You're the most like a dog!"

Strictly speaking, while Jian Lan had once carried the heavy hopes of her family on her shoulders, she had never formally entered the

harem and was never made a consort. So while Qi Rong's schadenfreude made no sense, Xie Lian still didn't know what to say.

He had never imagined that Feng Xin, who wouldn't even speak to a woman if he could help it, would actually...

The fetus spirit snapped the arrow that was nailing it down with a crunch of its jaws, and it lunged at Feng Xin once more. In a moment of carelessness, Feng Xin allowed it to sink its teeth deep into his right arm. Blood oozed nonstop from the wound.

Feng Xin's dominant hand was his right, but an injury to that hand was nothing to a martial god. Feng Xin had moved to strike with his left when Jian Lan cried out.

"Don't hit him!"

Feng Xin's hand abruptly stopped in midair, and a terrifying thought was born.

It wasn't just him—everyone present realized it at once. Feng Xin allowed the fetus spirit to gnaw at his arm like a man-eating fish as he looked at Jian Lan.

"Is...this...?"

76

I Decide the Path I Walk

XIE LIAN SUDDENLY REMEMBERED something—that fateful day at the Palace of Divine Might, Lan Chang had randomly accused everyone, but she had never pointed her finger at Feng Xin even though he was standing in the most conspicuous spot.

Jian Lan immediately denied it. "He's not!"

Disbelief was plain on Fu Yao's face as well; he seemed dumbfounded at the revelation that Feng Xin and this woman were connected. Hearing her speak, he finally snapped out of it.

"He hasn't even asked anything, so why did you answer so quickly?"

"Please! It's obvious what he was going to say," Jian Lan said. "And I'm telling you, he's *not*!"

However, Feng Xin was staring at the fetus spirit. "What did you call him? Cuocuo?"

That name, *"mistake,"* seemed to have a special implication. Jian Lan opened her mouth, then closed it, no longer willing to argue.

"What's a big man like you doing, talking so much?" she said instead, frustrated. "If I said he's not, he's not! Who the hell's so eager to recognize their bastard?!"

"What are you saying?" Feng Xin replied angrily. "If he is, then of course I'll…"

"Of course you'll *what*? Recognize him? Raise him?" Jian Lan countered.

"I..." Feng Xin was stuck.

He looked down at the deformed little monster hanging off of his arm. The fetus spirit seemed to bear a particularly deep hatred for him; it was latched on, tearing and chomping and crying *wah wah wah*. Feng Xin didn't know what to do; he couldn't hit it, nor could he *not* hit it. His bloodied hand clenched into a fist.

Seeing that he was stumped, that it looked like he couldn't accept the truth, Jian Lan *tsk*-ed at him. "I already said he's not, but you're still pushing! He's got nothing to do with you. There. Feel better?!"

"Bullshit! He has to!" Qi Rong yapped. "See, I wasn't wrong—it really is the spawn of a pleb! Everyone come check this out; Feng Xin's own son was carved out of his ol' ma's belly and turned into a little ghost, hee hee. I can't believe people actually pray to this shitty 'Son-Gifting' Nan Yang! Watch out, the more you pray, the more your sons are gonna be..."

Xie Lian raised his hand and Ruoye sealed Qi Rong's mouth. Jian Lan also stomped heavily on his head a few times, which led to some muffled screams.

Just then, Guzi blearily woke up to see Qi Rong getting trampled, and he lunged forward. "Don't... Don't step on my dad..."

With Guzi clinging to Qi Rong's head, Jian Lan couldn't stomp anymore. Instead, she changed course; she seized the fetus spirit by its little blanched legs and bolted, yelling at it angrily as she went.

"I told you to stop biting! So disobedient!"

Feng Xin was spacing out and didn't manage to catch them in time.

"Ruoye, chase!" Xie Lian cried on reflex.

Ruoye chased as commanded, but only once the white silk bandage flew out did Xie Lian remember that it had been binding

Qi Rong. He looked back, and sure enough, Qi Rong had leapt to his feet looking pleased, with Guzi still clinging to his head.

"This ancestor's free again!" he announced.

Seeing that Feng Xin had finally snapped out of it, Xie Lian changed Ruoye's orders.

"Ruoye, come back after all."

Thus, Ruoye came flying back to give Qi Rong a sound slap—*thwack!* Qi Rong had been singing the song of freedom, but now he was clobbered hard enough to spin in place three times. He tumbled to the ground, covering his face. After sprawling there for a moment, he went berserk and seized hold of Ruoye, shouting at it.

"Even a rag like you dares hit me?!"

This time, Ruoye was stuck in his clutches; it couldn't free itself no matter how it twisted. It was as if Qi Rong's strength had suddenly exploded. Xie Lian was about to take care of him personally when Qi Rong realized there was a small child on his head. He yanked Guzi down, holding him like a shield to protect himself.

"Don't come a step closer! Do it and I'll strangle him! Hey, hey, hey, look behind you, that dog Hua Cheng is gonna die!"

Shocked, Xie Lian whipped around. Sure enough, Hua Cheng's brows were tightly knit, and his hands were trembling at his sides. It seemed like he was forcing himself to endure something, but when he saw Xie Lian looking over at him, he immediately declared, "I'm fine!"

The agitation of ghosts!

The tremors this time seemed stronger than any so far. In a split-second decision, Xie Lian rushed back to Hua Cheng's side to hold him in his arms. Qi Rong took this chance to make his getaway with Guzi in his clutches.

Jian Lan also seemed to be suffering a throbbing headache, and she vainly covered her ears to muffle the tremors' calls. The fetus spirit bit and tore even more violently under this aggravation. Feng Xin had been bitten over a dozen times, and blood was pouring freely from the wounds, but he still didn't dare hit the creature; he instead reached out to tightly grab hold of Jian Lan's arm. The fetus spirit, however, didn't hold back, and swung its claws toward Feng Xin's face to give him a nasty scratch. Feng Xin grunted and covered the new wound; it wasn't clear if his eyes had been injured. Xie Lian was mortified and was about to send forth Ruoye, but Jian Lan furiously stomped her feet.

"If you keep this up, I'm going to get angry!"

Only after being scolded by its mother did the fetus spirit jump back into her arms, obediently curling up into a bundle. Jian Lan gave Feng Xin a look and gritted her teeth.

"He has *nothing* to do with you. I'm warning you, leave us alone!"

And then, with one hand hugging her head and the other hugging her son, the mother fled with her child in tow.

Fu Yao cried, "Let me go!"

Feng Xin knelt on the ground, covering half his face. Xie Lian crouched next to him with Hua Cheng in his arms.

"Are you all right? Let me take a look at your injuries. Was your eye scratched?"

Blood dripped through the cracks of his fingers, and Feng Xin replied with his eyes closed. "...No. And don't ask me."

"Feng Xin... Lan Chang... Miss Jian Lan, what was she talking..."

Xie Lian had only just started to ask when Feng Xin swung out his fist. With a loud *crack*, the tree beside them was punched in half.

"I *told* you not to ask me!" he roared.

That response sounded unexpectedly resentful, and Xie Lian could tell the resentment was directed at him. He couldn't help but be taken aback.

But Hua Cheng commented coldly, "Who turned your wife and son into ghosts? Go burn the right person with that fire of yours."

At this, Feng Xin raised his head slightly to stare at Fu Yao, his eyes red. Fu Yao was at first stunned, then furious.

"What are you looking at? You don't actually think it was m...my general? What is this terrible luck?! All he did was notice that the woman was a surviving citizen of Xianle and had some relation to the royals and nobility, so he lent her a helping hand. He had wanted to save that fetus spirit, but it refused to see sense; not only did it not want to be saved, it even turned into a fierce! Nothing good came of his help, and he ended up coated in crap. Had he known it'd end like that, he wouldn't have bothered! That little ghost doesn't even recognize who gave *birth* to it; you think it actually knows who *killed* it?!"

Perhaps it was because he had gotten tangled up in too many upsetting things lately, but his words were quite rude indeed.

"Your general calls a trifling incident like this 'terrible luck'? Should people who suffer worse luck simply die, then?" Hua Cheng said.

Feng Xin shook his head. "...How did things end up this way?" he murmured. "How did it get like this?"

"Why...don't you take care of your injuries first," Xie Lian tried. "Did you bring any balms?"

Feng Xin glanced at him and said darkly, "I'm fine. Don't worry about me!"

He didn't bother tending to his wounds. With one hand covering his injuries, he stood up and stumbled away. Xie Lian and Fu Yao called after him a few times to ask if he was going back to the Upper Court or planned on giving chase, but he didn't answer, and soon his silhouette disappeared.

Fu Yao struggled again. "Your Highness!" he cried angrily. "If you won't give chase, will you at least let *me* do it?"

Xie Lian snapped out of it. After weighing the options, he agreed, "All right."

And then he actually let go. Fu Yao didn't seem to think he would actually comply, and he humphed as he worked out the kinks in his wrists.

"Why are you so willing to let me go *now*?"

Xie Lian rubbed his forehead. "The...*situation*...in the Upper Court is probably even worse than I imagined..." He sighed. "Rather than advising your general to return, I now think he should continue to act on his own."

He paused briefly, then added, "What are you going to do now? I don't think the fetus spirit was throwing around that defamation as simply a means of escape. There might be someone directing it behind the scenes."

Fu Yao dusted off his sleeves. "Who cares? It's heading for Mount Tonglu, so I'll figure that out after capturing it!"

He rushed off. The inn, once lively with so many groups of people, was suddenly quiet and deserted. Xie Lian turned and went to check the collapsed cottage. He flipped and pulled aside the beams and straw to look around and made sure that those monks and cultivators really were only unconscious. Upon reassuring himself that they would probably come around soon, he left as well.

He and Hua Cheng traveled for a while, and once they had left the barren hills behind, they finally found a real inn and stopped to rest.

The past few days felt like a flurry of chaos to Xie Lian. He sat on the windowsill, lost in thought. Ruoye curled around his arm, rubbing against him gently as if it were purring, and Xie Lian scratched it absentmindedly.

Hua Cheng came to the window to bathe under the same moonlight. He spoke his mind.

"It has nothing to do with you."

Xie Lian was shaken out of his reverie. He soon understood what that meant, but he shook his head.

"I don't know if that's true… Feng Xin must've befriended Miss Jian Lan after the fall of Xianle and before his own ascension. That would've been during the years of my first banishment."

"But that doesn't mean you're at fault for how things turned out," Hua Cheng said.

After some thought, Xie Lian said, "San Lang, I've never talked about my first banishment, have I?"

"No," Hua Cheng said.

"I've never told anyone. I hope you don't mind if I make you listen to me babble," Xie Lian said.

Hua Cheng lightly pushed himself up onto the windowsill to sit there as well. "I don't mind. Go ahead."

Xie Lian began to speak, chasing his memories. "Back then, the only subordinate I had left was Feng Xin, and life was very difficult. The possessions I had while I was a martial god, while I was a crown prince, were all pawned off."

Hua Cheng chuckled. "Including Hongjing, right?"

Xie Lian smiled gaily. "Ha ha ha…that's right. Jun Wu can't know about that; do keep it a secret for me. And those dozens of golden belts—they were pawned too."

"Mmm. So Feng Xin took one of your golden belts and gave it to Lan Chang?" Hua Cheng asked.

Xie Lian shook his head. "I don't think that's true. Feng Xin wouldn't have taken my things so frivolously. I was the one who told him to sell it and to keep the money for himself."

That was essentially Xie Lian giving him a lot of money for no reason. Feng Xin had repeatedly declined the offer at the time, but Xie Lian was relentless, and in the end he had said, *"I'll keep it for you for now."*

"It's shameful to admit this, but the reason I made him sell those things and keep the money wasn't just out of guilt—it was also out of fear."

With all his devotees gone, only Feng Xin still treated him like the Flower-Crowned Martial God and His Highness the Crown Prince. Only then did Xie Lian realize that, even though they had grown up together and Feng Xin was his trusted servant and bodyguard, he had not once received any special reward.

Suddenly, Xie Lian knew fear—fear that Feng Xin would decide this life was too hard and stop following him.

Thus, that golden belt wasn't meant as a reward. It wasn't purely a gift or a show of appreciation—more one of compensation and ingratiation.

Xie Lian had seen a protection charm in the illusion created by the fetus spirit; it was probably something Feng Xin had given to Jian Lan. After Xianle fell, all of Xie Lian's temples and shrines were burned down. Not a single soul believed in the Crown Prince of Xianle anymore, and his protection charms were seen as trash. However, Feng Xin was still determined and tirelessly handed them out—all the while telling Xie Lian, *"Look, you still have devotees."* But Xie Lian knew deep down that all those protection charms were most likely thrown away.

"Even after so many years, I never knew if Feng Xin fancied anyone. I never asked, and I never paid attention," Xie Lian said slowly.

After all, he had been the darling of the heavens since birth, high and mighty and above all. Feng Xin naturally orbited around him like he was the sun, so how could he possibly have his own life and own heart?

"It might not sound great to give a girl something you yourself had been given, but that golden belt was genuinely the best gift Feng Xin could manage at the time. After all, we were frequently missing meals, and Feng Xin wasn't someone who'd spend wastefully. It's easy to imagine how much he liked Miss Jian Lan. But if he liked her so much...why did they split up?"

Whether or not the fetus spirit was Feng Xin's son, Xie Lian couldn't forgive himself if that time of poverty made Feng Xin lose the girl he loved.

"If he liked her but they separated in the end," Hua Cheng replied, "then it proves that what they had was only *like*."

Xie Lian smiled wistfully. "San Lang, things aren't always that absolute. Sometimes, it's not up to you to decide if the road is easy to walk."

"I might not be able to decide if the road is easy, but whether I walk it is entirely up to me," Hua Cheng said quietly.

Xie Lian blinked. He felt like a knot in his heart had been untied, and he stared wordlessly at Hua Cheng. Hua Cheng tilted his head.

"Gege, am I wrong?"

As he watched Hua Cheng's twinkling black eyes, Xie Lian suddenly grabbed hold of him and settled him on his lap.

"Ha ha ha, San Lang, you're very right!"

"..."

Hua Cheng seemed stunned by this and allowed himself to be lifted high in the air. Xie Lian laughed.

"Let me be blunt for a moment. The brash way San Lang said that—it quite resembled my younger self."

Hua Cheng seemed to have grown accustomed to being hugged and tossed around like this, and he quirked his brows. "Wow, what a dream."

They played around in the room for a while, then Xie Lian tossed Hua Cheng onto the bed before climbing on himself. He rolled over to face the ceiling and was about to speak when Hua Cheng abruptly sat up. His pupils shrank and his eyes turned sharp as he looked across the room.

Sensing something wrong, Xie Lian quickly sat up as well. He was awash in a cold sweat the moment he saw what it was.

Another person had silently appeared in their room. Somehow, neither of them had sensed a thing until now.

The person sat by the table, upon which there was a pot of tea brewed and ready, its fragrant scent permeating the air. And yet Xie Lian hadn't even noticed!

He couldn't help but feel a chill run down his spine as he leveled Fangxin in a defensive stance.

"Who's there?!"

"Do not be afraid," a man's voice replied evenly. "Tea, Xianle?"

"..."

That voice and figure were both suddenly very familiar. Even as his heart was still thumping, Xie Lian sighed a breath of relief. Some strands of hair had come loose during their play, and he brushed them back behind his ears.

"My Lord..."

Before he'd fully exhaled, he yanked up the blanket to hide both Hua Cheng and his own body.

"...Why has My Lord descended?"

The hand under the blanket grasped Hua Cheng tightly, gesturing for him not to worry. Jun Wu leisurely poured three cups of tea before he rose to his feet.

"You did not return, so naturally, I had to descend and see for myself what was keeping you."

He folded his hands behind his back as he spoke and slowly stepped out from the shadows to walk toward Xie Lian. Xie Lian's eyes traced up Jun Wu's white robes to land on the sword in his hand. Startled, he swiftly jumped off the bed.

"My Lord, I can explain..."

Unexpectedly, behind him, Hua Cheng pulled off the blanket and sat up. He wore a smile as he sat cross-legged with his arms casually resting on his knees.

"I don't think that's necessary," Hua Cheng said.

Xie Lian stood between them.

"I think we can probably sit down first and talk. Look at this child, My Lord, doesn't he look like—"

"Your son, correct?" Jun Wu finished the statement for him and smiled.

"...Ha, ha ha, ha ha ha ha..." Xie Lian laughed awkwardly for a bit. "How did My Lord know what I was going to say?"

Jun Wu finally moved his gaze off of Hua Cheng. He lightly patted Xie Lian's shoulder and, without another word, turned to sit at the table once more. Xie Lian understood this meant there would be no confrontation for the time being. He sighed an unconscious breath of relief.

If Jun Wu intended to kill, Xie Lian had personally witnessed just how terrifying he could be after he unsheathed his sword. Under no circumstances did Xie Lian want Hua Cheng to face that head-on.

Still, Hua Cheng's expression remained unfriendly, and his eyes never left Jun Wu. Jun Wu pushed the teacups forward.

"Good sir, although this is not the first time we have met, it certainly is the first time we have been in such close proximity. Since it is a peaceful occasion, why not take tea for wine and let us smooth over this situation?"

Xie Lian lightly cleared his throat and tried to appear as casual as possible while he donned his outer robe. Slipping on his boots, he asked, "My Lord, how are things in the Upper Court?"

Jun Wu didn't reply for a long moment. He set down his teacup and gazed out the window to watch the moon, then sighed. "I do not wish to speak of it."

"All right...I won't ask," Xie Lian said.

It would seem things were truly terrible. However, Jun Wu turned to look back and said, straight-faced, "I kid. Even if I do not wish to speak of it, I must. Xianle, leave your little friend for now and follow me outside for a moment."

Apparently, there were things to discuss that shouldn't be overheard. Xie Lian was about to comply when Hua Cheng made a leisurely comment from behind him.

"Your Upper Court is in complete chaos; it's not a secret. Even rube ghosts out in the countryside know that the ghosts' gathering couldn't be stopped this time, and they're howling nonstop in excitement. So why bother speaking in private?"

He climbed off the bed and languidly strolled to the table, then picked up a teacup to idly toy with—he seemed quite uninterested in actually drinking from it.

A few moments later, all three were seated at the table. Hua Cheng's current appearance looked young, but his expression and manners almost made one forget it.

"Nothing can deceive your eyes, good sir," Jun Wu replied evenly.

The tea had been poured by Jun Wu, and due respect must be given, so Xie Lian sipped from his cup. As he did so, he asked, "Isn't there still some time before Mount Tonglu's gates officially open and seal? Has it been confirmed that it's happening right now?"

Feng Xin had told him this as well, but Xie Lian suspected he was exaggerating. He doubted this was as certain as he'd claimed.

However, Jun Wu affirmed, "Indeed, it cannot be stopped."

"I suppose you had planned on doing what you've always done—deploy all the martial gods to blockade every road leading to Mount Tonglu and stop the ghosts en route," Hua Cheng commented. "But then Mu Qing broke out of prison and went on the run. His whereabouts are unknown, and his absence leaves a gap in the southern defense."

"Did Feng Xin return to the Heavenly Capital?" Xie Lian inquired. "How is he? Did he say anything?"

"He returned, but not in good condition," Jun Wu replied. "Nan Yang came back wounded and gave a rushed report of the situation, then pleaded for me to order all heavenly officials not to touch the female ghost Lan Chang and her son. He had wanted to descend again after reporting in, but his injuries were severe; he can barely move his right arm. I detained him to recover in the Heavenly Capital. However, that leaves the southern defense full of holes."

If this were any other matter—for example, if they needed someone to go kill a monster or steal spiritual pills or something—Xie Lian would volunteer in an instant. But one couldn't lead troops by charging ahead alone; one man might break through an army of millions, but there was no way he could defend against that army. Xie Lian had long understood that leading people and armies wasn't his strength. Rather than forcing himself to step up, it would be best if someone more suited for the position was nominated. Thus, he wasn't quick to volunteer.

Instead, he asked, "Is there no other martial god who can take up the task?"

"Other martial gods have their own domains and assignments to handle and can take on no more," Jun Wu replied. "Pei Xiu from the Palace of Ming Guang might have once been available, but he has long since been exiled. As for Qi Ying, he is the same as you: a free spirit who prefers to charge around the world alone, doing as he wishes—his whereabouts are also currently unknown, and that child never answers spiritual communication. The head official of the Palace of Ling Wen is also missing. There is a temporary chief, but while the other civil gods are certainly skilled in the arts...they are incapable when it comes to facilitating communication, making decisions, and coordinating management. These past few days..."

He made it sound like the Upper Court was about to fall apart. Xie Lian couldn't bear to hear it, and his sympathy only grew.

"I remember My Lord once said that there is another remedy to this, even if the gathering of ghosts can't be stopped. What can be done?"

"'Remedy'?" Hua Cheng echoed. "Probably a suicidal one, I bet."

Jun Wu gave him a look and sighed. "I also said that I did not want to take that step unless absolutely necessary."

It clicked in Xie Lian's mind. "Could it be...?"

"Correct. With things as they are, the only way to remedy the situation is to send a martial god to infiltrate the gathering of ghosts at Mount Tonglu," Jun Wu slowly confirmed.

If the slaughter couldn't be stopped, then they had to ensure that it was *thorough*—that not a single ghost was left behind!

Xie Lian crossed his arms into his sleeves and knitted his brows. "I'm not too familiar with Mount Tonglu, and I don't really know how the rules work. How should this be done—exterminate every last nefarious creature that reaches the mountain?"

But that was an inconceivable task. A god would have to conceal their identity to infiltrate Mount Tonglu, and they couldn't bring much help along. Otherwise, the ghosts would discover that there were heavenly officials in their midst and would surely surround and annihilate them. Mount Tonglu was also a locus of great evil; a heavenly official's spiritual powers would be severely restricted while in its perimeter. It would be even worse than the suppression they experienced at the Black Water Demon Lair.

"No," Jun Wu replied. "There is no need to make that much effort."

"I'm familiar with Mount Tonglu. Gege, look outside," Hua Cheng said.

Following where he was pointing, Xie Lian looked out the window. There was a large field outside planted with some flowers and herbs, and there was also a tiny flowerpot tucked into a corner. Hua Cheng hopped onto the windowsill and pointed at the flowerpot.

"In the heart of Mount Tonglu lies a giant kiln."

Just as the words left his lips, the little flowerpot fell over and rolled to the center of the field, then righted itself. The once-flat ground pulsed outward in waves from that flowerpot heart, and the field was transformed into an expanse of rolling mounds of various sizes.

"Mount Tonglu, the central volcano, is fully encircled by mountains," Hua Cheng continued. "These are the Tonglu Mountains, an area as big as seven cities."

Xie Lian watched, amazed, and then leapt lightly out the window. As he stood in the field among the tiny hills, it made him feel like a giant looking down upon the vast earth.

"The slaughter begins at the outer edges of the mountain range," Hua Cheng continued. "The goal is to reach the center and enter the mountain's heart—that is, the Kiln."

With a casual wave of his hand, many small things on the ground started to move. Xie Lian crouched for a closer look and discovered that dozens of weeds and leaves were twisting through the hills, as if they were tiny people crossing a mountain range.

"Which is to say, the ghosts are stronger as one approaches the center—as they close in on the Kiln?" he remarked.

"Yes," Hua Cheng said. "Because the weak weeds were already annihilated at the edges."

With another light wave, a breeze brushed by; the weeds were completely cleared away. The empty little hills became desolate, appearing almost sad. However, the flowerpot at the center suddenly emitted flashes of red light—looking very much the part of a tiny kiln, reddened by flame. As Xie Lian stared at it, he noticed a tiny red flower among the unremarkable weeds that had jumped onto the flowerpot. They all spun around the edges of the pot like people dancing, and the little red flower danced the wildest.

Hua Cheng half crouched next to him. "Only a handful of ghosts at most can enter the Kiln's interior. Once they've done so, the Kiln will close."

Those little "people" danced and danced, then fell from the flowerpot's rim one by one to be swiftly swallowed by the black soil.

"One ghost must break out of the Kiln within forty-nine days of entering," Hua Cheng continued.

The flowerpot shuddered violently, then a flash of blinding red light exploded from the pot with a *bang*, sending out a shock wave of dust.

The little red flower leapt out of the mud, fresh from its "earth"-shattering rebirth. It raised its two tiny leaves skyward as if shouting to the winds and announcing its might to the world. Xie Lian couldn't help but puff out a laugh at the sight.

However, perhaps it had gotten overly excited—the little red flower slipped and nearly fell from its perch on the edge of the flowerpot. Xie Lian hurriedly reached out and gently caught it, and he cradled it in his palms. The little red flower seemed dizzy from the fall. It shook its head, then raised its face to gaze at its rescuer.

Xie Lian brushed off some specks of dirt that had splattered onto his hair. "So this little one born from Mount Tonglu is the next generation's ghost king?"

Hua Cheng nodded. "Correct. The initial slaughter is a strengthening process; it cannot be skipped. If a ghost isn't strong enough and can't break out of the Kiln after it enters, it will be suffocated inside and burned to ash. It will become nothing but fuel for a more qualified candidate."

He rose to his feet and called to Jun Wu, who was still sitting inside.

"Your plan is to cut down the mighty and leave the weeds. There are only so many with the potential to become a ghost king—once those candidates are annihilated, the remaining weak ones might get into the Kiln, but they won't have the strength to leave. If they can't break out, they won't be recognized as ghost kings."

Xie Lian nodded. "Sounds doable. But will it work? Has it been attempted before?"

Jun Wu approached the window. "I do not know. And no, it has never been attempted before. In the past, the ghosts have always been stopped before they managed to assemble."

Hua Cheng crossed his arms. "I'm afraid it's impossible. Fighting under these conditions is suicide in all but name. I suggest the one who came up with such a brilliant idea go do it himself."

"I intend to," Jun Wu replied easily.

Xie Lian was taken aback. "My Lord?"

"Xianle, this is precisely why I descended," Jun Wu said. "I will be going to Mount Tonglu. I need you to return to the Upper Court and take up my duties for the time being."

Xie Lian dropped his hands and leapt to his feet. "There's no way! Temporarily take your place? *Me?* My Lord, please don't joke! No one will listen to me."

Jun Wu grinned. "Then this will be a very good chance for you to convince them to do so."

Xie Lian rubbed his forehead. "My Lord, pardon me, but I really cannot agree with you this time. This is too absurd. To use a vulgar example from the Mortal Realm, an emperor can ride forth onto the battlefield, but have you ever heard of an emperor infiltrating and assassinating? The Heavenly Capital can soar so high in the heavens because *you* are there to hold it up. No other heavenly official can do that; it is through My Lord's power alone. The sky will not fall if you are there to support it, but if you aren't there, it *will*."

"Xianle, the sky will not collapse for anyone in this world," Jun Wu replied, folding his hands behind him. "Once you become accustomed to the way the world works, you will understand that life goes on even without those lost along the road. There will always be new to replace the old. If a new ghost king is born, and they are another Crimson Rain Sought Flower or Ship-Sinking Black Water, there will not be an issue. But if they are another White-Clothed Calamity, the world will fall into chaos."

He looked Xie Lian in the eyes.

"You have witnessed for yourself how difficult it is to kill a supreme like him. If I do not go, there is no other way."

Xie Lian knew that Jun Wu wasn't being humble. Managing to accurately identify and subdue the strongest among millions of ghosts while trapped in a weakened state and sealed off from any hope of outside aid—Xie Lian couldn't say with any certainty that he could manage to do it himself. Jun Wu alone had a real chance at success. But he might be away for a decade—what about the outside world? What about the Upper Court?

Just then, Hua Cheng spoke up.

"Who says there's no other way?"

77
Gates Open to Mount Tonglu, the Mass Gathering of Ghosts

XIE LIAN AND HUA CHENG began their journey the next day.

Hua Cheng held Xie Lian's hand as they walked. "Gege, next time you see Jun Wu, don't talk to him. Turn and run away."

Xie Lian was puzzled. "Why?"

"I just know that whenever he comes looking for you, it's never for anything good," Hua Cheng said.

Xie Lian laughed. "What do you mean? He didn't even assign me this mission originally."

However, Hua Cheng said, "It's all the same in the end, whether you're going to Mount Tonglu or helping him manage the Upper Court. Neither are good assignments. The Upper Court is in complete shambles; might as well let it fall apart. What does he mean by dropping that mess in your lap? You're just choosing between suicide by saber or suicide by sword."

Xie Lian couldn't help but laugh, but once he finished, he said soberly, "Still, I never expected you to volunteer to accompany me to Mount Tonglu. I've been thinking for a while, and I feel this should be said: San Lang, please don't force yourself to do this."

He suspected that Hua Cheng had only volunteered to come because he knew what was going through Xie Lian's head—specifically, that Xie Lian felt it'd be much more gratifying to fight to his heart's content locked inside an oven than to get stuck ineptly managing the Upper Court.

But Hua Cheng replied, "Gege, I've already repeatedly sworn that I'm not forcing myself. Do you not believe me?"

"It's not that, of course..." Xie Lian said.

Hua Cheng nodded. "Then just relax, gege. I know my limits. You shouldn't feel like you owe me anything. Even just from my own perspective, I wouldn't mind stuffing the new ghost king back in before it's born."

Both the ghost kings and the heavens benefited from the way things were. But there was only so much rice, and everyone wanted a bite—there already wasn't enough to go around, which caused friction at times. No one wanted to let someone new barge in and share the pot. And if this new addition had an extreme personality, they'd all be left with nothing to eat if and when they went mad.

Jun Wu had heard out Hua Cheng's suggestion and considered it seriously. Xie Lian taking up the mission alone wouldn't go as well as Jun Wu handling it in person, but if Xie Lian was accompanied by a ghost king who had once journeyed to Mount Tonglu...well, it would certainly tilt the odds in their favor.

Of course, Hua Cheng wouldn't agree to help for free, and Jun Wu agreed to these terms for his assistance: all of heaven must give Ghost City a wide berth until the time of Mount Tonglu's next opening, and additionally, the Heavenly Court must publicize Crimson Rain Sought Flower's heroic deeds and sing songs of praise for an entire year... Xie Lian tried to imagine how those songs would go. They would probably be something along the lines of *"Foolish heavenly officials! Do you know who saved you?!"* This would practically be torture for the heavenly officials, who were already wary of Hua Cheng and had complicated feelings about him—he was all but stepping directly on their faces.

Hua Cheng smiled. "This journey will be much easier for you with me around."

Pulling himself back to the present, Xie Lian replied, "I still think we should set out after your period of aggravation is over—after you've returned to your normal self."

"You don't need to worry about that either. It'll be over soon," Hua Cheng assured.

Xie Lian was taken aback. "Huh…"

"What is it? Gege, what's with that face?" Hua Cheng questioned.

"…Does that mean San Lang's gonna grow up?" Xie Lian said, dejection clear in his tone.

Hua Cheng clasped his hands behind him. "Yes. I've endured this for too long. I can't wait any longer."

Just as he finished talking, Xie Lian slipped his hands under Hua Cheng's arms and lifted him. He raised him high in the air and laughed.

"It'll be such a shame! I won't be able to pick you up like this once you're grown again. I'd better hug you as much as I can right now. Ha ha ha ha ha ha ha…"

"…"

The Teleportation Array couldn't be used for the journey to Mount Tonglu, so they had to walk. Over a dozen days later, they finally left towns and signs of life behind them and entered a mountainous area covered with endless lush green forest.

As they walked deeper and deeper into the woods, they encountered more and more nefarious creatures. Their shapes and forms were bizarre, and the size of each swarm only grew larger. The path became more crowded as its pedestrians furtively hurried along.

Xie Lian walked hand-in-hand with Hua Cheng. "So many have come," he whispered.

"This gathering is certainly bigger than before. It's because the heavens didn't put up a blockade, so many who weren't planning on coming wound up doing so," Hua Cheng said.

It wasn't just solo combatants; many had come in groups. After a while, Xie Lian and Hua Cheng ran into a large group of ragged, disheveled-looking ghosts. They chanted as they marched with savage expressions on their faces.

"The universe is a crucible, and living creatures are the copper!"

"Infinite adversities abide within the abyss of suffering!"

"The universe is a crucible, and living creatures are the copper!"

"Infinite adversities abide within the abyss of suffering!"

They didn't seem afraid—in fact, they sounded eager. Hua Cheng's expression grew frigid as he and Xie Lian listened to their chants.

"They don't even understand what they're saying, but they certainly say it louder than anybody else."

Most of these nefarious creatures had never experienced this trial and didn't understand its cruelty—they thought becoming a supreme would be easy for them. They were filled with heroic aspirations, which brought understandable displeasure to anyone who *did* know what it was like.

"Can they enter as a team?" Xie Lian asked.

"Those teams are typically made up of individuals who already know each other. They plan to overcome the mountain together and swear beforehand to show each other mercy. But none of those promises will be kept. As you approach the mountain's heart, your strength increases with each opponent killed. Anyone spared leaves you with less chance to survive the Kiln. And the easiest targets are often the ones who trust you and are closest to you."

His brows knitted slightly, and he covered his right eye; it seemed there was another headache coming on. Concerned, Xie Lian quickly grasped him around the shoulders and pulled them both into the woods next to the road, then crouched low to better observe his condition.

"San Lang, we're about to reach the mountains. Are you really sure you're all right?"

Easing his brow, Hua Cheng replied, "Don't worry, gege, everything's fine. It'll be better soon."

But how could Xie Lian stop worrying just because Hua Cheng said to?

"Gege, come closer," Hua Cheng added. "I have something to tell you."

Xie Lian didn't know what he was planning, and he drew closer. Hua Cheng cupped Xie Lian's face in his hands and lightly touched his forehead with his own. Xie Lian blinked, stunned. He waited until Hua Cheng released him before asking for an explanation.

"San Lang, what are you…"

Hua Cheng smiled. "Done. There are only ghosts here, and gege is a heavenly official. His scent will be very conspicuous. This will help cover it a little."

So that was it—he was staining Xie Lian with his scent. Xie Lian couldn't help but remember how they had exchanged spiritual power and air. He was afraid Hua Cheng would be reminded too and bring it up, so he quickly acknowledged his statement.

"All right. Let's put on disguises."

Naturally, they had to disguise themselves to blend in with the swarm of ghosts, but a simple cloak would do just fine—there were plenty of ghosts and monsters who liked wearing masks and cloaks, so it wouldn't seem odd. After getting into their costumes, Xie Lian took Hua Cheng's hand in his own once more, and they slowly continued on their way.

After a while, they heard the faint noise of a commotion on the road ahead.

Unsure what was happening, Xie Lian asked, "Is there some sort of landmark that tells you that you've made it to Mount Tonglu territory?"

"There are landmarks," Hua Cheng answered. "But don't trust them."

Xie Lian was about to ask more questions, but the commotion ahead of them was growing louder. When the two left the forest, they found a large, dense crowd stuck before a steep bluff. There were at least three or four hundred nefarious creatures present, but that number was only the tip of the iceberg for this particular assembly.

"Why is the road blocked? Did we go the wrong way?"

"That can't be... Don't they say that any road will lead to Mount Tonglu?"

The crowd of ghosts was still mostly peaceful. Perhaps it was because they weren't yet within the boundaries of the Tonglu Mountains, and the slaughter hadn't officially begun.

Xie Lian found a random ghost to the side and casually asked, "What's going on over there?"

"Are ya blind?!" the ghost yelled. "There's a mountain in the way; we can't get through!"

"..."

Xie Lian took a look at the ghost next to him. Half of its head was sliced off; *it* was the blind one. But it wasn't his place to comment on that, so he asked instead, "Can't we go around it?"

Several ghosts rushed over from around the bend, shouting with long tongues dangling from their mouths.

"What the hell! There's something weird about this mountain! We ran around for over an hour and still saw no end to it! And then we had to run over an hour to get back!"

The ghosts turned to Xie Lian. "No."

"Can't we climb it, or fly over it?" Xie Lian questioned.

As soon as he spoke, a large bird, over two meters long, fell from the sky and crashed into the ground with a heavy *thud*. It appeared to have died on the spot.

"Dead!" a ghost cried out. "That bird spirit died from exhaustion! All that effort and it still couldn't fly over!"

The ghosts turned to Xie Lian again. "Nope."

Xie Lian tried once more. "Then can't we..."

But before he could finish asking his question, the ghosts all shushed him like they wished desperately to seal his mouth shut. "Stop asking, you jinx!"

"All right," Xie Lian complied.

Hundreds of nefarious creatures were blocked by this unpassable, unscalable, uncrossable mountain bluff. Their voices buzzed in an endless cacophony.

"I get it!" one exclaimed. "It's not a typical mountain—it's a barrier."

"Everyone," another announced, "the outskirts of Mount Tonglu must be right beyond this mountain. *This* one is probably a trial which we must pass before reaching the *other* mountain. If we can't even pass a simple test like this, we shouldn't even consider trying our luck at what will come after, and we might as well just go home."

"Wait!"

"Wait, what?"

A puzzled voice spoke up. "Why do I...smell something funny?"

"What smell? You sure it's not that human meat you got with you? Maybe it went foul."

"No, no. It's not the smell of dead flesh, it's the smell of living humans!" that voice said. "No, no, no, that's not right either! ...It's almost like...the smell of a heavenly official!"

The moment those words were spoken, noises of alarm rippled outward. The crowd of ghosts cried out.

"What?! You're shittin' me, why would there be a heavenly official here?!"

"Ahh, wait! Um... I smell it too!"

"How come *I* don't smell anything?"

"Now that y'all are talking about it, I think I smell it too... Did a heavenly official sneak in?!"

"That's impossible...! What heavenly official has the nerve to come to a place like this?"

Spurred on by the calling voices, uproar flared in every direction. Xie Lian felt some trepidation, but his face didn't give anything away. Hua Cheng had helped him cover his scent earlier, so how was there still a smell? No one should've noticed him mixing in.

Hua Cheng held his hand and whispered, "Gege, be careful. Something is deliberately muddying the waters to create chaos."

"It's also possible that some other heavenly officials really have snuck in," Xie Lian said.

The ghost who first mentioned the smell of humans jumped onto a boulder to give a speech.

"Everyone! Maybe those godforsaken heavenly officials in the Heavenly Realm saw that they couldn't stop us on the road, so they sent people to Mount Tonglu to ruin our celebration. To help uncover who has a spiritual aura, I suggest that everyone remove any masks, cloaks, or heavy layers for the time being. Everyone, announce your titles one by one. Don't give them the chance to infiltrate the gathering and lurk among us!"

The crowd applauded the idea, and that ghost continued.

"I'll go first! You may call me 'Demon of the Swift Life-Extinguishing Blade'—referring specifically, of course, to the blade an executioner used for beheading. He only ever used this one blade to chop off heads!"

"..."

In Xie Lian's experience, the more blunt and exaggerated the title—especially ones that contained "Unparalleled," "Thousand Hands," "Mighty," "Life-Extinguishing," and so on—the easier the owner was to wipe out. It usually only took a single hit, or even three with one blow. Hundreds of titles were being noisily thrown out, and Xie Lian shook his head as he listened. Suddenly, a nearby ghost elbowed him.

"Hey, why haven't you stripped off your cloak yet? What are you?"

The ghost didn't mean the latter question disrespectfully; if Xie Lian wasn't human, then he could only correctly be called a "what." As for the ghost's former question, there were plenty of ghosts that hadn't removed their cloaks and masks; there was even one not far from Xie Lian, watching them with his arms crossed. However, Xie Lian was the one who had been called out first. Seeing that all eyes were on him, he accepted his own bad luck and took off his cloak.

"I'm a Puppet Master," he said temperately.

The ghosts surrounded him.

"I see! No wonder you look so human. This is my first time seeing a Puppet Master!"

Xie Lian smiled without responding. Puppet Masters were nefarious beings with very weak evil qi. They would experiment with different kinds of materials in order to create the perfect puppet, so it wasn't strange for them to be stained with different scents. Since they particularly fancied the skins of humans, human scent was usually heaviest. The dream of all Puppet Masters was to steal hair from heavenly officials to use for wigs for their puppets, and some were even audacious enough to try their luck—so it also wouldn't be strange if he had the scent of a heavenly official on him.

"Then where's your puppet?" a ghost asked.

Xie Lian scanned the crowd, then bent and lifted Hua Cheng. The ghosts were in awe.

"Wow, exquisite!"

"What material did you use? *Tsk, tsk, tsk,* it looks so real."

"Feels like you're gonna be a tough competitor..."

"How can you say it looks real? I think it looks pretty fake. Isn't the skin too pale? Why would a kid have such long eyelashes?"

Hua Cheng had his arms crossed and his face was expressionless, but there were still many lady ghosts whose unmoving hearts were struck by his looks.

"I'm dying! What a handsome poppet!"

"Master, do you take commissions? Can I order one that looks exactly the same? We can talk about pricing."

Some even reached out to try to pet him, unable to resist. Xie Lian immediately pulled him back into his arms. The ghosts were visibly miffed.

"So stingy, treasuring him so highly that you won't even let us touch!"

Xie Lian held Hua Cheng even tighter, and his hand smoothed his hair.

"Of course. This is my puppet. Besides, he's got quite the temper. No one but me can touch him—otherwise, he gets very angry."

Hua Cheng quirked an eyebrow, and the ghosts laughed out loud.

"My, he can even raise his brows! He's got attitude!"

Just then, a voice spoke up. "I don't think that's it."

Xie Lian turned to look, and the one who had spoken was Demon of the Swift Life-Extinguishing Blade.

"The human scent on you is a little *too* heavy," he accused.

"He's a Puppet Master; it's understandable," the crowd of ghosts chided him. "He's got ghost qi on him too."

"No, no, look closer, everyone," Demon of the Swift Life-Extinguishing Blade countered. "The ghost qi on this 'Puppet Master' doesn't feel like it's being emitted from within. It feels more like it's only stained on the outside."

His surface coat of ghost qi should've been enough in most circumstances, but even the tiniest details would be brought under scrutiny once he became the focus of a whole crowd of ghosts. Much like Heaven's Eye, Demon of the Swift Life-Extinguishing Blade didn't look like he was very smart at first, and Xie Lian had taken him for an insignificant minor character—who knew he wasn't so easy to deceive?

"You seem like you're well versed on this topic, so is there anything concrete to what you're saying?" a ghost piped up. "How do we tell? Got any ideas?"

"Yes," Demon of the Swift Life-Extinguishing Blade replied. "There is a tool that can determine what he is!"

He pulled an item from his sleeve, and the crowd of ghosts instantly backed away the moment they saw it.

"The fuck?! You have a talisman on you?! You sure *you're* not the heavenly official mixed in here?!"

"No! I killed some cultivators on the way here and took their belongings, that's all," Demon of the Swift Life-Extinguishing Blade earnestly explained. "These are just typical talismans for dealing with little ghosts and irrelevant minions. Since you all made it here, I'm sure these won't harm you. Watch!"

He slapped a talisman on his own forehead. *Crackle, crackle.* The talisman burned up into nothing but a wisp of black smoke, leaving a black burn mark on his forehead.

"Even though this talisman can't harm me, it can still leave a mark on my face," Demon of the Swift Life-Extinguishing Blade said. "So this proves my identity, right?"

Paper talismans could be used to defeat or ward off nefarious creatures, so they could also be used to determine whether a person was, in fact, a person. Demon of the Swift Life-Extinguishing Blade pointed at Xie Lian.

"If you're really a Puppet Master, then stick this talisman on your forehead. We'll see whether it leaves a mark."

While Xie Lian didn't show any reaction, his mind was spinning rapidly.

However, Hua Cheng whispered, "Don't worry, gege."

Xie Lian knew this meant that Hua Cheng was confident he could handle things. He put Hua Cheng down and calmly approached, then took the talisman and pressed it to his forehead. *Crackle, crackle.* The talisman burned up into a wisp of black smoke. However, Xie Lian's forehead was still unmarred after the smoke had cleared, with not a trace left behind!

This proved that the ghost qi on him was only on the surface!

While that cloaked figure with crossed arms remained where he stood, hundreds of ghosts surrounded Xie Lian and Hua Cheng, yelling and howling and ready to unleash all sorts of bizarre weapons. However, they were repelled by an invisible barrier. The crowd of ghosts was left stunned.

"Well, well! Pretty skilled, aren't you!"

Xie Lian shrugged. "I didn't do anything."

Hua Cheng had been standing behind him, but now he approached with his hands clasped behind his back. "You ignorant rubes. Why do you look so surprised?"

"And you're a man of the world, baby ghost?!"

"It ain't a lie that he didn't have ghost qi on him. Just who are you? Declare yer identity now!"

"What a gaggle of fools. Of course there's nothing of the sort on *his* body—because *I'm* the real Puppet Master!" Hua Cheng answered.

As he spoke, the crowd of ghosts sensed an exceedingly sinister chill blow past them. It was like the entire field had frozen over. Despite their own bodies' ghostly coldness, they still shuddered.

"...What...? What's...going...on...?"

"Giving you a taste of the world, that's all," Hua Cheng said.

He rescinded his aura, and the crowd of ghosts finally stopped shivering.

"If... If you're the Puppet Master, and he's also a Puppet Master, then who's the real one?" Demon of the Swift Life-Extinguishing Blade asked with trepidation. "No, no, it can't be him, so what kind of creature is he?"

Before Hua Cheng responded, Xie Lian smiled and explained, "Obviously, the kind that belongs to him."

The crowd of ghosts were befuddled for a moment, then it finally dawned on them.

"So... So it's the opposite? He's the master, and you're the puppet?!"

Demon of the Swift Life-Extinguishing Blade was suspicious. "Then why did you say *you* were the Puppet Master? Why did you lie?"

Hua Cheng smiled. "Because I thought it'd be fun."

Xie Lian smiled too. "That's right. Master having fun is the most important reason in the world."

After the lady ghosts got over their initial shock, they tucked away their long claws and tongues and started circling around Xie Lian anew—only now it was to examine *him*. For some reason, the ghost women's commentary took on a completely different flavor from their observations of Hua Cheng; somehow, they were even bolder.

"So this little gege is the real puppet? *Aiyah*, I like this age better! Now I want one even more! Are you sure you don't take commissions?"

"Um... Thank you for your compliments," Xie Lian replied evenly. "But I'm actually *very* old..."

"This material is human skin, right? The treatment is done quite cleanly; there isn't any of that stinking, rancid man-musk that's usually on those burly brutes. Master, how do you maintain him? Do you use perfume?"

"It's human skin," Xie Lian confirmed. "No perfume. Just bathe frequently and drink lots of water."

"Wow! Feels like this puppet can do lots of things. All *sorts* of things! His face and body both look pretty good, eh? The feel of his skin is nice too. But he's a little skinny; I wonder if there'll be any meat on there after stripping off his clothes, hee hee hee hee..."

Xie Lian had maintained a polite and humble smile to this point, but his brows twitched when he saw that some of the lady ghosts were actually coming closer to feel his chest, their eyes glinting. Hua Cheng pressed two of his fingers together and lightly swung them upward—the circle of both youthful and wizened hands that had been closing in was flung back. Xie Lian quickly crouched behind Hua Cheng to hide, much to the annoyance of the ghost women.

"What, are you going to say that your puppet *also* has a bad temper and doesn't like other people touching him? He looks nice!"

Hua Cheng reached out and lifted Xie Lian's chin. "*His* temper is certainly nice, but mine is bad. No one but me can touch the things I love."

Xie Lian followed along and obediently raised his head, holding back his laughter so hard that his belly hurt. Still, he was very cooperative and gazed into Hua Cheng's eyes. "No. San...Master's temper is very nice too," he said earnestly.

Hua Cheng laughed as well, looking very pleased. The two went back and forth, singing the same tune and getting quite into their roles, but another ghost interrupted.

"I still think the human scent on him is too strong."

"What more do you want to do, then?" the lady ghosts questioned.

"I heard puppets made of skin aren't stuffed with real flesh, so they won't bleed if they're stabbed," a ghost said. "Let me stab him with a blade and see..."

But before he finished his thought, a death glare frightened him into silence.

"Try touching him, I dare you," Hua Cheng warned frigidly. "Do you think I would so easily allow you lot to touch my heart's dearest treasure?"

Earlier, the crowd of ghosts had been pushed back by the power of his aura alone. They were even more scared to make any rash moves now that he was making direct verbal threats. Without realizing it, they had backed away and vacated a large area around them.

Demon of the Swift Life-Extinguishing Blade had started this, but he was actually the first to try to smooth things over when he saw they were going downhill. "Please don't be angry, Puppet Master. We haven't even entered the boundaries of Mount Tonglu;

we can talk more once we're inside. Let's not start squabbling among ourselves now."

Hua Cheng's gaze swung to the side. "Rather than harassing my puppet, why not ask instead why *that* one still won't remove their cloak?"

The strange cloaked figure had been standing nearby this entire time, and still hadn't removed his cloak even after the ruckus started. He had been watching with his arms crossed like he was enjoying the show, acting like he wasn't associated with the hubbub at all. Now that Hua Cheng had pointed him out, he couldn't spectate the drama anymore—he had become its star. Demon of the Swift Life-Extinguishing Blade took a step forward.

"Friend, won't you also remove your cloak and let us see?"

The cloaked figure remained still for a long time. Just when Xie Lian was starting to suspect he was preparing to kick up dirt and run away, the cloaked figure extended a hand and pulled off his cloak in one clean motion.

Under the cloak was a man. He was somewhat handsome, but overall ordinary and rather forgettable.

If spotted in a crowd, a person like that wouldn't be an eyesore, but they'd be easily forgotten—their appearance would slip from one's mind the moment they weren't in view. While it seemed to disappoint the ghosts who saw this reveal, Xie Lian grew wary.

"Obviously a fake face," Hua Cheng said so that only Xie Lian could hear.

He nodded in agreement. When heavenly officials or ghosts of renown had business to do in the Mortal Realm, they'd sometimes create a fake face to avoid being inconvenienced by their real form. The most important element of this transformation was looking ordinary—it didn't matter whether it came out attractive. As long as it was plain enough to ensure that onlookers would forget the face the moment they turned away, that it would disappear from their mind no matter how long they stared, the transformation was a success. The cloaked figure's face perfectly matched the key component of such a transformation, which meant it was probably not his real appearance. His identity remained unknown.

Demon of the Swift Life-Extinguishing Blade handed him a talisman. The cloaked figure took it and stuck it on his forehead without hesitation. *Crackle, crackle.* Smoke, and then a mark.

It seemed he was also a ghost, not a human.

After all this ruckus, the crowd was growing agitated.

"So is there actually a heavenly official among us or not?"

"Who brought this up in the first place? You better not be wrong."

Demon of the Swift Life-Extinguishing Blade raised his hand in appeasement. "I was the first to notice, but it's true! I definitely smelled a heavenly official... *Aah!*"

He screamed and toppled over mid-sentence. Startled, Xie Lian rushed forward and found that he had been pierced through the abdomen, leaving a fresh, bloody hole. There was a faint but unmistakable residue on the wound—it was the kind of holy light that could only come from a heavenly official!

The crowd of ghosts was shocked. "Look at his wound!" one yelled. "There really is a heavenly official among us!"

Demon of the Swift Life-Extinguishing Blade covered the bloody hole with one hand and cried in terror, "Everyone watch out! They want to obliterate us!"

The crowd of ghosts lost their minds in terror. In an uproar, they all raised their weapons, ready to face enemies from any direction, yelling, "Who is it?! Who wants to wipe us out?! Where are you hiding?!"

It's just as I thought—the ones who give themselves such ridiculous titles are always the first to go down! That was what flashed through Xie Lian's mind when Demon of the Swift Life-Extinguishing Blade fell. Once the initial shock wore off, Xie Lian shouted, "Everyone saw just now, right? You were watching my master and me the entire time—we didn't do anything."

As he spoke, he shot a look at the cloaked figure. The cloaked figure also raised a hand, and his voice was low and quiet.

"Same."

Xie Lian bent down to check Demon of the Swift Life-Extinguishing Blade's injury. "It's a sword wound," he stated. "Whoever's using a sword right now is…"

When he turned his head, he was struck speechless. It looked like the sword wasn't just the most popular weapon in the Mortal and Heavenly Realms but in the Ghost Realm as well. Of the four-hundred-some ghosts present, at least three hundred wielded swords. They had innumerable suspects.

Xie Lian cleared his throat. "If only there were more talismans we could use, like the ones earlier. Then we wouldn't have to worry about who's who."

This was just an offhand comment, of course; he was trying to make himself sound helpful. If some of his heavenly colleagues really were infiltrating this crowd, he certainly didn't want to help identify them. Luckily, there was no way this Demon of the Swift-Blade individual had that many talismans at the ready.

Yet unexpectedly, as soon as Xie Lian made his comment, Demon of the Swift Life-Extinguishing Blade actually did produce several thick stacks of talismans.

"Oh! I do have more!"

"…"

Xie Lian couldn't help but want to take a look behind the creature's back. "Where exactly did you pull those from?"

"That's not important!" Demon of the Swift Life-Extinguishing Blade said.

"No, it's very important," Xie Lian said. "One normally doesn't carry such heavy burdens on the road. Those stacks are heavy enough to be hurled like bricks to kill people... How many cultivators did you kill?"

Demon of the Swift Life-Extinguishing Blade glared at him. "Maybe twenty or so."

No wonder. If every cultivator carried a few dozen talismans with them, then all together he'd gathered at least a few hundred!

The crowd of ghosts were anxious to find out who among them were heavenly officials, so without much ado, they devised a hasty plan. They formed into groups of two, then each stuck a talisman on their partner's forehead and observed whether the other had a burn mark. However, some small-time ghosts were still a little afraid of the prospect.

"Do I actually have to do this? Won't this shatter my spirit...?"

"Naw. It's exactly like those talismans they were using earlier. The power's weak, so they'll leave a mark at most."

"I see..."

Hua Cheng narrowed his eyes; he seemed to have noticed something. In the crowd of over four hundred ghosts, rows and rows of them now had talismans taped onto their foreheads—a peculiar and silly sight. However, nothing was happening.

The ghosts exchanged looks of dismay. "What's going on?"

"Hey, Swift-Blade demon, what kind of cultivators did you kill? Why are these talismans so crappy? They're not working."

Xie Lian had thought things were fishy from the start, and he knitted his brows. He was just about to speak when a lady ghost next to him pursed her lips and whined.

"I'm not doing this anymore! I'm ripping this off... Huh? What's going on? Why can't I get it off?"

Several ghost women started shrieking at once.

"Me too! Why won't it come off?!"

Crap!

Hua Cheng warned darkly, "Gege, get down!"

Xie Lian immediately followed his instruction, and Hua Cheng covered his ears for him. Not far from them, the cloaked figure pulled his cloak over his head and half knelt on the ground.

BOOM! BOOM! BOOM! BOOM! BOOM! BOOM!

Like fireworks exploding, loud rumbles roared to the skies.

Xie Lian could feel waves of violent tremors rippling from all directions. A peculiar, hard-to-describe stench permeated the air.

All the talismans had exploded!

As for the nefarious creatures who had them stuck to their foreheads... The ones with solid bodies had their brains blown out, splattering blood and flesh everywhere. The hollow-bodied ones were blown out of existence entirely, dispersed like black smoke. The mountain bluffs now overlooked a field of howling, wailing survivors. Hua Cheng uncovered Xie Lian's ears, looking unaffected by the chaos, but Xie Lian felt slightly alarmed as he rose to his feet. He had inspected those talismans one by one earlier; they were entirely normal exorcism charms. How could they have such a shocking effect?

A shredded piece of paper came fluttering down from the smoke-choked sky. Xie Lian seized it with a swift hand to take a look and instantly figured it out.

"How cunning."

It was a shredded corner from one of the talismans. He might not have noticed if it hadn't been torn, but it had two layers!

On top was a sheet of paper with the most ordinary of spells written on it, but beneath that was an extremely thin sheet of charm paper. It had been burned to the point where the spell was no longer recognizable, but it must have been a most vicious and aggressive one indeed.

Amidst the billowing, obscuring clouds of dust, many of the remaining ghosts were wailing—like someone had used this as a chance to ambush them. Xie Lian dropped low to the ground as he heard the ghosts shouting.

"Wait! The slaughter hasn't started! Why is everyone making their move now?!"

"Yeah! Didn't we agree that since we're all ghosts, we'd find a way to peacefully cross this mountain?"

A voice laughed savagely. "Idiots like you deserve to be annihilated in the first round! There's never been any rule about when the slaughter begins. We're all opponents, so obviously the faster you're dealt with, the better! Think I'm gonna warn you before I make my move?"

"Wait! Wait! I'm quitting! We're not in the Tonglu Mountains yet! Can't I back out?"

"Where do you think you are? Somewhere you can just enter and leave as you please? Not in the Tonglu Mountains yet, you say? Take a good look around!"

The clouds of smoke and dust began to clear, and once the ghosts could see, they were all mortified.

"*Huh?!* How did this happen?!"

It wasn't just them—even Xie Lian was a little stunned by the sight before him.

GATES OPEN TO MOUNT TONGLU

When they first arrived, there had been a tall mountain bluff blocking the road ahead, and it could not be bypassed. But now, somehow, the mountain had disappeared.

No, it didn't disappear. It migrated behind them.

It seemed they had crossed the boundary of Mount Tonglu without realizing it!

Earlier, Xie Lian had asked Hua Cheng if Mount Tonglu had any landmarks. And now, he understood why Hua Cheng had replied that the existing landmarks were not to be trusted—it was because those "landmarks" could move around on their own, like mischievous children playing pranks!

"I gotta see just what this puppet is made of," a voice suddenly said from behind Xie Lian in a sneering tone. "Or perhaps you're really something else?"

It was Demon of the Swift Life-Extinguishing Blade!

Xie Lian whirled around, yet before Ruoye could even fly out, a chilling light flashed. Demon of the Swift Life-Extinguishing Blade didn't even have the chance to scream before he was slashed in half at the waist!

Xie Lian rushed over. Sure enough, he had been chopped cleanly in two and couldn't be deader. Xie Lian looked up and saw that the one who had struck was that strange cloaked figure. The cloaked man slowly slid his sword back into his sheath as he walked over with steady, confident steps.

Xie Lian felt that the man and the way he walked were both somewhat familiar, and straightened up.

"And you are, sir?"

The man smirked and gave a low chuckle in response. He seemed about to answer, but he suddenly bent down instead. The unexpected action set off alarm bells in Xie Lian's head. He watched the man intently, preparing for any surprise attacks—however, the man only circled his arms around the slender waists of two lady ghosts.

"Are my ladies all right?"

"..." Xie Lian was struck speechless.

The two lady ghosts were both rather attractive. Because they didn't wield swords, they hadn't taken part in the talisman test and thus had escaped disaster. Nevertheless, the shock wave from the blasts had knocked them out. Feeling themselves embraced in someone's arms and addressed with such passion, they languidly came around with gratitude in their hearts.

"I'm all right, thank—"

Yet before those thanks fully left their lips, the two lady ghosts' faces changed abruptly. They shoved the strange cloaked figure away.

"Get outta here!"

The two quickly scrambled off. Even after being slapped twice, the man didn't seem annoyed—he only seemed confused as he stroked his chin and wrinkled his brow.

"That can't be right; this face isn't *that* ugly...?"

"..." Although he was still in disguise, Xie Lian already knew who he was. "General Pei, why are you here?"

The man turned to him and smiled. He swept a hand across his face and revealed his true appearance—it was indeed Pei Ming!

"Because the Heavenly Emperor asked me to give Your Highness a hand, of course."

"Really?" Xie Lian said. "Thank you, thank you. So very sorry for the trouble, then. It's quite dangerous here, as you can see."

"Gege, there's no need to be so grateful. He obviously negotiated some hefty rewards from Jun Wu," Hua Cheng said.

Pei Ming walked over and stopped in front of Hua Cheng.

Then he crouched down and reached out to measure his current height, laughing as he did.

"Do my eyes deceive me? Is this My Lord Crimson Rain Sought Flower? One certainly changes for the better with time, so what did you eat to grow backward? Ha…"

Only a single "ha" had left his lips when Xie Lian flung out his silk bandage; it whipped out so hard that Pei Ming was almost sent flying. He only barely dodged with a backward leap.

"Your Highness, just how deeply do you treasure Hua-chengzhu? Can't even take a joke?"

"Are you really General Pei?" Xie Lian demanded somberly.

Pei Ming patted the sword at his waist, flashing it for him to see. "Genuine and authentic; exchange if fake."

"No exchanges. If fake, refunds only," Xie Lian said.

"Gege, kill it. It's fake," Hua Cheng said.

"Hey!"

"If you really are General Pei, then why did that talisman leave a burn mark on your forehead?" Xie Lian questioned.

"It's simple," Pei Ming said. "It's all thanks to *this*."

He tossed a small item to Xie Lian. Since he was on guard, Xie Lian didn't catch with his hands; he instead used the tip of his sword to skewer it and bring it up to his eyes.

"Candy?"

On the tip of the sword, there was a shiny, black piece of candy. Pei Ming tossed another into his mouth.

"Ghost Scent Candy that I bought from Ghost City. Chew on one and you'll get a mouthful of ghost qi flowing from the inside out. Rather useful when pretending to be an inhuman creature."

Xie Lian twiddled the Ghost Scent Candy in his fingers, amazed. "You can buy such magical things in Ghost City?"

Pei Ming munched on the sweet in his mouth. "Ask your Huachengzhu right next to you. He knows better than anyone that you can buy anything in Ghost City if you know how. The flavor's not bad, Your Highness—wanna try one?"

Xie Lian was curious what ghosts tasted like. He turned to Hua Cheng. "Maybe we should've gotten some of those Ghost Scent Candies before we came."

However, Hua Cheng took the candy from his hand. "Gege, if you want anything from Ghost City, you need only ask. But don't eat stuff like this."

"Why?"

Even though Hua Cheng exerted no power on it, the candy shrieked and dissolved into a wisp of black smoke. "Everything in Ghost City is dangerous," he explained. "Take this candy, for example. It comes from a shady production mill, and the ingredients are mostly vulgar, puny ghosts of unknown origin. Eating it will damage your health."

"It's fine," Pei Ming said, sounding unconcerned. "They're only for emergencies—it's not like I eat them regularly."

"And the smell is extremely pungent," Hua Cheng went on. "Heavenly officials and mortals can't detect it, but such vulgar ghosts produce a rancid stench."

Pei Ming was speechless.

Hua Cheng snickered. "Now do you understand why those two ghost women told you to get lost?"

"..."

It was because of the incredibly vulgar, incredibly foul brand of ghost qi oozing from Pei Ming's body!

Xie Lian cleared his throat softly and made a polite suggestion. "General Pei, let's...not eat these anymore."

Pei Ming pulled out the leftover Ghost Scent Candies with a dismissive gesture and tossed them away. "Fine. But we've only reached the outer edges of Mount Tonglu's territory. As we progress further, we'll find much more powerful nefarious creatures who can tell we're suspicious with a single look. What shall we do then?"

The lady ghosts had swarmed around Hua Cheng like ducks; no doubt they really liked his scent. The ghost qi that Hua Cheng transferred to Xie Lian was assuredly of the highest quality, so there was no need to buy Ghost Scent Candies. However, to avoid anyone finding out that the qi was only a surface coat, they might need to press their lips together like last time and have Hua Cheng pass on something more tangible, like air or bodily fluids… Xie Lian immediately stopped himself from thinking about that any further.

"I don't know either. I'm just a puppet," he said matter-of-factly.

In other words, he would keep up his act.

"Fine. Your Highness, you'd best keep close to your master," Pei Ming said.

Xie Lian pretended not to hear that last bit and scanned their surroundings, humming. "I hadn't imagined casualties would be this devastating from the get-go."

The four-hundred-some ghosts that had gathered here originally were almost all dead or injured. Xie Lian couldn't help but recall the performance Hua Cheng had shown him nights ago; it wasn't an exaggeration. It really was like a gust of wind had blown through and uprooted all the weeds. Only a scattered few dozen had managed to escape this trial alive, and they were in terrible shape—there were severed limbs everywhere, and moaning and groaning all around.

Hua Cheng stood before the survivors. "Do you understand now what kind of place Mount Tonglu is?"

The ghosts that were fortunate enough to survive didn't dare make a sound.

"You're on the outer edges right now. There is still a chance to pull out," Xie Lian said gently. "If you don't want to continue on and meet even more frightening things, then stay here and look for a chance to leave."

The remaining ghosts intended to do just that. Seeing that Xie Lian and company didn't plan on wiping them out, they quickly pulled each other up and fled as fast as they could, leaning on each other for support.

Watching their retreating backs, Xie Lian mused, "Demon of the Swift Life-Extinguishing Blade was an exaggerated name to be sure, but he was an unexpectedly formidable character. Quite brutal."

"That creature was extremely good at manipulation. He'd stirred the pot from the very start," Pei Ming agreed. "He was also quick on his feet. Your Highness, that strike of yours gave him the perfect chance to use his injuries for trickery."

Xie Lian blinked. "Wait, *my* strike? What strike? I didn't unsheathe my sword."

"No?" Pei Ming wondered. "I meant the stab to his abdomen. If he hadn't whipped everyone into a panic thanks to that little gash stained with your holy light, none of the ghosts would've believed him and stuck those talismans on their foreheads."

Xie Lian was puzzled. "To be honest, I thought *you* had stabbed him, General Pei."

"Your Highness, do you have some sort of misunderstanding about me? I don't do ambushes or sneak attacks," Pei Ming said.

"If it wasn't you and it wasn't me, then was there a third heavenly official present? Or perhaps the holy light on that Swift-Blade demon's wound isn't what it seems…"

He turned, ready to inspect and verify again. But Demon of the Swift Life-Extinguishing Blade's corpse was gone.

Startled, he demanded, "Where's that Swift-Blade demon's body?"

"I clearly just slashed him at the waist." Pei Ming replied, blatantly baffled.

"Gege, be careful," Hua Cheng said darkly. "Within Mount Tonglu's domain, a slayer becomes stronger for each opponent killed."

And Demon of the Swift Light-Extinguishing Blade had just slaughtered nearly four hundred nefarious creatures!

78
Ambivalent Regrets, the Clear-Sighted General Snaps the Hateful Sword

THE THREE STOOD tense and on guard amidst the corpse-strewn field and dissipating black smoke.

Now that the tall mountain had migrated behind them undetected, the path ahead was finally visible. It plunged into the depths of a thick black forest; the strange squawking of crows echoed intermittently within the countless trees, exceedingly frightening. Xie Lian went on the alert and sharpened his senses, and yet at the same time he still unconsciously reached for Hua Cheng's hand. The moment their hands touched, he noticed an alarming sign.

Hua Cheng was of course a ghost, but his body temperature was blistering hot, like he had a high fever. Xie Lian was taken aback.

"San Lang...are you changing back?" he whispered.

Although Hua Cheng was burning up from his forehead to his fingertips, his expression remained unchanged.

"Soon."

Hua Cheng was going to transform back to his true form—wonderful news, considering their circumstances. However, the lead-up to the official return of his old self was inevitably the most critical, perilous time.

Making a split-second decision, Xie Lian cried, "I'll set up an array and shield you!"

And he went straight to it. He called forth Ruoye and had it form a large circle, twelve meters in radius, around Hua Cheng. Then he plunged Fangxin into the earth in front of the circle as the "lock" on the array's "door."

Hua Cheng sat on the ground to meditate. "Gege, keep Fangxin with you for protection."

"No, this array can't be sloppy; it must be sealed by a bladed weapon that's touched human blood…"

Before he could finish, he felt something rubbing against him behind his back. When he looked, he was rendered speechless.

A tiny silver scimitar was standing upright behind him. It blinked its big silver eye and nuzzled against him with its hilt, as if it was nominating itself for the task.

Xie Lian crouched down. "Eming, why are you like this too?"

The infamous scimitar Eming, a long, slender blade, bewitching and wild…had shrunk in size by at least half. Its silver eye used to be long and narrow, but now it was big, shining, and round, like a child's.

At Xie Lian's comment, it seemed to feel wronged and tried to push its hilt into Xie Lian's hand with renewed fervor.

Pei Ming also crouched to look. "So this is the infamous scimitar Eming?"

He looked like he was about to reach out and touch it. Eming changed face in an instant and pointed its blade at him threateningly. Fortunately, Pei Ming pulled away just in time—otherwise blood would have certainly spilled.

Xie Lian stroked Eming. "Fangxin is still better-suited."

Fangxin remained motionless. Eming had tried so enthusiastically to offer itself up but was so blatantly rejected. It hopped back to Hua Cheng's side, weeping. Hua Cheng didn't spare it a single look before he smacked it with a backhand slap.

"What are you crying about? This happened because you're useless! Trash!"

Eming fell flat on the ground like a piece of unwanted scrap metal, as if that strike had struck it dead. Xie Lian didn't know whether to laugh or cry, and he quickly scooped Eming into his arms to stroke it a few times.

"Nothing of the sort. Don't listen to him. You're not trash—you're very useful!"

Pei Ming couldn't stand the mood in the circle anymore and stepped out to stand at the boundary, unsheathing his sword once more.

"Things weren't supposed to be this tense. Who knew we'd run into such an impressive, difficult character right at the start? Your Highness really does have the very best luck…"

They had made the trip to Mount Tonglu in the first place to eliminate any inhuman candidates who had the potential to become supremes—that meant hunting down all of the most powerful ghosts. Xie Lian couldn't tell whether this counted as good luck or bad.

However, Hua Cheng said, "Why do you state so matter-of-factly that His Highness's luck is the problem, General Pei? Have you ever considered that the Demon of the Swift Life-Extinguishing Blade might have been targeting you?"

Pei Ming laughed out loud. "If he were a woman, I'd believe it."

He hadn't laughed for long before his expression suddenly changed, and he leapt backward. As he looked up, blood trickled down his cheek.

A bloody cut had appeared on Pei Ming's face!

He felt his cheek in disbelief, and his whole palm came away smeared with blood—this was no mere scratch. And although they were on high alert, Xie Lian didn't sense any killing intent directed toward him at all. He was unharmed.

And so, he said truthfully, "It seems…it really is coming for *you*, General Pei."

Pei Ming was about to speak, but once more he heard the sound of a sharp blade slashing through the air. This time he was ready and swung his sword—and the strike found its mark. A figure appeared hanging in midair, then split in half from the slash and fell to the ground with a thud, upper and lower body now separated. Its eyes were gloomy and vicious as it glared intently at Pei Ming.

It was Demon of the Swift Life-Extinguishing Blade!

Pei Ming walked over and stepped on the demon's chest, the tip of his sword pointed at the creature's throat.

"What are you?"

This being had claimed to be a spirit formed from the blade of an executioner. If that was true, then he should've shown his true form and ended this ridiculous charade after Pei Ming cut him in half. What kind of blade could still act with such arrogance even after getting snapped in two?

Suddenly, Demon of the Swift Life-Extinguishing Blade's eyes bulged, and he sneered. He reached up and snapped Pei Ming's sword with his bare hands!

Clang!

Pei Ming's eyes went wide. And it wasn't just him—even Xie Lian reacted the same.

Pei Ming was, at the very least, a formally ascended martial god. Even though he was trapped within Mount Tonglu's boundary and his spiritual powers had been suppressed to the bare minimum, his spiritual device shouldn't have been broken so easily!

Demon of the Swift Life-Extinguishing Blade gave a resounding laugh. "I can't believe you'd use such a trashy sword!"

With his weapon broken, Pei Ming resorted to using his fists.

But with a slap of his hand on the ground, Swift Life-Extinguishing Blade launched himself into the air. Pressing the fingers of his hand together, he shot out a blast from his palm. A bright, chilling, metallic light flashed on the edges of the blast as it hurtled past; it was a gust of power with a razor's edge. It seemed that the creature's true form really was some sort of sharp, bladed weapon!

Xie Lian stood up and made to leave the circle to help but was stopped by Hua Cheng.

"Gege, watch closely," he said with a low voice.

Pei Ming shouted to him as well. "No need to interfere!"

If the esteemed Martial God of the North couldn't even defeat a lowly ghost blade on the outer edges of Mount Tonglu, how could he live with himself?

Still, even with only an upper half, the Swift-Blade demon was extremely agile. No matter where Pei Ming struck, it seemed to predict his every move, which made Pei Ming's chances look rather poor. Hundreds of moves later, the Swift-Blade demon had inflicted dozens of deep wounds on Pei Ming. Xie Lian couldn't watch anymore and called out.

"General Pei, come back into the circle!"

Pei Ming's expression was growing grimmer and grimmer. He refused to retreat, and Xie Lian couldn't simply jump into the fight to make it two against one. Some martial gods would find it humiliating to require help in a one-on-one duel.

"General Pei, come back! There's something weird going on! Can't you tell?" Xie Lian tried again. "This creature knows your sword techniques and moves too well!"

Naturally, Pei Ming had also noticed—he just couldn't believe it yet. But since even Xie Lian had seen it while observing from afar, he had to accept it even if he didn't want to. Xie Lian pulled Fangxin out of the ground and opened a small gap in the array. Pei Ming took the chance to leap back into the protective circle, looking extremely upset.

Xie Lian plugged Fangxin back in. "General Pei, aren't you going to pick up your broken spiritual weapon?"

Pei Ming wiped away the blood on his forehead. "That's not a spiritual weapon," he replied darkly. "It's just a decent sword I grabbed at random."

Hearing this, Xie Lian sighed a breath of relief. While any sword Pei Ming randomly picked from his collection would still be a fairly valuable tool, it couldn't compare to a real spiritual weapon.

"Why didn't General Pei bring his spiritual weapon when coming here?" he asked.

"I haven't forged one," Pei Ming replied.

Xie Lian found that even more amazing. "Why not?"

Martial gods typically forged their favorite weapon into a spiritual device, which was much like adding wings to a tiger. Pei Ming had no answer for him, and Demon of the Swift Life-Extinguishing Blade scoffed.

"That's obvious. It's because his best sword no longer exists!"

Pei Ming frowned. "Who are you, exactly?"

"You're not asking *what* he is anymore?" Xie Lian asked.

Demon of the Swift Life-Extinguishing Blade humphed again. "Who am I? Ha! Pei Ming, when you snapped me in two with a blast from your palm, did you ever expect this day would come?"

Xie Lian's eyes widened. "General Pei, do you know him?"

Pei Ming pondered for a long while, and his expression grew more and more solemn. Finally, he hazarded a guess.

"You're...Mingguang?"

Demon of the Swift Life-Extinguishing Blade's smile faded at the mention of that name. He no longer looked like that common, puny little ghost from earlier.

"He's 'Ming Guang'?" Xie Lian questioned. "General Pei, isn't General Ming Guang your title?"

In an instant, countless possible stories of fraud and substitution flashed through his mind. They weren't outlandish assumptions, considering that there was now precedent in the heavens. He couldn't help but think, *Is this another Earth Master Yi?*

Pei Ming seemed to see through his worries. While covering his wounds with a hand, he said, "Your Highness, what are you thinking? I already told you I'm the genuine, authentic General Pei. I'm the real thing!"

"Then why did you call him Ming Guang?" Xie Lian demanded.

"Because his name *is* Mingguang. It's the name I came up with. He's my sword!"

Xie Lian made a noise of understanding. "Could you be...'The General Who Snapped His Sword'?"

"That's right," Pei Ming replied. "Mingguang was my sword when I was a mortal. And centuries ago, I snapped it with my own hands."

No wonder!

No wonder "Demon of the Swift Life-Extinguishing Blade" knew Pei Ming's sword techniques well enough that it was like he could predict every move. He was the sword that Pei Ming had wielded as he won countless victories from north to south, so he naturally knew Pei Ming's technique inside and out. And no wonder that even when he was slashed in two, he could still move so easily—like the injury had no effect on him whatsoever. It was because he had already been snapped in half!

"So that gash from before was from stabbing himself?" Xie Lian said. "Then the holy light on his wound was...?"

"My own," Pei Ming said. "Back then, I ascended as soon as I snapped him in half. I suppose that must have been when the light stained him. And it can't be cleaned away."

Demon of the Swift Life-Extinguishing Blade—no, Mingguang—started using his hand as a sword and began to slash at Fangxin. His expression was gloomy, like he was visualizing attacking Pei Ming himself.

Xie Lian couldn't help but ask more about this whole thing. "Um... General Pei, why does your sword resent you so much? What did you do to it? What's the story behind The General Who Snapped His Sword?"

Pei Ming felt around for his pill bottle. "Some raggedy story from hundreds of years ago—what's the point of talking about it now? Let's find a way to beat him first!"

Although Ruoye formed the protection circle, half the array would collapse if Fangxin was cut down; it was similar to breaking the lock on a door. Xie Lian glanced behind him and saw that Hua Cheng had entered a meditative state. His eyes were shut tight, and he seemed totally unaware of the outside world. Xie Lian was slightly reassured at the sight.

Pei Ming's voice pulled him back.

"Your Highness, will your sword hold?"

Xie Lian turned back. "I don't know. Fangxin's old, after all."

"That's all right," Pei Ming said. "Mingguang's pretty old too."

Xie Lian sighed in relief. "Then as long as he doesn't call for help, we should be able to hang on for a w—"

Before he could finish, heavy footsteps sounded from within the forest. A huge, burly, hideous man with dark skin appeared.

The burly man wore broken leather armor and was abnormally tall. The moment they saw him, both Xie Lian and Pei Ming felt a drop of cold sweat drip off them.

The burly man had noticed someone madly chopping at a sword with his bare hands; he seemed to find the sight surprising, so he walked over to investigate. Xie Lian and Pei Ming both covered their faces with their hands and turned around. As for Mingguang, when he noticed a giant corpse approaching who looked quite physically strong, he called out to him.

"Hey, big guy, give me a hand! Help me knock away this sword and break the array. I'll split the heads inside with you!"

But the burly man likely hadn't been a citizen of the Central Plains in life, and he hadn't died a ghost of the Central Plains, which meant a language barrier. He didn't seem to understand what had been said and shouted something incomprehensible in reply. The two shouted at each other for a while, but nothing was achieved aside from some new veins popping on both of their foreheads.

Pei Ming did his best to look natural and suave while keeping his face covered. "Your Highness, what's that brute yelling about?" he whispered.

"He thinks your sword is trying to provoke him, so he got mad. He's telling him to kneel and beg for mercy, lest he beat him to death," Xie Lian whispered back.

"Oh, good," Pei Ming said. "Hope they start fighting each other soon."

But the giant man heard their whispers and turned to stare, his brow wrinkling as he scrutinized them. Xie Lian and Pei Ming tightened the hands covering their faces, no longer able to care about appearing natural; but the burly man still recognized them. He stamped his foot, and the entire ground quaked with it.

"It's you! Scrap-collecting cultivator! Pei Xiu's boss!" he roared.

Since they had been recognized, the two dropped their hands. After some hesitation, Xie Lian replied with forced warmth in the Banyue tongue.

"General Kemo, please calm down."

The peculiar burly man was Kemo, who had escaped his seal after Mount Tonglu's tremors aroused millions of ghosts. He had been captured initially by Xie Lian, and he'd seen Pei Ming later standing next to Pei Xiu during his trial. His eyes went red at the sight of his enemies, and he kicked at Fangxin without another word. The blow knocked the sword off-center by a few centimeters!

Mingguang clapped and cheered and kept shooting out blast after blast. "Divine!"

Seeing that Fangxin was shaking harder and harder under their combined attacks, Xie Lian felt Hua Cheng's forehead, but his hand shrank back from the heat.

"What should we do?!"

Xie Lian needed to shield Hua Cheng with the array and couldn't be distracted, and Pei Ming posed no threat at all to the weapon with which he shared such a strange familiarity.

Just then, they heard Mingguang cuss.

"You bloody savage! Can you not smash where I'm smashing?! You hit my hand!"

Kemo ignored him completely. Noticing the friction between the two, Xie Lian grabbed hold of Pei Ming.

"General Pei! Kemo won't believe that you mean him no harm and will keep coming after you! Quick, press the fingers of both your hands together, cross your wrists above your head, then press downward from your head before opening your arms. This is the hand gesture his people use to ask for truce. Either way, just show him your goodwill and make him stop for now!"

Pei Ming was bewildered. "Huh?! You know full well that the resentment Kemo and Mingguang have for me isn't just some small misunderstanding. How could they be pacified with a simple hand gesture?"

But Xie Lian paid him no mind and grabbed hold of him. "Come, do it with me to make him stop!"

Pei Ming's hand was injured; the corners of his lips tightened as Xie Lian grabbed him. Even so, he was about to do as instructed—but Mingguang had already heard everything they said. He leapt in front of Kemo, then crossed his hands above his head and slid his arms down before opening them. He smirked smugly at the two in the circle.

"As if I'd let you!"

When Kemo saw that gesture, however, his eyes bulged, and thick veins surfaced on his dark skin. He opened his palm and swung his hand down like an iron cattail-leaf fan, sending Mingguang flying through the air.

As his slap flew, neither Pei Ming nor Mingguang understood what had happened. It was only a moment later that it dawned on Pei Ming, and he turned to Xie Lian.

"Your Highness, I thought Mingguang was cunning. I hadn't imagined you would be more cunning than him. I'm impressed."

Xie Lian wiped away his cold sweat. "It's nothing, it's nothing, much ashamed."

Although it seemed like his instructions were for Pei Ming, they were actually intended for Mingguang. When Mingguang overheard, he would obviously rush to show Kemo goodwill first and obstruct their plan. However, the gesture that Xie Lian described didn't really call for a truce—it was an insult. Indeed, it was the rudest provocation in Banyue culture, like a combination of "chop off your shitty head," "fuck your wife," "murder your whole family," and "level your ancestors' graves." Four power attacks all at once; how could Kemo not be outraged? Under any other circumstances, Mingguang might have been suspicious of Xie Lian's words, but because the situation was dire and Pei Ming had almost raised his arms, Mingguang didn't take the time to think carefully and was easily deceived.

Mingguang snapped out of it when Kemo sent him flying. He wanted to fix the situation, but they still couldn't communicate, and his instinctive reaction was to yell—so it looked even more like he was cursing Kemo. He tried a few other hand gestures, like a thumbs-up, but that was hardly convincing at that point. It simply looked like someone begging for mercy by faking goodwill after they'd just hurled the most malicious, vulgar abuse. It didn't feel sincere at all, and he got pounded a few more times for the effort. Kemo also knew some rough Central Plains profanities and he swore as he struck, so Mingguang was starting to get angry himself. They continued to escalate, beating each other harder and harder. Pei Ming almost wanted to cheer them on.

Mingguang glanced over, incredibly irritated. He waved a hand in front of Kemo. Then he pointed at himself, then at Xie Lian and Pei Ming inside the circle, before doing that crossing hand gesture again.

Kemo actually stopped and asked with a frown, "Are you directing that at me or *them*?"

Oh no, Xie Lian thought but didn't dare speak rashly—he couldn't be sure how to best influence Kemo. Seeing that there might be a way to turn this around, Mingguang tried harder. He turned to Pei Ming to repeat the gesture with a savage face, but when he turned back to Kemo he immediately put on a calm expression. Matching the emotions in his eyes to his repeated actions, Kemo finally understood what he was saying.

They had the same enemies!

Once they were unified, Mingguang and Kemo came charging at the array once more. Xie Lian's mind whirled rapidly. He inhaled deeply, then hollered at the top of his lungs in the Banyue tongue.

"General Pei Junior! Banyue!"

At the sound of those two names, Kemo stopped abruptly and demanded sharply, "Are they nearby too?!"

Xie Lian didn't answer, just focused on shouting. "General Pei Junior! Banyue! Kemo is here—don't come close! Hurry and run away! And don't come back!"

This naturally made Kemo think those two were nearby and that Xie Lian was telling them to flee. His fury flared.

"As if I'd let you!"

With that, he rushed off.

"Hey! Big guy!" Mingguang yelled. "What are you running for?! He must be lying! Come back!"

But Kemo was long gone. Mingguang stomped his foot in anger.

"*Dumbass!*"

Xie Lian wiped his cold sweat away for the second time and thought sincerely, *Learning another language is infinitely beneficial throughout your life!*

Seeing that Mingguang was about to attack Fangxin again, he raised his hand.

"Stop! Keep this up and we won't be so nice!"

"And how are you being nice to me *now*?" Mingguang countered.

"Did you forget something?" Xie Lian asked.

"Forget what?"

Pei Ming looked like he wanted to say something, but he stopped and pulled something out from behind him. "How could you forget something so important?"

The object he'd dragged out was the legs of Mingguang's lower half. The moment Mingguang saw them, his expression froze.

"Huh?! My lower body!"

This whole time, he'd been using his hands in place of feet, using his arms to prop himself up and jump around. It seemed he'd gotten used to moving that way without realizing it and had completely forgotten that he hadn't yet retrieved the rest of his body. While he and Kemo were fighting, Pei Ming took the chance to leave the circle and dragged his abandoned, immobile lower half into the boundary.

"You'd better not do anything unnecessary," Pei Ming threatened.

The thing was, this threat was obviously very awkward. If the hostage were a complete person, Pei Ming could sink his fingers into their neck or skull while making such a threat. The resulting picture would be much more effective at showing that he wasn't bluffing. However, they only had the lower half of the man's body on hand. Where could his hands go that could still strike fear without being awkward?

Pei Ming couldn't think of anything, so he simply stepped on one of the legs.

"Are you shitting me?" Mingguang said.

Xie Lian also didn't think this looked like much of a threat, and he courteously suggested, "General Pei, stepping on a leg isn't terribly convincing. Can you maybe...make him think you've got him by something more *critical*?"

"Your Highness, don't say something like that so lightly," Pei Ming said. "Do you think I'd choose to step on a leg if I didn't refuse to do something so classless? Why don't *you* come and grab him where it hurts?"

"..."

In the end, neither of them was willing to grab that critical place.

"Never mind," Xie Lian said. "Then why don't we do *this*!"

After huddling up for a moment, they each grabbed one of Mingguang's legs. Now this *definitely* looked much more threatening and less awkward.

"Please back off," Xie Lian demanded. "Otherwise your true body might suffer further damage."

Mingguang just sneered. "Ha! Did you actually believe my lower half is useless?"

As soon as he spoke, Xie Lian sensed a murderous aura rapidly crawling up his arm. He immediately tossed away the leg in his grasp.

"General Pei, watch out!"

The seemingly dead lower half suddenly swung its legs and kicked out without warning. Pei Ming threw the limb in his hands just in time and avoided being struck when those swift legs churned up blades of wind. The lower half flipped itself around in the air and landed with a single knee to the ground, then slowly straightened until it stood upright.

The moves were clean and impressive, and Xie Lian praised them in spite of himself: "Nice!" But then he immediately changed his tune. "*Not* nice!"

Not nice indeed. The protection circle that he had so arduously created was made to keep Mingguang out, but things had now become rather complicated. Even though Mingguang's upper half was still outside, his lower half was in!

Pei Ming also realized this. "We've been had," he muttered.

Some nefarious creatures with bisected bodies could only move if one half was leading, and others could move both parts at will. They originally didn't know which class Mingguang fell into, but his lower half had been rigid as a corpse, unmoving even when stepped on—and so Pei Ming had thought him to be the former. But it seemed he was only pretending that he couldn't move.

Mingguang was clapping in mirth outside the boundary. "That's right! This is what they call 'inviting a wolf into your home,' and 'catching turtles in the pot'!"

The three inside the circle each faced their own impairments. Hua Cheng was meditating with his eyes shut tight; it was a critical moment in his struggle. Pei Ming's sword had long since been broken by Mingguang. Xie Lian's Fangxin was acting as the lock to their protection array. The latter two had no weapons to wield.

With no other choice, Xie Lian called, "Eming!"

Scimitar Eming had been lying on the ground like scrap metal, but it instantly jumped up at Xie Lian's call and flew into his hand. Xie Lian gripped the hilt and swung. Mingguang's lower half raised a leg and kicked; while it blocked Xie Lian's strike, it was pushed back a couple of steps and almost fell outside the protection circle. His upper half watched from the outside, and its expression faltered, now looking rather wary. He clapped his hands, and the lower half returned to its true form—a verdant sword nearly a meter in length. It boiled with killing intent as it hung in midair.

Xie Lian didn't usually use scimitars, but Eming was agreeable in his hands. He was about to charge forth when Pei Ming spoke up.

"Your Highness, not to panic you at a time like this, but your Hua-chengzhu seems to be having a little bit of trouble."

Startled, Xie Lian whirled around. Sure enough, Hua Cheng's brows were even more tightly knit, and the hands that made seals while resting on his knees were shaking. Noticing Xie Lian's distraction, the broken verdant blade seized the opening to lunge—but Eming slipped out of Xie Lian's hand on its own and blocked the broken sword mid-attack with a resounding *clang*!

"Eming, please hold him off for a bit!" Xie Lian called, then he crouched in front of Hua Cheng. "Why is he like this? What went wrong?"

"Don't look at me, Your Highness," Pei Ming said. "I'm not as familiar with the ghost king as you are!"

"San Lang? Can you hear me? Come out! Stop subjecting yourself to this!" Xie Lian called out to Hua Cheng.

Mingguang shouted from outside the circle, "A little blade dares block my way?!"

During the previous exchange, the broken sword Mingguang and Eming had already parried countless times within the space of an instant, sending sparks flying. If this had been the normal scimitar Eming, it would have immediately gained the upper hand, but the shrunken Eming facing the longsword Mingguang really did look like a child getting beaten by an adult. Although it was ferocious, it simply wasn't long enough—its abilities were unavoidably hampered. Things had gotten perilous a few times, and Xie Lian spared glances while keeping his focus on Hua Cheng.

"Watch out!"

After he called out, Eming flipped and flashed, becoming a streaming silver whirlwind that successfully struck the broken sword. The Mingguang outside the circle gave a shout of pain; it must have been a substantial hit.

"Good Eming!" Xie Lian praised.

Pei Ming spoke up. "Wait, Your Highness. I think it got bigger when you complimented it."

Xie Lian looked closely. "Really?"

"Seems like it," Pei Ming said. "Why don't you try again?"

It was only some praise; no big deal. And so Xie Lian said, "Very well. Eming, listen closely! You are handsome and carefree, cute and kind, clever and intelligent, gentle and determined, number one in the world…"

He trailed off, then stopped entirely. Pei Ming applauded enthusiastically. Outside the circle, Mingguang's expression was one of disbelief; he was as flustered as he was furious.

"What kind of wicked spell is that?! How come I've never heard of it before?!"

Indeed! With every word of praise Xie Lian sang out, Eming's blade grew a little bit longer. If it looked like a ten-year-old child earlier, then now it was a youth of fourteen or fifteen!

The broken sword facing the now-grown Eming was in trouble. It could only awkwardly move left and right, while Eming was growing swifter and more unpredictable. With the way this would end getting clearer, Mingguang made a hand seal.

The moment Pei Ming saw, he called out, "No good—he's transferred all his spiritual power into his lower half!"

Sure enough, the black aura surrounding the body of the broken blade explosively expanded in size. When Eming struck, it was bounced away by the black aura and plunged into the ground at a slant. Xie Lian hurried to pull it out.

"Are you all right?"

"Don't worry. Watch this," Pei Ming said, then took Eming from Xie Lian's hands.

Xie Lian was puzzled, but he suddenly felt cold on his skin. *Whap!*

Pei Ming had pushed the scimitar into his face, the hilt touching his lips.

"..." Xie Lian removed Eming from his face. His lips were slightly numb from the impact of the cold silver, and he rubbed at them, baffled. "General Pei, is there a reason you did that?"

"Of course. An excellent reason," Pei Ming said. "Your Highness, please look down."

Xie Lian looked down and was struck speechless. Eming had grown even longer!

Mingguang couldn't hold back anymore, and he screamed at them from outside the circle. "What the fuck! And what wickedness is *that*? You might as well use all your tricks at once!"

"Truth be told, I also want to know what caused this," Xie Lian said.

Full of spirit once more, Eming stood tall and lunged at the broken sword Mingguang. Sword and scimitar battled relentlessly in the air. Xie Lian went back to check up on Hua Cheng, and Pei Ming watched Mingguang, who was bent over not far away. All of Mingguang's spiritual power had been transferred to the lower half that was battling Eming, so any threat from his upper half was greatly lessened. They all understood this, and Pei Ming rose to his feet to take him down.

However, another series of heavy footfalls came running up at top speed. Kemo had returned.

"You cunning Central Plain cultivators!" he cried hatefully. "You lied again! I hope you collect junk for the rest of your life! They weren't nearby at all!"

Xie Lian hadn't expected to keep Kemo away for long anyway, but he'd returned earlier than expected, and right at an inconvenient time. Mingguang was overjoyed, and he pointed at Fangxin.

"Big guy! Quick! Knock that sword over! Once the array is broken, the ones inside will be helpless!"

He didn't need to say anything. Kemo swung his hand down to chop, and Fangxin was knocked five more centimeters. Another chop, another five centimeters. Another chop, and Fangxin fell!

The protection array had finally been broken!

The broken sword stopped fighting Eming and flew out of the circle, returning to Mingguang's side. It transformed back into a pair of legs, and Mingguang stitched his two halves back together. He leapt to his feet and patted Kemo, then pointed at Pei Ming, then at himself. He pointed at Xie Lian, then pointed at Kemo. Kemo understood and nodded—this meant they were splitting the prey. As Kemo walked toward Xie Lian, who was shielding Hua Cheng, he cracked each knuckle on his iron-slab fists.

Mingguang stretched out his legs as he smirked. "Pei Ming, are you going to snap me in half again? Come give it a shot."

Pei Ming didn't speak.

Mingguang sneered. "The General Who Snapped His Sword. Heh. What a fine tale. The heavens are clearly blind if an incident like that could be turned into a beautiful story!"

"I never took it for a beautiful story," Pei Ming said.

"Bullshit!" Mingguang spat. "You know full well just how many you've killed. Brothers in arms, subordinates who followed you for years and years."

Meanwhile, Kemo had closed in on Xie Lian. Xie Lian gripped Eming tight. He wasn't afraid of Kemo, but he was worried that something could happen to Hua Cheng if he was careless.

Kemo noticed that his eyes were unfocused like he was thinking. "No need to come up with any more cunning tricks; I won't let you deceive me again!"

"I wasn't lying to you," Xie Lian said. "Banyue and General Pei Junior really were nearby earlier, but they fled after I told them about you. Huh? Banyue? Why are you here?!"

"Do you take me for an idiot?!" Kemo raged. "A foolish trick like this..."

Yet before he finished, a voice rang out from above him. "Kemo!"

That was the Banyue tongue—and a very familiar voice. Kemo looked up and came face-to-face with a large bundle of something wine-red falling on him from above. His face instantly dropped, and he hugged his head as he roared.

"*Go away!*"

It was a rain of those poisonous vipers found only in the Kingdom of Banyue, scorpion-snakes! And, naturally, the one who had flung them was the State Preceptor of the Kingdom of Banyue.

Banyue leapt down from a tree and landed next to Xie Lian. "General Hua..."

Xie Lian turned to Kemo. "I told you, Banyue really is here..."

Kemo didn't listen to him, just continued roaring at Banyue. "You threw them at me! You threw those scorpion-snakes at me! You know I hate scorpion-snakes, but you still threw them at me!"

Banyue crouched down. "I'm sorry...throwing scorpion-snakes is all I know how to do..."

Mingguang noticed that the situation was shifting and grew alarmed. "Who's there?!"

A shadowy figure leapt down from a tree and obstructed his path. "The former Deputy Martial God and Official of the Palace of Ming Guang, Pei Xiu!"

A miraculous cavalry had arrived, and Pei Ming was dumbfounded. "Little Pei? Why are you here too?"

"Banyue, weren't you with Lord Rain Master?" Xie Lian asked.

Pei Ming frowned slightly at the mention.

"Yes," Banyue replied. "We came with Lord Rain Master."

Mingguang evaluated Pei Xiu with a calculating eye. "You're Little Pei?"

"I am," Pei Xiu answered.

Mingguang narrowed his eyes and glanced at Banyue.

"I heard you threw away your heavenly official status for a little girlie," he taunted Pei Xiu. "Ha ha! Pei Ming, didn't you always proclaim that 'brothers are like limbs; women are like clothes'? Why's your descendant nothing like you? He doesn't even have a tenth of your eye for picking women! The State Preceptor of Banyue looks like a little quail; what the hell? Did you get cheated on and wind up raising someone else's spawn all those centuries ago? Ha ha ha ha…"

"Nothing but nonsense," Pei Xiu stated, then shot a blast from his palm.

Kemo leapt into the air, roaring, "You are my sworn enemies!"

"Hey! Big guy, we're on the same side!" Mingguang shouted.

Kemo turned his head and saw Mingguang jump up and transform into a long verdant sword that flew into his hand. Kemo opened his large hands, his palms like iron fans, and clutched the hilt. A black aura exploded from his giant body.

A menacing corpse taking up a demonic sword was like a savage beast growing venomous fangs!

When Pei Ming tapped Xie Lian's face with Eming, it had given Xie Lian an idea. Although he couldn't quite understand why, he felt that maybe the same trick could help Hua Cheng. He would sneakily transfer some of his breath to him while no one was looking to see if it would bring him some relief. However, as the dire situation continued to unfold, he couldn't help but shout.

"Watch out!"

It was awkward for Pei Ming to join the fight, so Pei Xiu and Banyue banded together to attack. One was sharp and direct, and the other agile and unpredictable; however, form alone wasn't enough. Pei Xiu had no spiritual power, and Banyue lacked brute strength. Kemo had both in spades, and they felt the strain as they continued to fight.

After being berated by Kemo, Banyue was too embarrassed to throw any more scorpion-snakes. But Pei Xiu had no such concern and threw out snakes like rain, enraging Kemo—the man roared ceaselessly in protest. It was only due to the protection of Mingguang's sword qi that none of the snakes dared approach.

Despite all that, after watching the fight for a while, Xie Lian began to relax. This was because he could tell that Kemo and Mingguang didn't match well.

Kemo grew up in the Kingdom of Banyue and was used to wielding a mace. He was accustomed to large, heavy weapons, so he wasn't used to swords. Even though he possessed unimaginable strength and the weapon in his hand was incomparably sharp, he couldn't necessarily unleash their full potential as a pair, nor could he immediately learn the tricks of the trade.

Thus, Xie Lian seized his chance and clapped his palms together in a prayer toward Hua Cheng.

"Forgive me!"

However, Xie Lian felt frozen as he stared at Hua Cheng's handsome, snow-white, little face, with its eyes shut so tight. Finally, he made up his mind and shut his own eyes to press close. But in his nervousness, he missed and ended up kissing Hua Cheng's forehead. While it was light and gentle, his heart was crushed.

A voice spoke up next to him. "Your Highness, you're doing it all wrong. What's the use in kissing his forehead?!"

Xie Lian almost fell over from shock. When he turned his head to look, Pei Ming was crouched next to him.

Sounding unusually indignant and resentful, Xie Lian said, "General Pei, can you not look?!"

Pei Ming raised his hands in defense. "All right, all right, all right. I won't look."

Then he turned around to watch the ongoing fight instead. After observing for a while, he shouted to Kemo, "You don't use swords like that. If you don't know how to wield a sword, then don't wield one at all!"

Naturally, Kemo didn't understand, but the Mingguang in his hands was all too eager to reply.

"Says the guy who snapped his own sword and can only stand around uselessly criticizing others!"

As he yelled, Pei Ming flew in and entered the brawl, landing in front of Kemo. Kemo swung the sword, but there was an incredibly crisp *clang*!

The strike didn't hit anything. When he looked down, he was dumbfounded.

The Mingguang sword in his grip had been snapped once again!

Seizing this chance, Pei Xiu hurled over another large wave of scorpion-snakes. It was like he had spilled a huge vat of dye that covered Kemo in dark wine-red from head to toe. He growled as he desperately tried to smack those slippery snakes off his body.

Pei Ming, on the other hand, looked down at Mingguang. "You know my techniques inside and out. And naturally, I know where you'd break the easiest."

Banyue plummeted from the sky with two pots raised high. Without a word, she flipped the pots so their mouths were facing down and captured the shocked Mingguang and the roaring Kemo within them.

With this, Xie Lian finally breathed a sigh of relief, inwardly remarking, *More people definitely get things done faster!*

Banyue sealed the clay pots and shook them in her hands, pressing her ear close to listen for the echoes inside.

"Banyue, stop playing around," Xie Lian hastily chided. "Put them away, and be careful not to let them escape."

Banyue nodded. She crouched in front of Xie Lian and looked at Hua Cheng.

"General Hua, is this your son?"

Xie Lian smiled. "Regrettably, he's not."

But soon, the smile fell from his face. Banyue gave an *oh* and said, "I saw you kiss him earlier and thought that he was."

Xie Lian covered his forehead with his palm, not wanting to bother explaining things any further.

Banyue seemed to find Hua Cheng rather adorable. She pulled at one of his little braids and commented on him with deep concern.

"He seems sick. Should I put him in a pot to help him recuperate? I felt better really quickly after I went into General Hua's pot."

Pei Xiu finally walked over. "No need. Don't worry about him; His Highness will take good care of him."

"Oh," Banyue said.

Pei Ming glanced at her. "You're the State Preceptor of Banyue?"

He stared down at Banyue, his disdain apparent. Shrouded in his shadow as she crouched on the ground, Banyue nodded. Intentionally or otherwise, Pei Xiu took a step forward to stand in front of her, but Pei Ming pushed him aside and approached her as if he wanted to scrutinize her more closely.

When he was only about two steps away from her, Banyue's face changed color drastically and she hurried to hide behind Xie Lian—

it was like she couldn't get away fast enough, but judging from her expression, she didn't seem scared. Everyone was puzzled, but Xie Lian soon understood.

"General Pei, um...the Ghost Scent Candy..." he courteously hinted.

Pei Ming blinked, then his face turned a little dark. It seemed the Ghost Scent Candy's...*perfume* hadn't yet dissipated. Since Banyue was a female ghost, she couldn't tolerate that vulgar ghost qi and fled from the stink...

Xie Lian snorted in spite of himself but quickly schooled his expression. "Why has Lord Rain Master also come to Mount Tonglu? Where is he now? Why aren't you traveling together?"

"Due to the agitation of ghosts, large numbers of inhuman creatures swarmed toward Mount Tonglu. When they passed Yushi Country, they captured some farmers to use as rations. At the time, neither Lord Rain Master nor the Guardian Steed were present; after learning of the incident, we've come in pursuit," Pei Xiu explained. "We were all traveling together at first, but on the way, we heard Your Highness calling for us in Banyue tongue. We split off to come investigate."

Xie Lian had simply been yelling random things due to the urgency of the situation and hadn't actually thought they were close by—he'd hit the mark by accident. And Yushi Country looked like a small, quiet village from the outside, so it wasn't unusual for ghosts to pass by and stupidly try to grab people.

"I couldn't find you in the Mortal Realm before," Pei Ming said with a frown. "How did you end up with Lord Rain Master? Don't tell me you were chasing after the State Preceptor of Banyue."

Pei Xiu lowered his head slightly. "No. It was Lord Rain Master who saved me."

Pei Xiu had been wandering the Mortal Realm after his exile, and since he had the time, he smashed up a few of Qi Rong's little lairs. Irked by this, Qi Rong rustled up a gang of who-knew-what in an attempt to surround and destroy him. If Pei Xiu had still had his spiritual power, that rabble wouldn't have been able to harm him. But he now possessed a mortal body, so when he was attacked by hundreds of ghosts, he sustained injuries and was stuck in a difficult predicament. As he fought with all his might, hanging on by a thread, the Rain Master happened to ride by on an ox and lent a helping hand. After the Rain Master ensured that his identity and story checked out, Pei Xiu was taken to recover in Yushi Country.

"Lord Rain Master didn't give you trouble?" Pei Ming asked, seeming astounded.

According to Shi Qingxuan, Yushi Country and the Palace of Ming Guang had been at odds in the past. Hundreds of years ago, the Rain Master knocked out Pei Ming's previous deputy general. It seemed Pei Ming didn't think the Rain Master was the generous sort.

"No," Pei Xiu replied. "Lord Rain Master never gave me a bit of trouble. On the contrary, I've received much support."

Just then, an echoing voice sounded out. "Rain Master? Is the Rain Master from the Kingdom of Yushi?"

"That's right," Xie Lian replied without thinking.

It was only after he responded that he realized the voice belonged to Mingguang—although he was locked in the pot, he was still listening intently to everything outside. He clicked his tongue at Xie Lian's answer.

"Pei Ming! You've slept with so many women, but that useless descendant is the best you can produce?! He actually needed the protection of someone from the Kingdom of Yushi to survive, and he's even speaking well of them?! Honestly, each generation is only getting worse! *Ha!*"

Pei Ming looked a bit uncomfortable at his jeering. Xie Lian didn't understand the joke—or what was worth being angry about—so he asked Banyue in a whisper, "Do you understand what he's saying?"

"Not really," Banyue replied. "But I think I heard Pei Xiu-gege say that before his general ascended, he was a general of the Kingdom of Xuli."

"..."

Was there anything wrong with Pei Ming being a general from Xuli?

There absolutely was!

Because, as far as Xie Lian knew, the Kingdom of Yushi had been flattened by the iron cavalry of the Kingdom of Xuli!

"Lord Rain Master was the last ruler of the Kingdom of Yushi," Banyue added.

"..."

No wonder Pei Ming always looked odd whenever the Rain Master was mentioned, and no wonder the Rain Master didn't hold back when disciplining that former deputy heavenly official. It seemed both parties held a long and ancient grudge.

It must be known that heavenly officials considered it quite natural for the Mortal Realm's kingdoms to fight and annihilate one another. It was always the same old story being played out over and over, century after century. But it was often hard to let things go when their own turn came. It had to be vexing to be forced to stand in the same court as a man who had annihilated one's own kingdom, and be forced to watch said man cavort and strut around the heavens.

Pei Xiu added a talisman to the surface of the pot, and Mingguang's voice came to an abrupt stop.

"Why has the general come too?" Pei Xiu asked.

"Isn't it so I can drag you back sooner?" Pei Ming replied.

Xie Lian remembered Hua Cheng's words. It seemed *this* was a "benefit" Pei Ming had negotiated with Jun Wu when being dispatched to Mount Tonglu.

Pei Ming patted Pei Xiu's shoulder. "Since you're here, make me proud. If you perform well, perhaps you can return to the Upper Court early."

The talisman on the pot in his hand burst into flames before Pei Xiu could answer. The imprisoned Mingguang's fury was so hot that he burned it.

"Pei Ming! Do you still remember what you said back then?!"

Pei Xiu was about to add another talisman to shut him up, but Pei Ming stopped him.

"I've said too many things over the course of this lifetime. What are you referring to?"

"Do you still remember your excuse when you killed all those men who had followed your command for years? 'Some people can be killed, some can't. Some things can be done, some can't.' Sounding like you possessed the heart of Buddha, forgiving of all!" Mingguang spat hatefully. "And now? Do you think no one knows what despicable deeds your Little Pei has done? Word has already spread! And here you are, trying to wipe his ass and help him hide his past! The brothers who followed you in battle from north to south deserved to die, but when it comes to your descendant, he doesn't? You toss away clothes once you've used them and break limbs after they've served their purpose! What, so your Little Pei is a gem, and the rest of us are weeds?!"

He roared furiously and mindlessly, but Pei Ming listened to the end.

"You're not Mingguang," he suddenly said.

The pot instantly fell silent. A moment later, Mingguang's voice resounded once more. "What bullshit are you spouting? Have you not witnessed that I'm Mingguang? Did you not see my form with your eyes?!"

However, Pei Ming stated with conviction, "No. You're not Mingguang."

The voice inside the pot was grouchy. "Then who else could I be?"

Pei Ming took the pot from Pei Xiu's hands, sounding sure in his response. "I think you're Rong Guang."

When that name was said, the pot went completely silent. Pei Xiu's eyes widened slightly upon mention of the name.

"General Pei Junior, who is this Rong Guang?" Xie Lian asked.

Pei Xiu snapped out of it, hesitating slightly before he answered. "Before the general ascended, Rong Guang was the deputy general who'd followed him the longest, and his most capable subordinate."

And thus, Xie Lian finally learned the story of the General Who Snapped His Sword.

Back when Pei Ming was still mortal, he was successful on the battlefields of both love and war—as a general, he was constantly victorious for decades, without a single defeat to his name. Naturally, his own courage and skill were to credit, but the support of his deputy general couldn't be ignored. This deputy general was named Rong Guang.

Rong Guang was famous for cunning, deception, and manipulation. The two had very different personalities and styles, but they had known each other since they were young and their collaboration was unexpectedly good. One in the light, one in the shadows, their friendship spanned years and was made of iron. Pei Ming's sword "Mingguang" was a name they had come up with together and was a combination of the pronunciations for "Ming" and "Guang" from their own names.

Pei Ming was good at fighting wars, and in a turbulent period of history, that was much more important than knowing how to make money or anything else. Naturally, he only continued to rise in rank. However, no matter how high he climbed, the position of general was the highest he could go. There might be endless honorable and esteemed titles added before the word "general," but there would always be another sitting on his head. Before the king, he must bow and kneel.

Pei Ming had no particular opinion on the matter. However, as he conquered city after city and the glory on his armor shone brighter and brighter, the troops under Rong Guang's command grew restless. While Pei Ming never had so much pride that he forgot his roots and principles, his subordinates had swelled infinitely with it on his behalf.

The worst offender was Rong Guang. Since he was closer with the soldiers, it was extremely easy for him to fan the passion in their hearts, planting ideas in the minds of those former subordinates. *"General Pei deserves more than he's been given!" "General Pei is oppressed, just as we are!" "The Kingdom of Xuli needs General Pei to save it, and it needs us to help him do it!"* They planned to invade the Imperial Palace of Xuli and declare Pei Ming king, then have him lead the elite troops to further greatness, towering over all as the strongest kingdom. They dreamed of the grand future that awaited once they flattened all four seas with their iron cavalry—a world unified under one nation.

Unfortunately, Pei Ming himself had no interest whatsoever in becoming king.

His greatest joys in life were fighting victorious battles and sleeping with beautiful women, and he didn't need to be king to accomplish either of those things. Besides, while the King of Xuli had no great achievements, he didn't do anything particularly wrong either—and Pei Ming knew that he might not do better if he took over. The potential for chaos had more drawbacks than benefits, so why bother with mutiny for no reason? And so, Pei Ming skillfully thwarted Rong Guang every time he dropped his eager hints.

But not only was Rong Guang unconvinced, he became more and more obsessed with every failed attempt at persuasion. Until finally, the soldiers resolved one day that they would revolt regardless and worry about the consequences after the fact. If the insurrection was successful, there was no way Pei Ming could back down from the position.

Having listened to this point, Xie Lian was left speechless. *Can you actually force that on someone, like ushering ducks onto a perch...?*

Pei Xiu saw his confusion and said, "Rong Guang may not have truly wanted to crown Pei Ming king, but he needed to borrow the general's name to incite a revolt. He didn't have the level of prestige that the general did, so he might not have been able to earn the people's support if he raised his own flag."

Xie Lian pondered this. "That might not have been the only reason."

They were using Pei Ming's name to put him on the throne, and with that banner raised, the man himself couldn't pretend not to know what was going on. And so he picked up his sword at once and led a small, trustworthy troop of soldiers to rush the palace.

It was the last battle of his life.

79
Panic Left and Right, East or West Road Undecided

"DID GENERAL PEI win or lose?" Xie Lian asked.

"Won. And lost," Pei Xiu answered.

All the insurgents died by Pei Ming's sword. There were many of his former subordinates among them, men who he'd shared decades of friendship with. Pei Ming had always used his sword Mingguang to fight by their side. Now it was the weapon he used to butcher them.

As the slaughter was coming to an end and the results of the battle were clear, it was unsurprising that the King of Xuli ordered for the injured, nearly immobile Pei Ming to be surrounded and charged with treason.

Pei Ming was good at fighting wars, but legal battles were never his strong suit. He had clearly been fighting for and defending the throne, but in the end, he only earned a declaration that he should be put to death.

Pei Ming held the pot in his hand. While he heard what Xie Lian and Pei Xiu were discussing, he didn't have the energy to care. "I should've known it was you. This is very much your style."

Rong Guang's resentment must have possessed the broken sword that had been so thoroughly dyed by the blood of millions. He'd connected with its bitterness, which had allowed him to survive this long.

However, the voice inside the pot was cold. "Your brothers are long dead. I'm nothing but a sword."

Xie Lian knew that he might never admit to it and that continuing to question him would be fruitless. "Never mind, General Pei."

Pei Ming nodded and returned the pot to Pei Xiu.

Thus, they subdued two particularly nasty ghosts. Setting aside everything else, this could be considered a good start.

"General Pei and I will continue further toward Mount Tonglu," Xie Lian said. "Banyue, how about you two? Will you go and find Lord Rain Master?"

"Lord Rain Master has already gone on ahead to chase the evil creatures who kidnapped the farmers," Pei Xiu said. "To catch up, we'll need to head in the same direction as the general and Your Highness, so we are willing to join you and assist."

Pei Ming snapped out of it and knitted his brows slightly. "Then we'd best hurry. The Ruler of Yushi isn't a martial god, and the road ahead is likely full of dangers."

And so Xie Lian picked up Hua Cheng, Banyue tucked the two pots away, and the party hastily made their way deeper into the dense woods.

Since they were still situated on the outer edges of Mount Tonglu territory, they didn't run into any impressive characters—most were nothing but weeds. They weren't interested in picking pointless fights, so they ignored the rabble. Some of those weeds were foolish enough to challenge them, but they were quickly scared away by Banyue and Pei Xiu's scorpion-snakes.

After a day of journeying, they finally emerged from the forest and reached the second layer of Mount Tonglu.

Here the trees gradually became sparser, the roads grew progressively wider, and there were more traces of habitation. Xie Lian even saw a broken-down, blackened little house on the side of the road—an exceedingly bizarre sight in this isolated land.

"How are there houses here?" he couldn't help but wonder.

Banyue and Pei Xiu both shook their heads to indicate they also didn't know.

"I'm afraid that's something you'll have to ask the Lord Ghost King in your arms," Pei Ming replied.

The same thought crossed Xie Lian's mind as soon as he asked the question. Had Hua Cheng been awake, then he'd surely have the answer. He glanced down. Hua Cheng's unusually hot body temperature was gradually cooling, but his eyes were still tightly shut. Xie Lian couldn't help but worry.

"Your Highness, we're about to enter the next layer," Pei Ming reminded him. "The things we'll run into further ahead will be even more powerful. Shall we take a break and wait for Hua-chengzhu to wake?"

The group had come to a fork in the road. One path headed east, and the other headed west. Xie Lian contemplated, then stated his decision aloud.

"The night has deepened. Let's camp here for now."

After traveling for a day, it was high time to rest—to focus on protecting Hua Cheng and helping him recover.

"That's good," Banyue spoke up. "Pei Xiu-gege also needs rest."

Only then did the group remember that Pei Xiu was mortal at the moment and required both rest and sustenance; he had been silent about his discomfort throughout the whole trip. The cursed shackles on Xie Lian's body meant he had similar needs, but his worry for Hua Cheng had pushed any other thoughts from his mind.

The group stopped at the fork in the road and set up camp. Banyue started a fire, and Pei Xiu went hunting. Seeing that everyone was busy with their own matters, Xie Lian stared at Hua Cheng's face again.

A moment later, instinct made him whip his head around, and sure enough, Pei Ming was watching the two of them. They stared at each other, and Pei Ming huffed a dry laugh.

"Fine. I'll go away."

"No, it's fine," Xie Lian said.

It wasn't like he was thinking of doing anything unfit for the public! Why did Pei Ming have to make it sound like he was sneaking around?!

Just then, Banyue walked over holding a pot. "General Hua…"

Xie Lian and Pei Ming both turned to look.

"What is it?" Xie Lian asked.

Banyue showed them a terrified wild chicken that was tied up and stuffed inside the pot. "Pei Xiu-gege caught this for me to cook, but I don't know how."

After Pei Xiu had finished hunting, he left to scout the area. Pei Ming seemed dissatisfied with Banyue no matter how he looked at her.

"Aren't you a girl?" he berated her presumptuously. "Fighting and killing things all day! Never mind not bothering to paint your face—how come you don't even know how to cook?"

Xie Lian and Banyue were both speechless. Banyue wasn't a delicate girl raised in a normal household, and she hadn't a clue of how Pei Ming judged beauty. She couldn't understand his comments and was left quite puzzled. As for Xie Lian, he had pretty much figured Pei Ming out by now—he was simply impossible when it came to women.

"Put it down, Banyue. I'll teach you," Xie Lian said.

Banyue already had great faith in him, so she happily followed his instructions. An incense time later, Xie Lian was plucking the colorful feathers from the wild chicken, and Pei Ming was staring at his own blood-smeared hands.

"There could be some new famous tales now—the Chicken-Killing General and the Feather-Plucking Crown Prince," he lamented.

Xie Lian had watched him kill the chicken with his bare hands; it had been a bloody and grimy sight.

"General Pei, couldn't you have used a knife or something? It would've been cleaner."

"Is there one lying around?" Pei Ming retorted.

As soon as he spoke, they both glanced at the two pots sitting on the ground. Rong Guang seemed to have noticed the two peculiar looks even from inside his prison, and the pot shuddered violently.

"Get outta here! Scram, far away! Careful, I might just smear venom on my blade and poison you all!"

They hurried away. Once they were sure the pot couldn't hear them, Pei Ming shook his head and said to Xie Lian, "And he keeps denying it. He's always had that temper. It's him for sure."

Xie Lian had heard Rong Guang cussing ceaselessly at Pei Ming, and he had long since developed an odd sense of sympathy.

"I understand completely. I have a little cousin who's somewhat like General Rong. He knows more curse words, but he doesn't know how to do much other than spew them."

At least Rong Guang could help Pei Ming fight battles. If Qi Rong was to help Xie Lian fight, he'd ruin Xie Lian long before he had a chance to be killed by the enemy.

Pei Ming seemed to have imagined what Rong Guang would be like if he couldn't fight, just cuss, and he earnestly remarked, "That's honestly terrifying."

Xie Lian threw the fully plucked wild chicken back into the pot, filled it with water, and started cooking it atop the fire. Every now and then, he'd toss in some wild fruit or herbs for flavor. Banyue copied him and tried very hard to find something that looked edible to stuff into the pot. Pei Ming didn't understand what they were doing, but he didn't see any glaring problems since he'd never entered a kitchen himself. He helped by adding firewood to the campfire.

"Your Highness, I have a question I've always wanted to ask you. It's never been an appropriate thing to ask, since we haven't had more than a passing acquaintance."

It was true that they'd never been close. Xie Lian's early impression of Pei Ming was that he was a skilled martial artist, but a villain and a womanizer. They'd even faced off against each other more than once. Now that they'd crossed paths a few times, his opinion had changed without him realizing it, and their relationship had grown somewhat friendlier.

"By all means, General Pei, please ask."

"You've been banished twice and bear two cursed shackles on your person," Pei Ming said. "You could've asked the Emperor to remove them after you ascended the third time. So why didn't you?"

Xie Lian watched as Banyue scrunched her face up in deep thought. She then brightened up and cheerfully pulled out a few long, wine-red scorpion-snakes to put into the bubbling pot.

"Then, General Pei, I've also got a question I want to ask you," he replied, appearing unperturbed.

"Please," Pei Ming said.

"After you snapped Mingguang, why didn't you forge a new spiritual sword?" Xie Lian asked.

Pei Ming raised his brows. "What an unpleasant question."

Xie Lian matched his expression. "Likewise."

The two shared a chuckle.

Suddenly, Pei Ming said, "I never thought it was a beautiful story."

"I get it," Xie Lian said.

He was about to elaborate when there was movement behind him. He sensed something and looked back.

"San Lang?"

Sure enough, Hua Cheng had sat up! Surprised and delighted, Xie Lian went over to help hold him up by the shoulders.

"San Lang! You're awake! You seem…bigger?"

Before, Hua Cheng had looked like he was only a little older than ten, but now he appeared to be at least thirteen or fourteen. When he spoke, his voice had changed from that of a child to a teen's slightly raspy tone.

"Yes. Thank you, gege, for giving me relief."

"What a joyous occasion," Pei Ming commented.

"No need to thank me, I…" Xie Lian replied, trailing off as he realized that he had said the word "relief." His smile froze, and he wondered to himself, *That doesn't mean what I think it does, right?*

A moment later, Hua Cheng grabbed his shoulders. "Your Highness, listen to me," he said darkly. "Something is rapidly approaching from the east. You must get out of its way!"

Xie Lian was taken aback. They both looked to the east, like they could see through the endless black night and spot any figures skulking in the darkness. Although Xie Lian didn't sense anything, still he said, "Very well! We'll leave."

"Where to?" Pei Ming asked.

The road only forked into two paths, and Xie Lian answered, "The west!"

Banyue grabbed the pot that was cooking over the flames, looking like she planned to bring it along. "Pei Xiu-gege hasn't returned yet!"

Just as she spoke, a shadow came hurrying from the road to the west. It was Pei Xiu, who had returned from scouting.

"General! Don't go down this road! There's a large group of nefarious creatures coming this way right now!"

"How many?" Hua Cheng demanded.

Pei Xiu was momentarily stunned when he noticed that Hua Cheng was the one who'd asked.

"Judging by the ground tremors, at least five hundred!"

A martial god would never consider retreat unless there was absolutely no other choice.

"Do we go west or east?" Pei Ming demanded.

"West!" Hua Cheng said with conviction.

Xie Lian also replied, "West."

For some reason, although there were more ghosts coming from the west and not a single shadow in the east, Xie Lian's instincts told him the west was the safer choice.

Without further ado, the group hurried on their way. Xie Lian was originally prepared to kill without hesitation if they ran into any roaming hordes, yet he hadn't spotted a thing even after running for several kilometers. He couldn't help but find it strange.

"General Pei Junior, where and when did you hear that over five hundred ghosts were approaching?"

"Not far from here," Pei Xiu said. "They were only a few kilometers behind me at the time and moving with great speed."

"Then this is very strange!" Xie Lian commented.

The group was running westward, and the horde of five-hundred-some ghosts was rushing eastward; both parties were moving quickly, so they should've run into each other by now. So why wasn't there a single ghost—and not even any commotion?

"Little Pei wouldn't have heard wrong," Pei Ming said. "Maybe they went back the way they came?"

"I don't think that's likely," Pei Xiu said. "Their pace really was extremely fast. It sounded as if they were…"

"Running for their lives," Hua Cheng said.

Suddenly, Xie Lian stopped in his tracks. And not just him—the entire group stopped. Just ahead of them, a field of corpses was blocking their way.

Of those corpses, some were beasts and some were men, their bodies in all shapes and sizes. There were even battered souls, wisps of black smoke and ghost fires floating in the air. It was an exceedingly chilling sight.

Xie Lian crouched to check. "They really were running for their lives. They just…didn't succeed."

When Pei Xiu heard this horde's approach, he'd turned back to inform Xie Lian and the others. And right after he left, something had chased them down and killed them all at once.

"This is the work of one person," Hua Cheng said.

Xie Lian nodded in agreement. If the clashing parties were both great in number, the kill wouldn't have been this clean, and the battle wouldn't have ended so straightforwardly.

Killing over five hundred nefarious creatures in such a short period of time… The perpetrator of this massacre was doubtlessly stronger than Demon of the Swift Life-Extinguishing Blade. It seemed this was another one they should keep an eye on.

"I hope Lord Rain Master didn't choose this path…" Banyue said, holding her soup pot.

"No need to worry. My Lord has the Guardian Steed," Pei Xiu said.

Just then, Xie Lian heard a strange clacking noise from not far away. When he went over to look, he found a skull whose jaws were chattering—the noise was coming from it.

When it realized that it had been discovered, it cried out in terror. "Mercy! I'll never come again; I wanna go back, I wanna go home!"

Xie Lian cupped it in both hands and spoke to it gently. "Don't be scared, we're only passersby. Can you tell us exactly what happened here?"

The skull's jaws continued to chatter as it bit out a reply. "Y-you're passersby? Don't go any further onward, there's someone really scary ahead... Counting us, he's already killed over a thousand ghosts, and he's still dissatisfied... He's still, he's still..."

Over a thousand! That was far more than they'd imagined.

"Who is it that you speak of?" Xie Lian asked. "Do you know his name or his moniker? Or what he looks like?"

"N-no," the skull said. "I didn't get a clear look. It didn't take long for him to kill us. I only faintly saw that he was a man clad in black, very young, his face very pale..."

"Sounds a bit troublesome," Pei Ming said. "Your Highness, Hua-chengzhu, are you sure we should be heading westward right now and not east?"

The skull heard that and shrieked. "The east won't do either! *Not the east!*"

"What's wrong with the east?" Xie Lian asked.

"We...didn't dare go east, which was why we chose the west," the skull said. "On the road to the east, there's a young man dressed in white who has killed over two thousand ghosts in a single day. He's far more terrifying than the one in the west..."

Over two thousand!

Everyone's expressions stiffened.

Xie Lian glanced at Hua Cheng. "It seems the west road was the right choice."

The skull sighed through its chattering teeth. "Either road is a mistake! There is no path to take!"

Indeed, for normal little minions, either direction was oblivion. East or west, they would be crushed easily; no matter which road they chose, in the end they would be blown to smoke and become someone's fertilizer. After howling a few more dry wails, the ghost fires in the skull's empty sockets gradually went out.

Xie Lian gently placed it down on the side of the road. "San Lang, do you know what the creature in the east is?"

"Can't be sure right now," Hua Cheng replied. "But it's coming this way. Under the current circumstances, I don't recommend we face it head-on. This one to the west is a little easier to deal with."

Xie Lian nodded. "Very well. Then we'll continue westward."

The group crossed through the field of corpses and hurried on their way. They traveled all night but never encountered the black-clad man the skull spoke of, nor did they see any trace of the Rain Master. Xie Lian couldn't help but start to worry.

As they journeyed on, the houses and buildings alongside the road increased in number. Soon, they could even recognize general locations—these were the city's impoverished slums, this was the theater house, this was a general store, this was the courtyard of a wealthy household... The road beneath their feet had been paved by human hands, and the patterns of the bricks could still be faintly seen. This had once been a prosperous little town, but it was now empty of the living, strangely desolate, and deafeningly quiet.

There was an old well by the roadside, and when they pulled up water it was relatively clean, so the group decided to rest there for a while. Xie Lian and Pei Xiu both drank some water and took the chance to wash their faces. When they looked up, they were greeted by the sight of Banyue coming their way.

Banyue had held on to the black clay pot the entire time and had been waiting for them to finish. "General Hua, Pei Xiu-gege, eat something."

"All right. Thank you for the trouble," Pei Xiu said.

"Everyone's worked hard traveling today. Let's all give this a try," Xie Lian said.

The group gathered around, but their faces froze the moment Banyue opened the pot.

Although "smell" was something colorless and formless, it was as if some mysterious, tangible force had twisted the air around the mouth of the pot the moment Banyue removed its cover.

The group stared into the pot for a long time. Their eyes reflected an endless, bottomless darkness; it was as if they were about to be pulled into the abyss. No words could describe the sentiment expressed on their faces. A moment later, Xie Lian patted Banyue's shoulder and gave a thumbs-up.

"Not bad. It's good for a first attempt."

Pei Ming looked at them in disbelief. "It's her first time, but is it Your Highness's first time too? If I recall correctly, you made her follow your every step, and you did more than her. I *knew* something didn't seem right with what you two were doing. So it wasn't just my imagination."

Hua Cheng spoke up. "Is that right? Well, since gege made this, I gotta try it."

Pei Ming and Pei Xiu's heads both jerked to look at him. Their eyes were full of awe, terror, respect, and other such emotions.

"Gege, what's this dish called?" Hua Cheng asked.

Xie Lian lightly cleared his throat. "...Toppled Phoenixes."[1]

---

1 [顛鸞倒鳳] Toppled Phoenixes: an idiom that means either "the world is ever changing" or "to mess around (sexually)."

"Good name," Hua Cheng earnestly complimented, then reached into that infinitely dark pot.

The way Pei Ming and Pei Xiu watched him, it was like they were anxious he was going to be swallowed whole by the pot. However, Hua Cheng calmly and easily took out a small, burnt piece of something that resembled a broken corpse and serenely placed it in his mouth.

"How is it?" Pei Ming asked.

"Tastes like its name," Hua Cheng said.

Pei Ming turned to Pei Xiu, whose expression was unreadably complicated.

"It was made for you. Enjoy."

"..." Pei Xiu commented stoically.

His face expressionless, he took the pot from Banyue's hands and reached inside.

Xie Lian used the cold well water to wash his face again and fixed his hair, then turned away from the others. He surveyed their surroundings.

"How come this place has so many traces of settlement, even though it's so isolated from the rest of the world? Could the area within the Tonglu Mountains actually be habitable?"

He had already asked this question the day before, but there was no one who could answer him at the time. Now there was.

"It *was* habitable, but that was a long time ago," Hua Cheng replied. "Mount Tonglu's territory is the size of seven cities, spread out far and wide. These houses are the remains of historical cities and towns from an ancient kingdom. As we get closer to the Kiln, you'll see more relics and more prosperous sites."

Xie Lian believed him without a doubt. "I see."

Just then, Pei Ming's voice came from behind them. "Little Pei, what are you doing? Men don't kneel so easily—get up!"

Xie Lian didn't turn around. "What's the name of this ancient kingdom? San Lang, do you know?"

Hua Cheng didn't turn around either; his hands were clasped behind him. "The Kingdom of Wuyong."

"Your Highness? Your Highness, do you have an antidote or something? You can't just kill someone and not bury the body. And *you*!" Pei Ming admonished Banyue. "Is this how you cooked for him? What's with this snake? It's still moving even after it was cooked for so long—is it a spirit now?!"

Banyue seemed to be ceaselessly kowtowing in apology. "I'm sorry…I'm sorry…I'm sorry… It's indeed turned into a spirit, I didn't know how long a spirit would need to be cooked for…I'm sorry…"

Xie Lian propped up his cheek with one hand in thought. "I'm ignorant and ill-informed; I don't recall ever hearing this particular kingdom's name. How ancient is it?"

However, as soon as the words left his lips, he wasn't so sure anymore. Wuyong, Wuyong… It did sound foreign without context. But when he thought deeply, he felt that he had heard someone utter that name a long, long time ago.

"The details aren't clear," Hua Cheng said. "But it must predate the Kingdom of Xianle. It's likely at least two thousand years old."

Xie Lian scanned their surroundings. "These buildings don't look like they're millennia old."

"Naturally," Hua Cheng replied. "Mount Tonglu's perimeter isn't open most of the time, so it's like they're sealed in a massive mausoleum. Since they're isolated from the outside world, they of course remain in a pristine state."

Xie Lian bowed his head and grew pensive. Pei Ming finally left Pei Xiu to his own devices and came over.

"Lord Ghost King sure knows everything. But isn't this information a little too wild to believe? Might I ask what your source is? I've never heard a single word about this on the outside."

Hua Cheng didn't look at him. "And might I ask General Pei something? What kind of person could enter Mount Tonglu to gather this sort of information?"

"Logically, any ghost could," Pei Ming said. "But if they wished to obtain a wealth of valuable information, they would have to gather it over a considerable amount of time. And taking Mount Tonglu's rules about slaughter into consideration, your source would have to be a powerful individual."

"And after gathering that information, what kind of individual could emerge from Mount Tonglu?" Hua Cheng asked.

"They would have to be a Supreme Ghost King, like My Lord," Pei Ming said.

"So I gathered the information myself, and there won't be any words spread for you to hear if I'm not the one saying them." Hua Cheng finally turned his head to look at him, and his tone became slightly mocking. "Perhaps for a heavenly official of the Upper Court, keeping a secret is more difficult than passing a Heavenly Tribulation. But that is not the case for me."

"..."

He wasn't wrong. If a heavenly official in the Upper Court had stumbled upon knowledge of such importance, not even two hours later it would have spread to excited and open discussion in every spiritual communication array. Yet Hua Cheng had kept this under wraps for centuries, never selling it to anyone or boasting about it. It showed the magnitude of his ability to play things close to his chest.

"I get it," Pei Ming said. "It appears that when it comes to His

Highness, Hua-chengzhu is all-knowing and will tell him all that he wishes to learn."

"That's not right," Xie Lian suddenly said.

Everyone turned to look. "What isn't?"

Xie Lian had been thinking hard for a while, and now his right hand folded into a fist and lightly tapped his left palm. "I said that I hadn't heard the name Wuyong before, but I was wrong. I *have* heard that name!"

Hua Cheng became a little serious. "Gege, where did you hear of it?"

Xie Lian turned to address him. "When I trained at the Royal Holy Temple of Xianle in my youth, my master was the state preceptor. When he first took me in as a disciple, he told me a story."

It wasn't actually a proper *story*; it was more like he was trying to instill some grand, glorious, legendary imagery in Xie Lian's young mind.

Once upon a time, there was an ancient kingdom. In that kingdom, there was a crown prince who was ingeniously talented, intelligent, and clever. He was skilled in both martial and literary arts. He was a scintillating character, the kind that would only appear once in history. He loved his people, and his people loved him. Even long after he died, his people never forgot him.

"My child, I hope you will become a person like him," the state preceptor said, solemn and tender.

Young Xie Lian sat there poised and proper, and he said without thinking, "I don't want to become a person like him. I want to become a god."

"…"

"If that crown prince was really as amazing as you say, how come he didn't become a god?" young Xie Lian went on.

"…"

"If the people really never forgot him, then how come I've never heard anyone speak of this crown prince before?" young Xie Lian continued.

"..."

Xie Lian still swore that he had never intended to be provocative or rebellious when he raised those questions. He was genuinely curious and looking for answers to his queries. However, when the state preceptor heard him, his face turned quite the shade.

Why could Xie Lian recite *Dao De Jing* forward and backward as if it were a simple feat? Because the state preceptor made him transcribe *Dao De Jing* a hundred times that night, to do good by its name and "cultivate both the body and mind." Xie Lian sincerely suspected that if not for his status as the honorable crown prince, the state preceptor might've had him kneel on nails as he wrote.

In any case, every word of *Dao De Jing* was deeply burned into Xie Lian's brain after that incident, and a faint impression of the "Crown Prince of Wuyong" also remained.

Xie Lian had always enjoyed reading, but he had never come across records related to the Kingdom of Wuyong in any old scrolls. So he figured the story was something the state preceptor had fabricated on the fly to educate him—or perhaps the state preceptor had played too many games of cards and mixed up some of the details. However, he didn't feel the urge to blow his cover, nor the urge to copy *Dao De Jing* another hundred times, so he didn't take it seriously nor to heart.

"Your Highness, it sounds like the state preceptor of your Xianle had quite the background and was very knowledgeable," Pei Ming said. "Might I ask what happened to him?"

After some hesitation, Xie Lian replied, "I don't know. After Xianle fell, there were many people who I never saw again."

Just then, he felt something tighten around his ankle and froze. "Who's there?!"

He was about to stomp and break the bones of whatever it was, but he looked down first. He breathed a sigh of relief.

"General Pei Junior, what are you doing announcing yourself like this? That was close—I almost ruined your hand."

The hand did, in fact, belonged to Pei Xiu. His entire body was sprawled on the ground, face planted in the dirt. His arms were outstretched, one hand gripping Pei Ming and the other Xie Lian. The two of them crouched to hear him speak.

"What are you trying to say?"

Banyue was still holding the cooking pot. "I don't know. Pei Xiu-gege has been crawling all over the ground, and it seems like he's discovered something important."

"Oh?" Pei Ming was amazed. "You managed to detect something even in your current condition? As expected of Little Pei. So what did you find?"

Pei Xiu loosened his hand's grip and pointed in a direction. Xie Lian looked where he pointed.

"These are..." Xie Lian said.

The group all gathered to examine them.

"Ox hoof marks?"

Pei Xiu finally lifted his head from the mud. "These, are...marks left behind by, Lord Rain Master's, Guardian Steed," he croaked out.

"Pei Xiu-gege, your sentences are broken," Banyue remarked.

"I'm, all right," Pei Xiu replied. "Lord Rain Master, Lord, Lord..."

He was stuck on the word "Lord" and could no longer continue.

"Could he have been...poisoned by a scorpion-snake?" Xie Lian wondered.

"Their poison doesn't work like this..." Banyue said.

"The Rain Master already ran into the black-clad man in the west and fought him," Hua Cheng said.

"Really? How can you tell?" Xie Lian asked.

Hua Cheng was about to speak when Pei Xiu, whose speech was now fully broken, extended a shaky finger and started to write on the ground. Out of some odd sense of respect, the group gathered to watch him. The words "battle formation" were scrawled in crooked characters by his finger. Once he was done writing, it was like he had exhausted the last bit of his energy; he clenched his hand into a fist and moved no more.

Hua Cheng looked back up. "That's it exactly. The Rain Master's steed is a black ox transformed from one of the golden beasts on the gate knocker of the Kingdom of Yushi's Royal Cultivation Hall. The steed is usually steady and leaves no traces when it walks, but it changes form when it enters battle. And this hoof print's shape is different from its normal hoof marks—it's much bigger."

"Lord Ghost King is shockingly well informed," Pei Ming commented.

Hua Cheng pointed at the marks on the ground and continued to speak to Xie Lian. "Gege, look here."

Xie Lian moved his head closer. "Yeah, you're right... These hoof marks show up very abruptly, so the enemy must have caught them by surprise."

"Yeah," Hua Cheng said. "And the mark is deep, so it's obvious the enemy was strong. The ox grappled the enemy with his horns and was pressed deep into the earth during the confrontation—at least half a dozen centimeters."

They simulated the fight scene that had occurred, and Pei Ming also didn't back down.

"But in the end, it was a draw."

"That's right," Xie Lian agreed.

There was no trace of blood nearby, nor ghost qi dispersing in the air. It appeared that when they met, their match was quick and fierce, but they both abandoned the fight once they found the other too tough to handle.

Hua Cheng informed them that the movement of the creature in the east had changed direction, and the group continued westward, though at a slower pace. Soon, they came upon a peculiar-looking giant building on the side of the road. Looking at it from afar, it was more impressive than all the other houses around. Even though some of its enclosures and eaves had collapsed, it was still a sight to behold. Xie Lian unconsciously paused in his steps.

"What is this place?"

Hua Cheng gave it only a glance. "A holy temple of Wuyong."

Pei Ming had one of Pei Xiu's arms hooked over his shoulders to drag him along. "And how does Hua-chengzhu know it's a holy temple?"

"Because that's what's written on it," Hua Cheng said.

Hearing this, the group looked up. A row of giant characters was engraved on the stone beam hanging before the gates of this building. While worn from age and scratched by strange marks, they were still quite clear.

However, after some silence, Xie Lian said, "There's certainly writing, but…"

But he couldn't understand this writing at all! He was stunned that not even something like this could trip up Hua Cheng.

Hua Cheng turned to Xie Lian. "The gist of the meaning is, 'The Eminent Crown Prince descends with shining light to eternally protect the Land of Wuyong.' Nothing but nonsensical praise.

Gege, look at the last two characters at the end—don't resemble the modern characters for 'Wu' and 'Yong'?"

The mention of "The Eminent Crown Prince" stirred something slightly within Xie Lian. Taking a closer look, the row of characters looked like a child's drawings, all circles and curves mixed with odd symbols. However, the word "Wuyong" was in shapes and strokes he was familiar with, as if this writing was a variant of his own language.

"Hua-chengzhu can actually read and interpret the lost writing of an ancient kingdom. I am truly in awe," Pei Ming said.

Hua Cheng cocked an eyebrow and gave a fake smile.

"I stayed at Mount Tonglu for ten years. Much can be done in a month; if I can't even interpret a few words after ten years, then what am I doing on this earth? Am I right?"

Not even the top ten civil gods in the Upper Court would dare proclaim such things, so as a martial god, what could Pei Ming do? He could only give his own fake smile.

"Perhaps."

Xie Lian puffed a light breath. "Thank goodness San Lang is here."

"I can only translate some rough Wuyong phrases," Hua Cheng said. "If we run into anything difficult, gege will have to help me. We'll evaluate it together."

Xie Lian felt himself sweat nervously. "Um... I'm definitely not as good as San Lang at this. But was the god worshipped by Wuyong also their crown prince?"

Hua Cheng folded his arms. "I think so, yes."

Xie Lian frowned as he voiced his thoughts. "If my master knew of the Crown Prince of Wuyong, then he must also have known that he ascended. So why did he tell me that the crown prince died?"

"There are three possibilities," Hua Cheng said. "First, he didn't actually know. Second, he was lying. Third, he didn't lie—the Crown Prince of Wuyong really did die, but it wasn't a typical death."

"If the Emperor were here, perhaps we could ask him if he knew of this kingdom, or of such a person," Pei Ming said.

"Unlikely," Hua Cheng replied. "The Kingdom of Wuyong disappeared over two thousand years ago. Jun Wu is a youngster in comparison; they're of completely different generations."

Jun Wu ascended around one thousand, five hundred years ago. He was a famed general of a warring era who later proclaimed himself king and, after ruling for some time, successfully became an immortal. As the top martial god who had ruled for over a thousand years, his background was completely out in the open. As for the "generations" Hua Cheng spoke of, he was referring to the dynasties of the heavens.

Jun Wu was the ruler of the current heavenly dynasty, and hundreds of heavenly officials formed the current Upper Court. The gods and government that preceded them belonged to a different generation. Just as regimes changed in the Mortal Realm, the Heavenly Realm also went through dynastic changes. It took considerably longer, but it was fundamentally the same. New worshippers replaced the old, and so too did new gods replace the old.

Sometimes, a god's decline wasn't the result of mistakes they made or a resulting banishment. Sometimes it was because another, more powerful god appeared. And sometimes it was for no reason other than gradual changes in people's lives and beliefs, and the inevitable irrelevance that resulted.

For example, a heavenly official who managed horses was likely quite comfortable in their position. People always needed reliable transportation, and they couldn't very well leave the condition of their horses and carriages to the whims of fate; who wouldn't want their horses to be strong and healthy, and their travels safe? Thus, this sort of heavenly official would always see regular devotion.

However, what if one day mortals discovered something completely novel that ran faster than a horse? When this new invention inevitably overtook horses, worshippers of the heavenly official who presided over horses would decrease in turn. Heavenly officials such as these made up most of the heavens, blinking to life and flashing by like shooting stars.

This was the cruelest way gods declined because the process could not be reversed. A heavenly official in that situation was destined to watch their own decline until they disappeared entirely—unless they jumped down from the heavens, returned to being mortal, re-cultivated a new path, and then ascended once more as a brand-new god. Not everyone possessed the courage and fortune to do something like that.

The gods of the previous generation had faded in such a way. Some said it was because they caused a great calamity and waged a chaotic war, which was why they all fell from grace at the same time—but nothing could be proven, and it was no longer important regardless. A few centuries later, Jun Wu was born, and he heralded a brand-new heavenly era. An endless number of heavenly officials rose after his arrival, filling in the gaps for worshippers. Gradually, the stable Upper Court of the current day was formed.

Which meant that unless there was a heavenly official who was older than the one-thousand-five-hundred-year-old Jun Wu, there was no one who could know of the god worshipped in the Kingdom of Wuyong or how he had been silently wiped from history.

Their group crossed through the mostly collapsed wall that once enclosed the premises and entered the darkened great hall.

They hadn't gotten too far inside before Xie Lian noticed something amiss.

He had initially thought the great hall was dark because the interior hadn't seen light for years and all its windows were shut. But the more he looked around, the more he found their surroundings peculiar.

He walked to the wall and lightly brushed his fingers over it. When he brought them to his eyes to look, he blurted, "This is…"

"Black," Hua Cheng said.

It wasn't that the light was dim—it was that the walls of this immense holy hall were completely black!

"Based on what I've seen, almost all the holy temples on Mount Tonglu are like this," Hua Cheng said.

It was a chilling sight. Why would the walls of a holy temple be painted a hellish black? The color alone would make one anxious; how could anyone worship the divine with a sincere heart when surrounded by it on all sides?

"All of them are like this?" Pei Ming wondered. "Rotted away from neglect, perhaps?"

"The houses we passed by earlier weren't black," Xie Lian said. "Logically, those houses are the same age."

As he spoke, he continued to feel lightly around and explore the walls of the holy temple. Not only were the walls horrifyingly black, they were also rugged in texture, covered in terrifying scars like a woman's ruined face. They were also extremely solid. Something clicked in Xie Lian's mind.

"This holy temple was burned by fire."

"How can you tell?" Pei Ming asked.

Xie Lian turned around. "The walls would've originally been covered in murals. They would have been done with a special type of paint in a very heavy layer. After fire burned them, they would turn black and parts would melt and change shape, and they would feel rugged and hard like this after cooling and solidifying again."

"Your Highness certainly knows a lot. I might as well be in awe of you too," Pei Ming said.

Xie Lian rubbed his forehead and lightly cleared his throat. "This...isn't anything to be impressed by. I only know because many of my crown prince temples ended up like this after they were burned."

At that, the group fell silent. Xie Lian suddenly remembered another thing.

"And that stone beam outside! There were scratch marks all over the praise engraved on it. It didn't look like regular wear and tear; people must have slashed at it with blades."

Pei Ming frowned. "Why would they do that?"

"Because they didn't agree with the words," Hua Cheng coldly replied.

"That's right," Xie Lian said. "It's the same as smashing an establishment plaque."

Banyue was slightly taken aback. "So this holy temple was burned down by the people of Wuyong themselves?"

They fell into silence again. Xie Lian was about to speak when Pei Ming said, "What is the meaning of this?"

Xie Lian turned to see. Pei Ming had his left arm raised, and a scorpion-snake was biting deeply into his hand. Its tail was also swinging vigorously, attempting to sting him.

Banyue was about to kneel again. "I'm sorry, I have snakes all over my body..."

Xie Lian didn't know whether to laugh or cry and held her upright. "Banyue, don't get into the habit of kneeling to apologize. General Pei, how did you get yourself bitten by her snakes?"

Pei Ming's face was dark. Still holding up his arm, he replied, "How should I know? I only put my arm around her, and *this* happened."

"Then, General Pei, what were you doing putting your arm around her?" Xie Lian asked patiently.

Pei Ming fell silent; it was only as he started to contemplate the question that he seemed to notice the problem. A moment later, he answered, "Habit. Isn't it normal to hold women in your arms in a dark, creepy place like this, to comfort them and calm their fears?"

"I'm sorry, but I wasn't scared," Banyue said.

"..."

Xie Lian understood. This was nothing more than a tragedy inflicted on Pei Ming by his own itchy hands. Pei Ming finally yanked off the scorpion-snake, but his left hand was already hugely swollen.

"Give me the antidote, quick."

"I'm sorry, I already used up the shanyue ferns I had on me," Banyue said.

"It's all right," Xie Lian said. "General Pei, you're a heavenly official. The swelling will go down soon enough."

Then he turned around and continued to examine the walls. As his eyes swept over a blackened area, he froze.

"Everyone, come see," he called. "There's still a face on this wall!"

80
Four Heavenly Kings Hidden on Darkened Walls

THERE REALLY WAS A FACE. Perhaps the flames hadn't consumed it entirely, or maybe the melting paint had flowed down and shielded the image from ruin. Whatever the case, beneath the tip of Xie Lian's finger there was a chunk of an illustration depicting a human face. He began to carefully scratch away the solidified black material.

"Is Your Highness really that fascinated by some mural?" Pei Ming asked, holding his very swollen left hand.

"It's not fascination," Xie Lian replied. "But rather that I have a daring idea."

"Let's hear it," Pei Ming said.

"We've gotten a rare chance to enter Mount Tonglu territory. While we work to stop the rise of a new ghost king, perhaps we can also find out more about the position itself. For example, who created the role? What kind of power is supporting all of this? Perhaps we might even be able to destroy it in one sweep and rid the world of this disaster for good. We'd never have to worry about another ghost king being born."

"That really *is* a daring idea," Pei Ming said. "But if Hua-chengzhu never discovered anything while he was here, we'd probably only be wasting our time. I don't recommend trying it in our current circumstances."

Hua Cheng spoke up. "I didn't make any such discoveries because my talents are dull and my abilities limited. Besides, last time, I was too busy killing. The results will be different if gege takes the lead on this investigation."

"No, no, no. I'm the one whose abilities are limited. San Lang is much more capable than me," Xie Lian said.

"..." As if he couldn't listen anymore, Pei Ming tossed Pei Xiu over to Banyue and turned to walk outside. "I think I'm gonna go get some fresh air."

It was surprisingly easy for Xie Lian to chip off a few chunks of the black, hardened substance. He blinked.

"This can actually be..."

The hard layer of charred material could actually be peeled off in large pieces!

In the short span of those few words, he had already peeled off a significant amount to reveal a human face about the size of a baby's fist. The lines were simple, but the face's expression was lively, like it was chasing after something; the passion in the eyes was as clear as crystal. The hard black material seemed to have acted as a protective layer atop the mural proper, and the colors underneath were as vibrant as the day they'd first been painted.

Xie Lian turned his head. "San Lang, let's do this together..."

Hua Cheng didn't move, but a field of shimmering silver light began to gleam in the darkness. Hundreds of silver butterflies silently appeared, then fluttered to rest on the blackened walls. Xie Lian heard small chipping sounds as they flitted their wings in unison. Innumerable small cracks crawled across the black walls, like a fracturing mask.

With a crumble, the black material covering the walls completely shattered, revealing the true image behind.

It was a giant, colorful mural!

Raising his head to look at the wall, Xie Lian felt chills.

The mural was divided into four levels. The highest level shimmered with golden light and was crowded with clouds, but no people were present.

On the second level, there was only one individual depicted: a handsome young man dressed in white. Golden light surrounded him; the artist had used the same gold paint as on the top level.

On the third level, four characters were depicted. Each of their faces, apparel, expressions, and gestures were different, and they were half the size of the white-clad young man on the second level.

The fourth level, which was the lowest, was covered with countless figures, and they were half the size of those on the third level. Each of their faces were exactly the same; their expressions were open and full of passion, worship, and rapture. The first face Xie Lian had discovered was one of these on the very bottom.

The lines of the mural were elegant and mature, and Xie Lian was stunned for a long time before he found his voice.

"San Lang, have you...ever seen this before?"

Hua Cheng's response was hesitant. "I traversed half of Mount Tonglu's domain and walked through almost every one of Wuyong's holy temples, but I swear I've never seen anything like this before."

Xie Lian came back to himself. "I don't think this mural is from two thousand years ago."

"There's no way it can be," Hua Cheng said. "Look at how well the colors have kept, as well as its overall condition. I'd say it's at most a hundred years old, or maybe even newer than that."

Which meant that this mural had been painted after the kingdom's destruction!

Xie Lian pointed at the highest level. "That level must be depicting the heavens, since the 'Law of Heaven' presides above all sentient beings."

Then he pointed at the second level. "This level must show the Crown Prince of Wuyong. Since this holy temple was made to worship him, he's naturally the main subject of the mural—which is also why he's the biggest figure in this painting and surrounded by the same color light as the heavens. He's only slightly below the 'Law of Heaven.'"

Then he pointed to the fourth level. "The figures at the lowest level are the smallest, and all their faces are the same. They must be the people of Wuyong."

Finally, he pointed at the third level. "But who are these four? Regardless of their poses or expressions, they're situated above the people of Wuyong and below the crown prince. That means they likely all have the same status. Ministers? Vassals? Or..."

Hua Cheng took a few steps closer. "Gege, look, they also have a sheen of spiritual light on their bodies."

Sure enough, they did. The light radiating from the Crown Prince of Wuyong was so strong that it far outshone their spiritual light in comparison.

The answer dawned on Xie Lian. "They're heavenly officials the crown prince appointed after he ascended."

Which meant they were the same as Feng Xin and Mu Qing, once upon a time.

Xie Lian made a round of the great hall and confirmed it was only this wall facing the gates that hid secrets. The other three walls were thoroughly burnt from crust to core.

Who left this mural behind, and for whom was it left? What kind of message were they trying to communicate?

Xie Lian couldn't deduce much from just one painting. He hummed for a moment, then turned to Hua Cheng.

"As we continue on the road, let's pay more attention to the other holy Wuyong temples. I have a feeling that...there can't be only one mural like this."

Hua Cheng inclined his head. "I intend to."

The two of them and Banyue, who was supporting Pei Xiu, left the holy temple. It was only then that Xie Lian remembered their other team member.

"Where's General Pei?"

Pei Ming had said that he needed some fresh air and went outside. Even though they'd dallied in the great hall for a good while, he still hadn't come back. Xie Lian called out a few times but received no response.

"I hope he hasn't gotten lost at a time like this."

The four looked around the small, desolate town, but their search was fruitless. Furthermore, they couldn't use the spiritual communication array in Mount Tonglu. Just as Xie Lian was beginning to feel desperate, Hua Cheng spoke up.

"Gege, don't worry. I have a way."

He extended a hand. In his palm there was a tiny silver butterfly which started lightly flapping its wings. It flew around Xie Lian, circling him a few times. While Xie Lian thought it was charming, he didn't know how it could help.

"What..."

Just then, he heard labored breathing. A few moments later, a man's voice came from the silver butterfly.

"I never thought I'd see you here," the man said.

Pei Ming!

Xie Lian looked at Hua Cheng, who snickered.

"Yesterday, I planted a silver butterfly on everyone."

Pei Xiu arduously raised his head. "...So, you can use, silver butterflies, to, monitor, everyone's movement, without them, noticing, you? As expected, of Crimson Rain, Sought Flower."

"Don't speak if you don't know how to form sentences," Hua Cheng sniped.

"..."

Xie Lian cupped the little silver butterfly in his palm and called out to it. "General Pei? Where are you? Who's in front of you?"

"I'm sorry, gege," Hua Cheng said. "You can only listen, not speak through it."

Xie Lian gave it a thought and acquiesced, "Fair enough."

If the listener's voice could pass through, then it could easily give its presence away to the other party, couldn't it?

Soon after, the frigid, exhausted voice of another young man spoke. "Ol' Pei, a word of warning—you'd better not spew any ridiculous nonsense right now. Be careful, or I might start smacking you around."

Xie Lian's eyes widened at that voice.

It was the voice of Ling Wen's male form!

"I see!" Xie Lian exclaimed. "So the man in black who killed so many along the way...was Ling Wen in his male form."

"Is, it Ling Wen-qianbei, who took General, Pei away?" Pei Xiu asked.

"I don't know. I'm still listening," Xie Lian replied.

On the other end, Pei Ming said, "Noble Jie, why the temper?"

"Shut up," Ling Wen said. "I told you not to speak. *I'm* not the one with a temper, it's someone else. I'm warning you—I can't control my body right now, so I won't be responsible for any injuries you sustain by my hand."

"Who are you trying to scare? We're both in the same predicament; we can't move a muscle," Pei Ming said.

Xie Lian looked up. "It's not Ling Wen who caught General Pei. Someone else has trapped them somewhere." Then he pondered somberly, "They even suppressed the Brocade Immortal. Who could it be?"

"Are you still wearing...?" Pei Ming asked.

He didn't say it out loud, but everyone knew what he was referring to.

The Brocade Immortal!

"Yeah. He really doesn't like you, so watch what you say," Ling Wen replied.

"How would you know what he's thinking?" Pei Ming wondered. "Honestly, I can't believe you. What's gotten into you, starting trouble like this? So audacious, going so far as to steal from the Temple of Divine Might. You broke your own golden bowl,[2] and now you've come running to Mount Tonglu. What, did *he* tell you to do all this?"

"He didn't make me. I'm the one who wanted to come," Ling Wen said. "Ol' Pei, stop asking questions! He's getting mad. I can feel it."

Pei Ming shut up. After a while, Ling Wen puffed a light breath; it seemed that the Brocade Immortal had finally calmed down, so he picked up the conversation again.

"And what's with you, Ol' Pei? What are *you* doing, coming to Mount Tonglu? And were you stung by a million hornets on your left hand or what? That wound looks horrid."

Pei Ming's voice was extremely sullen and woeful. "Got off to a bad start...it's a long story. Little Pei isn't making my life easy either. I shouldn't have wound up in such pathetic circumstances, but who could've known I'd be jinxed the moment I arrived? If I weren't

---

2 "Golden/steel bowl" is an expression meaning "steady job."

injured, do you think I'd let someone drag me to this hellish place? I didn't even see who it was."

Can't you specify which *hellish place already?* Xie Lian thought. *Say whether you're in a cave or a house or what, so I'll at least know where to look.*

It wasn't like there were no clues whatsoever, though. The Teleportation Array couldn't be used in Mount Tonglu, so Pei Ming mustn't have gone far. Their voices sounded somewhat hollow and echoed faintly, so they had to be somewhere spacious. And Xie Lian could vaguely hear the sound of water.

They hadn't run across any rivers or lakes along the way, and there weren't any buildings around that were more spacious than the nearby holy Wuyong temple. Therefore, there was only one place they could be—

Underground!

But that didn't tell them much; this small town wasn't all that small. They were underground, but where exactly?

"And what about you?" Pei Ming asked. "I hear you killed over a thousand nefarious creatures—everyone's terrified. Congratulations. Well, you can't be the number one civil god anymore, so why not change careers and join us martial gods? What manner of creature managed to bind you here?"

Ling Wen laughed bitterly. "I don't know what it was either. I accidentally clashed with Lord Rain Master and was dizzy afterward, so something took the chance to ambush me from behind. No need to ask me, it'll show itself sooner or later. Just remember not to expose your identity."

Just then, a third voice interrupted their conversation.

"Pei Ming, Nangong Jie, you nasty couple. You can stop your smug calculations. You think I don't know what's under your fake skins?!"

81

Why Not Xuli, Why Not Jing Wen

It was a man's voice, one that sounded very foreign.

Even though Xie Lian knew that he couldn't be heard from the other end, he still hushed his voice. "Someone's there. I don't know if he'll harm General Pei. We have to find where they are as soon as possible."

The two on the other end seemed completely stunned by the newcomer, and it took a moment for Pei Ming to speak.

"Might I ask who My Lord is? Why hide your face if you've gone this far?"

"You should ask yourself that question," the voice said.

"They must have a grudge against you," Ling Wen said. "Probably another ghost woman you ruined."

"Keep spouting drivel with your eyes wide open, why don't you…? Just which part of this…*thing*…looks like a woman? Besides, he didn't just capture me—maybe he's got a grudge against you."

"Never mind all that. At a time like this, let's not discuss where the blame lies—let's overcome this obstacle together," Ling Wen said. "It's also possible he's got a grudge against both of us. Do you recall anyone like that?"

"Not specifically. There're too many," Pei Ming said.

The man must have approached them, as his voice became louder. But strangely, there was no accompanying sound of footsteps—there was instead a series of odd thumping sounds.

"Can you two be a little less shameless and stop flirting in front of me?" he griped.

His words and tone seemed to reveal something, and after a brief silence, Ling Wen spoke.

"You're...Jing Wen-zhenjun?"

The voice didn't respond. Pei Ming seemed to be a little taken aback as well.

"Jing Wen-zhenjun? No way. Did Jing Wen-zhenjun ever speak so impolitely?"

Ling Wen humphed. "He's always been like this. He puts on one face in front of others and another in front of me. Of course you don't recognize him."

On his end, Xie Lian furrowed his brows. "Jing Wen-zhenjun?"

He thought he could faintly remember the name, but he couldn't be sure. The name sounded like a civil god; there were far too many civil gods who used the same collection of words in their titles: "literature," "respect," or "tranquility."³

Pei Xiu explained in a low voice. "Jing Wen-zhenjun, was, the, previous top-ranking civil god, who first, appointed Ling, Wen-zhenjun to the, heavens!"

With this, Xie Lian finally remembered. The first time he ascended, Ling Wen was still a junior civil official in the Lower Court—not yet the top-ranking civil god of the Upper Court. And apparently Jing Wen-zhenjun was the previous number one. However, Jing Wen had long since declined as a god; there was not a single Temple of Jing Wen to be found within a four-hundred-kilometer radius.

"Everyone knows each other, so why can't we just talk peacefully?"

---

3 文 / wen means "literature." 敬 / jing means "respect." 静 / jing means "tranquility."

Xie Lian couldn't help but wonder aloud. "Must we bring out the weapons and the ropes right at the start?"

"It's *because* everyone knows each other that the knives come first." Hua Cheng replied.

The words had only just left Hua Cheng's lips when Jing Wen spoke again on the other end. Since his identity had been revealed, it seemed he felt the need to put on a front, and he changed his tone to something more polite. Nonetheless, his words were still barbed.

"Nangong, weren't you *pleased* with being the top-ranking civil god in the Upper Court? Why did you break your golden bowl and come running here?"

Pei Ming piped up. "You see? His grudge is against you. It's your fault I got dragged into this."

"General Pei," Jing Wen continued, "don't think that you're off the hook just because I'm seeking vengeance against Nangong. This wench insulted and harassed my worshippers and secretly desecrated my Temples of Jing Wen, adding fuel to the fire. But don't think I don't know who loaned her the martial officials who helped her!"

"…"

"Don't you laugh either, Nangong," Jing Wen continued. "And to think I appointed you back then because I valued your talent! This is how you repay me? You ungrateful, venomous wench. I've waited for this day for too long—*too long!*"

Xie Lian covered his forehead with his palm. *The Three Tumors certainly live up to their name—each nastier than the last!*

Unexpectedly, Ling Wen gave a flat reply. "Jing Wen-zhenjun, there's no one here but us right now, and you've had your say. Why keep up the act? Did you actually appoint me as a deputy official because you valued my talent? Others might not know what really happened, but I'm sure you remember the details. Just why *did* you appoint me? And do you recall how you treated me afterward?"

Xie Lian was growing more curious the longer he listened. "What happened between Jing Wen-zhenjun and Ling Wen? General Pei Junior, do you know the story behind this?"

Pei Xiu was also listening intently. "I'm sorry. I had yet to, ascend, at, the time, so I don't, know much."

His broken sentences are probably beyond saving, Xie Lian thought. Hua Cheng spoke up.

"Gege, no need to ask others. Just ask me."

Xie Lian was amazed. "San Lang, you know about heaven's past scandals too?"

As it turned out, that was no exaggeration—when it came to the shady history and associated hearsay of every major heavenly official in the Upper Court, Hua Cheng certainly did his homework. He nodded and told Xie Lian what he knew.

The story was this: Jing Wen and Ling Wen were both civil gods born of the Kingdom of Xuli. Jing Wen was older than Ling Wen by many centuries, and he had a deep foundation in the Kingdom of Xuli. Originally, the two weren't supposed to cross paths.

However, one year, the Kingdom of Xuli conducted a ceremonial festival to revere and worship the civil gods. As a part of the festival, there was a small contest. Young scholars were to compose anonymous essays that would be hung in the kingdom's largest civil god temple—at the time, the Palace of Jing Wen. The Kingdom of Xuli itself was the subject, and the content of the essays was unrestricted. The compositions would be judged by the people, and the best of the bunch would be selected as the winner and afforded much commendation.

At the time, Jing Wen-zhenjun had descended to dally about the Mortal Realm, and on impulse he thought it'd be fun to transform into a scholar and join the contest. With an easy swing of his brush, he wrote a jaunty, elegant piece, singing praises of the glory of the Kingdom of Xuli. He was quite confident that his composition would stand out from the crowd and take first place. He imagined that if he revealed his true form once the results of the contest were revealed, showing all onlookers that the winner was actually a clone of Jing Wen-zhenjun, surely his story would be passed down as a beautiful tale for future generations.

If things had turned out that way, it would've been a happy ending. However, the results were far more awkward.

After the ceremony ended and the ranking board was revealed, the winner was not Jing Wen's "Ode to Xuli" but a piece of critical political discourse entitled "Need Not Xuli."

This turn of events might have been awkward, but the bystanders did find it rather interesting.

"Has San Lang ever read 'Need Not Xuli'?" Xie Lian inquired.

"I've flipped through it," Hua Cheng said. "If gege wants to read it, I'll recite a summary for you another time."

"No, it's okay," Xie Lian said hurriedly. "I imagine it must've been very well written, if it defeated the already-ascended Jing Wen-zhenjun."

"It's not bad, but it wasn't groundbreaking," Hua Cheng commented. "It's just that the political situation in the Kingdom of Xuli wasn't great at the time. The people were full of complaints, so a piece like that matched their tastes. Essays like 'Ode to Xuli' were rampant, and people were tired of them. When comparing the two, naturally 'Need Not Xuli' won."

Xie Lian gave a light nod. "There is no such thing as number one in literature; it's all subjective. A win like that wouldn't really matter—especially if the content wasn't even similar."

"Correct," Hua Cheng said. "Jing Wen thought so too, at first."

The people of Xuli looked everywhere for the author of "Need Not Xuli," but of course no one claimed it—who would dare claim such a piece? Those who were greedy for fame and came forward with false claims of authorship were all quickly exposed. Soon government officers took notice, and the top-ranking essay was removed from the festival.

Jing Wen-zhenjun wasn't too pleased with the results of the contest and sniffed at them, but after a few months he'd forgotten about the whole thing. The tragedy was that after a few months, shocking news spread among the civil gods in the Upper Court: the individual who had authored "Need Not Xuli" and won the Civil God Ceremonial Festival of Xuli had been found, arrested, and locked up in prison. And this individual was a young woman who sold shoes on the streets!

How could this be?! Unacceptable!

"A...shoe seller?" Xie Lian was amazed.

"Yes," Hua Cheng replied. "That's what Nangong Jie did while she was mortal."

No wonder he'd heard people call the Palace of Ling Wen a "Palace of Shitty Shoes" under their breath on more than one occasion. Since Xie Lian didn't think it right to inquire about the root of such things, he'd never learned where the term came from.

Originally, there was no way anyone would connect "Need Not Xuli" with a shoe-selling maiden. However, the young woman would sometimes help others scribe letters or poems to make some extra income. One of her commissioners discovered that her writing was similar to the style of that infamous winning essay and reported her, which was how she was eventually caught.

After learning of this news, Jing Wen-zhenjun immediately

appointed the young woman Nangong Jie to the heavens with a swing of his brush.

It must be known that female heavenly officials were already few in number at the time. They weren't entirely absent from the heavenly ranks, but most of them oversaw things like flowers and plants, crafts and embroidery, singing and dancing, or other such skills. Even as deputy officials of the Lower Court, no one wanted to appoint a woman. Female civil gods were rarer still. The women within the temples of civil gods were all identically beautiful, and none of them controlled anything scholarly; they were usually soft, gentle souls who ground ink and set out paper. They were hardly considered "real" heavenly officials; at most they were seen as objects to be appreciated.

Jing Wen-zhenjun's actions garnered praise from the other civil gods. Everyone said this young woman had the best of luck for his wise eyes to fall upon her. Not only did she escape the trial of prison, she was able to climb above the trees to become a phoenix; truly a beautiful tale.

In reality, the main characters of this "beautiful tale" were at each other's throats.

"I thought so highly of you, but you make it sound like I had ill intent," Jing Wen accused.

Ling Wen always treated others politely, never sounding servile nor overbearing. But in that moment, his voice had an air of derision.

"Please. There's no need for you to go around telling everyone how highly you thought of me. If you really regarded me so *highly*, you wouldn't have made me serve tea and water to everyone in the palace for so many years. Or made me wipe tables, walk hundreds of kilometers just to collect poetry manuscripts, and ceaselessly deliver gifts to other heavenly officials on every holiday."

Thinking back on it, Xie Lian thought Ling Wen's complaints sounded accurate. Back when he first ascended, Ling Wen was always on an errand every time he saw her. It was precisely because she ran so many errands that Xie Lian was able to vaguely remember such a character.

"At the end of the day, you were just upset that I refused to promote you," Jing Wen retaliated. "But did you ever consider *why* I didn't promote you?"

"Why?" Ling Wen echoed. "I want to know why too. When I was a mortal, I had time to read and write. Even when I was locked up in jail, I could at least face the wall and tranquilly reflect. After I was appointed, there wasn't a day I didn't work like a horse for you, running errands for you and prostrating to you and everyone in heaven. If you had wanted to grind me to death, you couldn't have thought of a better way to do it."

"Nangong!" Jing Wen barked. "You dare refuse to admit your wrongs, even now?!"

"And what wrongs have I committed?" Ling Wen countered.

"Are you saying it's all my fault?!" Jing Wen demanded. "The things I made you do were obviously in your best interests! If you can't even handle such trivial matters, what right do you have to take on more important duties? I gave you so many training opportunities in order to toughen you up. How can you blame me for not promoting you when *you* were the one lacking in ability? You think too highly of yourself! No matter what, you're still a woman—you can't reach such heights. You have to admit that is the truth!"

Ling Wen laughed out loud, yet he seemed furious. "Very well!" His voice dropped. "You said I can't reach that high. Then, might I ask—at the highest peak of its prominence, did the Palace of Jing Wen even reach the *knees* of today's Palace of Ling Wen?!"

Xie Lian could smell the roiling brew of their past resentment growing thicker, and he didn't think he could let them keep talking much longer. With no other choice, he employed a very brutish method.

He punched the ground with a powerful fist. A large crater formed with him at the center, accompanied by a massive *boom*!

Hua Cheng instantly understood what he wanted to do. "Gege!"

Xie Lian flapped his hand to disperse the dust in the air and coughed a few times. "This is the most direct way! I'll take care of this side! San Lang, you and General Pei Junior...go lie down over there!"

He'd initially wanted Hua Cheng and Pei Xiu to try the other direction, but in their current states he wasn't sure they were capable. But Hua Cheng was hardly going to listen to him and laze around willingly. He positioned himself opposite Xie Lian's chosen direction, summoned Eming, and plunged the blade into the ground.

This strike and Xie Lian's fist both created the same effect. The pair took turns producing huge noise after huge noise, moving farther and farther away from each other as they went. After pounding a few times, Xie Lian stopped to listen, but Pei Ming and Ling Wen didn't react; it looked like they hadn't heard the booming sounds he was creating.

As for Jing Wen, Ling Wen had clearly hit him where it hurt. He sneered as the mask of politeness was ripped off, and he returned to the sharp, sour tone he had employed when calling them a "nasty couple."

"Nangong Jie, don't get cocky just because you've had a taste of success, you little rat! If it wasn't for me appointing you to the heavens, who knows how many men you would've bore spawn for in jail!"

Now *that* comment was quite ungentlemanly, and Xie Lian's hand almost slipped. Even Pei Ming couldn't listen anymore.

"You were once a civil god! Have a little class!"

"See, Nangong," Jing Wen accused. "See how your good lover is shielding you! General Pei, who are you to accuse *me* of being classless?"

"In your mind, who isn't my lover?" Ling Wen spat. "You're looking for retribution? Then let's talk retribution!"

Xie Lian had leapt quite a distance by now. He once again slammed the ground, and this time, Jing Wen's alarmed voice sounded on the other end of the silver butterfly.

"What's that noise?!"

Xie Lian cheered inwardly—he was headed in the right direction!

Pei Ming and Ling Wen both heard too.

"Did someone start fighting up above?" Pei Ming hesitantly wondered.

This time, Xie Lian dashed for several meters and landed an even stronger thunderous punch.

"It's closer now!" Pei Ming exclaimed. "What destructive power! It came from right above us!"

He'd found the spot!

Xie Lian didn't throw another punch. Instead, he pulled out Fangxin and thrust the sword downward.

The aura of the sword erupted, and the ground rumbled as it caved in. A moment later, Xie Lian fell into an eerie underground cave. He silently prayed that he hadn't crashed in right over Pei Ming and Ling Wen's heads. He waved away the dust in the air as he rose to his feet, turning around with sword in hand.

"Jing…" he called.

The moment Jing Wen-zhenjun's figure entered his sight, Xie Lian's eyes went wide.

Jing Wen was alarmed at the sight of an intruder.

"Who are you?!"

But the one questioning Xie Lian wasn't actually a man. It was a stone statue of a man, extremely coarsely made, its body bare but wrapped with cloth. It was bizarre—and completely absurd.

No wonder there was no sound of footsteps when he walked, only strange thumping sounds. No wonder when Pei Ming and Ling Wen saw him, they were both shocked. And no wonder Pei Ming said Ling Wen was spouting drivel with eyes wide open, because this thing looked absolutely nothing like a female ghost.

Pei Ming and Ling Wen were both tied up with what looked like scrolls; they were in Jing Wen's clutches and unable to move. Xie Lian finally snapped out of it.

"Me...?!"

Jing Wen asked, "You're the Crown Prince of Xianle?"

Xie Lian was taken aback. "Huh? You actually recognize me? Well, that's truly..."

But it wasn't really that strange; Xie Lian's first ascension was an earth-shattering event. *He* might not have known every Upper Court heavenly official, but every one of them knew him. And even now, it was the same—he didn't remember Jing Wen's original appearance whatsoever, but Jing Wen still remembered him.

"Of course. Your Highness's journey of godhood had such ups and downs, it'd be difficult not to recognize you!"

Xie Lian felt oddly touched. "I'm honored... But how did you turn into..."

"How did I turn into *this*?" Jing Wen finished for him.

Xie Lian cleared his throat softly and nodded, feeling that his question was a bit impolite. However, Jing Wen used this chance to start ranting again.

"It's all thanks to that wench Nangong Jie! When the Palace of Jing Wen declined, my spiritual powers grew progressively weaker, and then she added insult to injury by hunting me down and trying to kill me. In order to survive, I had absolutely no choice but to possess this stone statue!"

"I wasn't that bad compared to you," Ling Wen said. "You would order me to stay in the Palace of Jing Wen until midnight, then turn around and tell everyone I stayed behind until late to entice you. Words murder without form. I was much nicer, responding with blatant violence."

Then Ling Wen suddenly kicked out and struck Jing Wen's lower body. To Xie Lian, this move didn't really look like it would do much—since she was kicking a stone statue instead of a flesh body, it would at most maybe rip a few of the cloths wrapped around Jing Wen. Yet unexpectedly, Jing Wen let out a tragic wail like he really had been kicked in the gonads, and he hastily covered his lower half.

However, it was too late. Ling Wen's kick had torn off the layer of white cloth wrapped around his crotch, and Xie Lian swiftly saw the truth. Under that white cloth, there was...nothing.

Nothing... In other words, what was *supposed* to be present in the crotch area of this bare-naked stone statue...wasn't.

This was a eunuch statue!

It's a statue of a eunuch slave! Xie Lian thought.

This sort of stone statue was often found in the graves of the powerful and wealthy. They were burial effects steeped in extremely heavy yin energy, so they were indeed a good choice for possession. But it was extremely ironic that a male heavenly official like Jing Wen, who was so small-minded about losing to a woman, would find his final resting place in a stone statue of a eunuch slave!

Ling Wen burst out laughing. "And here I was, wondering why you were so worked up! So *this* is why! You said I can't reach that high? Well, I can't wait to see how high *you* can reach in your current state! Ha ha ha ha ha ha…"

Now that the cloth covering his shame had been torn off and trampled underfoot, Jing Wen was going mad with fury. He grabbed Ling Wen's hair and yelled.

"Shut up! Who knows how many heavenly officials you slept with to get where you are? What's there to be proud of?! Apologize, right now!"

The yanking nearly tore a large chunk of Ling Wen's hair from his head, but he endured the pain without begging for mercy, never mind apologizing.

"Are you really a civil god?" Pei Ming commented with disgust. "Such a lack of character and culture; even shrews on the streets act better than you!"

Xie Lian only silently cried his grievances, scared that Jing Wen would strangle the two to death on a whim. However, he couldn't help but call out a "Hey!" to gain his attention and raised his hand.

"Please calm down, Jing Wen-zhenjun! It actually makes no difference whether you have *that* or not! Really! It's true!"

Jing Wen had Ling Wen in one hand and the other covering his groin. "Lies!" he roared. "It makes no difference?! Why don't you get rid of yours and see?!"

"It's true! Believe me!" Xie Lian said earnestly. "Even though I have *that*, I might as well not have it at all! Because I'm…*that*!"

He once again sacrificed himself, offering his own person as proof. Hearing this, Jing Wen calmed down a bit.

"You're *what*?!"

"Just...*that*! You understand," Xie Lian said. "And even if I have it, I never use it! *Cough*, actually, all such things are mere worldly possessions when it comes to male heavenly officials or female heavenly officials, or...other heavenly officials. It's nothing to be so preoccupied with..."

Jing Wen cut him off. "If you don't think it matters, why don't you chop yours off to prove it?"

Xie Lian was flummoxed into silence.

"Didn't you say it makes no difference?" Jing Wen pressed. "Hypocrite! You're obviously reluctant to lose it, so don't you use that bullshit to cajole me! I'm no young'un who'll repent in tears just because you've given me a couple candies! But it's fine if you won't chop yours off—I'll chop off *his* instead!"

He gestured toward Pei Ming, who stood there, dumbfounded. "What the fuck?!"

Well, this was a disaster. While there were plenty of people out there who wanted to cut off General Pei's *thing*, Xie Lian hardly wanted Jing Wen to get his way.

"Jing Wen-zhenjun!" he said hastily. "It was wrong for Ling Wen to bully you after your decline, but if you bullied her too, you're technically even. There's no need to go to such extremes!"

As he tried to talk him into distraction, he secretly released Ruoye, and it slithered behind Jing Wen like a snake.

"*Even?* It's not that simple," Jing Wen countered. "But now you've reminded me that there's something I need to grill that wench on! Nangong, did you play a part in the fall of Xuli?!"

Jing Wen was a civil god who the Kingdom of Xuli had placed on the holy altar, which meant that Xuli was his foundation. If his foundation was destroyed, he would of course be affected and potentially go into decline. Thus, it was reasonable for Jing Wen to suspect Ling Wen.

But after he posed the question, Ling Wen kept his lips sealed and refused to answer.

"Just 'fess up! Did you do it?!" Jing Wen yelled. "I just know it was you! It must've been you, otherwise the kingdom wouldn't have fallen so fast! It's all this insidious bitch's fault! That idiot general must've fallen into your hands!"

Ling Wen hasn't even responded, and you're answering your own questions... Xie Lian thought. *Wait, what? Which general?*

Ling Wen started snickering under his breath. Had Jing Wen not been possessing a statue with a completely immobile face, he would've been gritting his teeth.

"What are you laughing about?"

Ling Wen lifted his head slightly to give a lighthearted reply. "Do you know the consequences for calling him an idiot to his face?"

Jing Wen hadn't yet grasped the situation when the scroll binding Ling Wen suddenly ripped apart. Amidst the whirling shreds, a hand emerged from within Ling Wen's black sleeves and seized Jing Wen by the head. Jing Wen hadn't had the chance to speak a word before he was subdued. A crack appeared upon his coarsely hewn face. And then another, then another...

With three cracking sounds, his entire body shattered!

As for Ling Wen, he had broken free of his bonds and stood in place, enveloped by streams of black qi that emanated from within. A pile of crumbled stone lay at his feet.

It turned out the "ancient kingdom" in the legend of the Brocade Immortal was Xuli, and Bai Jing was also a citizen of that land. Xie Lian was just organizing his thoughts when he heard Pei Ming, who was still tightly bound by the scroll, speak up.

"Ling Wen? Stop."

Ling Wen had turned around and was stalking toward him, step by step. Remembering that Ling Wen had told Pei Ming that the Brocade Immortal really didn't like him, Xie Lian thought, *Oh no, is he going to kill him?*

Ling Wen tried to appease him as he walked. "Bai Jing, he's already dead. It's all nonsense—none of it was true."

But it wasn't working. Ling Wen addressed Pei Ming.

"Ol' Pei, I have no way to stop him. He heard Jing Wen say you're my lover and has steeled his mind to kill you. Your Highness, lend me a hand!"

No need to ask. Xie Lian had already swung his sword and slashed through the scroll binding Pei Ming, who jumped to his feet. The two leapt out of the underground cave, returning to the ground above. Looking back into the cave, they saw that Ling Wen had punched right into the rock where Pei Ming had just been sitting. His strength was considerable, and debris flew. The punch was even stronger than Xie Lian's strikes when he was hammering the ground to scout for them!

Xie Lian tucked Ruoye away by wrapping it around his forearm, and Pei Ming worked out the kinks in his wrist. After being bound for so long, the swelling on his left hand had gone down somewhat; it now looked like he'd been stung by five hundred thousand hornets instead of a million.

"What is this fucking injustice..." he started.

But before he could even finish, Ling Wen appeared right in front of him in a flash!

The two exchanged a blow, and both were pushed a few meters back. Xie Lian and Pei Ming exchanged a look. This situation was too complicated—so they bolted. Xie Lian turned his head and yelled behind him as he ran.

"Ling Wen! Can you try to talk to General Bai again?!"

Ling Wen was hot on their tail. "I tried! But he doesn't believe me anymore!"

"It must be because he's hurt that you lied to him!" Pei Ming shouted.

"Ling Wen!" Xie Lian cried. "Can you change back to your female form?! The destructive power will be reduced in a woman's body!"

"No!" Ling Wen answered.

"Why not?!"

"He won't let me!" Ling Wen replied.

"I get it!" Pei Ming said. "The bastard's afraid of clinging to a woman's body! What a wimp!"

Rrrumble! A roof came crashing toward them, almost crushing Xie Lian and Pei Ming.

"I didn't throw that!" Ling Wen cried. "It's your fault for insulting him; now he's even madder! You're both in danger!"

"Huh?! What's it got to do with me?! I've said nothing!" Xie Lian cried hastily. "Ling Wen, can you tell him to count me out of it, please?!"

"Better to count you in—it's easier with more people to shoulder the burden!" Pei Ming yelled. "Your Highness, where's Little Pei? The State Preceptor Banyue? Your Crimson Rain Sought Flower?!"

"Don't count on them showing up! They went in the other direction to search for you two!" Xie Lian yelled back. "We've already covered over a dozen kilometers; run first, talk later! He's absorbed over a thousand nefarious creatures; it wouldn't be smart to face him head-on right now!"

Yet unexpectedly, just as the words left his lips, his feet went light as his entire body was hoisted up. And not just him—Pei Ming was caught too. As he looked around, he realized that they'd both been captured by a large net and were now hanging in the air.

What an unexpected disaster. The net must've been made of some special material, and bare hands couldn't rip it apart. One or two hundred ferocious, savage-faced ghosts and yao jumped out from the woods all around them, clapping in joy.

"Caught them!"

"Ha ha ha ha, how many is this now? This trap is so good!"

"Let's see what we caught! How many heads!"

They had paid no attention to the road they'd followed during their panicked escape, and in a moment of carelessness, they had fallen into a trap set by these third-rate minions. Xie Lian reached for Fangxin to slash through the net, but when he found his back empty, he realized that Fangxin had fallen from his grip when he was yanked up. Ling Wen had already chased them to the net, and Fangxin lay at his feet.

The mob of little minions hadn't yet realized what had approached, and they were overjoyed.

"Another one!"

Ling Wen raised his hands, and two balls of black ghost fire ignited in his palms. He looked up to address Xie Lian and Pei Ming.

"You two, this...really isn't up to me."

Xie Lian puffed a breath. "Ling Wen, can I ask what will happen if we're hit by those?"

"Last time I used ghost fires that big, I was attacking His Highness Qi Ying. He was injured, but it wasn't too bad; he could still hop around and run."

It sounded like the damage wouldn't be severe—even if they were hit, their injuries wouldn't be too dire. Xie Lian and Pei Ming both sighed in relief.

"Thank goodness..."

But as soon as he said that, the ghost fire in Ling Wen's hands suddenly erupted to ten times its original size—into two giant pillars of flame, blazing to the skies!

Xie Lian was speechless.

Pei Ming was also speechless.

"...But if you get hit by flames of *this* size, I can't say how things will turn out," Ling Wen said.

"Wait! I'm really not your lover, though!" Pei Ming roared.

"I know that! But it doesn't matter if we're the only ones who believe it!" Ling Wen exclaimed.

The nefarious creatures were startled by the blazing ghost fires, and they quickly drew their weapons. They shouted with arrogant indignation as they circled Ling Wen.

"You bastard! You've got guts, trying to steal our kill when you're about to die yourself! Get him!"

However, pathetic little minions like these posed no threat to the Brocade Immortal—they were nothing but another round of fresh nourishment. Ling Wen inclined his head slightly, his eyes reflecting the vibrant light of the ghost fires. He looked quite ready to receive a set of new heads from those who were so eager to sacrifice themselves.

At that moment, a wild whirlwind blew by.

In the blink of an eye, the mob of little minions was blown into the sky with a chorus of terrified wails! Rather than being tossed skyward by wind, it was more like an invisible giant hand had snatched them into the air.

The Brocade Immortal seemed to have sensed something that alarmed it, and the ghost fires blazing in Ling Wen's hands calmed as he scanned the surrounding area. Xie Lian looked up with arduous effort, but the dense tree cover blocked his view. The wails of those ghosts had come to an abrupt stop, so he couldn't figure out what had happened above.

Pei Ming was also alarmed. "Who's here?"

Ever alert and watchful, Xie Lian suddenly said, "Do you smell that?"

"What?" Pei Ming asked.

"The scent of flowers," Xie Lian replied.

Pei Ming was confused. "Flowers?"

Xie Lian closed his eyes. A moment later, he said with conviction, "Yes. It's the scent of flowers."

It was mellow, peculiar, fresh, and cool. He didn't know the name of the bloom, nor its source. It was exceedingly light, exceedingly soft, and so faint it was as if it weren't even there.

Pei Ming furrowed his brows. "I don't smell flowers, but I definitely smell…"

Before he could finish, he felt something drip onto his face. He wiped it with his hand without thinking, and his pupils shrank.

It was blood.

A few drops fell onto the ghost fire in Ling Wen's hands, and the flames' intensity instantly weakened. His expression grew even more apprehensive, and his head shot up.

Right at that moment…

…a torrential rain of blood fell from the heavens!

Pei Ming was hanging higher than Xie Lian, and the blood deluge drenched him until he was like a red-dyed drowned rat, leaving only a pair of eyes that were black and white, round and bulging. The ghost fire in Ling Wen's hands was completely extinguished, and he scurried under a tree to avoid the same fate as the defenseless Pei Ming.

As for Xie Lian, he felt the net tear and his body drop, and he plunged downward. He flipped in the air as he fell and landed steadily just as the bloody rain was about to descend upon him.

There was no time to dodge, so Xie Lian raised his sleeve to block as much as he could. After things went dark, he heard the soft, low rumble of laughter.

The air was awash in the mysterious, alluring fragrance of blossoms.

Xie Lian lifted his head and looked up. He didn't feel any raindrops hitting his face; instead, something soft gently brushed past him.

He reached out and caught it. Looking down, the thing that had quietly fluttered into the heart of his palm was a small, vibrant, red flower petal.

He looked up once more, and his breath hitched. He couldn't believe it.

The bloody rain that had darkened the sky had been transformed into a shower of fluttering flower petals.

There was no need to guess who had come. Xie Lian curled his fingers to clutch the flower petal as the name blurted from his lips.

"San Lang!"

He turned around and saw that Ling Wen had fallen soundlessly to the ground. A tall, slender young man stood there, chuckling softly. With hair of raven black and robes of crimson red, he could be none other than Hua Cheng.

Blossoms fell like blood; blood danced like petals on the wind. His face was as spirited and handsome as the first time they met, and his eye was bright and lively. He languidly sheathed that long, slender silver scimitar and spoke with a deep voice.

"Your Highness, I'm back."

82
A Long Way to Travel, Blocked on Narrow Road

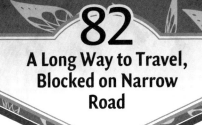

TREADING ACROSS THE GROUND strewn with exquisite fragments of crimson, Xie Lian slowly approached Hua Cheng. He saw that the man's shoulders had a few red blossoms scattered on them, and he wanted to brush them off for him, but he realized that gesture would be overly intimate. So he forced down the urge and tucked his arms behind his back, smiling.

"Not only can you call forth blood rain, you can also make a flower shower. I didn't know that. How fun!"

Hua Cheng walked toward him wearing a smile, easily dusting the petals from his shoulders. "This was something spontaneous, a trick I only came up with today. Originally it was going to be the usual blood rain, but then it occurred to me that gege was present. And wouldn't gege blame me if I drenched him? So I held back at the last moment and transformed it into flowers. I'm glad you found it fun."

While Xie Lian wasn't drenched, Pei Ming was completely soaked. He called out from high in the air, "Excuse me, you two. Let me down, won't you?"

A few silver butterflies fluttered upward and slashed the net with their shimmering wings, allowing Pei Ming to finally break free and land steadily on the ground. Xie Lian looked down and saw a silver butterfly resting on Ling Wen's back between his shoulder blades.

"San Lang? Ling Wen and the Brocade Immortal are both okay, right?"

"They're fine," Hua Cheng said. "I've only temporarily put them to sleep."

Xie Lian was amazed. "The Brocade Immortal was going berserk, but you managed to subdue it so quickly."

Hua Cheng raised his brows. "It was fine. For some reason, it didn't seem to want to fight me."

Xie Lian hummed. "That's true. When you put it on before, it didn't do anything to you—it even showed itself."

Pei Ming walked over. "Save the chitchat for later, you two. Aren't you going to peel that robe off him first?"

"Um… Wouldn't that be inappropriate?" Xie Lian said.

Pei Ming didn't seem to think anything of it. "He's in his male form right now, so what's there to be embarrassed about?"

His hands moved as he spoke, but just as they touched Ling Wen's collar, it was like something jabbed him hard. His expression dropped, and he yanked his hands back—they were covered in blood.

"This robe! It bites!"

Only then did Hua Cheng lazily explain, "The Brocade Immortal won't let Ling Wen go. You won't be able to take it off of him."

Pei Ming looked at his bloodied hands. "If something like this happens again, will My Lord Ghost King please warn me sooner?"

"General Pei, it's not that he didn't want to warn you. Your hands moved too fast," Xie Lian said evenly.

Hua Cheng snickered. "That's it exactly."

"…"

Their will remained strong even after being wounded, and the three headed back the way they came. Someone had to carry the male Ling Wen, and Pei Ming took up the responsibility without a word.

Pei Xiu and Banyue were waiting in the same small town as before. The group reconvened near the holy temple of Wuyong, and Pei Xiu strode over to greet them when he saw them return.

"General, Your, Highness, the mural, in that, temple, has disappeared!"

Pei Ming was carrying Ling Wen in one arm while the other hand slicked back his blood-soaked hair. "What mural?"

Banyue's eyes widened at the sight of Pei Ming covered in deep red. Xie Lian gave Pei Ming a brief account and went back into the temple with Pei Xiu to investigate. Sure enough, the wall from earlier was now exactly the same as the other three burnt ones—it was as if the mural had never existed.

Hua Cheng dropped his hand from the wall. "The mural was created by magic."

Xie Lian nodded. "Perhaps the one who left it had reason to fear its discovery and didn't dare leave it for too long."

Banyue was hesitant for a long time but eventually mustered up enough courage to ask Pei Ming, "Are...you okay?"

Pei Ming gave her a look and began to bluff. "Why don't you ask your snakes if I'm okay, since they bit me?"

Pei Xiu opened his mouth to defend her, but he wasn't sure whether he should go against Pei Ming. Banyue's eyes widened even further, and she mumbled as she tried to argue.

"But...a scorpion-snake bite doesn't fester in the whole body like this..."

Pei Ming raised the left hand that bore the bite mark and waved it in front of her, proving that he had indeed been bitten. This "ironclad proof" was as solid as a mountain, and Banyue could only apologize.

"I'm sorry..."

Pei Xiu couldn't watch anymore and patted her shoulder. "Don't, take it to, heart. This wasn't, caused by the bite of your, snakes."

Xie Lian couldn't watch anymore either, so he spoke up in exasperation. "General Pei, can you not tease little girls at a time like this?"

But that was the very source of Pei Ming's life. He used his spiritual powers to cleanse himself of all the blood and grime, and his face was glowing again as he laughed out loud.

"Aren't little girls made for teasing? Besides, what 'little girl'—the State Preceptor of Banyue is how many centuries old now? Still worried she might get embarrassed?"

"..."

No one wanted to talk to him anymore.

While Pei Xiu's broken sentences hadn't healed, he could now move normally, so he took over the task of carrying Ling Wen. The group of them passed through the small town and continued down toward the next layer of Mount Tonglu.

A day later, the group reached a small valley. There were steep, tall mountains with rocky bluffs on either side and a path in between. Only when they arrived did Ling Wen finally, groggily, wake. Although he was conscious, he still couldn't move due to the silver butterfly that remained resting firmly on his spine. He didn't react to discovering that he was being carried on someone's back.

"...Why are there so many people?" he asked in confusion. "How come you're all here? Isn't this Mount Tonglu?"

"This is 'many'?" Pei Ming asked. "Let me tell you, there'll be more later—you haven't even seen everyone yet. There's enough of us to set up some tables for a round of cards."

Xie Lian wholeheartedly agreed with the sentiment and couldn't help but smile. After a pause, he spoke up.

"By the way, Ling Wen, Qi Ying chased after you back at Puqi Shrine. Where is he now?"

"Don't know," Ling Wen replied. "After I reached Mount Tonglu territory, there were too many inhuman creatures swarming around, and I lost His Highness Qi Ying in the crowd. I have no idea where he is right now."

Pei Ming sighed at Ling Wen. "I can't believe you didn't tell me you were the one who snipped Xuli's last lifeline. Harsh."

Only then did Xie Lian remember that Pei Ming was also from the Kingdom of Xuli. However, he didn't seem particularly attached to the kingdom—after all, he was only a general, not a king, and he was even backstabbed by the ruler before he ascended. So there was no trace of grief or anger in his voice; he was just poking fun. However, Xie Lian still worried that talking too much about Xuli would provoke the Brocade Immortal, so he swiftly changed the subject. He turned to Hua Cheng.

"San Lang, I'm curious about something."

Hua Cheng had been keeping an eye on the two tall mountains ever since they entered the valley. "What is it?"

"The Kiln of Mount Tonglu. What is it, exactly? Is it really just a giant stove?" Xie Lian asked.

Hua Cheng smiled faintly and returned his gaze to Xie Lian.

"Of course not. But that's a good question, gege." He raised his hand and pointed. "It just so happens that we can see it now."

The group looked in the direction he was pointing, and they unconsciously stopped walking.

"That's...the Kiln?" Xie Lian asked.

Hua Cheng crossed his arms. "That's right."

A large mountain was reflected in his inky black eye, standing extremely far in the distance. It sat at the edge of the world and was so tall it touched the heavens. It was condescendingly enthroned above all the surrounding peaks. Painted a deep, abyssal blue, the mountain's summit was surrounded by a sea of clouds and heavenly winds. A layer of snow could be faintly seen, an eternal field of unmelting ice.

"The Kiln is a live volcano in the heart of Mount Tonglu," Hua Cheng leisurely said. "It wakes when a new ghost king is born."

"With a volcanic eruption?" Xie Lian asked.

"Correct," Hua Cheng replied. "All Supreme Ghost Kings are born accompanied by blazing fires, lava, and ruinous disasters."

Imagining that fiery scenario made one's eyes glow red. Xie Lian was lost in thought, and Pei Ming spoke up.

"That's too far away. If we continue at this speed, it's gonna take a long time to get there. And that's not even factoring in having to slay ghosts en route."

Xie Lian nodded. "It's like an arduous childbirth every time Mount Tonglu opens its gates for slaughter."

Hua Cheng chuckled. "Gege's metaphor is brilliant." He stopped suddenly. "We're here."

"...?!" Xie Lian was dumbfounded. "So fast?"

"Not at the Kiln," Hua Cheng explained. "We've come to a holy Wuyong temple."

Sure enough, there was a large temple in the center of the valley ahead, the building listing to one side. This was the second holy Wuyong temple they had come across. Xie Lian was perplexed—he almost wanted to rub his eyes.

"Is that temple real?"

He couldn't help the question slipping out. In fact, almost everyone doubted that it was real—it seemed so out of place.

It shouldn't have been built somewhere like this. Who had ever seen a temple or shrine constructed in such a narrow valley, smack dab in the middle of a small mountain road? What was this crappy feng shui?

Even if its construction was an act of obstinance, or if the temple had to be built in this location no matter what, it should at least have been placed off to the side. But this holy Wuyong temple was bluntly constructed right in the middle of the valley road, like a brainless little tyrant brazenly blocking the mountain path!

Pei Ming lowered his voice. "Where there is abnormality, there is evil. Everyone, be careful."

Ling Wen was leaning heavily on Pei Xiu's shoulder and arduously lifted his head.

"Everyone, if you don't want to go inside, you can just leap and run across the cliffs."

But Xie Lian responded, "No. We have to go in and see if there are any murals."

"Don't worry, gege," Hua Cheng said. "Go inside if you want to. It's fine."

For some reason, since Hua Cheng was the one assuring them, everyone relaxed, and the group resumed their approach. Nothing odd happened while they walked, nor when they reached the entrance. As they passed through the temple doors and entered the great hall, they found that, sure enough, the walls inside this temple were that same blackened color from the aftermath of a blaze. With a light scratch, a small fragment of hardened material fell from the wall just like in the previous temple.

Xie Lian was tense and alert at first, but he relaxed a bit once he was sure there wasn't anything hiding in the darkness.

"Let's do this."

The ashy protective layer on the wall was cleaned off bit by bit, and soon enough, they'd revealed the mural behind. Xie Lian and Hua Cheng began to examine it closely.

The subject of the mural in this holy temple was completely different from the previous one. They started studying it from the highest level, the top of the painting. A white-clad young man sat poised upon a jade divan, his face quietly handsome—the Crown Prince of Wuyong. His eyes were shut tight, and judging from his posture, he seemed to be meditating.

However, he wasn't tranquil. The brow of This Highness the Crown Prince was deeply furrowed, and there were even a few drops of cold sweat dripping down his forehead. Surrounding him were four individuals, their expressions heavy with concern. They were the four guardian deputies that served under the crown prince, as pictured in the previous mural. Their accessories and attire were exactly the same as in the other painting.

Progressing downward, the protective ash layer was still gradually falling apart and had not yet been fully cleaned away. Xie Lian could only make out a chaotic field of red, and he frowned slightly.

"That's odd." He reached out and lightly touched the wall, puzzled. "Was this mural poorly kept?"

Although he couldn't quite tell what the mural was depicting, he could see that this spread of lines and colors was blurry and hazy, like it was fading away, trapped behind a veil of mist. But if this mural was created by magic, how could it deteriorate like a normal painting?

Hua Cheng also observed it intently, knitting his brows. "Let's give it another minute."

The two exchanged glances. Once the burnt, black, hardened material was thoroughly cleaned away and the mural was laid bare, they took a few steps back and stood side by side to look. The full mural was reflected in Xie Lian's eyes. His breathing stopped, and he felt chills.

He wondered out loud in shock, "Is this…hell?"

"No. It's the Mortal Realm," Hua Cheng said darkly.

It was indeed the Mortal Realm—the painting was packed with houses, dense forests, and crowds of humans—but they were all submerged in a vast, endless sea of flames and flowing lava. The haze of red that Xie Lian had seen earlier was the color of fire.

The houses and trees were ablaze; the people's bodies were alight with flames. They were screaming. Those twisted faces were drawn so realistically that Xie Lian could almost hear their wails in his ears.

At the center of the painting, there was a vibrant red mountain—it looked like a giant kiln glowing red with heat, absolutely horrifying. Fire and lava spewed from that volcano.

"The meaning of this mural is…a volcanic eruption brought down the Kingdom of Wuyong?" Xie Lian pondered.

"Yes. And no," Hua Cheng said.

It dawned on Xie Lian. "That *isn't* completely right, because this is…a dream."

The Mortal Realm's tragedy portrayed at the bottom of the mural was likely a depiction of a dream once had by the Crown Prince of Wuyong.

The Crown Prince of Wuyong and his four guardian deputies were surrounded in golden light, meaning he had already ascended at this point. The mural showed him as he was tormented by a nightmare, which was why the dream landscape's lines and colors were hollower than those of "reality."

Some heavenly officials possessed enormous spiritual might and abnormally incredible talents. Seeing even the smallest omen was enough to let them peek into the future. In other words, they could have prophetic dreams. Had the dream of This Highness the Crown Prince become reality? Was this how the Kingdom of Wuyong fell?

Humming for a moment, Xie Lian remarked, "Someone must want to tell us something. The story in this mural seems like a continuation of the previous one. I think the closer we get to the Kiln, the more questions will be answered."

Ling Wen was watching something outside the windows and spoke up just then. "Everyone, I need to ask you something. Isn't this strange?"

"What is?" Pei Ming asked.

"I'm not sure if I remember wrong, but were those two mountain bluffs always so close?"

Everyone looked out the window. When they had entered, the mountain bluff outside was about three meters away. But now it was extremely close, as if it was going to press into them at any moment. Xie Lian was about to go outside to check, but then he heard a series of odd cracking and creaking sounds—like earth and trees being disturbed, or bricks and stones under pressure.

Now everyone had noticed.

"What's going on?"

The bricks under their feet were quivering; the ceiling above their heads was shaking. One piece, two pieces—chunks of debris and clouds of dust began to fall.

"An earthquake?" Pei Ming wondered.

Only a moment after he spoke, the walls began to crack and wrinkle from the pressure.

"It's not an earthquake!" Xie Lian exclaimed. "It's…"

The mountain bluffs on either side were pressing into the holy temple of Wuyong that sat in between!

There was no time to explain.

"Run!" he shouted.

He didn't need to say anything. Pei Ming had already kicked down a wall, creating an exit. The group pushed through and dashed out of the main hall. However, they were still running within the holy temple of Wuyong—the temple was extremely long, and beyond the great hall there were many side chambers, small alcoves, incense rooms, training halls, and so on. Thus, the group had to keep running, breaking down walls and kicking down doors as they went. At times like these, a martial god's typical way of getting things done really shined. But they had only crossed through two short halls when a giant boulder, half the size of a man, crashed through the roof and fell heavily at Xie Lian's feet.

Huge boulders were tumbling down the mountain bluffs on either side!

The rumbling noises were endless as more and more rocks fell from the sky. The big ones were as large as water vats and collapsed massive chunks of the building's ceiling. The small ones were the size of human heads, but they also fell with astonishing force as they dropped from high in the sky. Fortunately, there was still one last bit of ceiling hanging in there, and everyone's considerable physical prowess allowed them to dodge in time. Only Hua Cheng was at ease; as Xie Lian ran and dodged, he heard him beckon him to his side.

"Gege, wanna come here?"

He turned his head to look. Hua Cheng was following closely behind him, his steps so steady it was like he was flying. He was holding a red umbrella he had produced from who-knew-where and was grinning at Xie Lian from underneath it. The falling rocks were crashing hard on the surface of the umbrella, but Hua Cheng held the handle steady with just one hand!

Xie Lian quickly took cover under his umbrella. *"Phew*, that was close. Thank goodness for you, San Lang."

Hua Cheng flashed a smile and very thoughtfully tilted the umbrella more to Xie Lian's side. "Come closer."

Even though it really wasn't the time, Xie Lian still felt a little touched. "Are you tired of holding the umbrella up? I can help you hold it..."

The others were fleeing and dodging, running like mad. They couldn't stand the sight of their two companions having such a lovely time, so they started to shout at them.

"Hey! Isn't that unfair?!"

"Hua-chengzhu, may I ask if you have any spare umbrellas?!"

"Can I hide under that umbrella too?!"

Hua Cheng smiled fakely. "No. And no."

Xie Lian felt a little embarrassed at the others' objections. "Oh, this mountain certainly is strange!" he mumbled, trying to slip away. Hua Cheng had slid an arm around him unnoticed, however, which stopped him from doing so.

"Gege is correct, this mountain certainly is strange. Strange in the spiritual sense," he explained leisurely. "There are three large mountains near Mount Tonglu, called Old Age, Sickness, and Death. They can move as they will within Mount Tonglu's perimeter, but they're otherwise no different from normal mountains. This is why some take them as landmarks of Mount Tonglu."

Falling rocks continued crashing violently around them, but there was nothing but peace and harmony under the umbrella.

"I see!" Xie Lian replied. "So when Rong Guang was disguised as Demon of the Swift Life-Extinguishing Blade, the mountain blocking our way was one of those three mountain spirits?"

Ling Wen was being jostled up and down on Pei Xiu's back

but still arduously tried to join the conversation. "No wonder this holy temple of Wuyong was constructed in such an odd place in the center of a valley. Its original placement was probably not so strange—those two mountain spirits sandwiched it afterward!"

"But Birth, Old Age, Sickness, and Death[4] are a set," Xie Lian said. "Since the last three are present, where's the first?"

"Regrettably, there's no Birth. At least, not that I've seen," Hua Cheng replied.

"Meaning there's no chance for life here, is that it? How cruel!" Xie Lian said.

A moment later, Banyue exclaimed, "The mountain bluffs are still closing in!"

When they'd first entered the valley, the mountain path was dozens of meters wide, but it grew narrower as they walked further in. By the time they reached the gates of the Wuyong temple, the road was no more than thirty meters wide. Now the space between the two mountain bluffs was less than ten meters. The building and walls were cracking and bending from the pressure. Since the holy temple of Wuyong was made of stone beams and other such solid construction materials, it acted as a wedge between the two mountains as they pushed closer—but they might not last for much longer.

"We can't go forward or backward, so let's break through the roof and go up!" Pei Ming yelled. "The shower of rocks is nothing; just knock them to pieces!"

"We can't!" Xie Lian exclaimed. "Right now, there's a temple wedged between the mountain spirits. If we go upward, what if they manage to hit us? We'll be squished and killed!"

---

4   In Buddhist belief, birth, old age, sickness, and death are the four causes of physical suffering. Greed, anger, and ignorance are the three causes of mental suffering.

During their exchange, the sides began to push closer even faster, rumbling and quaking. The space they were in was now less than six meters across. Ling Wen was still immobile, and he couldn't help but cry out.

"Can everyone please come up with something more quickly?! If not, can you release me so that *I* can take my own measures?! I don't want to get squished *or* killed, thank you!"

Fire was burning their behinds, but ideas didn't come so easily. As the space shrank to only the length of a person, Pei Ming suddenly gave a loud shout and leapt sideways. His arms pushed against the mountain on the left and his legs against the one on the right. He used his entire person to become a wedge, bracing himself sideways between the two large mountains.

"Even if I'm gonna get squished, I don't wanna get squished by these fucking things. I'll hold them back for now; you guys hurry and think of something!"

"..."

Everyone was stunned by his deed. Ling Wen arduously gave him a thumbs-up.

"Ol' Pei—what a man!"

Pei Ming forced out a reply through clenched teeth. "...y'r w'lcome!"

There was no need to describe the strength of a martial god. The two mountain bluffs were still trying to press closer, but Pei Ming's tactic had halted their movement and forced a stalemate. However, Pei Ming was exerting all the spiritual power he possessed and would surely not last long. As Xie Lian rapidly spun his wheels trying to come up with a way to escape, the two mountain spirits were slowly gaining the upper hand and forcing Pei Ming's knees to bend.

Seeing the situation was not going in their favor, Pei Xiu cried, "General I, will come assist, you!"

Ling Wen was leaning on his shoulders, but Pei Xiu tossed him to Banyue before joining the ranks as a flesh wedge. However, he was just a mortal at the moment and couldn't use spiritual power. The Brocade Immortal on Ling Wen could've been useful, but the person himself was too much of a risk; releasing him might add oil to the flame, or be like stepping on a venomous snake after falling into a nest of jackals.

Banyue put Ling Wen down. "Me too..."

She had the body of a little girl, and her limbs were nowhere near as long as grown men's. Too short to wedge herself between the walls, she instead clapped her palms onto Pei Xiu's back and transferred her spiritual power to him. Their combined power exploded, making their faces turn red and veins bulge on their skin.

As for Hua Cheng, whose powers were the strongest in the group, he watched without the slightest hint of concern as he twirled the red umbrella in his hand.

Suddenly, Xie Lian pounded his fist into his palm and cried out, "I've got it! I've got it, I've got it, I've got it!"

He had an idea!

"Since going forward, backward, or upward won't work, we'll go downward!" Xie Lian said. "Let's dig a hole and hide for now!"

Ling Wen instantly latched on. "A good idea! Will you please start on it right now?!"

"And...please...*hurry*...!" Pei Ming choked through gritted teeth.

"Okay, okay, okay!"

Xie Lian was already stabbing crazily at the ground with Fangxin to drill a pit—sand and earth was flying all over the place. Beside him, Hua Cheng held the umbrella over Xie Lian's head; not only wasn't he helping, he was coaxing him to stop.

"Gege, stop digging. Sit down and rest."

No one could take it anymore, and they cried, *"Hua-chengzhu!"*

"Hmm? What?" Hua Cheng said.

Ling Wen lay on the ground in a heap. "Hua-chengzhu, you and His Highness are here as well. If you have any tricks or ideas, won't you contribute? None of us want to be crushed into pancakes, after all."

He didn't voice the following words that no one dared say: *"And if you don't have any ideas, can you please go be a flesh wedge too?"*

Although Xie Lian was anxious, he still trusted Hua Cheng instinctively. As he kept digging, he asked, "San Lang, you have a plan, don't you?"

Hua Cheng chuckled. "Gege just has to wait. You don't need to do anything. It'll be fine in a moment."

Fire was scorching their behinds, and they couldn't help but feel the burn even though they knew Hua Cheng must have a plan. Ling Wen was about to say more when Xie Lian suddenly voiced a question.

"What's that noise?"

Amidst the loud rumbling of falling boulders came another strange sound—and it was approaching them rapidly. *Krsh, krsh! Krsh, krsh! Krsh, krsh!* It was incredibly fast and coming closer and closer. Xie Lian thought the sound seemed familiar, like he'd heard it before somewhere, and he stopped his mad digging.

"This... Could it be...?!"

A spot beside his feet caved in as the words left his lips, revealing a black hole that was big enough for two people to drop in. The head of a shovel peeked from the depths of the hole, reflecting a bright white light.

It was the Earth Master Shovel!

The shovel peeked up for a moment but then quickly withdrew back into the hole.

"A little late, but at least he made it," Hua Cheng commented. "Let's go."

Without another word, Xie Lian picked up Ling Wen and threw him down the hole, then did the same with Banyue and Pei Xiu, then Pei Ming. With the "wedges" bracing the walls gone, the mountain spirits began moving much faster. Amidst the sounds of scratching and quaking, Hua Cheng circled his arm around Xie Lian's waist and held him tight.

"Let's go, quick!"

With Xie Lian in his arms, he jumped into the hole. Xie Lian was plunged into darkness. A moment later, a thundering boom echoed from above.

The two mountains had finally fully pressed themselves together!

If they had still been above ground, they would've been crushed into meat pancakes for sure. After taking a moment to catch their breaths, a few small balls of flames ignited in the darkness.

Xie Lian inspected the underground path they found themselves in. It was neither wide nor narrow, and was neat and orderly—as expected of a path dug by the Earth Master Shovel. The ones who had dropped in first were sprawled on the ground, panting slightly.

Hua Cheng released Xie Lian's waist, and Xie Lian dropped the arm that had unconsciously gripped Hua Cheng's shoulder. He turned his gaze to the black-clad man holding the shovel.

That man was also panting, leaning against the shovel and wiping away cold sweat. Xie Lian took a few steps closer, inspecting him closely. He looked like a neat and tidy young man, and somewhat handsome—maybe a seven out of ten. But his looks didn't have much personality to them. He seemed like the sort of person who had very little presence.

Xie Lian approached him, and the black-clad man looked up.

"Your Highness…"

But before he finished, Xie Lian had already seized his wrist.

"Where's Lord Wind Master?"

The black-clad man was shocked. "Huh? I…I don't know."

Xie Lian huffed a sigh, then said sternly, "My Lord Black Water, why keep up the act? Your revenge is none of my business, but Lord Wind Master was once your friend, and he never committed a crime or harmed a soul. So I hope…"

Ling Wen interrupted. "Black Water? Your Highness, why do you think he's Black Water? Their faces are different."

Xie Lian looked back and replied doubtfully, "Because he's holding the Earth Master Shovel. Besides, don't we all know the key to a good disguise? That face is so ordinary—it wouldn't be noticed in a crowd at all. It must be fake."

As discussed previously, the first rule of disguise is to make the face as plain as possible, and the black-clad young man before them was in perfect compliance. Even if one stared at his face for an hour or more, they would completely forget his appearance by the next morning. There was no doubt—this face was a fake!

"…"

However, a moment later, the black-clad young man said, "I'm sorry, Your Highness, but this…this is just how I look," the young man replied.

"…"

Hua Cheng walked over and cleared his throat lightly. "Gege, this really isn't Black Water."

"…"

Pardon?!

"This is his real appearance," Hua Cheng said.

So this was a true, natural-born pedestrian face!

Xie Lian slapped his forehead with his palm, then quickly pressed his hands together in prayer and bowed an apology.

"...I'm sorry."

He'd been so certain of his theory, he'd bluntly told the man to his face that he was so plain he was completely unnoticeable. It couldn't be helped—that face really was the model for a perfect disguise!

The black-clad young man also felt extremely awkward, and he waved off the apology. "Don't worry, it's nothing, I'm already used to it..."

"Your Highness Yin Yu, thank goodness for your assistance," Ling Wen said.

Upon hearing that name, Xie Lian blinked. It was only then that he realized the young man's voice was a little familiar; he must've heard it a few times before. His eyes moved downward to look at the young man's wrist. While it was covered by his sleeve, Xie Lian was sure that it bore a black cursed shackle.

Pei Ming also rose to his feet to double-check the black-clad young man's identity. "His Highness Yin Yu? Well, I'll be. I didn't think we'd run into you here. What are you..."

Yin Yu scratched the tip of his nose with his finger and returned the greeting. "Ling Wen-zhenjun, General Pei, General Pei Junior."

Suddenly, a voice humphed. "Yin Yu? You're *that* Yin Yu, the one who was thoroughly and *miserably* defeated by his own shidi?"

The heavenly officials' expressions stiffened, but that voice continued.

"I gotta say, aren't you a little too pathetic? Banishment aside, I can't believe you'd turn your back on heaven and become a ghost's errand boy just like that. Compared to Quan Yizhen, you really did badly; to think you're his shixiong..."

The voice was coming from Rong Guang, who was imprisoned inside the pot. Pei Xiu stuck on a talisman to shut him up.

Whether he was serving Jun Wu or Hua-chengzhu, Yin Yu was a petty official regardless; there was functionally no difference. Still, being in the same room as his former heavenly colleagues now that he had become a ghost officer was like a constable-turned-thief getting caught in the act by old comrades. The awkwardness in the air was stifling. No one knew what to say, so Yin Yu could only turn around silently and continue digging the path with the Earth Master Shovel. The group continued onward as a path was dug.

Pei Ming still had his friend's brother on his mind. "Since Hua-chengzhu managed to get the Earth Master Shovel, does this mean the two ghost kings communicate with each other? When I asked His Highness before, His Highness excused My Lord by stating he wasn't close with Black Water Demon Xuan and certainly didn't know his whereabouts. If it's possible, will you please give Demon Xuan a shout? Ask him to please release Qingxuan, if he hasn't killed him yet."

"You're mistaken," Hua Cheng replied. "I don't know Black Water's whereabouts."

"Then where did the shovel come from?"

"I found it on the ground," Hua Cheng said.

"..."

So he would unapologetically admit to nothing, but what could be done about that? No one could do anything to him, and everyone was depending on him in their current circumstances. Pei Ming could only snort.

"All right, fine. Hua-chengzhu sure was lucky to come across a spiritual device so easily."

Ling Wen was being carried on Pei Xiu's back and said out of habit,

"That shovel belongs to a heavenly official of the Upper Court. Will Hua-chengzhu return…"

Before he finished, he realized he was no longer part of the Upper Court, so there was no need to collect debts on its behalf. He shut up.

Xie Lian rubbed his forehead, wondering whether he should ask after the matter in secret, when Hua Cheng spoke softly in a voice only he could hear.

"Black Water really did ditch it. After he stopped disguising himself as the Earth Master, he tossed the shovel away in Ghost City and fled. I thought it might be useful, so before we entered Mount Tonglu territory, I sent someone to collect it."

"I see," Xie Lian replied. "And here I thought I might uncover Lord Wind Master's whereabouts… This shovel is perfect for dealing with the mountain spirits, though. San Lang really does think of everything and makes perfect plans."

"I only thought of it because I had a rough time when I was chased by those mountain spirits, that's all," Hua Cheng replied.

Xie Lian couldn't help but imagine Hua Cheng at Mount Tonglu for the first time, charging through obstacles like a novice. Just then, a few tiny balls of silver lit up the darkness; it was the shimmering wraith butterflies acting as lights. Xie Lian held his palm under a small silver butterfly and looked upward.

"Just what are these mountain spirits? Why do they attack us?"

"It's hard to say what they are," Hua Cheng replied. "When I first came here, they'd already existed for a long time. It's not that they're attacking us specifically—they'll try to stop anyone who wants to reach Mount Tonglu. If they can't block them outright, they will attack."

"Attack indiscriminately?" Xie Lian wondered. "If you think about it, their purpose is exactly the same as ours. But Lord Rain

Master and His Highness Qi Ying are both here as well—I hope nothing happens to them."

Yin Yu had been diligently digging and opening the path, but he faltered for a moment when he heard Quan Yizhen's name. Xie Lian noticed and glanced at him. He remembered that Yin Yu had encountered Quan Yizhen while wearing a mask; at the time, he had acted like they were strangers. If Quan Yizhen had known it was his shixiong standing before him, what would've happened?

Ling Wen raised his head with difficulty. "Your Highness Yin Yu, have you seen His Highness Qi Ying? He's come to my Palace of Ling Wen many times to ask for my help in searching for you."

Yin Yu was stumped for a moment before he stammered a reply. "R-really?"

"Yes," Ling Wen said. "When you first descended, he came almost every day. Then, since there was never any news, he came once every three days, then once every month. Until recently, he'd come at least once a year. He always felt there was a misunderstanding between you two about the Brocade Immortal affair, and he wanted to hear your side of the story so he could help you explain it to the others. But there was never any sign of you, nor any word."

Yin Yu fell silent. He heaved a sigh before focusing on digging with renewed vigor.

He doesn't want to talk about it anymore, Xie Lian thought.

Ling Wen was perceptive enough to see this too, so he didn't say anything more and allowed Yin Yu to concentrate on digging. It was some time later when Yin Yu finally spoke again.

"Chengzhu, Your Highness, we've already dug fifteen kilometers. Do we continue?"

The Earth Master Shovel worked as fast as the wind, tearing through the ground as if it were cutting tofu and leaving not a single mound of loose earth behind. And since their group ran like they were fleeing, they moved even faster than they'd managed above ground. Surprisingly, they had covered fifteen kilometers in the blink of an eye.

Xie Lian noticed that Yin Yu had included him in the question, which confused him. "You don't need to ask me," he replied gently.

"It's all the same," Hua Cheng said. "What does gege think?"

Xie Lian thought it over. "Since we were almost out of the valley by the time the mountain spirits came crushing in, fifteen kilometers should be far enough. The air underground isn't sufficient; if we stay down here, we might get dizzy. Let's start digging upward."

"Yes, sir!" Yin Yu acknowledged.

He instantly changed directions, digging upward at a slant and even erecting beautiful mud stairs as he went.

This man really is an outstanding assistant. Quick and efficient, and he speaks exactly as much as necessary, Xie Lian remarked to himself.

Everyone followed behind Yin Yu. After climbing dozens of steps, Xie Lian stepped on something hard sticking out of the ground. It didn't seem like mud or a rock, so he looked down and crouched, using his hands to scrape at the ground. A moment later, his brows knitted slightly.

Hua Cheng noticed and exclaimed, "Gege, don't touch!"

But it was too late. When Xie Lian stood up again, he already had a skull dangling from each hand.

"Everyone, a question. Did we dig into a mass grave?"

Pei Ming sighed as he pulled a femur out of the earthen wall, marveling at his find. "Probably. Look at the structure of this bone. It must've belonged to an exquisitely beautiful woman with long, slender legs. What a shame for her bones to be buried here."

"Regrettable indeed," Hua Cheng said. "The leg is long, true. But it's the bone of a man."

Once Pei Ming heard it didn't belong to a woman, he lost interest and tossed the femur away.

"To be more accurate, it's the bone of a man who was deformed after turning into a ghost. So there must be corpse poison on it," Hua Cheng added.

Pei Ming opened his palms, and sure enough, the places where his hands had touched the bone now oozed with green corpse qi.

"Can you ever manage to keep your hands to yourself? *Can* you?" Ling Wen berated.

"Corpse poison, won't do any, harm. General is a, heavenly official. It'll be, fine in a, while!" Pei Xiu said.

That femur wasn't just long and slender, it was also rather sturdy—robust and light when swung. Pei Ming picked it back up and wrapped the end with a cloth to hold it. It seemed he planned on using it as a weapon.

"Your Highness, how come you're fine holding those two skulls?"

Xie Lian put the two skulls down gently and showed his hands to the others. As it turned out, his palms were radiating that same green, but the color was rapidly fading.

"Truth be told, I've been poisoned by corpses many times," Xie Lian explained. "At least eight hundred, if not a thousand. I'm quite immune to it now; this level of poison is manageable."

His explanation was oddly silly, and their companions almost laughed. Hua Cheng, however, didn't seem amused at all. He walked over and crushed the skulls to pieces under his boot.

Xie Lian had spoken calmly, but he could tell Hua Cheng was upset when he heard the violent, furiously brutal sound of crushed bones. He wanted to ask what was going on, but he couldn't help but feel that Hua Cheng's foul mood was his fault somehow. He didn't dare to pry further.

A little later, Hua Cheng demanded quietly and flatly, "What's taking so long?"

The surface shouldn't have been more than six meters away. Even if their slanting course made the distance slightly farther, it still shouldn't have taken this long.

Yin Yu was also baffled. "I'm confused too… Wait, there it is. We've dug through!"

Right after Hua Cheng's inquiry, the Earth Master Shovel pierced the surface. Yin Yu cleared a large hole and leapt out first.

"We're…out?"

Everyone climbed through. But they were all puzzled the moment their feet touched the "surface."

"Are we back above ground? No, that's not right. What is this place?" Pei Ming asked.

They definitely hadn't emerged outside, as the light was extremely dim.

"It was still daytime when we were walking through the valley. There's no reason the sky would turn dark so fast," Ling Wen commented.

A few shimmering wraith butterflies flew out and circled the area. The group could finally clearly see where they were.

It was an enormous cave, empty and spacious. The domed ceiling was extremely high and wide and looked like an ink-black night sky. They were surrounded by countless smaller caves, each of which led in a different direction.

Xie Lian was amazed. "Is this place man-made or naturally formed?"

Hua Cheng took a glance, his arms crossed. "It's natural."

Even though he still answered Xie Lian's every question, Xie Lian kept his previous moment of oddness in mind.

"The point we picked to dig upward earlier happened to be right under this mountain," Hua Cheng added. "We dug into it."

Xie Lian nodded. "I see. Then let's hurry and find the exit."

"But which, way?" Pei Xiu asked.

That was the question of the hour. There were many tiny caverns that no person could possibly crawl through, but there were still at least seven or eight other cavities that were large enough for exploration. Xie Lian crossed his arms and contemplated.

"Split, up into, groups? It's the, fastest way," Pei Xiu said.

Xie Lian dropped his arms. "No. Splitting up is the worst thing we could do right now. If there's anything hiding in the shadows, it'd be too easy to ambush us. I'd rather take our time finding the right path than divide our power."

Pei Ming wielded his new femur weapon. He seemed addicted to swinging it, and he spoke as he swung.

"Then we'll stick together. Let's try this way first."

Thus, the group picked a path and followed it together. Hua Cheng and Xie Lian took the lead.

After walking in silence for a while, Xie Lian ventured in a whisper, "San Lang?"

Hua Cheng had long since stopped showing any sign of upset, and he answered, "Does gege have a question?"

Xie Lian couldn't bring himself to ask if he had been angry earlier, so he replied offhandedly. "No, it's nothing. Just...this tunnel is so winding and twisted, like intestines. I'm a little dizzy."

"Do you want to take a break?" Hua Cheng instantly replied. He didn't sound like he was joking at all.

"No need, no need," Xie Lian hurriedly said.

Behind them, Pei Ming piped up. "Did I hear that right? Your Highness, you get dizzy from a little walking?"

"..."

Xie Lian was a bit embarrassed by what he'd said, and he felt like he was forcing conversation, so he pretended he didn't hear Pei Ming's comment.

"Everyone, do follow closely," he said sternly. "This tunnel has many twists and turns, so it would be easy for something to go wrong..."

As he spoke, he turned to look back and immediately stopped in shock, grabbing Hua Cheng to stop him as well.

"San Lang!"

"What is it?" Hua Cheng asked, and when he turned to look as well, he frowned.

There was no one behind them!

Pei Ming had not been far behind when he teased them. Now the dark cave was empty except for the two of them. Hua Cheng immediately gripped Xie Lian's shoulder, his voice dark.

"Gege, stay close to me. Don't run off anywhere."

Xie Lian held his breath, tense and alert. "Is there something hiding in the mountain?"

"No," Hua Cheng said. "But it's even more worrisome that there's nothing here."

For that meant they were dealing with something that could come close undetected and steal everyone away right under their noses!

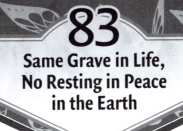

83
Same Grave in Life, No Resting in Peace in the Earth

"There's no way it could have snuck up behind us and accomplished something so major without us noticing," Xie Lian said in a low whisper.

Even if Xie Lian didn't believe in his own abilities of observation, he believed in Hua Cheng's. And when it came to gut instinct for danger, he honestly did trust himself quite a bit.

"Let's retrace our steps and see," Hua Cheng said.

The two walked side by side and returned the way they came, turning and rounding corners for a while before they came to a stop.

It wasn't that they stopped voluntarily; rather, they were forced to stop because there was no more path. Even though the tunnel wound and turned in all directions, it was still only a single road. But before they had reached their original starting point, they were blocked by a cold, hard stone wall that hadn't been there earlier!

The two were unsurprised. Xie Lian wondered, "Is this an illusion, or is this real?"

A silver butterfly flew languidly over and tapped lightly on the rugged stone wall. The wall seemed completely normal, and the butterfly was forced back.

"It's real," Hua Cheng said.

Xie Lian nodded. "Then this is tricky."

There were two common types of devil walls. The first type was an illusion, meaning one would see a wall where there actually wasn't one.

This type was easy to get rid of; just touch it and give yourself a slap, or douse yourself with a bucket of cold water to wake up and then touch it.

The second type muddled one's sense of direction and memory, and this type was a little more daunting. For example, at a fork in the road, they could confuse you—make you think you had chosen the left path when you had actually turned right. This so-called "Devil's Roundabout" was nothing more than a petty trick; there is a slight natural deviation to every person's gait, and inhuman creatures can confound the mind to distort the perception of this deviation. They can make someone think they're walking in a straight line when they're actually making a large circle. Once they made it back to their original starting point, they would be puzzled: *"Huh? How did I end up back here again?!"*

Both methods were paltry tricks to the two of them. As for the cold stone wall before them, it was an unexpected third type: it was real.

Xie Lian was considering whether to give the wall a brutish punch to see what was behind it when Hua Cheng spoke up.

"Gege, give me your hand."

Xie Lian was puzzled, but he still obediently gave Hua Cheng his hand. Hua Cheng gently took the hand he'd been offered and held it in his own palm. His other hand hovered over it like he was putting something on it.

Xie Lian held his breath for a moment. Then he raised his hand, curious.

"This is...?"

On the third finger of his left hand there was now a thin red string, carefully tied there by Hua Cheng. The red string extended outward and connected to a red string knotted around Hua Cheng's finger.

Hua Cheng smiled and raised his own hand to show him that they now had identical tiny red butterfly knots on their fingers.

"Now we're joined together."

Xie Lian could feel his face grow hot. Maybe he was a little too self-conscious. He hurriedly rubbed his cheeks hard before he smiled back, scared that Hua Cheng might notice his heart was beating faster than normal.

"Is this some sort of spell?"

"Yes." Hua Cheng straightened his expression and dropped his hand. "Even though we won't separate voluntarily, this is a precaution. The red string won't break and won't grow shorter. As long as this red string remains unbroken, it means the person on the other end is all right. It will surely lead us to each other, unless one of us is no more."

"What do you mean by 'no more'?" Xie Lian asked.

"Dead or dissipated," Hua Cheng explained.

Xie Lian was about to speak when he heard the faint sound of tremors in the distance. He listened intently and wondered, "Is someone throwing fists?"

Considering the power and frequency, it seemed like someone was throwing heavy punches at the mountain itself.

"Such power definitely couldn't belong to an ordinary mortal; it must be a martial god," Xie Lian remarked. "Could it be General Pei?"

"It's coming from ahead of us," Hua Cheng observed.

"Ahead" meant the direction they had intended to go but that they had to turn back from because Pei Ming and the others disappeared. But Pei Ming and the others had been behind them when they vanished—how could they suddenly reappear ahead? And if it wasn't Pei Ming, who could it be?

The two exchanged a look and walked toward the noise side by side, ready to check it out. But when they were about halfway back, the mountain-punching sound disappeared. They couldn't tell whether it stopping was intentional or if the energy fueling the punches had been depleted.

Since they had already come this far, why turn back? Xie Lian and Hua Cheng continued to walk in the direction from where the sound had come. A few silver butterflies danced in the blue-toned darkness of the cave ahead of them, lighting their way. Xie Lian's sharp eyes caught sight of something odd on the stone wall.

"What's that? A red string?"

They couldn't tell what it was from afar, but it was extremely bizarre. It looked like a red string, but much thicker. It kept twisting around, looking more like a long red worm the closer they got. Xie Lian approached and examined it carefully.

"Isn't this one of Banyue's scorpion-snakes?"

Sure enough, it was the bottom half of a wine-red scorpion-snake, twisting and throwing its body around. Its upper half was buried in the stone wall.

"Did it crawl into a hole that it couldn't get out of?" Xie Lian wondered.

"Probably not," Hua Cheng said.

The scorpion-snake's body was dangling in the air; snakes didn't climb walls, so how could it have slithered up so high before crawling into a hole? Besides, there were many small crevices in this stone wall; if it had wanted to crawl into a hole, why pick such a small one? The "hole" was also strange—it was almost the exact same shape as the snake's body, which was why the serpent had gotten so thoroughly trapped.

Xie Lian wanted to grab hold of the snake and pull it out to see, but the snake was abnormally active and swinging its tail madly; it was attacking randomly with its stinger and kept almost hitting

Xie Lian. So Hua Cheng flicked it. The motion seemed completely casual, but the snake seemed shocked by this and was too stunned to move. Xie Lian didn't know whether to laugh or cry, and he was just about to speak up when he quickly shut his mouth.

"Do you hear that?"

"I do," Hua Cheng said.

The two looked ahead at the same time.

From within the darkness, they could hear the low sound of breathing: very steady, very calm.

Two wraith butterflies dallied and danced around each other and fluttered toward the breathing sound, flying higher and higher and lifting their silver light upward. Gradually, a pair of hands was illuminated.

They were the hands of a person—the hands of a man. They were spotted with blood and covered in gashes, and they drooped like a corpse's. As the glowing butterflies moved upward, the person's messy head was revealed, which also drooped as if he was dead.

However, there was no lower body.

That's right—the person "hung" so high on the stone wall didn't have a lower body. He only had an upper half, like he had grown straight out of the wall!

In the past, Xie Lian had seen nobles and aristocrats hunt for rare game and take the head as a trophy. They would treat it with chemical solutions to prevent decay, then hang it on the wall of their residence. The sight before him reminded him of those neatly displayed trophies—the heads of tigers, bucks, wolves, and other such beasts. However, this man was obviously breathing—he was still alive!

Xie Lian took a step closer. "What is this creature? Is this the true body of the mountain spirit?"

But there was no response from beside him. Xie Lian felt chills crawl up his spine. He whipped his head around—and sure enough, Hua Cheng was gone!

"San Lang?!" Xie Lian cried.

Naturally, no one answered, but the man hung on the wall mumbled like he was talking in his sleep and about to wake. Under the current circumstances, however, Xie Lian had no interest in him whatsoever. He spun around a few times in his search, then remembered the red string tied around his finger and raised it in renewed cheer. Sure enough, the red string was still there—and it was unbroken. Xie Lian relaxed a little at the sight and picked up the red string, tugging on it as he walked. He walked and walked until he reached the end of the thread.

The red string was strung through a stone wall!

Xie Lian couldn't believe it. He yanked at it a couple times, but his efforts only pulled out an endless length of red string from within the stone wall. It almost made him suspect that Hua Cheng was inside.

The moment that idea occurred to him, Xie Lian raised Fangxin and was ready to shatter the wall without another word. But the tip of his sword hadn't even touched the stone when his sight went black. It was as if the wall before him had opened a giant mouth, and it howled as it swallowed his entire body whole!

The blackness didn't recede—it only grew darker and darker as Xie Lian was swallowed. He was surrounded by sand and mud, crushing him with their weight and suffocating him. Everything moved endlessly; it felt like he had been swallowed into the stomach of a giant yao beast that had gobbled down a mishmash of things and was tumbling it all around in its stomach to digest. It also felt like he was sinking into quicksand—he couldn't exert any power even though he had the strength, and the more he tried to struggle, the deeper he sank. Xie Lian wanted to break the wall to escape, but then he realized that Hua Cheng could also be trapped here. And so, instead of backing out, he moved forward, swinging his arms to break away the earth and sand as he pulled at the red string and arduously continued onward.

A hand reached out and firmly seized his wrist. Xie Lian was alarmed.

"Who?!"

Mud poured in the moment he opened his mouth, and he miserably spat it out. As for that hand, it grabbed him and pulled him into a pair of arms. A familiar voice came from above.

"Gege, it's me!"

At the sound of that voice, Xie Lian completely relaxed and hugged Hua Cheng tightly. "Thank goodness...the red string didn't break. I really found you!" he blurted.

Hua Cheng embraced him firmly back and said with conviction, "It didn't break! I found you too."

As it happened, they both experienced the same strange incident. Xie Lian was observing the half-bodied man hung high on the wall, and Hua Cheng was keeping an eye on their surroundings, guarding against anything that might ambush them from the shadows. Xie Lian had been standing right next to him, but it only took a split second, the blink of an eye, for him to disappear, a stone wall looming where he once stood. Hua Cheng had pulled at their red string, following and searching, and he went inside to look for Xie Lian when he discovered it was threaded into this wall.

Though there had probably only been a single wall between them, they had both feared that the other was trapped inside and entered at the same time. Xie Lian mentally repeated for the umpteenth time that Hua Cheng really always thought of everything.

"Thank goodness we're linked by a red string! Otherwise, who knows if we would have found each other. And no wonder General Pei and the others disappeared so abruptly—they weren't ambushed, they were instead…swallowed by the mountain spirit."

"That's right," Hua Cheng said. "We picked a bad spot to dig and wound up breaking right into the mountain spirit's stomach."

Xie Lian unconsciously cleared his throat.

This was true—they were currently, without a doubt, in the stomach of one of the three mountain spirits. When Yin Yu had asked Xie Lian whether they should start digging upward, their chosen location just happened to be where one of the mountain spirits was resting, and Xie Lian had cheerfully agreed. He had the world's most unbelievable luck, no lie. The sand and mud were crushing in on them, monopolizing more and more of the space around them, and the air was getting increasingly suffocating. Xie Lian felt they really shouldn't stick around here much longer.

"How do we get out?" he asked.

"The mountain spirit got dug into from the bottom, so it's not very happy," Hua Cheng replied. "It's trying to digest us right now. A bit annoying, but rest assured, gege, we'll get out eventually." Then he joked, "This must be what 'same grave in death' feels like."[5]

Xie Lian was slightly shocked by the comment, but the corners of his lips curved upward. He hastily suppressed himself the moment he noticed.

"The half-bodied man outside was probably also swallowed by the mountain spirit. The punching sound we heard must have been him

---

5   [生同衾，死同穴] "Same quilt in life, same cave [grave] in death." A quote from the second half of a verse from "The Propitious Pavilion of Romance," one of the tales recorded in the Mount QingPing Hall Novella Collection. It describes a married couple who are intimately in love and has a similar sentiment to "not even death shall part us."

pounding at the stone walls trying to escape. He and that scorpion-snake are the same; they were only half swallowed."

Which was why the effect was so terrifying.

"But he's not someone from our Mount Tonglu traveling group," Hua Cheng pointed out.

Xie Lian recalled that messy hair. "Wait, I know who that was. It was probably Qi Ying!"

Hua Cheng thought for a while before he seemed to remember. "Oh, the one with the curly hair. I guess that was him."

"I wonder if he's all right," Xie Lian said. "Did he pass out? He wasn't responsive earlier."

"He's fine, just asleep," Hua Cheng said.

"...How do you know?" Xie Lian asked.

"I left a few silver butterflies outside," Hua Cheng said. "I sent one over to him just now. My right eye can see through it."

As soon as he spoke, he made a soft sound of interest, as if he'd seen something strange.

"What is it?" Xie Lian asked.

Hua Cheng didn't respond, only bowed his head slightly and gently lifted Xie Lian's chin so they could touch foreheads. Xie Lian's eyes instantly widened, but then he closed and reopened them.

"This is...truly magical."

His right eye was seeing a completely different scene from what was before him. It was dark, but he could see rough silhouettes. The silver butterfly that was monitoring the outside seemed to be hiding behind a bunch of weeds. A black shadow was slowly approaching from below.

"Someone's coming. I wonder who it is," Xie Lian whispered. "Where is your silver butterfly hiding? Will it be discovered?"

"It's in his hair," Hua Cheng said. "Its light is concealed—it won't be discovered."

The black shadow finally came close enough to be distinguishable. The man lifted his head to reveal a ghastly pale face.

"Yin Yu?" Xie Lian said.

84

This Jade Refuses to Be a Thrown-Away Brick[6]

IT WAS INDEED Yin Yu.

He was still holding the Earth Master Shovel. Even if he'd been swallowed by the mountain spirit, he could still swiftly dig a path to escape with that holy device in his possession. It wasn't strange that he was making an appearance here, especially considering Quan Yizhen's furious, earth-shattering pounding.

The images that Xie Lian was seeing in his left and right eyes were different, and it was incredibly uncomfortable. He blinked lightly, which made him discover that his right eye could still see the scene outside even while closed. So he kept his eyes shut.

Just then, his field of vision shuddered; it shook wildly and swung from left to right. It appeared Quan Yizhen had finally come around and was shaking his head.

Seeing that he had raised his head, Yin Yu swiftly reached up to cover his face with his ghost mask. However, Quan Yizhen didn't have the attention to spare for him—the moment he woke, his entire body was violently yanked backward and another piece of it sank into the wall.

---

[6] This chapter title is a derivative of the idiom 抛砖引玉 / "pao zhuan yin yu," or "throwing out a brick to attract a jade." It describes the act of making a rudimentary suggestion that is intended to prompt others to come forward with better ideas. Yin Yu's name is written the same way as "attract a jade."

The mountain spirit had swallowed another large portion of Quan Yizhen's body!

When his arms were still out, Quan Yizhen had relentlessly smashed at the wall with his fists, working hard to pull himself free. However, the mountain spirit was probably thousands of years old, and its yao powers were equally immense. It opened its mouth wide and swallowed again, and Quan Yizhen sank deeper and deeper until the sound of wall-pounding disappeared—when both his arms were dragged into the stone wall. The mountain spirit seemed to stop, but Quan Yizhen was left with only his head exposed.

That was when he realized there was someone standing below him.

"Who are you?" he demanded without thinking.

Yin Yu didn't respond, but the sharpness of his eyes could be seen through his mask. His gaze was chilling. Xie Lian couldn't help but think, *That certainly isn't the expression of someone who wanted a reunion.*

Quan Yizhen continued to speak without thinking. "Is that a shovel in your hand? Help dig me out of this wall. I want to get out."

He had always spoken this way—naive, matter-of-fact, fearless, and unconcerned of consequences, almost like a child. He didn't even ask who the stranger was before demanding his help, completely disregarding the question of whether the peculiar shadowy figure who appeared under such circumstances was there to kill him.

Hearing his demand, Yin Yu's grip on the Earth Master Shovel grew firmer. A moment later, with that gleaming shovel in his grasp, he slowly approached Quan Yizhen. One step, then another step, like he was a murderer about to commit an unspeakable crime. For some reason, Xie Lian grew alarmed and unnerved as he watched this play out.

"...Wait. Why do I feel like he wants to chop off Qi Ying's head with that shovel?"

"He might," Hua Cheng said.

Xie Lian had no words.

"But for the time being, we can't let him kill Quan Yizhen," Hua Cheng added. "The mountain spirit can only swallow things raw at the moment, and they aren't digested easily. A corpse would be much easier for it to absorb. If Quan Yizhen dies and gives the mountain spirit a chance to devour a heavenly official, its powers will grow exponentially. It'd add more trouble to our escape."

"Wait, wait, wait, wait," Xie Lian quickly said. "San Lang, easy digestion aside, Yin Yu is your subordinate. From what you know about him, do you think he'll kill Qi Ying? Is there some deep grudge between them?"

Qi Ying had been so determined in his search for Yin Yu. Since they were a shixiong and shidi of the same sect, it was impossible that he didn't understand his character after all these years. Xie Lian thought the reason behind his search was obvious: Quan Yizhen believed Yin Yu was worth searching for. And with Quan Yizhen's personality, what could he have done that would make someone want to kill him?

"There's no major grudge," Hua Cheng replied. "But the desire to kill someone doesn't always come from one or two particularly agonizing incidents; it can stem from small matters. Especially small matters that otherwise go unnoticed."

"What do you mean by that?" Xie Lian asked.

Just as he spoke, the scene in his right eye changed. He wasn't seeing Hua Cheng's red robes *or* a man facing a head on a stone wall—it was a large street. Xie Lian was just about to ask what this was when he heard a commotion ahead.

There was a crowd of cultivators gathered in a circle on the road, and they seemed to be yelling furiously at someone. When Xie Lian looked closer, he discovered a small child crouching on the ground at the center of the crowd. He was crowned with a head of thick, curly hair, and his face was covered in blood.

Any normal child would have surely been terrified and crying at being surrounded and yelled at like this. But while this child was only about ten years old, not only was he not scared, he seemed *excited*—his eyes darted around, and his little fists were clearly itching to be tested.

A young cultivator pushed through the crowd and approached the child. "Let it go, stop yelling at him! He must know he's in the wrong by now."

Xie Lian made a soft noise of wonder. The young cultivator had bright eyes and a glowing, spirited face. His back was straight, and he stood tall. This was, shockingly, Yin Yu.

Maybe it was because he was at the height of his youth, or maybe because he was in high spirits, but he didn't have the dim color of one worn down by the passing of ages. He was much more vibrant here than in the fading impression he'd left in Xie Lian's mind when they met. Anyone would praise him as an impressive young man. The boy of the past and the man of now were practically two different people.

"He wasn't so ordinary and plain-looking back then!" Xie Lian remarked.

Hua Cheng laughed out loud. "Who wasn't young once?"

Only then did Xie Lian realize that he had accidentally spoken his mind out loud.

"San Lang's right eye can see such things?"

"Not exactly. Something else saw it, and I'm just borrowing that for viewing."

"Amazing. Incredible." Xie Lian said with true astonishment.

"It's simple," Hua Cheng said. "One must do a thorough background check when picking a subordinate. I'm fairly good at running such checks, so if gege ever needs one, come find me anytime."

In the scene that their right eyes were showing, another clean-cut young man around Yin Yu's age ranted furiously at him.

"'Know he's in the wrong,' my ass! Look at him—does it *look* like he knows he's in the wrong? This brat doesn't look like he knows anything at all! We were doing our morning training and minding our own business, and he ruined the session by chucking rocks and mud at us! We've gotta teach him a hard lesson!"

Yin Yu stopped him. "Let it go, Jian Yu. You already beat him up; I'm sure he won't dare do it again. You've all vented your anger, so what more is there to accomplish? You'll kill him if you discipline him any more. Look at this child; considering the way he's dressed, there mustn't be anyone at home, and he surely has no one to teach him manners. Just ignore him. Everyone, go back inside and calm down."

"I'm telling you, that stinkin' brat is insane—he's not normal!" Jian Yu spat as he turned around. "Look at him, looking so happy while getting beaten up! I think he wants to go another round!"

Yin Yu pushed them away, urging them to leave. He sighed. "You said yourself that he's insane, so why bother with him?"

It was easy to see that Yin Yu's words held weight with his peers at this point in his life. Although the crowd was still upset, they left as told. Yin Yu glanced at the child sitting on the ground, and he crouched to join him. Before he even opened his mouth, the child scooped up a handful of mud and threw it at his head with an excited expression.

The mud hit Yin Yu squarely in the face, and he was left speechless for a moment before he could even think to wipe himself clean.

"Why are you so mischievous, little guy? Why did you hit the cultivators from our temple?"

The child leapt up and struck an attacking stance. "Come at me!"

Yin Yu stood, thoughtful for a moment. "That's an attack stance from our sect. Who taught you?"

But the child still only urged, "Come at me!"

He bounced in place like a silly little monkey, and he even grabbed for more handfuls of mud and rocks from the ground to throw at his "opponent" with incredibly accurate aim. Yin Yu was older than him by a few years and mindful of his own status; he couldn't fight a child. He wound up running around to dodge the attacks.

"And that throwing posture *also* came from our sect. Did you climb the walls to spy and learn in secret every day...? Stop hitting me! I said, *stop hitting me!* I didn't even hit you! Do you really like fighting so much?!"

Unexpectedly, when Yin Yu said those words, Quan Yizhen actually came to a sudden stop. He nodded as he rubbed his muddy, grimy little hands together.

"I like it."

He said those words so seriously. Both Xie Lian and Yin Yu were stunned.

There was no need to say who this child was. Xie Lian was in awe.

"Qi Ying really is a martial fanatic. He was born to be a martial god."

Even though everyone else thought Quan Yizhen was an insane child, Xie Lian felt like he could relate. An obsession like this was necessary to achieve godhood.

A person who could understand this feeling of obsession had potential; they had a chance, even if slim. Those who couldn't understand—who would only mock and jeer these "insane idiots"—had no hope of walking this path from the very start.

Yin Yu blinked, then laughed. But he didn't laugh for very long before another ball of mud splattered on his face.

"Hey! I said stop hitting me... Listen to me! How about—do you want to enter our sect and learn how to fight?" he quickly called out.

Quan Yizhen's movements stopped when he heard this, and the ball of mud in his hand paused too. But Xie Lian didn't find out whether he wound up throwing it anyway, because he heard a resounding *clunk* sound upon the stone wall outside.

Yin Yu hadn't actually broken Quan Yizhen's neck with the shovel, but the sharp metal did scrape past Quan Yizhen's face. It was an extremely dangerous move.

The silver butterfly hidden in Quan Yizhen's hair was very steady. While it wasn't shocked into flight by the surprise strike, the image Xie Lian saw in his right eye shook and he blurted in spite of himself, "Don't!"

But Hua Cheng seemed to have expected this. "Just watch. He certainly does have the inclination, but his intent to kill isn't strong enough yet."

Only Quan Yizhen's head was exposed on the outside of the wall. "You want to kill me?"

Yin Yu didn't respond.

Quan Yizhen seemed very confused. "Have I done something wrong?"

Xie Lian also wanted to know. "*Did* he do something?"

"It's difficult to say," Hua Cheng said. "Gege, watch for yourself."

Xie Lian's right eye now showed him a cultivation hall with long, white walls and a black tiled ceiling. Yin Yu looked a few years older than in the last scene; he was hunched over his desk, fervently writing something. Next to him was a large crowd of his fellows, filled with angry indignation and crying their grievances.

"Yin Yu-shixiong, the way Quan Yizhen eats is unbearable! He sprays his rice everywhere at mealtimes, and he eats three times as much as everyone else! It's like he's a starving ghost or something. No one can eat well with him hogging the rice bucket like that!"

"Yin Yu-shixiong, I can't live with him anymore, I want to change rooms. He's always so cranky in the mornings—I worry every day that he'll kick me and break my ribs. I can't deal with him!"

"Yin Yu-shixiong, I don't want to be in his group anymore. That jerk never cooperates with others, and he's so inconsiderate of everyone! He only cares about showing off and randomly throwing his fists around. I'd rather be paired with the weakest shidi than with him!"

Yin Yu was getting overwhelmed by all the complaints. "All right, all right. Then how about this—I'll look into everything and determine the best course of action when I'm done. Head back for today."

The one who slapped the table and complained the loudest was of course Jian Yu, and he obviously wasn't satisfied with this response.

"Yin Yu, you really shouldn't have made shifu take in that brat in the first place! Trouble came in through the front door, honestly. Look, how long has he been with us now? And since he arrived, has a single day passed without him causing chaos? Has a single day passed without him destroying something?!"

The crowd was trying to force his hand, so Yin Yu attempted to pacify them.

"None of these complaints are anything major..."

"Nothing major?! He's killed our peace and quiet! Cultivation requires peace, they always say. How can we cultivate without it?!"

"Yeah, there were never this many issues in the past!"

Yin Yu could only say, "Yizhen doesn't have bad intentions. He just genuinely doesn't understand the ways of the world very well, and he doesn't know how to get along with others."

"Ignorance isn't an excuse! If he doesn't know, can't he learn? We all live in a world full of people, and we all have to learn how to get along with others. How old is he now?! He can't act like a child forever! Some people are dads at his age!"

"Shifu's favoritism aside, that brat has only been here a few years! And from the moment he came, he hogged all the benefits—he was given the best training hall, he's given the best cultivation supplements from every season's batch, he can even skip morning and evening lessons and is exempt from reciting scriptures. Even when shifu catches him misbehaving, he only gets a light reprimand—no lectures at all! What's so good about him?! Yin Yu-shixiong! *You're* the eldest disciple; if you acted like that, we would let it slide with no complaints. But who the hell is *he*? No education, no manners. So what if he's talented? None of us will accept him!"

His complaint was an attempt at sowing discord, and the crowd eagerly rallied to agree. Yin Yu's face turned grim at this, and he gripped his brush. Xie Lian couldn't help but think that things were going south.

A person with an ordinary level of patience would have been easily baited; if they were narrow-minded, they would've already been on their feet even without a hook. Would he explode when such a lure was flashed?

After some contemplation, Yin Yu put down his brush. Unexpectedly, he admonished them in a stern tone.

"Shidi, the things you're all saying aren't right."

The crowd was taken aback.

"I'm going to say something unpleasant," Yin Yu continued. "No matter what path we cultivate, talent truly is an incredible thing. And he is not only talented, he's willing to work hard. If you really think shifu is playing favorites, then let's work harder to keep up with him—maybe even overtake him. And then things like training halls and supplements will naturally be open to everyone. Rather than wasting time being angry at him, your priority should be training harder. Am I right?"

His reprimand punctured everyone's indignation and made them a little embarrassed, but they still said, "Shixiong is being generous by giving him the benefit of the doubt."

"Your magnanimity alone makes you millions of leagues better than him."

Jian Yu gave a warning. "Yin Yu, you defend him today, but watch out—he may very well screw you over in the future!"

In any case, neither side was happy after the round of complaints was over. Once the crowd of disciples left, Yin Yu closed the door of his study, and he was about to shut the windows when he discovered someone and jumped in surprise.

"Who's there?!"

Quan Yizhen was perched on the windowsill. His head drooped.

As soon as Yin Yu recognized him, he asked, "When did you get here?"

He tugged at him, but Quan Yizhen didn't move.

"Yizhen, if you want to perch somewhere, find a different spot. I'm going to shut the window."

Quan Yizhen suddenly asked, "Shixiong, am I annoying?"

Yin Yu puffed a dry laugh. "You overheard all that?"

Quan Yizhen nodded, and Yin Yu's expression grew complicated. He scratched the bridge of his nose.

"...You're...not...that bad...I guess..."

Any normal person would've picked up on how forced the words were, but Quan Yizhen seemed to take them at face value.

"Oh."

Yin Yu could tell he took it for the truth, and he smiled briefly before giving him some encouragement. "You really don't need to mind them. You didn't do anything wrong. It's fine like this."

Anyone with clear eyes could see that the other disciples couldn't stand Quan Yizhen. They found fault everywhere, and it wasn't because of his big appetite, or because he wasn't a morning person, or because he was inconsiderate and a poor teammate who only cared about showing off.

At the end of the day, what they really couldn't stand was this: he was the last to enter the school, but he received the most.

Quan Yizhen nodded. "I think so too."

Yin Yu patted his shoulder. "Go train! That's what's most important. Don't think about anything unnecessary."

Quan Yizhen hopped off the windowsill. Looking at the direction he was headed, he was indeed going off to train. As for Yin Yu, he shut the window, picked up the books on the desk, and started studying anew.

After watching the two scenarios, Xie Lian praised Yin Yu. "San Lang, that subordinate of yours really is a rare character. What a good heart."

But then he remembered that in the present, Yin Yu had almost chopped Quan Yizhen's head off with the Earth Master Shovel. He quickly asked, "Is everything all right out there?"

Hua Cheng showed him the view of outside. Yin Yu had calmed down; he had pulled the Earth Master Shovel out of the wall and seemed to be contemplating what he should do with Quan Yizhen's head. Xie Lian relaxed a little.

"I suppose the problems between them started after ascension?"

"Correct," Hua Cheng replied.

A magnificent great hall appeared before Xie Lian's eye.

Yin Yu sat, poised and proper, at the center of the great hall. Jian Yu and Quan Yizhen stood guard behind him—one on the left and one on the right. Many gods milled about the hall; they were all heavenly officials of the Upper Court. Xie Lian saw several familiar faces—a male Ling Wen, an apathetic Pei Ming, Lang Qianqiu with his perfect smile... They were all in formal attire, and junior officials trailed behind them holding large red gift boxes.

This was clearly the Heavenly Court and the Palace of Yin Yu. It was the palace's Opening Ceremony—the grand, propitious day his divine residence was formally established.

Xie Lian was slightly amazed. It made sense that Hua Cheng could easily see scenes from the Mortal Realm—it was his domain. When he wanted to cast his net, any travelers, wandering ghosts, or birds and beasts could become his eyes as he wished. But the Heavenly Capital was within heaven's boundaries—how could he see it as well?

Hua Cheng seemed to have guessed what he was thinking. "Gege, take a look at the nook near the entrance."

Xie Lian listened to him and looked over. The "nook" was actually quite large in size, because the grand hall was grand indeed. There were at least ten people milling around in that corner.

"Guess which one is Black Water?" Hua Cheng asked.

Only then did Xie Lian remember that He Xuan had been undercover in the Upper Court for years and years—he must've sold this information to Hua Cheng. Xie Lian stared hard and tried to guess, and a moment later, he found one that seemed to match.

"The one in black?"

"Incorrect—too conservative of a guess. Try again," Hua Cheng said.

Xie Lian tried again. "The one over there who's not smiling or speaking?"

"Wrong again," Hua Cheng said.

He made more guesses, but they were all wrong. Just then, an entrance announcement was made.

"Presenting the Lord Wind Master!"

Xie Lian instantly looked to the entrance of the grand hall. Shi Qingxuan strolled over the threshold, ostentatiously fluttering the Wind Master Fan, his face bright as a spring breeze. He tossed a gift box to the side and gave a courteous salute.

"Congratulations to the Palace of Yin Yu for its grand opening! I've come late; I'll take a penalty drink, ha ha ha ha!"

Yin Yu smiled from his spot on his throne. "Nonsense, My Lord is not late. Lord Wind Master, please, this way!"

Hua Cheng finally revealed the answer. "That one."

Xie Lian was quite confused. "...Lord Wind Master is Black Water?"

Now *that* was too incredible. Hua Cheng laughed.

"Gege misunderstood me. Not *that* one, the one behind him."

Xie Lian looked closer and saw that there was a low-ranking heavenly official standing behind Shi Qingxuan beside the hall's entrance. He was responsible for receiving gifts from guests. His appearance wasn't distinguished, but an enthusiastic smile hung upon his face. Shi Qingxuan crossed into the hall looking very pleased and casually tossed the heavenly official a small pearl as a tip. The heavenly official's eyes shined brightly, and he looked every part a fawning servant as he thanked the Lord Wind Master profusely and caught the pearl with both hands.

Xie Lian couldn't help but comment, "...That's Black Water? With such a bright smile?"

"That's him," Hua Cheng said. "The smile is fake, that's all. The man has at least fifty clones stationed throughout the Heavenly Court, each with a different identity. All so he can directly monitor over eighty Upper Court officials and over three hundred Middle Court officials. The Earth Master identity alone was far from enough."

"..." Xie Lian was in absolute awe of Black Water's acting, his ability to plant pawns, and his inconceivably exuberant energy. "Where are those fifty-some clones now?"

"Jun Wu is probably pulling out those nails one by one," Hua Cheng replied.

Just as he spoke, a sharp voice came from the outside.

"Your Highness Yin Yu, you'd better give us a good explanation for your shidi!"

All of the heavenly officials' smiles dropped, and they looked to the source of the sound. It appeared there was someone outside who had intended to barge in but had been stopped, and he was now shouting relentlessly.

"Aren't you going to discipline your shidi Quan Yizhen, who assaulted heavenly officials who outranked him?"

Yin Yu's light smile disappeared, and he lowered his voice to question the two behind him. "What's going on? Yizhen, you picked another fight with someone?"

"Yeah," Quan Yizhen replied.

Jian Yu's eyes bulged in rage, and he gritted his teeth. "*Again*, you stinkin' brat?!"

Shi Qingxuan was always the first to speak when these incidents happened. He tucked his whisk into the back of his collar and asked, "What's going on? Today is this palace's grand opening, so what is it that can't wait?"

To cause trouble on someone's propitious day—they were either blind and ignorant, or they were trying to pick a fight on purpose.

"Oh gosh, is it My Lord's joyous palace grand opening? We didn't know!" the mob outside the palace said. "But he didn't choose an appropriate time to come looking for a fight, so why do *we* need to schedule a time to settle the score? Quan Yizhen belongs to the Palace of Yin Yu. It was His Highness Yin Yu who personally appointed him. Who else can we seek out if not him?"

There it was—they were here to pick a fight.

Ling Wen furrowed her brows slightly. "Why must it be this way?"

Yin Yu resignedly rose to his feet. "I understand. However, it's really not a good time right now. Can we talk afterward?"

The mob outside snorted. "We can only hope the Palace of Yin Yu won't cover this up!"

They hadn't even explained the details of the situation at hand, but accusations of cover-ups were already flying. They were blatantly the aggressors. Shi Qingxuan seemed ready to speak up again when Quan Yizhen jumped down from behind Yin Yu's throne.

"Are you leaving or not?"

The troublemakers were obviously confident that he wouldn't dare retaliate during the event, and they shouted at him without fear. "Why? Are you gonna fight us again if we don't leave? All your heavenly colleagues are watching..."

But Quan Yizhen wasn't someone whose actions could be predicted by common sense. Without another word, he raised his fists and dashed out. Terrible wails came from outside the palace, and every heavenly official inside the hall was stunned!

It was only after a while that Ling Wen spoke up.

"Guards, go stop him, they're going to die!"

Yin Yu was also dumbfounded for a moment before he hurried out. "Stop this instant!"

But the troublemakers only yelled, "Think your Palace of Yin Yu is hot shit?! Yeah, right! Shixiong and shidi are ganging up and bullying people!"

That evening, Yin Yu paced back and forth in a side chamber of the Palace of Yin Yu while Jian Yu stomped in rage.

"A perfectly good grand opening ceremony was completely ruined by that stinkin' brat!"

Xie Lian could understand Jian Yu's anger completely. While he didn't care much for things like palace grand opening ceremonies, many heavenly officials considered them significant. This was a ritual that validated a heavenly official's formal induction into the Heavenly Court. For lack of a more appropriate example, today's incident was like a mortal emperor's crowning ceremony being ruined. Who wouldn't be angry?

Yin Yu sighed. "Let it go. The others must have provoked him first. Besides, he wasn't the one who started the trouble today; *they* chose to come pick a fight at the ceremony, so what could we have done?"

"There are so many people in the Upper Court—why don't they pick on anyone else? Why do they always have to provoke him specifically?" Jian Yu demanded.

"You know why," Yin Yu said. "He's never one to take a beating without fighting back. It's not that they don't pick on anyone else, it's that everyone else understands how to endure that kind of provocation, but he doesn't."

"This is the Heavenly Capital," Jian Yu ranted. "It's not the Mortal Realm. Is it so hard to keep your head down and stay low profile?! If he behaved and didn't pick fights, today's incident would've never happened! Now look at us. We've lost all face! So many heavenly officials were watching! Once word gets out, who cares who started it? They'll only say that the Palace of Yin Yu was being unreasonable and beating people up in public; who's gonna debate who's more in the right?! Do you think he has a reason for acting like this?! *He doesn't!* When things go down, you become the unreasonable one the moment you raise a fist! He doesn't understand shit! He only knows how to cause trouble for us!"

After his blowup, Jian Yu stormed out of the side chamber in a rage. Yin Yu was left sitting where he was, his heart heavy with worry.

A while later, he looked back to see the shadow of a figure perching on the windowsill. When confronted by this familiar scene, Yin Yu jumped in surprise once more.

"Why are you perching there again? When did you get here? What is this habit of yours?"

Quan Yizhen didn't answer his questions, but said instead, "They cussed at me first."

Yin Yu opened his mouth to reply, but then he closed it. Instead, he comforted Quan Yizhen. "Yizhen, don't take what Jian Yu said to heart."

Quan Yizhen kept going. "They cussed at me first. I don't even know them. They said I was a low-ranking heavenly official and yelled at me for no reason, then they laughed at me and told me to scram and not to block their way. I told them to apologize, and they wouldn't, so I beat them up. They only shut up when I beat them up, otherwise I wouldn't have hit them."

Things were considerably more peaceful in the current time, but in the early days, some heavenly officials—from both the Upper and Lower Courts—would throw their weight around and bully lower-ranked officials with less experience. Yin Yu sighed.

"Are low-ranked heavenly officials beneath other people?" Quan Yizhen asked.

"No," Yin Yu replied.

Was that true? It was obvious that he didn't believe his own words, and Quan Yizhen noticed.

A good while later, he said bluntly, "I don't like it here."

Yin Yu said nothing.

"They think I'm annoying, but I think they're even *more* annoying," Quan Yizhen continued. "Before, I could train at least sixteen hours a day. Now half of that time is taken up by talking and listening to nonsense, by greeting and visiting people. There are people who yell at me and hit me for no good reason, without apologizing, and I can't even fight back. This isn't heaven. I don't like it here."

Yin Yu sighed. "I don't like it here either."

"Then let's go back," Quan Yizhen said.

But Yin Yu only shook his head. "Even though I don't like it here, I want to stay."

Quan Yizhen couldn't understand. "Why do you want to stay if you don't like it here?"

Yin Yu was stumped, and chuckled in spite of himself. He didn't know what to say, unable to explain it to him. How could he convey to Quan Yizhen that reaching the Heavenly Capital was the dream of so many people who sought the path of cultivation, the ultimate end goal? Or just how difficult it was for someone his age to achieve ascension?

Yin Yu tried instead, "It's...because ascension is really hard. Since it didn't come easily and we finally made it here, I want to try to do better."

Quan Yizhen, however, didn't think much of that reason. "Ascension isn't that big of a deal! It doesn't matter if you don't ascend."

Yin Yu found him both exasperating and a little funny. "What do you mean, it's no big deal?! Why don't you give it a try, then?"

Watching up to this point, Xie Lian commented, "People really shouldn't make jokes like that so casually."

"Indeed," Hua Cheng said. "Half a year later, he won't find it so funny when Quan Yizhen actually ascends."

"Can we watch that part too?" Xie Lian asked.

"We can. Hold on," Hua Cheng replied.

The scene changed. It was still the Heavenly Capital, but the occasion was a banquet beneath the moon. Xie Lian watched for a moment.

"The Mid-Autumn Banquet?" he wondered aloud.

"That's right," Hua Cheng said.

"Where's Black Water hiding this time?"

"Just look for whoever's eating."

At the banquet, every heavenly official was busy making toasts, greeting the others, or playing games. There was only one exception—a person whose face was practically buried in the giant bowl in front of him. This time, He Xuan wasn't hiding. He was openly sitting in the corner in the guise of the Earth Master, but still, no one noticed him there.

Yin Yu and Jian Yu were seated next to the "Earth Master." Their assigned seats were considered the edge of the banquet. Yin Yu wasn't eating or talking to anyone.

Next to him, Jian Yu muttered under his breath, "Thank god that insane stinkin' brat didn't come!"

Yin Yu heard him and whispered back, "He's been ascended for a while now. You shouldn't let others hear you talk about him like that, so be more mindful."

"It's the truth; am I wrong to speak it?" Jian Yu said. "So what if he ascended? His brain won't get any smarter no matter how many centuries he lives."

As they conversed, a new group of heavenly officials arrived and began to seat themselves. They were mostly new faces, and they welcomed each other with simple greetings.

A heavenly official inquired offhandedly, "And this lord is...?"

Another heavenly official gave an offhanded answer. "This is the martial god who rules the west."

Hearing this, the heavenly official who made the inquiry instantly grew more enthusiastic and stood up to make a toast.

"Oh! Oh, oh, oh! What an honor! I've long heard your great name, My Lord!"

Yin Yu quickly stood up as well, smiling. "Please, it hasn't been long."

"Oh, don't be so humble, My Lord!" the heavenly official replied. "I've indeed heard *so much* about you! I've long heard that His Highness Qi Ying of the west is young and capable, and that he has already earned the deep love of his devotees only a few years after his ascension. You even made it to the top ten in this year's Mid-Autumn Battle of the Lanterns! You dominate the west, your status is immovable, your future is boundless. Boundless, I say! Seeing

My Lord today, you seem a bit older than I imagined? But still fairly young and worthy to be praised as capable! Young and capable!"

The smile on Yin Yu's face froze, and the matter of whether the toast should be accepted became extremely awkward. The other party fervently continued to try to build a connection, even addressing him like they were brothers.

"I'll be honest—I rarely meet people who I like, but brother Quan, you feel so much like family! My domain is also in the west, so, my brother, as long as you think well of me, by all means let me know if you have any needs in the future! We should all help each other out, eh? Ha ha ha..."

He laughed heartily, and those nearby who knew Yin Yu laughed heartily as well. Xie Lian could almost cross through time and feel the suffocating awkwardness in the air.

Jian Yu's face was growing dark from rage, but Yin Yu was still somewhat composed. While his hand trembled for a second, he managed to steady himself.

"Unfortunately..."

Just as he was about to clear away this misunderstanding, someone called out.

"Qi Ying is here!"

A commotion started at the other end of the banquet, and the heavenly official next to Yin Yu was shocked.

"Huh? You—you're not His Highness Qi Ying?!"

Only then did the others explain through their laughter, their hands hugging their bellies.

"You got the wrong person, my brother! Did you forget? There are two martial gods ruling the west; one is Yin Yu and the other is Qi Ying. They're shixiong and shidi of the same sect! The one in front of you is His Highness Yin Yu. Ha ha ha..."

"Oh, oh, oh, I've gotten the wrong person, how embarrassing! Ha ha ha, I'm too ill-informed and only heard about Qi Ying..." the heavenly official quickly said.

He trailed off, but Yin Yu had already closed his eyes like he was too tired for words and had given up on socializing. Someone had noticed things were not going well and elbowed the heavenly official, and only then did he notice that what he had said was hurtful. He laughed awkwardly to smooth things over, then cleared his throat.

"*Ahem, ahem,* I'll take my leave now, Your Highness Yin...Yin Yue—ah! No, no, no, Your Highness Yin Yu! Let's get together again sometime, happy Mid-Autumn, ha ha ha..."

While he said he was taking his leave, he raised his cup and headed in the direction that was cheering Quan Yizhen's arrival. At the other end of the banquet, there was already a large crowd of heavenly officials fighting to greet Quan Yizhen. The surrounding crowd had completely blocked the person in the center from sight.

It appeared that this was soon after Quan Yizhen ascended and established his own palace. He was at the height of his popularity in Heaven, in contrast to how he was disliked by most of the present court. Although the two were both the Martial Gods of the West, he was significantly more prominent than Yin Yu. The attendees all swarmed over, leaving the table where Yin Yu sat empty and quiet. Only He Xuan remained there, drinking his soup.

It was awkward whether he stood or sat.

Shortly after, Yin Yu abruptly said, "Let's head back."

The two left their seats, and no one noticed. Jian Yu was outraged.

"Bunch of brownnosers! And they're heavenly officials, no less! Back when that brat first joined the Upper Court, they gave him the cold shoulder and complained to you about him all day, every day. Now look at them. The brat ascends and gets some lanterns, and now they praise him to the skies! They change their attitude faster than flipping a page! Immovable status, they say? Young and capable, they say? His devotees are all insane, just like him! Only idiots would worship someone with brain damage!"

Just then, Shi Qingxuan walked over with a cup of wine.

"Don't say any more—let's get out of here!" Yin Yu hissed.

Jian Yu finally shut his mouth when he saw someone approaching. Shi Qingxuan was puzzled.

"Yin Yu, are you heading back? Didn't Qi Ying just get here? I recently heard him say that he hasn't seen you in a long while; he even asked me what you've been up to. Aren't you going to go catch up with him a little?"

Yin Yu forced a smile. "No. I'm not feeling well, so I'm heading out."

Shi Qingxuan didn't think too deeply on it and laughed cheerfully at the sight of the "Earth Master" sitting behind them.

"Then you go and rest easy, and we'll get together next time. Ming-xiong! I told you not to sit all the way over here! Come, come, come—come over to my table..."

Jian Yu waited until Shi Qingxuan walked away and stopped paying attention to them before he continued to grumble.

"Catch up, my ass! That brat won't be smug for long. He'll suffer a crushing defeat soon enough. I eagerly await the day!"

He kept grousing, aggravating Yin Yu's silent frustration.

"Just drop it, and stop being so resentful."

"Drop it, drop it, that's all you say, 'drop it,'" Jian Yu complained. "How can I drop this? When he first came here, he would've been kicked out almost immediately if it wasn't for you always going around wiping his ass and smoothing things over for him. I really can't watch this anymore; I'm frustrated for you!"

The two swiftly returned to the Palace of Yin Yu. Compared to the exceptional liveliness seen at the palace's grand opening ceremony, the halls were now desolate and deserted, with only a few lower-ranked officials milling around. After closing the gates, Yin Yu's voice grew louder.

"Don't say any more! I don't want to hear it! It's very normal for an ascended heavenly official to establish a palace, so he didn't do anything wrong. Since you get irritated just talking about him, why must you constantly bring him up?"

"Please don't think that I'm speaking out of turn, but someone must remind you. Yin Yu, the west is only so big, and there are only so many devotees. He's already taken so much. That wolf yao kill should've been yours, but he stole it! Look at the state of you now—your domain's shrinking smaller and smaller. How much do you have left? Can you maintain your standing if this keeps up?"

"How is what he's done *theft*? It's not like he's forcing anyone to worship him at knifepoint—everyone's willing. Besides, that wolf yao..." Yin Yu sighed and said frankly, "I couldn't have defeated it. It was useless praying to me, so of course they went to him."

"I just... I'm just worried that if this fight continues, he'll win and leave us with nothing," Jian Yu said bitterly. "Fuck, even those lower-ranking officials only care about their own advancement—each one of them coming up with empty excuses to quit and then slipping away to serve under other heavenly officials. What a bunch of no-good asshats!"

Yin Yu sighed again and sat down on a prayer cushion. "What fight are you talking about...? Why care for such things? Those who want to leave will always leave in the end, and those who want to stay will naturally remain. I didn't ascend to fight for power with anyone, nor squabble over domains, nor quarrel, so why can't you let this go?"

One mountain has no room for two tigers, or so they say, and one need only look at the present example for proof: Feng Xin and Mu Qing were both stationed in the south and had been at each other's throats for years. Things might have been a little better if they weren't in the same territory, but enemies are destined to meet, and one's domain is where one is renowned and ascends. After ascension, the people from one's past mortal life will often end up crowding together. In and below the heavens, as gods and as humans—life is just awkward like that. There was no reason for Quan Yizhen to abandon the west and move to a different territory.

The two were in the middle of their argument when someone banged loudly on the doors.

"Who is it?!" Jian Yu called.

"It's me," the person outside replied.

Jian Yu turned angrily to Yin Yu and hissed under his breath, "Why did that stinkin' brat come knocking?"

Yin Yu gestured for him to go to the back of the palace, and he schooled his expression before moving to open the doors. Sure enough, standing just outside was Quan Yizhen. He seemed to have grown taller since the last time they met; he was now about the same height as when Xie Lian first met him. And he had finally stopped perching on windows.

When Yin Yu spoke, he sounded fairly calm. "Yizhen, it's you. Aren't you going to attend the Mid-Autumn Banquet? Why have you come here instead?"

Quan Yizhen followed him into the grand hall, and his first words were as blunt as expected.

"It's my birthday."

"…"

As it turned out, the Mid-Autumn Festival was Quan Yizhen's birthday, and he had come looking for his birthday present.

Xie Lian had heard that Yin Yu, as Quan Yizhen's shixiong, would always give him a present on his birthday. But with all the awkward incidents lately, there wasn't one that year. Judging by Shi Qingxuan's words back at the Mid-Autumn Banquet, Yin Yu had been avoiding him on purpose for some time. Someone with a bit more sensitivity would've noticed when someone started avoiding them and stopped giving gifts—they certainly wouldn't have gone to ask for a present in person. Yet here Quan Yizhen was, knocking on the door with full confidence, no idea that anything was wrong. Xie Lian had never witnessed anything more tragically awkward. If he wasn't touching foreheads with Hua Cheng right now, he would've slapped his own face to cover his eyes so he wouldn't have to watch anymore.

Yin Yu puffed a dry laugh. "...Ah, that's right, today's your birthday again. It's been busy here in the palace recently, so..."

Quan Yizhen's eyes widened. "There's nothing?"

Yin Yu seemed to think it wasn't right to leave things like this, so when the words reached his lips, they immediately reversed.

"No, I didn't forget. It's in the back, just wait a moment."

Quan Yizhen sat himself down on the spot, resting both his hands on his knees. He nodded energetically, looking very hopeful. Yin Yu fled to the side chamber, and Jian Yu was sitting there with a grim expression. Of course Yin Yu hadn't prepared a gift, so the moment he entered the room he started searching through all the drawers and dressers, the chests and shelves—but he couldn't find anything appropriate for the occasion.

"Quick, help me find something. Something that can be temporarily used as a gift," he called out to Jian Yu.

Jian Yu grabbed a cleaning rag and threw it onto the ground. He stomped on it twice before saying hatefully, "Give *this* to him."

"Jian Yu!" Yin Yu berated.

"This is still more than he deserves," Jian Yu spat. "I can't believe he's shameless enough to come asking for a present!"

"He doesn't get it," Yin Yu said, resigned. "I've always given him something in years past. If I don't give him anything this year, it'll seem too deliberate. Anything will do, as long as the intention is there. How about this—go find me that Golden Exorcism Bracelet we just received. It's not quite appropriate, but at least it's something."

He had to urge him a few times before Jian Yu finally stormed off. Yin Yu returned to the grand hall and sat in front of Quan Yizhen.

"Just wait for a moment. Things are a bit disorganized right now, so I sent Jian Yu to look for your gift. By the way, what have you been up to lately? Things have been going smoothly, I presume? I heard the number of worshippers of your palace has increased fivefold these past few months. Congratulations."

"I don't know about any worshippers," Quan Yizhen replied. "I've just been doing my own thing, and they came crowding into my temples for some weird reason. I killed a wolf yao the other day."

Yin Yu's smile became stiffer. Quan Yizhen so effortlessly managed everything he couldn't. It was like being ignored by a girl you loved, and nothing you did could win her over—and then, when she tearfully ran into someone else's arms, they couldn't even be bothered to spare her a glance; instead, they turned around and told you that she was only average, nothing special. Truly, what a bitter feeling.

Quan Yizhen rambled for a bit, then suddenly said, "I saw you at the Mid-Autumn Banquet. I wanted to talk to you, but you left so quickly."

When he finally stopped talking with such excitement about the recent battles in his domain, Yin Yu could finally breathe a sigh of relief. "Oh, a little something came up, so I headed back early."

Quan Yizhen nodded. "Someone told me it was because they greeted you as the wrong person."

Yin Yu's face dropped at this. But Quan Yizhen didn't notice at all, his lips curving upward.

"That's too funny—so stupid!"

Xie Lian couldn't bear to watch anymore, and he buried his face in Hua Cheng's arms. "This...this...this...this is too tragic to watch."

Xie Lian wholeheartedly believed that Quan Yizhen genuinely thought it was funny that someone had made such a silly mistake, and that he genuinely did not realize just how unfunny it was to Yin Yu. But that didn't change the fact that he was going to die from suffocation if those two continued this awkward conversation. Thankfully, Jian Yu finally came around with a gift box before he suffocated. He passed the gift box to Yin Yu and returned to the back of the palace without a word. Yin Yu looked like he had been saved and passed the box on to Quan Yizhen. He seemed ecstatic and hopped up on the spot to receive it, but Yin Yu's smile was already laced with fatigue.

"Why don't you open it back at your place?"

Quan Yizhen nodded. "Okay. I'll head back now. Oh, I'm going on the patrol next month. If shixiong is free, come with me."

Yin Yu couldn't listen to anything else he said, and he placated him with an offhanded "All right." Once he was sent off, Jian Yu came out, cussing and slamming doors.

"Who does he think he is?! Did his mother drop him on his head hundreds of times as a child?! If not, he came here to mock you on purpose! 'I don't know about any worshippers,' what nonsense! And that patrol, is he trying to show off?! How evil!"

When he yelled this time, Yin Yu didn't stop him. He silently headed to the back chambers and did not reemerge.

Xie Lian could tell instinctively that the gift box Quan Yizhen had taken was the problem here. "Was the Brocade Immortal in that box?"

"You guessed it," Hua Cheng said.

"Then Jian Yu should've been considered responsible for the Brocade Immortal incident. Why was Yin Yu's punishment so severe?" Xie Lian asked.

"Gege will find out. The next part takes place three days later," Hua Cheng replied.

He said three days, and three days went by. Rays of sunshine shone startlingly through the quiet Palace of Yin Yu. Yin Yu sluggishly walked into the side chambers and started hunting for something. He searched through the chests and delved into the drawers. As he rummaged through a desk, he fumbled out a shining gold bracelet covered in charms and spells. He didn't care about it at first and set it aside, but a moment later, he picked it up and called out.

"Jian Yu?"

Jian Yu entered the room. "What is it?"

Yin Yu held up the bracelet. "Why is the Golden Exorcism Bracelet here?" he asked, puzzled. "Didn't you give it to him? Didn't I have you wrap this up in a gift box?"

Jian Yu humphed. "Give him a gift? He doesn't even deserve a drop of your spit!"

Yin Yu was exasperated. "You didn't actually give him that foot-cleaning rag, did you? Why must you purposely offend him?"

But Jian Yu only smiled cryptically. "I didn't. I gave him something better."

His tone was odd, and Yin Yu frowned.

"What exactly did you give him?"

"That robe you captured last time," Jian Yu replied.

Yin Yu's face instantly changed, and he clearly didn't think the situation was so casual anymore.

"What? I was wondering why I couldn't find it anywhere. That robe can manipulate minds; it can suck blood!"

He turned to hurry away, but Jian Yu grabbed him.

"Why so worried?! Sure, that thing can manipulate minds, but you're the one who gave it to him, so only you can control him. As for the blood-sucking, maybe it's effective on mortals, but I doubt it'll do anything to a heavenly official. Listen, it's been three days and nothing's happened to him!"

Yin Yu thought it over. Then he thought it over some more while pacing back and forth in the side chamber.

"Besides, isn't that brat *capable*?" Jian Yu continued. "Young and capable, right? Let's see just how *capable* he is."

In the end, Yin Yu still threw his hands up and sighed. "No! We don't know how dangerous that thing is—if anything happens, we're done for! My gosh, how can you take this so lightly?!"

With no regard for Jian Yu's calls, he dashed out. He bumped into many heavenly officials as he rushed to the Palace of Qi Ying. When he arrived, the person in question wasn't there, so he grabbed hold of random people and anxiously asked after him.

"Where's Qi Ying? It's urgent—where is he?!"

"Qi Ying?" the others said. "His Highness Qi Ying is in a meeting at the Palace of Divine Might! All the top-ranking martial gods of the Upper Court are there today…"

Yin Yu didn't stay to hear the rest of the sentence and ran off. It was only after he reached the Palace of Divine Might that he realized he couldn't enter—this meeting had only summoned the "top-ranking martial gods of the Upper Court," and he hadn't been called. Furthermore, even if he could get in, he wouldn't be able to talk about the matter in front of everyone. He could only wait outside.

Xie Lian glanced through the windows, and sure enough, there were a number of familiar faces listening intently in the hall—Feng Xin, Mu Qing, Pei Ming, and so on. But the person Yin Yu was looking at was Quan Yizhen, who was dressed in impressive, shining armor.

There was nothing odd about him. It was instead Ling Wen who appeared a little odd as she stood next to Jun Wu, who sat on his throne. She was clearly distracted and making frequent mistakes. It grew so noticeable that Jun Wu had to speak up.

"Ling Wen? Ling Wen?"

He called to her a few times before she snapped out of it.

"What? What is it?"

Jun Wu chuckled. "Whatever is the matter with you today? You keep staring at Qi Ying. Are you perhaps like me and think that his new armor is quite nice?"

The martial gods in the hall started laughing. Ling Wen mumbled an apology, subtly wiping away the cold sweat on her forehead. However, the hand that she used to grip her brush seemed to be trembling.

If Xie Lian had been present at the time, he probably would've smiled as well. However, he was perfectly aware now that Ling Wen must've been quite unsettled to see Quan Yizhen confidently wearing the bloody robe that she herself had created centuries earlier.

Yin Yu paced outside the hall, sometimes squatting, sometimes standing, agitated and jittery. At last, the meeting ended, and Quan

Yizhen was the first to come out. When he saw Yin Yu outside, he greeted him.

"Shixiong, why are you here?"

Yin Yu instantly rose to his feet. He made a few inconsequential remarks, then jumped straight to the point.

"Your armor..."

"It's great!" Quan Yizhen replied. "Both the Emperor and Ling Wen complimented it. Thank you, shixiong."

"..." Yin Yu spoke with forced calm. "It's great indeed, but the person who forged the armor said there's a little problem and wants you to bring it in for repairs."

If he directly ordered Quan Yizhen to "take off that armor," he would risk Quan Yizhen discovering he was being manipulated. It would be bad if the truth was discovered, so Yin Yu couldn't afford for him to notice anything amiss—thus he could only make the request in such a roundabout way. However, this meant that Quan Yizhen was only puzzled by the demand.

"What problem? I don't think there are any problems."

After all, it was also awkward to ask to have a gift returned. Yin Yu was thinking hard on how to counter this statement when Quan Yizhen spoke again.

"By the way, shixiong, next month we can go out on patrol together."

Yin Yu's head shot up, and he looked a little bemused. "What?" That almost made him forget about the whole business with the Brocade Immortal. He said hesitantly, "I don't think my name is on the list for the patrol?"

Quan Yizhen, however, looked quite happy and excited. "It is. I mentioned you, and the Emperor said he would consider it."

"..."

In that flash of a second, Xie Lian could almost see the waves of hot blood rushing to Yin Yu's face. Years of built-up resentment and pent-up grievances finally exploded at that very moment.

"What is *wrong* with you?!" Yin Yu yelled.

This was the very first time Quan Yizhen had seen Yin Yu so angry, and he blinked as confusion colored his face. A few heavenly officials who were passing by also snuck glances at them.

Yin Yu clutched his head. "Did I say that I wanted to go?! What does the Patrol of Martial Gods have to do with me?! I didn't ask you to do it, so who are you to mention me to the Emperor?!"

Outsiders might not know why Yin Yu was losing his cool like this, but Xie Lian could understand perfectly. After all, this was great humiliation to any proud martial god.

The Patrol of Martial Gods was a ceremony that only the top martial gods of the Upper Court could participate in. During the procession of this patrol, the chosen martial gods would demonstrate their might by subduing and dispersing evil. Not only could this help spread their names and expand their base of worshippers, but there were also opportunities to spar with the other participating martial gods, to improve their skills and build relationships. It was a grand affair by any estimation, and there were extensive prerequisites for the martial gods in attendance—a prominent foundation and high-level skills, for example, or having at least four thousand temples, or ranking in the top ten at the Mid-Autumn Banquet.

With Yin Yu's qualifications, he wasn't eligible to participate in the Patrol of Martial Gods. Even if he could attend and was able to gain from it, those who knew his status would gossip. Those with thick skins might not care; there were countless small-time heavenly officials who would fight to squeeze themselves in.

But Yin Yu clearly wasn't thick-skinned. He knew deep down that he wasn't qualified, so how could he possibly depend on someone else's connections and force himself in? And that "someone else" was Quan Yizhen, who had once depended on *him* to escape expulsion from heaven!

Quan Yizhen didn't understand at all. He probably thought he had done a good deed. He had mentioned Yin Yu, and that was all. He didn't think there could be problems beyond that. However, Yin Yu looked truly furious, and for the first time Quan Yizhen seemed to want to say something—but he stopped, looking like he didn't dare.

A moment later, he managed to mumble, "Shixiong, why are you mad? Did I do something wrong?"

"…"

Those words again!

Xie Lian practically wanted to beg him to stop talking. As for Yin Yu, veins popped on his forehead. He was teetering on the edge of a breakdown, and he pulled at his own hair.

"Enough! I've had enough! I'm going mad! I'm going fucking *mad* because of you!"

Then he pointed at the Palace of Divine Might.

"Quan Yizhen, stop talking to me! Go and take back your recommendation right now! Stop adding to my troubles! Do it! Right this second!"

Quan Yizhen instantly turned and dashed back into the Palace of Divine Might without another word. Yin Yu blinked, and only then did he remember that Quan Yizhen was still wearing the Brocade Immortal. His actions weren't because he knew himself to be wrong and wanted to rectify things, but because he was being controlled!

Within the Palace of Divine Might, the few martial gods who hadn't yet left watched in confusion as Quan Yizhen came blazing back in. Yin Yu stood outside the hall, trembling slightly, and he yelled again.

"Stop!"

Quan Yizhen had almost made it to Jun Wu when he abruptly halted and came to a hard stop. It took a good moment before he came to, bewildered.

"What was up with me just now?"

Jun Wu knitted his brows. "Qi Ying, do not move! Come here and let me take a look at you. Your eyes were unfocused and you are surrounded by an evil aura. It seems you have been bewitched by an evil spell."

Quan Yizhen scratched his head, feeling confused. "All right."

And he then moved forward. Without any choice, Yin Yu had to yell another command.

"Come back! Leave!"

Quan Yizhen turned around the moment he gave the order, madly running out of the hall in Yin Yu's direction. Perhaps it was because rage had rattled his mind, perhaps he had gone crazy from distress, but the few moves Yin Yu had made were all extremely terrible. Yin Yu himself also started running in confusion, looking very much like a fleeing criminal. Jun Wu couldn't possibly pretend he didn't see, so he rose to his feet.

"Bring them both down!"

The martial gods all acknowledged him. "Yes, My Lord!"

Yin Yu was falling deeper into despair, his mind in complete disarray, and he roared while covering his face with his hands, "Leave! Leave right now! Take off your clothes!"

Quan Yizhen's eyes were wide and blank, and he stripped off

his armor in the middle of his mad dash. A group of martial gods surrounded them halfway and attempted to arrest them outright. Seeing that there were people obstructing him from obeying his orders, ferocity flashed in Quan Yizhen's eyes. Taking the dozen martial gods in his sights as his targets, his fists flew out and punched a chain of holes right through them!

"*Aaaaaaaah! Murder!* Murder in the Upper Court!"

Screams echoed through the air as blood had spilled. Yin Yu was already petrified, his face white as a sheet. Only Ling Wen wore a face paler than his.

He had never imagined that the Brocade Immortal was so powerful, so incredibly evil! This had gone completely out of control!

The lower-ranking officials that had charged forward to apprehend him couldn't block Quan Yizhen's fists, and they were all completely annihilated on the spot. Seeing how perilous this situation had gotten, Feng Xin, Pei Xiu, and Lang Qianqiu all leapt in to surround Quan Yizhen, ready to attack.

"Ignore him!" Yin Yu cried. "Don't touch him! He won't kill any more!"

As long as they didn't prevent Quan Yizhen from completing his orders, he wouldn't harm anyone. But Quan Yizhen had already killed over a dozen martial officials, so who would let him run free? Of course no one believed Yin Yu's words. If he were someone who reacted quickly and remained calm in emergencies, he would've shouted "drop to the ground, surrender, and don't move," or a similar command. But things were happening so quickly, and there was no time to react. Yin Yu had probably never experienced a situation like this, and he was already in distress, his decision-making ability completely broken. With just one misstep, they had been sent careening down a terrible path.

He was still wholly distracted by his confusion when Mu Qing suddenly appeared behind him.

"Trying to get away?"

Only then did Yin Yu realize he was also fleeing with no direction in mind. He quickly halted, trying to explain himself. "I wasn't..."

But Mu Qing didn't wait for him to finish before he twisted his arm behind his back. Xie Lian heard a crisp *crack*, and Yin Yu's face twisted.

As a martial god, being subdued by another martial god whose abilities and strength were greater was a double whammy—a blow to both the body and the mind.

Pei Ming was watching the fight without participating, and he commented from the back, "Why's it like his strength suddenly exploded?"

He was referring to Quan Yizhen. It was only natural; Quan Yizhen was already very capable in combat, and his power had increased twofold while wearing the Brocade Immortal. When the other martial gods faced him one-on-one, it was actually two against one—he had an unfair advantage. But since no one knew the truth, they were too embarrassed to attack him in a group. Wouldn't that be pathetic? So Quan Yizhen fought his way down the main street of the Heavenly Capital, covered in blood from head to toe. When he saw a palace on the road, he barged right in headfirst.

"He's entered the Palace of Yin Yu!" the crowd shouted.

The command Yin Yu gave him was to "leave," but he didn't say where to go, so Quan Yizhen chose somewhere at random. Several martial gods followed him inside. Since everyone else was clear of mind, they held back while fighting Quan Yizhen, but he didn't care and fought with all he was worth against anyone who obstructed his orders. This apparent callousness enraged the other martial gods.

"There's something really wrong with this brat," Feng Xin barked. "Let's beat him down first and talk later!"

The moment Feng Xin shouted, the other gods lost their reservations—they wouldn't show restraint any longer. They all rushed in and surrounded him to beat him to a pulp. Swords swung, palms blasted, fists flew, legs kicked, and with a loud rumble, half of the already-deteriorating Palace of Yin Yu collapsed!

Yin Yu was still being restrained by Mu Qing, but his eyes bulged, and he cried out when he saw his palace falling apart around the brawl.

"Please stop fighting!"

That would never stop the other martial gods, but Quan Yizhen heard his order and his fists stopped. Now he'd done it—all those swords, blasts, fists, and kicks rained down hard on him. Another tragedy!

Lang Qianqiu didn't have the time to halt the swing of his greatsword, and it struck deep into Quan Yizhen's shoulder. Thank goodness his sword was dull and that he was able to quickly pull back his strike—at least Quan Yizhen wasn't sliced in half.

"Stop fighting—I don't think he can move anymore!" Lang Qianqiu shouted.

Feng Xin wiped the blood off his face. "Fucking finally!"

Quan Yizhen lay stiffly on the ground like he'd been trussed up with rope. Mu Qing tied Yin Yu's wrists with an actual Immortal-Binding rope before letting him go. Yin Yu fell to the ground in a daze, and he stared dumbly at the mess that was left of his Palace of Yin Yu. After taking in the room, his gaze fell back onto Quan Yizhen, who had dropped to the floor in front of him. Quan Yizhen clearly had a very stubborn life force; even after being beaten to a pulp by several martial gods and pulverized beyond recognition, he didn't lie still for long before suddenly sitting up straight, clearly confused.

"What's going on?"

"..."

The martial gods were going to go mad from rage. They all shouted at the same time, "You're in big trouble now!"

Ling Wen had been following behind and watching closely, and she finally exhaled, her face still pale. She somehow had the presence of mind to coordinate help and raised two fingers to her temple as she called out to the spiritual communication array.

"Medical officials, emergency aid, now!"

Quan Yizhen was still very confused. When he turned his head and saw Yin Yu sitting on the ground, he crawled to his feet, seeming to want to help him up. At the sight of that completely oblivious face paired with the background of his smashed divine palace, Yin Yu was speechless. However, his face was slowly contorting.

Quan Yizhen didn't remember anything of what had transpired. "Shixiong, what are you doing?"

"..."

It was as if Yin Yu had lost all sanity. He puffed an abrupt laugh, his eyes brimming red, then cried:

"Quan Yizhen, why don't you just go die?! *Go die, will you?!*"

Hearing that cry, Xie Lian's eyes went wide, as did those of the many heavenly officials present. Upon receiving the order, Quan Yizhen took immediate action without a second thought. He grabbed a sword off the ground, and with the sword in one hand and the other yanking his own head up by the hair, he aimed for his own throat.

The moment he moved, the martial gods' assumed that he was going to make a sneak attack, so they leapt dozens of meters away to get out of his reach. They never expected him to slit his own throat, and by then it was too late for them to snatch the sword away.

They all roared at him. Yin Yu was also shocked, but he hadn't yet come to his senses and could only avert his gaze.

Mere seconds before blood could splatter, Jun Wu's figure suddenly flashed behind Quan Yizhen. *Crack, crack, crack, crack*—all four of Quan Yizhen's limbs were dislocated in an instant. Jun Wu then chopped precisely at the back of Quan Yizhen's neck, knocking him unconscious and sending him tumbling backward to the ground in a heap. He was broken beyond recognition, so wrecked that he looked like a pool of blood and pulp.

Everyone, Xie Lian included, sighed a breath of relief.

Everyone except Jun Wu.

Jun Wu turned around to regard Yin Yu. His expression was gravely solemn, showing neither rage nor joy.

"With things having progressed thus, I trust you have an explanation?"

Yin Yu's head was buried in his hands, and he subconsciously looked up at the question. "I don't know anything. It wasn't me. It's...!"

His whole body jolted midway through his rambling, like he had only just realized what had come out of his mouth.

He had told Quan Yizhen to "go die" in front of so many witnesses—and Quan Yizhen had tried to do it!

It was impossible not to notice something amiss.

Mu Qing spoke up. "My Lord, Qi Ying's reaction indicates that he must've been cursed with some wicked spell. There must be something forcing him to follow Yin Yu's commands. But we don't know exactly what it is."

Ling Wen naturally knew exactly what had caused this, but she didn't dare speak a word from where she stood in the crowd. Coordinating helping hands on the scene was the most she could do.

"Something like that exists?!" Lang Qianqiu said in disbelief.

Someone pushed through the crowd to rush forward—it was Jian Yu. It was obvious that he had been out looking for Yin Yu before returning to the palace and that he didn't yet know what had happened.

"What are you all doing? What...what happened to the Palace of Yin Yu? How did this happen?! Who smashed it up?!"

Jun Wu languidly approached Yin Yu. "How are you controlling him?"

His tone was not harsh, but it carried a suffocating, oppressive air of authority. Being looked down upon from so high above struck fear into one's heart. Xie Lian had certainly made many major mistakes, but he had never seen Jun Wu like this before. It seemed he really had let Xie Lian off easy back then and treated him with unusual kindness.

As far as Xie Lian could tell, Yin Yu didn't have strong composure to begin with, and his ability to react in stressful situations was weak. At a time like this, with his mind already a mess, he was even less capable of giving an answer.

Seeing that he wasn't responding, Jun Wu said, "Just as well. Even if you do not answer, I already know. It is that armor, correct?"

He was done for. Finished. Doomed.

Yin Yu sat on the ground, clutching his head anew as waves of talk crashed down all around him.

"Astonishing... Over all my centuries in heaven, I have never witnessed anything more inconceivable!"

"A heavenly official manipulating another heavenly official to slaughter without reservation... He made him murder over a dozen officials and then told him to kill himself?!"

"How vile..."

When Jian Yu discovered that something so major had happened, his face also blanched. Still, he gritted his teeth and charged forward from the crowd to kneel on the ground.

"My Lord! That armor was...was... It was me who gave it to Quan Yizhen! It had nothing to do with Yin Yu!"

Only then did Yin Yu stir. "Jian Yu..." he croaked.

Jian Yu braced himself and cried loudly, "I only wanted to teach that brat a lesson, but I didn't think...that it would cause something so horrible..."

Quan Yizhen was still unconscious, lying in a pool of his own blood. The medical officials who had rushed to the scene surrounded him, as did the rest of the crowd.

"I've always hated that brat, but Yin Yu has always treated him with courtesy—many here can bear witness to this. He didn't know anything about the armor!" Jian Yu said.

But it was too late at this point. No one would believe that Yin Yu wasn't involved. Instantly, someone piped up.

"You're only a low-ranking official in the Palace of Yin Yu, yet you already hate him to the point where you mean him harm. It's easy to imagine that the heavenly official you serve isn't any better."

There were even those who taunted them. "He didn't know anything? If he didn't know anything, why would he tell him to 'go die'? Are you going to try to tell us he was joking?"

It could've been argued that Yin Yu's reactions were understandable, that he had become flustered by distress, but those last words negated everything—*"go die."* Those words had doomed him to condemnation.

When Ling Wen first told Xie Lian this story, she'd said that Yin Yu "played a prank." Xie Lian could now appreciate that she'd said that to cover for Yin Yu.

Jian Yu couldn't believe it. "What? Stop talking nonsense. How could he have said anything of the sort? He's always been perfectly polite with that brat, so why would he tell him to 'go die'? Yin Yu, you didn't say it, right? You didn't say anything like that? You wouldn't have said it!"

But Yin Yu didn't answer him; he closed his eyes instead. The onlookers were speechless at the sight of Jian Yu refusing to concede the truth.

"We all heard it with our own ears. How can it be denied?"

"There must've been a misunderstanding!" Jian Yu exclaimed anxiously. "There's so much you don't know!"

"No matter the misunderstanding and no matter what we know, I don't think there's any matter so severe that it should make someone want to kill their own shidi."

Yin Yu and Jian Yu were both silenced by this. Thus, the heavenly officials on the sidelines continued their commentary.

"I heard that ever since Quan Yizhen went solo and established his own palace, the people of the Palace of Yin Yu stopped caring for him. Every time Quan Yizhen visited, they always gave excuses and said no one was around. I was confused at first, but it turns out it was because they couldn't stand him, huh…"

"Speaking of, didn't someone mistake him for Quan Yizhen at the Mid-Autumn Banquet the other day? I saw how upset he was at the time."

Those were undeniable truths, but they led to the wrong conclusion.

"Oh, I know about that incident too. It was pretty awkward, but it still wasn't bad enough to justify harming someone…"

"Yeah, that's a little too small-minded…"

Jian Yu's eyes were going red, and he shouted, "I already said that His Highness had nothing to do with this; I'm the one who committed the crime! I admitted to everything, so what are you all still going on about?!"

But at this point, there was no hope of clearing Yin Yu's name. In the others' eyes, this only proved that Yin Yu had a malicious but loyal subordinate. And one argument alone was enough to shut down all his defenses:

"Well, there was only one person who told Quan Yizhen to 'go die'!"

Things were becoming more and more heated.

"Take them both away," Jun Wu said grimly. "Ling Wen, stay here and watch over Qi Ying."

Ling Wen inclined her head to acknowledge the command, and Jun Wu stalked out of the Palace of Yin Yu with his hands clasped behind him. Several martial officials pulled the heart-stricken Yin Yu to his feet.

"Let it go, Jian Yu. Don't say any more."

Jian Yu was also pulled to his feet and bound with Immortal-Binding rope.

"It's always 'let it go, let it go' with you. This time you absolutely must not let it go!" he cried. "Let it go and you're finished! You'll be banished! You'll be banished for sure!"

But Yin Yu only sighed. "Let it go. If I'm banished, then so be it. Even if I stay here...it doesn't mean anything."

"...You...you should have never ever cursed him," Jian Yu cried bitterly. "Just those two words, and you lost all hope of turning this around! You've never cursed him before, so why did you have to say it now? Of all the times! *Those words!*"

It was like Yin Yu had aged ten years in an instant, and his eyes had lost their light. He seemed a little lost, and he shook his head.

"I don't know why either. At the time, I was just...*sigh*. I don't want to argue anymore."

They started to take him away, but he'd only stumbled a few steps when Jian Yu suddenly cried out.

"*Why?!*"

Everyone turned to look at him.

"It's not like you didn't work as hard!" Jian Yu cried. "You're stronger than him by ten thousandfold, better than him by a millionfold! Quan Yizhen is nothing! So what if I hate him? Why is he like that, and you're like this? Why isn't he the one who gets banished?!"

He gritted his teeth hatefully, hating with every bit of genuine emotion he could muster—so absolutely filled with hate that tears rolled down his cheeks.

There were many times when hard work just wasn't enough. Perhaps he knew that deep down, but he just couldn't accept it, unable to swallow his resentment.

Listening to his cries, Yin Yu couldn't move another step. He buried his face in his hands and slumped to the ground in a heap before the Palace of Yin Yu.

"*Enough!* I already said not to say any more! Please, just let me go!" he yelled. He covered his ears and cried until he was hoarse. "Please stop reminding me over and over—stop talking, *please*, I beg all of you to *stop talking*!"

Xie Lian couldn't bear to watch this any longer. "...That's enough!"

Hua Cheng dispersed the scene, and the two gently separated their heads.

Having been pressed together for so long, Xie Lian's forehead was a little numb, a little itchy, and overly warm. He wanted to reach up and rub at it, but his limbs couldn't move. Hua Cheng seemed to have noticed even this subtle discomfort, and he raised his hand to rub it for him, like it was the most natural thing in the world, before dropping his arm.

Outside the stone wall, the ghost-masked Yin Yu had been pacing back and forth. After a while, he turned to Quan Yizhen.

"You want to come out?" he asked coldly, intentionally disguising his voice.

Quan Yizhen nodded.

"I do."

"Very well. Look here!" Yin Yu replied.

In the blink of an eye, with blinding speed, he whacked the shovel against Quan Yizhen's head!

Clunk! Quan Yizhen instantly fell silent. Xie Lian was stunned.

"No way. He whacked him dead?! He really killed him?!"

Hua Cheng laughed heartily. "Don't worry, gege. He's not dead, just knocked out."

After swinging the shovel, Yin Yu exhaled. In the end, it seemed he decided to dig Quan Yizhen out of the wall after all. He raised the Earth Master Shovel and began to dig through the wall bit by bit. Xie Lian now understood the situation.

If Yin Yu chose to save Quan Yizhen but they ended up fighting, he wouldn't be able to win. He also risked exposing his identity, which would be harrowing. The relationship between the two, shixiong and shidi, was distressing to the extreme, and there was no comparing who was worse off. It was best for Yin Yu to pretend not to know him.

"San Lang, should we also think of a way to get out of here?" Xie Lian said.

Hua Cheng seemed to be enjoying himself where they were. "Hmm? Already?"

Xie Lian didn't know whether to laugh or cry. "Well, yes. Do you want to live in here?"

"If it's with gege, I don't see why not," Hua Cheng said. "All right, fine. I was joking."

He schooled his expression and reached out to cover Xie Lian's ears.

"What are you doing?" Xie Lian asked.

Hua Cheng smiled. "I'm too lazy to walk out, so I might as well just blow the whole place up."

"..."

Xie Lian was just wondering whether this would blow up everyone else who had been swallowed by the mountain spirit when his expression suddenly changed.

"Wait."

Hua Cheng wore the same expression and dropped his hands. The two listened intently.

A moment later, Xie Lian whispered, "Do you hear that?"

Hua Cheng also lowered his voice. "Yes."

On one side of the stone wall, Yin Yu was digging with the Earth Master Shovel. On the other side, there was another person—and they were talking.

There weren't any silver butterflies listening in; they heard the voice directly, because the person in question was standing extremely close to the stone wall, almost pressing against it as he spoke. Xie Lian held his breath to listen but could only hear muffled, intermittent, indistinct words, like *"ate them," "Upper Court," "martial gods."* His mind whirled, and he exchanged a look with Hua Cheng. He then tried, with difficulty, to move closer to the voice.

The voice belonged to a man. He seemed to be conversing with someone, since every time he said something, he paused for a moment. Yet Xie Lian didn't catch any replies from whoever he was speaking with—perhaps because the other one was too far away?

Once they silently shuffled closer, the voice became somewhat clearer. Words were still blurred here and there, but Xie Lian could at least hear some full sentences.

"His Highness the Crown Prince has also come," the man said. "I don't want to take this step; I'm sure you agree. But he's beyond saving."

Xie Lian wondered inwardly, *Me? How am I beyond saving? Wait, this voice...*

The voice was very familiar. He knew he'd heard it somewhere before, and for a long time—not just once or twice. But it was a memory from a long, long time ago, so he couldn't match the voice to its identity that quickly.

Just as he was racking his brain for answers, the man added, "Then let him end here."

And Xie Lian suddenly remembered who the voice belonged to. He twitched his lips and muttered without a sound, *State Preceptor?!*

The person on the other side of the stone wall had the exact same voice as his mentor from the Kingdom of Xianle!

85
Riddle of the Mysterious State Preceptor Confounds Minds

Xie Lian's heart raced wildly, and even his fingertips trembled. However, he remained composed and didn't make a sound, only lifting his head a little to whisper in Hua Cheng's ear.

"...San Lang, don't move. The voice out there sounds a lot like the state preceptor's. Let's not allow ourselves to be discovered..."

It certainly sounded like him, but he couldn't say for sure. There were people in the world who shared similar voices, not to mention that he hadn't seen the state preceptor for centuries, so he could be remembering wrong. There was no need to make any reckless moves right now. If they just quietly observed to see how things progressed, perhaps they would learn more secrets. Hua Cheng bowed his head slightly and hugged Xie Lian's waist.

"All right... You don't move either," he whispered in his ear.

Rocks and earth crushed at them from all around, forcing them to press tightly against one another, their faces nuzzling and their ears warming at the contact. While it was hardly the right time, a thought nonetheless flashed through Xie Lian's mind: *It doesn't feel so bad to share a grave.*

Just then, that voice sounded again. "What about the other two? Where did they go?"

The other two?

Xie Lian's first thought was that he was referring to himself and Hua Cheng and was slightly startled. He wanted to listen closely to find out who exactly the other participant in the conversation was, but there was something quite strange occurring. After the state preceptor—he would address him as this for now—posed the question, there was no response of any kind.

It really was strange. At such a short distance, both Xie Lian and Hua Cheng could hear the state preceptor's questions. His voice wasn't loud, and he wasn't yelling at the top of his lungs, so the other party couldn't be too far away. If that person replied to him, their voice should be audible. And yet there was no response to be heard.

The state preceptor spoke again. "Thank them for their efforts, but there's no need to worry about the small fry anymore; they'll amount to nothing. We have more important things to attend to right now."

It was then that Xie Lian understood that "the other two" did not refer to him and Hua Cheng, but rather the state preceptor's other two companions.

Things were becoming increasingly bizarre. It was clear from the state preceptor's tone that he had received a reply, but it sounded like he was talking to himself or to the air. An eerie idea appeared in Xie Lian's head, but he brushed it off. It was possible that the state preceptor was the only one who could hear the other participant's voice.

Suspicion was growing thicker and thicker in his mind, and he held his breath as he listened more intently. To Xie Lian, every word the state preceptor uttered was more peculiar than the last.

"Is everyone inside the mountain now?" he asked. "Bring them to the Kiln first; I'll think of a way to take care of them individually at that point. The faster, the better. They must get there within two days."

The Kiln! And within two days. The Teleportation Array couldn't be used within Mount Tonglu territory, so how could they get there so quickly? And what was that about "taking care of them"?

After a pause, that voice continued, "Call the other two over. Let's go to the Kiln together. None of us can be missing if we are to face His Highness the Crown Prince. He hasn't fully awakened yet, but if he does…it's hard to imagine what he will do this time."

Xie Lian was stunned. Was the state preceptor talking about him?

Right then, the sounds of explosions echoed throughout the mountain's body. Xie Lian could feel the rocks faintly shuddering all around him. From the outside, the state preceptor asked, "What's going on?"

Inside the stone wall, he turned to Hua Cheng with the same question. "What's going on?"

"Something happened on the other side of the wall," Hua Cheng said, hushed.

The two touched foreheads once more, and the ongoing situation with Yin Yu and Quan Yizhen appeared again in Xie Lian's right eye. It was probably showing him what had happened a few moments ago.

Yin Yu had finally dug Quan Yizhen out of the stone wall, and he panted as he dragged him down. He heaved a sigh. But unexpectedly, the "unconscious" Quan Yizhen suddenly leapt to his feet and yanked the mask off Yin Yu's face!

Quan Yizhen had only pretended to faint!

Now that Xie Lian thought about it, Quan Yizhen would be extremely familiar with Yin Yu's habit of pacing while thinking, the way he spoke, and his strength when he struck. Perhaps he already knew who was behind the mask the moment Yin Yu's shovel swung down. But it was inconceivable that Quan Yizhen even understood how to deceive someone—who would've thought they'd ever see the day? It was the simplest of tricks, but when he used it, it was completely unexpected. No one was prepared.

Underneath the mask was Yin Yu's pale, terrified, obviously shocked face. Quan Yizhen was fiercely thrilled and bounced in place with his head covered in blood.

"Shixiong!"

Yin Yu's lips twisted; he looked like he had seen an indescribable horror. He abruptly clutched his head.

"You've got the wrong person!"

With that roar, he bolted. As he ran, he blasted at the person behind to hamper his pursuit.

"Don't follow me! *Don't follow me!*"

Quan Yizhen dashed after him, completely ignoring the blasts. He only yelled, overjoyed, "Shixiong! It's me!"

Yin Yu couldn't help but roar out an expletive. "Goddammit, it's *because* it's you that I'm terrified! I said, *don't follow me!*"

The two ran and fought the entire way, making the mountain rumble with the blasts. The state preceptor was puzzled.

"What are they doing over there? What's all that ruckus?" There was still no audible answer, but the state preceptor seemed to have gotten a response. "I see. Kids these days, honestly. So energetic. I'll take my leave first; there are still some preparations to be made. Let's reconvene once you're closer to the Kiln."

He was going to leave. Hua Cheng covered Xie Lian's ears anew, and Xie Lian closed his eyes. A moment later, there was a violent tremor from all around, and the stone wall that had been pushing against their bodies was finally blown apart. The two leapt out together, landing lightly on their feet, and breathed fresh air once more.

However, on the outside, there was only an empty cave. There was no state preceptor, nor any mysterious second person, nor any trace of them left behind.

Xie Lian and Hua Cheng exchanged a look. They weren't in any hurry to give chase, and they hadn't yet separated when a black-clad man came charging out of the cave adjacent to them—Yin Yu. He waved the Earth Master Shovel as he dashed madly toward them.

"Chengzhu! Your Highness!"

Quan Yizhen came rushing after him, his head covered in blood from Yin Yu's blows. Hua Cheng didn't bother looking up and only flicked his hand. Quan Yizhen raised both arms to block, but the move Hua Cheng had used couldn't be warded off with fists. Red smoke blasted around Quan Yizhen with a resounding *boom*. After the smoke dispersed, there was only a very round, red budaoweng spinning in place where Quan Yizhen once stood. It looked very innocent thanks to its big, wide eyes.

This was the same trick Hua Cheng had once used on Lang Qianqiu. Only then did Yin Yu stop his crazed flight. He wiped away his cold sweat as he approached.

"I'm eternally grateful, Chengzhu."

"Did you really have to be so scared?" Hua Cheng asked.

Yin Yu was still shaken, and he smiled miserably. "Truth be told, when I see His Highness Qi Ying now, I only want to run as far away as possible."

Xie Lian found that a little funny, but he could sympathize. Quan Yizhen's personality quirks must have severely traumatized Yin Yu. The budaoweng sat on the ground, watching them pathetically with its wide eyes. It swayed heavily back and forth without anyone paying it any mind. Xie Lian felt pity for it and was about to pick it up when he felt the ground shake. He nearly fell over with the tremors—they almost shook harder than that rocking doll.

He quickly steadied himself. "What's going on? Earthquake?"

Although Xie Lian didn't need help, Hua Cheng still held his arm to steady him, then he turned to Yin Yu.

"Go take a look outside."

Yin Yu recovered quickly and acknowledged the command. "Yes, sir!"

Then he picked up the Earth Master Shovel and rapidly and cleanly dug a hole. Sunlight shone through from the outside. When Yin Yu took a look, surprise filled his face.

"Your Highness Yin Yu, is it an earthquake, or is the mountain collapsing?" Xie Lian asked.

"It's neither!" Yin Yu answered. "The mountain spirit... It's running!"

Running? Xie Lian and Hua Cheng exchanged a look, then both ran over to look outside the mountain spirit. They were rendered speechless by the sight that greeted them.

It really was running!

Outside the mountain's body, the scenery was whizzing rapidly past, reduced to nothing but colorful streaks. It was like they were riding a speeding carriage pulled by galloping horses or sitting on the shoulders of a giant as it ran wild!

Hills, rivers, clearings, forests—they were all trampled beneath the mountain spirit's feet, crushed to make way. Whooshing winds whirled in from the hole, and their hair and belt ties began to dance with them.

"At this speed, it'll probably only take two days to reach the Kiln..." Yin Yu remarked.

Two days? Hearing this, it dawned on Xie Lian.

No wonder! No wonder they couldn't hear any responses to the state preceptor's one-sided conversation, and no wonder the state preceptor asked that they be brought to the Kiln impossibly quickly.

Because all that time, the state preceptor wasn't talking to another human—he was talking to the mountain spirit!

Hua Cheng must've also figured it out. "Just as well. By borrowing its strength, we won't need to move so slowly anymore. He said they would reconvene at Mount Tonglu. We'll know what he wants once we're there."

However, Xie Lian looked somber, and Hua Cheng noticed.

"Gege, what's wrong?" he asked.

"What did he mean, 'hasn't awakened yet'?" Xie Lian asked.

That voice from earlier had said, *"He hasn't fully awakened yet, but if he does…it's hard to imagine what he will do this time."*

"If that man really was my master, and he was talking about me, then what did he mean by all that?" Xie Lian said.

"Gege, don't think too much right now," Hua Cheng said. "That man might not be your master, and the crown prince he spoke of might not be you. Don't forget, the Crown Prince of Wuyong is also a royal highness."

"But if it was?" Xie Lian urged. "I have some hunches. Will you hear me out and see if they make sense?"

"Very well. Gege, do tell," Hua Cheng said.

"There are three great mountains within Mount Tonglu territory: Old Age, Sickness, and Death. Birth is the only one missing," Xie Lian began. "If that man really is my master, and the one he was talking to is a mountain spirit, and he has the ability to communicate with mountain spirits, then it's possible that when he mentioned 'the other two,' he was referring to the other mountain spirits."

"I agree. And?" Hua Cheng said.

"And I wonder if the three mountain spirits possess human consciousnesses," Xie Lian continued. "Or perhaps they were originally transformed from humans. Why is there no Birth? Because Birth has yet to materialize as a mountain. Birth is still a person, and that person...is the state preceptor!"

The more he thought, the more he felt it made sense. With his heart racing in his chest, he continued.

"Mount Tonglu used to be part of the Kingdom of Wuyong. Birth, Old Age, Sickness, Death, they're a set of four; the Crown Prince of Wuyong also had four guardians. Coincidentally, there were also four state preceptors who taught me when I was growing up in Xianle—one chief and three deputies! Do kingdoms typically have so many state preceptors? I didn't think anything of it in the past, but now I realize there normally aren't so many. Do you think this is a coincidence? Or are they all connected somehow?"

"It could easily be a coincidence," Hua Cheng replied. "Aren't there four Famous Tales? And when there weren't four Calamities, one more had to be forced into their ranks."

"For some reason, I have a strong feeling," Xie Lian said. "Birth, Old Age, Sickness, Death. The four guardian deputies of Wuyong and the four state preceptors of Xianle... Perhaps they're all the same people."

Xie Lian followed along with this train of thought. "But if it's true that my four masters were the four Guardian Deputies of the Crown Prince of Wuyong, why did they come to Xianle to become state preceptors? Why did they come to teach me? Why did Master tell me the story of the Crown Prince of Wuyong? Why did he say he wanted me to become someone like that prince? Is there something about me that I wasn't even aware of? What did he mean when he said that I'm not yet awakened? Could I actually be..."

He was rambling like someone possessed. Hua Cheng gripped his shoulders as he assured him with conviction.

"It's not possible! I can swear that you are you. You're no one else. Trust me. Don't read too much into this and imagine things that aren't real."

It was then that Xie Lian came to his senses. "...You're right. I'm letting my mind run a little wild..."

After his own parents, the state preceptor was the person Xie Lian knew best. While the state preceptor often scolded him for not listening and was often reserved due to Xie Lian's position, he was a good teacher overall. It confounded the heart to so suddenly discover that someone he thought he knew was something so terribly foreign.

Moreover, there was another point—they were too similar. While the temple murals' story was not yet complete, the experiences of the Crown Prince of Wuyong depicted upon them gave him a vague but terrifying sense of reincarnation.

Hua Cheng's tone softened. "But, gege, think carefully. What was the State Preceptor of Xianle's background?"

Xie Lian mulled over the question. "...I'm not sure."

It was true. He couldn't remember where his master came from.

After a moment of contemplation, Xie Lian said, "The state preceptor had held that position since before my birth. I only know that he was called Mei Nianqing, but needless to say, that must be a false name. I thought this many times: Master is such an incredible individual, so why hasn't he ascended? If that really was him just now, then he's spent many more years in this world than I have. If he wants to deal with us..."

"It's all right. Who cares if he's been alive longer?" Hua Cheng said with nonchalance. "No matter what he is, we'll take care of things as they come. Remember that if anything happens, I'm here. I will always be on your side."

Xie Lian was a little stunned by that.

Yin Yu's presence was already faint, and since he hadn't spoken this whole time, he had practically been forgotten. Only now did he speak up. "Chengzhu, do we need to go find the others?"

They'd gotten out of the wall, but Pei Ming and the others had been swallowed too—who knew in which hidden corner they were being digested by the mountain spirit?

"Yes! Let's go find them together," Xie Lian quickly replied. "Please wait, Your Highness Yin Yu."

"Your Highness, there's no need to call me Your Highness... I haven't been a heavenly official of the Upper Court for a long time now," Yin Yu said.

Xie Lian smiled. "Then you can just call me by my name as well; no need to be so polite. I also haven't been a crown prince in a long time."

Yin Yu glanced at Hua Cheng, who was standing behind Xie Lian. "I...daren't," he hastily replied. "I shouldn't. I can't."

"What's the concern?" Xie Lian asked.

He took a couple of steps forward to pick up Quan Yizhen the budaoweng when a figure suddenly dropped from the ceiling and landed heavily before him. The sound of bones cracking was loud and crisp in the air.

Xie Lian's first reaction was to reach for Fangxin and strike. It was fortunate that he had good martial habits; he looked before he struck and forced himself to halt mid-swing.

"General Pei?"

The man—indeed Pei Ming—flipped over and leapt to his feet. He dusted off his shoulders, looking amazingly at ease, and glanced at them.

"Looks like His Highness and My Lord Ghost King have been enjoying themselves here."

"We're not too bad, not too bad," Xie Lian said. "But, General Pei, are you all right? I thought I heard a cracking sound…"

"Oh, that was nothing," Pei Ming said. "Though I appreciate Your Highness's concern. That cracking sound wasn't from my own bones but from this one."

He raised an object, and it was the femur of that unlucky man; the bone was bent out of shape.

"It was this good brother's help that allowed me to dig a path to safety through this mountain spirit's body," he added. "Even though it's a man's bone, he's a solid, good man."

Just as he finished, a second figure dropped from the ceiling not far away, also crashing in heavily. The group of them walked over to see, and this time it was Pei Xiu. He was shielding Banyue in the cradle of his arms, and Banyue was holding the two black clay pots that contained Kemo and Rong Guang. The two of them were ashen-faced and disheveled, but they didn't seem to have any serious injuries, and they quickly crawled upright.

Pei Xiu spat out a few mouthfuls of dust. "Gen, eral! Your High, ness."

"Looks like the mountain spirit didn't think we were tasty enough and spat us out," Pei Ming commented.

Hua Cheng and Xie Lian exchanged a look.

"Not necessarily," Xie Lian said quietly. "Perhaps someone told it to spit you out."

Pei Ming took a few steps and noticed the unusual tremors

shaking the ground, and he furrowed his brows. "What's with this mountain? Why is it shaking so hard?"

"Because it's currently running, carrying us toward the Kiln," Xie Lian replied.

Pei Ming walked to the hole Yin Yu had dug and glanced outside. "So fast! Excellent. That'll save us some walking."

However, there was still one person missing.

"Where's Ling Wen?" Xie Lian asked.

Hua Cheng used his right eye to take a look. "The silver butterfly on his back was swallowed by the mountain spirit. He's gone."

Which meant that Ling Wen and the Brocade Immortal could now move as they wished. That was no laughing matter.

"Let's go find him!" Xie Lian hurriedly exclaimed.

Thus, the group started running around once more inside the body of the mountain spirit. Hua Cheng released nearly a hundred wraith butterflies to conduct a search, and in the end, it led them to another hole.

This hole had been forcibly blown out of the mountain, its edges jagged. Beyond it, they could see the landscape flying by. Wild winds were flung into the mountain's body, making howling, demonic-sounding cries. After Ling Wen was spat out by the mountain spirit, he probably made this hole for his subsequent escape. Peering down from the edge of the hole, Xie Lian frowned.

"What should we do now? The Brocade Immortal's destructive power is too strong; we can't just leave it be."

"Don't worry," Hua Cheng said. "He's heading for the Kiln too. We're just taking different paths to the same destination."

Once everyone gathered around, Xie Lian briefly gave an account of what he had overheard earlier, although he left out some fine details. After he was done, they all sat down to let their minds drift.

There weren't any monsters to fight right now, and they didn't even need to make the journey themselves, so this downtime was rather boring.

Since Yin Yu said he really didn't know how to communicate with Quan Yizhen and just seeing his face gave him a headache, Xie Lian felt it wouldn't be wise to release him—so he was temporarily kept in budaoweng form. Pei Ming was bored, so he continued to play with the doll by slapping it down.

Xie Lian saw how heavily the doll was wobbling, like a little kid being physically abused, and felt sorry for it. He softly cleared his throat, then chided, "General Pei, please stop playing around."

Pei Ming briefly complied, but when Xie Lian grew drowsy and dozed off leaning against the mountain wall, with no one to stop him, he started slapping at it again. Yin Yu, who was guarding the hole and keeping track of how much distance had been traveled, watched this from nearby. He kept looking like he wanted to say something, but he stopped himself in the end. And yet, tragedies are born in the midst of extreme joy. Pei Ming's slapping session was interrupted by a sudden *thud*—Pei Xiu had keeled over. Since Pei Xiu was his blood descendant, Pei Ming instantly forgot all about playing and grabbed him.

"Little Pei? What's wrong?!"

Yin Yu took this chance to quietly walk over and pick up the budaoweng, then set it down next to Xie Lian.

Hua Cheng was annoyed. "What's with all the noise? He's not going to die. Can't you see His Highness is asleep?"

Sure enough, Xie Lian was roused. He groggily realized he'd somehow ended up leaning against someone's shoulder when Hua Cheng's voice sounded right next to his ear.

"Gege is awake?"

Xie Lian rubbed his eyes. The budaoweng Quan Yizhen was swaying back and forth next to him, so he quietly tucked it away. "I fell asleep on you? Sorry about that... What's going on?"

"It's nothing," Hua Cheng replied, looking calm and composed. "If you're sleepy, you can take another nap. We'll be there soon enough."

Across from them, Pei Ming was violently shaking Pei Xiu by the collar. The sight shocked Xie Lian a little, and he was now quite awake. Thinking something was wrong, he went over to try to help.

Once he finished his examination, he said, "Oh, don't worry, General Pei. General Pei Junior is just overwhelmed by fatigue and hunger at the moment."

Pei Xiu was mortal right now, after all. He'd been struggling all this time without food and water, and he didn't have Xie Lian's wealth of experience with starvation and beatings. He couldn't hang on anymore and had finally collapsed.

Pei Ming had a bone to pick with the way Xie Lian had described it so offhandedly. "What do you mean by 'just overwhelmed by fatigue and hunger at the moment'?"

That couldn't be helped. He didn't like to brag, but Xie Lian could go three days on one meal, and he could get beaten down ten times and be back on his feet and collecting scraps like nothing happened. What other heavenly official had more experience with this?

"Umm." Xie Lian coughed. "Does anyone have anything to eat?"

No one responded. Banyue took out a pot.

"I'm sorry, but I only have this..."

The moment that Pei Ming saw it was the pot of Toppled Phoenixes, he yelled, "Why are you still holding on to that thing?! Who are you trying to kill? Throw it out, now!"

While they were getting noisy and rowdy, Hua Cheng turned to Xie Lian.

"See, I told you it was nothing. So why not take another nap?"

The mountain spirit had been running the whole day with them on its back, and Xie Lian could see that the sky was turning dark outside.

"How far have we traveled now? How much longer until we reach Mount Tonglu?"

"We've run nearly four hundred kilometers," Yin Yu answered.

That was definitely much faster than walking. Xie Lian rose to his feet and approached the edge of the hole where Yin Yu had been keeping watch. He was only going to take a casual look, but when his eyes swept over their surroundings, he saw something that made his hair stand on end.

"What's that?"

Looking down from the mountain spirit, through the darkness of the night, he could see a giant human face on the ground below!

The face had closed eyes that curved into crescents, and its lips curled upward in an eerie smile. Xie Lian took a step back in spite of himself; Hua Cheng caught him from behind as he did. After pulling himself together, he took a closer look. As it turned out, that "face" was merely an image formed by hills and ravines—an optical illusion. However, the illusion looked very real, and it was a shocking sight when caught in a passing glance.

"What's that gully that resembles eyes and a mouth?" Xie Lian wondered.

"That's the Wuyong River. It was called the 'Mother River' by the people of the kingdom," Hua Cheng replied. "Its source was in the high mountains, and melting snow from the mountaintops supplied its waters. Of course, it's completely dried out now. But if we've reached this area, it means we're very close to Mount Tonglu."

Xie Lian nodded. "Then the 'nose'?"

"A bustling city on the shores of the Wuyong River," Hua Cheng answered. "Wanna go down and see?"

Xie Lian inclined his head. "Is there anything worth seeing down there?"

"There's another Holy Temple of Wuyong in the city," Hua Cheng said. "I imagine gege might want to go check it out."

If there was a temple, then there might be another mural.

"Let's go!" Xie Lian immediately said, eager to learn more about the Crown Prince of Wuyong.

Pei Ming chimed in.

"Let's go! We have to find some food and water for Little Pei. How do we get down, though? My sword's broken again."

Hua Cheng waved, and silver butterflies appeared around each of them in a flurry of shimmering light. They rested on their shoulders, backs, heads, and sleeves. Anyone else who saw these little silver butterflies might grumble and question whether they could possibly bring them anywhere, but Xie Lian didn't say a word before releasing Ruoye and tying everyone together so they wouldn't lose each other mid-flight. Yin Yu widened the hole to allow at least five or six people to go through at the same time. Preparations complete, Xie Lian and company stepped toward the edge of the hole.

"Everyone, get ready—"

"Wait," Pei Ming called out.

Xie Lian turned to look. "General Pei, is something the matter?"

"What's that on your hands?" Pei Ming asked.

Following his gaze, Xie Lian looked down at his hand. Only then did he realize that his and Hua Cheng's fingers were still connected by the red string.

"..." Xie Lian softly cleared his throat. "Th-this is...a spiritual device, of sorts. For keeping in contact."

"Oh," Pei Ming said. "Doesn't it make moving around difficult? It's a string, after all. What if you trip on it or it gets tangled on something? Accidents might happen."

His comment made a lot of sense. A martial god should never allow anything to hamper their movement; it wasn't as if Xie Lian didn't know that. But for some mysterious reason, Xie Lian really didn't want to cut the string. Seeing the hesitant expression on his face—like he was caught in some internal struggle—Hua Cheng looked at the red string and chuckled.

"It certainly is a little inconvenient like this."

Xie Lian saw the red string disappear between them.

"Now it's much more practical," Hua Cheng said.

Xie Lian stared at the empty air where that red string had once been, a little dumbfounded. It had only connected them for a short while, and now it was gone. This wasn't a big deal—really, it was extremely minuscule—but he was still a little forlorn. Afraid someone would notice, Xie Lian quickly squeezed out a smile.

"Let's go! Ready...*jump!*"

The mountain spirit was still charging forward and didn't notice that little people the size of grasshoppers had surreptitiously leapt from its body. Enveloped by a circle of wraith butterflies, the whole group landed light as feathers, not a hair on their heads harmed. They had landed on the bridge of the "nose" of that giant smiling face.

After straightening up, Xie Lian scanned the area, perplexed.

"San Lang, is there a Wuyong temple and city here?"

"Yes," Hua Cheng said.

"But...there's nothing around," Xie Lian remarked.

It was true. He had thought that when they landed on the ground, he would see the same small-town sights that had surrounded the first holy temple—streets, shops, residences, wells, temples, and so on. But before him now was an open clearing, empty and barren, without a trace that a city had ever existed. Pei Ming was holding Pei Xiu upright, and he propped up one leg on a boulder.

"Where's this 'bustling city'?"

"Under your feet," Hua Cheng said.

"What?"

The group crowded around, studying the boulder under Pei Ming's foot.

"Is there some sort of secret mechanism?" Xie Lian asked.

Hua Cheng put his hand on the hilt of his scimitar and walked over. "Come, come, come. Stand here."

The others did as he said. He pulled out the scimitar Eming, aimed the tip downward, and stabbed the ground right next to the boulder with a strike as fast as lightning. The tip of the blade pierced the earth. There was a cracking sound, and small, cobweb-like fractures spread outward rapidly. The cracks grew bigger and bigger, the fissures deeper and deeper. Finally, the entire section of the ground caved in with a *boom*, revealing a chillingly dark hole.

Hua Cheng jumped in first. Xie Lian hadn't realized he would take the first leap, and he dove for the edge of the hole.

"San Lang?!"

Hua Cheng's voice came from below a moment later. "Everything's fine down here. You can come down now."

It turned out he'd gone down first to scout. Xie Lian sighed a breath of relief and immediately jumped in as well. Hua Cheng reached for Xie Lian's hand and pulled him upright.

"It's so dark in here," Xie Lian noted.

He had just spoken when several silver butterflies lit up the darkness, dancing languidly in the air as shimmering specks of light.

A number of ghost fires also appeared to illuminate the deeper parts of the hole.

What appeared before them was a long street. A thousand years ago, this would've been a bustling place, packed full of shops and large buildings. The boulder that Pei Ming had stepped on was the roof of one of those very buildings.

The others jumped down one by one as well.

Xie Lian looked up.

"I see. So this city was buried? Buried by what? Earthquake? Landslide? Or…"

"Volcanic ash," Hua Cheng said.

Xie Lian quickly turned to look at him.

"The entire city was buried beneath volcanic ash about seven meters thick," Hua Cheng specified. "What you see right now is a portion that was dug out by nefarious creatures who came to Mount Tonglu for past trials. There's still more of it buried deep within the ash."

Xie Lian instantly thought of the mural inside the second Divine Temple; its vivid red glare seemed to materialize before his eyes again. This meant that the apocalypse foretold by the Crown Prince of Wuyong's dream had really come true!

Pei Ming set Pei Xiu down on the roadside. "Never mind all that for now. Is there water? A few sips of water would be good for him."

"The river on the surface has long since dried up, though I recall that there's water in the deeper parts of the city underground. Let's see if we have any luck finding it," Hua Cheng said.

Thus, Pei Ming, Banyue, and Yin Yu left to go find water. Xie Lian was still deep in thought when Hua Cheng walked over.

"Gege, look at your hand."

Xie Lian automatically did as he asked. When he raised his hand, he saw that the bright red knot on his third finger—personally fastened by Hua Cheng—was still there, even though the red string connecting the two of them was gone. It was like a tiny red butterfly had perched on the back of his hand.

Hua Cheng had explained that if the red string between them broke, the knot would disappear. Xie Lian couldn't help but blurt out a noise of surprise.

"This..."

Seeing him stunned, Hua Cheng smiled.

"Just a little camouflage spell, that's all. The red string is hidden. The distance is unlimited and you don't have to worry about tripping over it, but it wasn't actually broken." He raised his own hand to show Xie Lian an identical knot. "As long as the affinity knot is still there, the person on the other end of the red string is safe. Things will only get more dangerous as we approach the Kiln, and we don't yet know what's ahead of us. So I thought untying the red string would be a bad idea. What does gege say?"

Upon learning that the red string was still there, Xie Lian's lips curved upward in spite of himself—but he straightened his expression the moment he noticed and replied very seriously.

"Oh, yes. With this, we'll both know whether the other is safe at all times. Excellent. It's a very practical spell."

Hua Cheng also flashed a smile, though it quickly disappeared. "But Your Highness, there's something I must say, and I hope you'll listen."

Seeing him suddenly turn solemn, Xie Lian grew solemn as well. "What is it? Go ahead."

Hua Cheng gazed into his eyes. "I know you can't die, and that you aren't afraid to die. But no matter how tough you are, remember that you can still get hurt."

Xie Lian was stunned.

"Not dying doesn't mean not getting hurt," Hua Cheng continued, "and it certainly doesn't mean that it *doesn't* hurt. When you see something strange or dangerous, don't touch it. Find me. Let me take care of it."

When he had touched those skulls covered in corpse poison, Xie Lian remembered Hua Cheng's expression turning dark in a flash. Could this be why Hua Cheng was so angry? Just because Xie Lian had nonchalantly picked up something dangerous?

If that were truly the case, then he really didn't know what to say. It took him a moment to reply.

"All right... I won't do that anymore."

His answer sounded sincere, and that seemed to satisfy Hua Cheng. He nodded and was about to turn and continue onward when Xie Lian called out.

"San Lang, wait!"

Hua Cheng stopped and looked back.

Xie Lian chewed on his words before he finally, arduously squeezed out a quiet request. "You...you too. If there's something dangerous, I won't touch it, but you don't touch it either. Neither of us will touch it. All right?"

One side of Hua Cheng's mouth quirked up. Once he said it, Xie Lian was a little nervous and unconsciously let out a laugh, only to see Hua Cheng take a step closer. He was just about to speak when they heard Pei Ming's voice from not too far away.

"What is this?"

"They look like people," Banyue said.

"Indeed!" Pei Ming remarked. "But how could people turn into something like this?"

Hua Cheng and Xie Lian exchanged a look and walked toward their voices.

"Turn into what?" Xie Lian asked.

86
Saint Born Under the Ominous Star

PEI MING AND COMPANY had entered the yard of a residence, probably in search of a well.

Xie Lian followed after them and commented offhandedly, "The houses on this street are all so big and impressive."

"Mount Tonglu is situated in the imperial capital, at the heart of the Kingdom of Wuyong," Hua Cheng replied. "This place is close to the mountain—or rather, close to what used to be the imperial capital two thousand years ago—so it was once a wealthy area. Since mostly prominent figures and government officials lived here, the homes are naturally impressive."

There was, in fact, a well there, but the sight near that well was horrifying. There were seven or eight people sprawled over the edge, as if they had been dying of thirst but perished after struggling to make it there. Upon closer inspection, Xie Lian blinked.

"This... I wouldn't call them people—they're more like stone statues?"

They weren't live humans, of course, but they weren't corpses either, and they definitely weren't skeletons. They were coarsely made, ash-white stone statues. Xie Lian was about to reach out and touch when Hua Cheng gave him a look. He immediately remembered that they had just promised each other that they wouldn't touch anything strange or dangerous, so he forced down the impulse.

Thinking about it, who in the world would sculpt so many terrifying statues? They had to be people, but they had been transformed into this state for reasons unknown.

The front doors of the residence were wide open. Xie Lian looked inside the house and saw that there were two more people lying on the ground, their forms twisted into a tight embrace. While their faces were blurred and their expressions were unclear, judging by the pose, one could sense that terror had filled their hearts. There was a bundle between them that they were hugging tightly; on closer inspection, Xie Lian realized that it must've been a baby.

What had happened was more than clear.

"The ones outside were the household's servants, and the ones inside were most likely the master's family of three," Xie Lian said.

"Mmm," Hua Cheng said. "After the volcano erupted, the Wuyong River ran with lava. The citizens who lived on high ground weren't burned to death by the lava or blazing fires, but they couldn't escape the blanket of volcanic ash and died of suffocation."

The volcanic ash had enveloped their entire bodies in an instant and formed a hard shell, preserving their last moments and transforming them into stone statues. At the very instant their lives ended, this husband and wife had fearfully embraced each other and their child, and had thus become one in death.

The old well had long since dried out, of course. Pei Ming wasn't interested in studying the faces of the dead, so carrying Pei Xiu with him, he left to continue the search for water.

Suddenly, Xie Lian noticed something strange. He leaped into the house and crouched next to the stone bodies of the family.

Hua Cheng entered as well. "What did you want to see?"

Xie Lian slightly furrowed his brows. "I just think their positions are a bit strange. The two adults are holding each other tightly with one arm, but the other arm…"

Their other arms were tucked against their chests, like they were gripping firmly onto something.

"You want to see what's in their hands?" Hua Cheng asked.

Xie Lian had barely nodded when Hua Cheng tapped once on the joined stone statues.

"Wait, isn't this disrespectful to their remai—" Xie Lian exclaimed.

But Hua Cheng moved faster than he did, and the family of three broke into a pile of shattered ash-white shards.

"No need to be too concerned," Hua Cheng said evenly. "They're long dead. Their remains are already gone."

There was nothing left in the shattered shells. The "stone statues" were hollow on the inside.

Although the volcanic ash formed a solid protective cocoon, the corpses sealed inside still decayed and broke down. And after the rotting was done, only the ash husk remained.

All that once lived would eventually pass away, leaving behind only that which had never lived at all.

Amidst the shattered ashen pieces that had scattered across the ground, there were some pieces of cloth that had not yet fully rotted through. The jewelry and accessories had also remained intact—rings, earrings, necklaces, and so on. Xie Lian highly doubted that this couple was clutching jewelry in the face of death, and he was picking through the pieces when Hua Cheng plucked something from the pile and handed it to him.

"What's this?" Xie Lian asked.

"It's what they were clutching in their hands," Hua Cheng said.

It was a pendant—a shimmering golden plate and something that resembled bone were hanging off of the chain. Patterns were engraved on the golden plate, and Xie Lian lightly dusted off the ash on its surface to examine the details.

"The Ominous Star?"[7]

A celestial drawing was etched on the golden plate—the gold represented the heavens, and inlaid agate represented the stars. The stars were laid out in a very particular pattern, depicting the sign of the Ominous Star, the celestial phase in which the Star of Glowing Befuddlement stays motionless in the Heart Constellation.

The Star of Glowing Befuddlement had historically been seen as the Star of War and Death. And when it rested within the Heart Constellation, it was an even more ominous sign, especially toward rulers and emperors and other such leaders. Why was a celestial drawing like that engraved on an accessory?

No, this couldn't have been an accessory... Xie Lian fumbled through the ash shards again and found two more identical pendants. There were three in total; even the baby in the couple's arms had one. Under what circumstances would the same accessory be purchased three times...?

"This isn't a protection charm, is it?" Xie Lian wondered.

Only a protection charm would be gripped tightly by those teetering on the brink of death, prayed over frantically in a last grasp at hope in the face of terror.

---

[7] [荧惑守心] "The Star of Glowing Befuddlement Resting in the Heart Constellation," or "the Ominous Star" in this translation. Ancient Chinese astrologers believed Mars was unstable in both position and light, thus they called it the "Star of Glowing Befuddlement." It symbolized ruin, pestilence, death, famine, war, and other such bad omens. The Heart Constellation sits in the east, and its three main stars symbolize the Crown Prince, the Emperor, and the Commoner. Thus, when Mars enters the Heart Constellation, it is often interpreted as foretelling major changes in politics and dynasties, or the fall of greatness.

"It is," Hua Cheng said. "I've dug through parts of this city in the past, and I discovered this same protection charm on quite a number of statues."

Xie Lian hummed. "The people of Wuyong worshipped their crown prince, so this should be his protection charm. But why draw this particular celestial phase on it? Does the crown prince have any connection to the Ominous Star?"

"He was born under the celestial phase of the Ominous Star," Hua Cheng said. "The people of Wuyong used it to symbolize him."

"How did San Lang find this out?" Xie Lian asked.

Hua Cheng flipped the gold plate over. "It's written on this."

Sure enough, there was a line of engraved characters on the back, which Hua Cheng translated for him.

"These words mean 'Saint Born Under the Ominous Star.' In recent times, the Star of Glowing Befuddlement resting in the Heart Constellation is a grave omen, but things might have been different two thousand years ago."

Xie Lian mulled over those words, his heart slowly sinking—for he was also born under that very same celestial phase: the sign of the Ominous Star!

Wasn't this too much of a coincidence?

He rose to his feet. "Let's go to the holy temple."

The two walked down the long street side by side. Pei Ming and the others hadn't had any luck in their search of the area, so they followed along as well. The remnants of many carriages were strewn across the streets—some rested by the roadside, others were completely overturned. There were also more stone people scattered on the ground in various poses. Most citizens had run back to their residences to escape the disaster, so the ones on the street were likely homeless beggars or travelers who couldn't make it home in time—their cries and struggles in the moment before death were preserved. The group traversed this strange, grotesque display.

Hua Cheng pointed out to Xie Lian which homes were the residences of wealthy merchants and which ones belonged to the entertainment district. Xie Lian couldn't help but ask after this knowledge of his.

"San Lang, the Kingdom of Wuyong fell over two thousand years ago; none of its descendants remain. How did you learn to read their script?"

He couldn't have just forced his way in from nothing; there must have been a door to his method.

"It wasn't too difficult," Hua Cheng said. "As gege can see, some Wuyong characters are very close to today's characters."

"That's true," Xie Lian said. "The two characters that make up the word 'Wuyong' are indeed very close to how one would write it today."

"Right. So those two characters were the first Wuyong script I learned," Hua Cheng explained. "There are a few more like this, and when they are mixed into a given phrase together, the other words can be determined from context. There are some that use a familiar character but give it a different meaning—that's not too common, though."

Xie Lian nodded, and Hua Cheng continued.

"And then there are words that show up more frequently. Like those two."

He pointed at two buildings on the street.

"It's obvious what those places are. The words on the signs have different beginning characters but the same ending characters. Therefore, one can easily deduce the meaning of the ending words:

they're either taverns or restaurants. And there are many similar methods. If gege wants to know more, I'll tell you all about it when there's time."

So that was it. There were actually people in this world who could figure anything out through their own power, without any help—Xie Lian couldn't help but be awed.

The holy temple of Wuyong was still the grandest and most impressive building in the city. The party arrived at the temple, but before they entered, Pei Ming spoke up.

"What's that noise?"

Squeak, squeak, squeak. Squeak, squeak, squeak. The noise echoed from afar, then dispersed.

"Rats?" Xie Lian wondered.

"Not your typical rats. But if there are rats, that means there's water nearby," Hua Cheng said.

When they entered the temple, there was no burnt material on the walls this time. They could see the vibrant colors of the immense mural simply by raising their heads. However, there wasn't just one mural, but murals left, center, and right—a set of three! There was a mural on each of the walls!

The group stood before the first mural and looked up. The Crown Prince of Wuyong was sitting upon the clouds with golden light shining around him. However, his expression was severe. In his left hand there was a ball of light, and within its glow was a small mountain spewing flame. The fingers of his right hand were pressed together, the palm facing outward, seemingly waving in dismissal.

A palace was depicted below, and over a dozen people stood within. Their attire and accessories were incomparably lavish, and each was making unique gestures. Some had their arms wide open, some were wearing armor and carrying bows, and some were pointing into the far distance with agitated expressions.

The details of the mural were complex and abundant with information. Xie Lian studied it for a good while before turning his head.

"May I tell you what I've gathered from this painting?

"The ball of light held in the Crown Prince of Wuyong's left hand contains a small volcanic eruption, indicating that he told his dream to those down below. As for the gesture made with his right hand, it's obviously one of negation; he must be rejecting something."

"What is he rejecting?" Pei Ming asked.

"That we find out from the actions of the people below," Xie Lian replied. "This palace is situated in the Mortal Realm. It's magnificent, so it's likely the royal palace. These people must be the royalty and nobility of Wuyong. Look at this one with his arms wide open—it seems he's making a gesture for 'expand.' But expand what? We learn this by looking at what's in his hand."

The group looked closer. The man held a map, and Pei Ming was more than familiar with what that meant.

"Expand territory!"

"Yes," Xie Lian said. "And these generals are dressed in armor, looking ready to be dispatched into battle. There are others to the side pointing the way. Look, their directions are very obvious—it's like they're saying 'go there, fight there.'

"With this information, the meaning of this mural becomes easy to understand. To roughly summarize: It seems the Crown Prince of Wuyong told his prophetic dream to the ministers inside the royal court. Once the volcano erupted, the consequences would be severe; it would be a disaster that could bring ruin to the Kingdom of Wuyong. The kingdom's territory wasn't big enough because the volcano was situated right at its center; all of its important cities would perish. So how could this be solved?"

"If their own territory wasn't big enough, take over someone else's," Hua Cheng said.

"Right," Xie Lian said. "The ministers suggested opening up the borders and invading neighboring countries. However, the Crown Prince of Wuyong didn't agree with this method, which is why his right hand is in a gesture of rejection."

After analyzing the first mural, the group moved to the second. The colors of this mural were much gloomier than the one previous—perhaps because it depicted a scene of slaughter and war.

Blood flowed like rivers through the battlefield, and the soldiers on both sides killed relentlessly. Xie Lian could tell which side was Wuyong, since their soldiers' armor was the same as that of the generals from the previous mural. The Wuyong soldiers looked savage and aggressive, trampling the heads of their enemies under their feet, raising corpses up on their halberds. Arms and legs and flesh flew, the scene bloody and cruel. There were soldiers who wore savage smiles as they reached for cowering women and children. The horrors of war.

Thick clouds of gloom blanketed the skies above the battlefield, yet from within peeked a sliver of white light. Half of the Crown Prince of Wuyong could be seen through the clouds, and he was watching the scene below. His expression was that of fury. One of his arms was extended, and his palm released many pillars of golden light. The Wuyong soldiers touched by the light were being sucked upward.

This painting's meaning was easier to analyze than the previous one. Xie Lian studied it for a moment.

"It seems the generals and ministers didn't listen to the crown prince's advice and dispatched armies to invade neighboring countries," he said softly. "The soldiers killed indiscriminately and excessively. They even harassed women, children, the weak, and the old. When the crown prince found out, he was furious, and he put an end to the Wuyong soldiers' aggression."

"How touching," Pei Ming said flatly in response to his interpretation. "But to be frank, if one kingdom must perish, then they can't be blamed for choosing to protect their own land's future. If the soldiers on the front lines didn't die at the hands of their enemies, they probably died from the rage of their own crown prince—or their own rage at him. I certainly wouldn't want to fight for someone like that."

Xie Lian gave a dry chuckle and said a little woefully, "General Pei is, uh, quite right."

Hua Cheng only snorted at the comment.

"So the volcano's about to erupt. What does This Highness the Crown Prince plan to do?" Pei Ming continued. "He can't just leave his own people to wait for their deaths."

"Let's look at the third mural," Xie Lian said. "It should have the answer."

The group finally came to the last mural. The colors were again in enormous contrast to those of the last mural; this image returned to bright, vibrant tones and was filled with holy light. But with only one glance, Xie Lian was shocked to the core. His eyes went wide.

Pei Ming observed the piece. "My god, is this the idea the Crown Prince of Wuyong came up with? Ha! Daring. Worthy of admiration."

At the bottom of the third mural was the Kingdom of Wuyong. The Wuyong River wound across the earth. The crown prince and his four guardian deputies were also depicted. But none of that was the focal point of the piece—the most prominent object was a bridge at its center.

The Crown Prince of Wuyong and his four guardians were holding up a massive bridge that radiated white light. The people on the ground were swarming toward the bridge with smiles on their faces.

The Crown Prince of Wuyong had built a bridge that connected the heavens and earth to bring his people to the Heavenly Realm!

Xie Lian was struck speechless by what he saw.

"Is that possible?" Pei Ming wondered.

"Why not?" Hua Cheng countered.

Everyone looked to him, and Hua Cheng continued.

"Isn't appointing a general just bringing a mortal to the Heavenly Realm? He's simply taking everyone near the royal capital to the heavens temporarily, then sending them back once the disaster is over. Why couldn't he do that?"

"Crimson Rain Sought Flower, please don't make it sound so easy," Pei Ming said. "My Lord should know that it takes spiritual power to appoint generals. And he's appointing *how* many with such a feat?"

In reality, appointing a general was nothing more than using one's spiritual power to keep a mortal in the heavens, who would then have to labor in their service. If there were no restrictions, what would stop a heavenly official from appointing all the people they wanted? An emperor might as well bring up his full harem and court; a general might as well appoint his entire army.

"Judging by the relics left behind, the Kingdom of Wuyong had a population of only a few hundred thousand. And some tens of thousands lived in the vicinity of the royal capital."

"While it would be tough...it's possible. Though just barely," Xie Lian said quietly.

"Even if it's *only* a few tens of thousands, no heavenly official would dare appoint so many," Pei Ming said. "If he really went through with it...well, then I don't know if he should be congratulated on his courage or extreme stupidity. There's definitely no one else like him in history, at least."

Xie Lian studied the bridge on the mural, completely engrossed. The faces of the white-clad crown prince and his four guardian deputies were looking more and more bizarre to him—more and more like his own face and those of his four State Preceptors of Xianle.

That, plus the celestial phase of the Ominous Star…this was the stuff of reincarnation, of history repeating itself. He wanted to know what happened next, but perhaps he already knew.

He turned his head away, afraid to keep his eyes on that mural any longer.

"Have we found water?" he asked.

Banyue dragged Pei Xiu along as they walked. "That gege went to look."

She was referring to Yin Yu. Xie Lian glanced at Pei Xiu, who had his eyes closed. Humming for a moment, he decided to speak up.

"When we go onward to the Kiln, I think it would be best that General Pei Junior stays here."

Pei Xiu was presently in a mortal body after all, which was inconvenient in many ways. Furthermore, they didn't know what awaited them ahead. Pei Ming squatted and looked Pei Xiu over.

"Yeah, I agree. But will Your Highness please not tell him the reason to his face? The boy will understand. Just leave it to me to tell him."

"Rest assured, General Pei, I understand," Xie Lian said. "Otherwise I wouldn't have said it while he was unconscious."

Pei Xiu was once a young martial god with an infinitely bright future in the heavens, but now he had to stay behind because he couldn't keep up. Of course he'd feel bitter. However, mistakes must be punished, and that's how exile *should* feel. He had no choice but to accept it.

They remained in the temple and discussed their situation for a while longer.

"Where's Yin Yu?" Xie Lian wondered, puzzled. "It's been a long time—why hasn't he come back yet? Has he still not found water?"

Hua Cheng was staring intently at a few wraith butterflies resting on his fingertips. The butterflies had been very useful earlier, but now they had all returned to him, tucked away to conserve energy. He looked up slightly.

"He shouldn't be taking this long."

Xie Lian grew alarmed and stood up. "Let me go take a look. General Pei, watch over things here. San Lang, will you come with me?"

Of course he would go with him. Xie Lian left Ruoye behind to tie a protection circle. Then the pair left the temple and headed toward the deeper part of the underground city.

There were plenty of houses and all sorts of random things along the way; Xie Lian picked up a jar that he rather liked, and Hua Cheng seemed to find it funny.

"What are you doing picking that up?"

"If we find water later, we can use this to bring some back for General Pei Junior," Xie Lian said. He'd grown used to collecting scraps, and he patted the jar in his hands in spite of himself. "Come to think of it, this is an antique—thousands of years old."

Hua Cheng laughed. "If you like stuff like this, come to my place later. I've got a few antiques of my own; you can see if you find anything you fancy."

An incense time passed before the two finally heard the faint sound of water flowing. Soon after, Xie Lian exclaimed, "Over there!"

There was indeed a subterranean stream down below. Xie Lian set the jar he'd picked up in the water and started washing it with gusto. Two millennia's worth of ashes had formed a thick shell that couldn't be washed off, but rinsing the loose dust from the surface would make it usable, at least. He filled it with water and lowered his head, ready to take a sip himself. Hua Cheng had been surveying the area with a keen eye and turned just in time to see what he was about to do.

"Don't drink that," he immediately said.

Xie Lian had already put his face to the jar and was confused by the caution. "What?"

"So hot," a voice said.

There were only the two of them here, so where did that third voice come from? Xie Lian subconsciously looked down, following the sound—it was coming from the jar in his hand!

He quickly peered inside the container. There were two tiny scarlet dots lurking in the water, watching him.

Those had to be eyes! Could someone be hiding in there?!

The moment the eyes met his, the thing inside the jar lunged straight at Xie Lian's face. The water inside was disrupted by the movement and splashed out. Xie Lian's hands moved swiftly and flung the jar meters away in an instant. It smashed against a wall and the thousand-year-old antique shattered into pieces! As for the thing that had been hidden inside it, it wasted no time scurrying off into the darkness. In his rush, Xie Lian hadn't clearly seen what it was, only that it looked like a big bundle of something black.

"What was that thing?"

Hua Cheng stood in front of him to shield him, and Xie Lian frowned.

"It wasn't in that jar before, was it?" he asked.

And why had it said "so hot"? Shouldn't it have been cool inside the water?

"No," Hua Cheng said. "It swam into it from the river. There are creatures that flock together and swim in this subterranean stream. That's why I told you not to drink."

But you'd let General Pei Junior drink it... Xie Lian thought.

All of a sudden, he felt a chill on his back, and he shouted, "Who's there?!"

He had just heard someone cough in the distance!

It definitely wasn't a delusion, and he tensed in alarm. Soon after, hushed chatter came pouring in like the tide. Pair after pair of red dots lit up around the two and surrounded them in a circle.

"Don't worry, they're not human," Hua Cheng said.

It's because they're not human that we have to worry... Xie Lian thought.

When he listened closely to the whispers, Xie Lian could discern what the voices were saying.

Cough, cough, cough...

"So hot, oh, it's so hot..."

"I'm boiling..."

"Waaaagh..."

"I'm suffocating... Is anyone there...?"

"I can't move, can't move!"

The voices were tiny, but clear and full of pain. They were like ants vigorously crawling into his ears. Xie Lian was just about to reach for Fangxin when a voice cried out sharply.

"Your Highness! Your Highness, where are you?! Save me, *save me!*"

That last cry made the hair on Xie Lian's neck stand on end—for an instant, he thought the voice was calling for him. However, Hua Cheng released thousands of wraith butterflies with a fierce wave of his hand, and they charged at the glowing red eyes!

The silver butterflies shimmered and illuminated the countless creatures that were whispering in the dark. Sure enough, they weren't human—they were rats!

Hua Cheng grabbed him. "I mentioned there are a lot of rats here. Let's go!"

Even as he rushed along, Xie Lian was still stunned. "Are those rats? Why do they look more like cats to me...?"

It was true. These rats were each larger than a cat, and their hair was black as ink and thick as needles. Ferocity glinted in their little red eyes. Many were perched on the walls, watching them closely from the darkness. They were speaking in human voices, creating a scene that was creepy to the extreme.

Once the silver butterflies charged at them, the slaughter began. Red and silver lights flashed and crossed. The tide of the battle was unknown, but it was clearly vicious and violent.

"Yin Yu couldn't have been dragged off somewhere by those creatures, right?" Xie Lian wondered.

"He wouldn't be so useless. There's probably something else tripping him up," Hua Cheng replied.

The first part made Xie Lian relax slightly, but the latter part made him tense again. "Never mind how big the rats are; why are there so many? What do they eat to grow so large?"

"Simple," Hua Cheng replied. "The dead, of course. Those are corpse-eating rats."

When volcanic ash blanketed the city, the humans had nowhere to hide, and it was the same for their large domesticated beasts—oxen, horses, lambs, and so on. But the rats could burrow deep underground. They survived disaster by relying on the air and food in the underground caves.

Once the dust settled, they reemerged from the underground and scoured the now-hellish city for food. However, everything was destroyed; it had all been entombed in lava or buried in volcanic ash. They gnawed through many things but couldn't find food for the longest time.

Until one day, they smelled the scent of rot.

The putrid smell came from those humanoid stone statues. Some corpses had a thinner ash shell, and when they started to rot, they emitted a rancid stench and began to leak fluids.

The starving rats surrounded the statues and set about creating small holes with their teeth, allowing them to scurry inside and feast upon the corpses within.

The lowest, scummiest creatures often survived the longest. The bodies of the dead were cocooned in those ash shells, as was their terror, rage, frustration, and other such powerful emotions. When the rats ate their corpses, they consumed those emotions too. They gained the ability to speak with human voices and express what those people had yearned to say at the moment of their deaths.

Xie Lian was enlightened. "I see; so that's why they were saying those things. I was wondering why they would say stuff like that..."

"What was that?" Hua Cheng unexpectedly asked.

Xie Lian blinked. "Hmm?"

Hua Cheng stared at him. "What did they say? What did you hear?"

Xie Lian was confused. "San Lang, you didn't hear them?" He then repeated, "'So hot,' 'it's suffocating,' 'can't move,' 'save me,' things like that..."

But before Hua Cheng responded, it dawned on Xie Lian.

That wasn't right!

The corpse-eating rats could only repeat the ravings of the Wuyong people before their deaths. Which, naturally, would be in the Wuyong tongue.

So why could he understand them?!

87
Jealous Ghost King, Three Questions on Where the Friendship Lies

Hua Cheng had used his own abilities of inference and capacity for learning to pick up the Wuyong language. He could decipher the meaning of words, but since there wasn't anyone alive who could read the words aloud to him, he couldn't match written words with sounds. That meant he couldn't understand the murmuring of the corpse-eating rats.

But Xie Lian, who had never visited Mount Tonglu before, understood. What could this mean?

Hua Cheng could tell what Xie Lian was thinking with a single glance, and he was quick to reassure him. "Gege, don't panic just yet. I'll repeat those words to you. Give them a listen."

"...All right," Xie Lian said.

Hua Cheng's memory was exceptional, and he clearly and precisely repeated the words as soon as they left the area where the corpse-eating rats had gathered. Xie Lian stared intently at his lips as he pronounced a series of moderately paced and somewhat bizarre-sounding phrases. The words had a strange, ancient rhythm to them. Hearing them spoken with such steady control through Hua Cheng's lips made the notes deep, beautiful, and pleasing to the ears.

After concentrating on the words for a moment, Xie Lian said, "I don't understand them."

Now this was very strange—he could understand the words the corpse-eating rats had spewed, but he couldn't parse them when

Hua Cheng repeated them exactly. Still, that moment of comprehension couldn't have been a figment of his imagination.

"When you heard those voices, you easily understood what they were saying, right?" Hua Cheng asked.

Xie Lian nodded. "Right. There was never a translation process in my brain."

He hadn't even realized it was a different language.

"I get it," Hua Cheng said.

"What do you get?" Xie Lian asked.

"What you understood wasn't the Wuyong tongue but the emotions of those who died."

Xie Lian understood, but at the same time he didn't.

"Meaning that a long time ago, someone heard these same dying voices. They understood them and remembered them, and then somehow transplanted this memory into you and infected you with their feelings," Hua Cheng explained further. "*They* knew the Wuyong tongue and had already completed the 'comprehension' step, which is why you don't need to know the language to understand. Those voices have always been buried deep within your mind, and you were brought directly into their emotions the moment you heard them."

Xie Lian thought this explanation sounded fairly plausible. "I see... But the question is, who could pass such memories and emotions to me? And when did they do this?"

After a pause, he murmured, "...The state preceptor?"

"We can't be sure," Hua Cheng replied. "Gege, you're already assuming your master is from Wuyong. But if that's the case, shouldn't they have been communicating in the Wuyong tongue when we were in the stomach of the mountain spirit? Why weren't they?"

That wasn't hard to explain. Xie Lian said, "The Kingdom of Wuyong was destroyed two thousand years ago. They would need to use modern language to survive in the world for the past two millennia. It's only natural for them to use the language they're more fluent in now."

Hua Cheng gripped his shoulders, his tone growing harsher. "Gege, stop letting yourself think this way."

Xie Lian finally turned to face him. "Fine. San Lang, what does it usually take to transplant memories and emotions to someone?"

"There are two conditions that must be met. First, you must trust this person absolutely and without reservations. When necessary, you are willing to be led by them," Hua Cheng answered.

After a brief moment of contemplation, Xie Lian had picked the candidates in his mind.

"Second, it is someone you are powerless to retaliate against. The one implanting the memories must hold absolute power over you, and you must fear them deeply," Hua Cheng said. "Gege, think carefully. Over the years, who has matched these requirements?"

Xie Lian contemplated for a while, and after some hesitation, answered slowly. "I suppose there are three in total."

"Very good. Who are the three?" Hua Cheng asked.

"The first one is the State Preceptor of Xianle," Xie Lian said.

While he loved his parents deeply and never guarded against them, he knew deep down that he and his father walked different paths—thus, he couldn't say he was willing to be led by his father. However, the state preceptor guided him at the beginning of his education and taught him everything. He met both conditions.

This was expected, so Hua Cheng prompted, "And the second one?"

"Jun Wu," Xie Lian answered.

He held immense respect for Jun Wu, and was constantly in awe of him, no need to say more on the subject. He also met both conditions. Hua Cheng didn't look too impressed, but he didn't comment.

"And the last one?"

"The third one," Xie Lian said, "doesn't match the first condition, but the second."

Hua Cheng understood. "...White No-Face?" he said darkly.

Xie Lian closed his eyes and nodded, a hand covering his brow. "...I won't lie to you. I never revealed this to anyone—not even Feng Xin and Mu Qing. I never said anything dispiriting to them back then. But I actually..."

But actually, deep down, he profoundly feared that creature.

There was a period of time when even hearing the name would set him trembling nonstop. But Xie Lian had never dared to allow anyone to notice, because he was the only hope they had for defeating White No-Face. If even *he* was scared, then wouldn't everyone else fall deeper into despair? If that happened, everything would collapse!

Of course, it was all much better now. Hua Cheng gripped his shoulders even harder.

"It's all right. There's nothing shameful about being afraid of something."

Xie Lian gave a small, flickering smile. "I'm just not brave enough, that's all."

"You don't need to be so hard on yourself," Hua Cheng comforted. "Without fear, there is no courage."

Xie Lian was slightly taken aback.

Hua Cheng continued without pause.

"Is it only those three?"

Xie Lian nodded. This meant that someone among those three had planted within him the Wuyong people's memories and emotions at the moment of volcanic cataclysm. Hua Cheng mused on it, furrowing his brows.

Xie Lian was silent for a while before he suddenly spoke up. "That's not everyone."

Hua Cheng turned his head to look at him. "What?"

Xie Lian drew a small breath. "...It's actually not just those three. There's a fourth person who fulfills the first condition. But I'm certain he has nothing to do with the memories and emotions of the dead."

Hearing this, Hua Cheng turned toward him completely. "Oh? How do you know? Have Your Highness and this person shared many years of deep friendship?"

Not so many years, Xie Lian thought, *but a deep friendship.* He believed this person counted, but he was too embarrassed to say it out loud, so he replied ambiguously.

"In any case...he might be the one I trust the most. Even more than my master and Jun Wu."

"How does that count?" Hua Cheng asked.

Xie Lian lightly cleared his throat. "It's embarrassing to say," he said shyly. "Because...if I were to make a grave mistake, or find myself in trouble after upsetting a huge hornets' nest, he's the first one I'd think to call... And my trust for him isn't quite the same as what I have for my master and the Emperor..."

Before he could finish, he noticed Hua Cheng's odd expression. He trailed off.

"San Lang?"

Only then did Hua Cheng come around. He quirked an eyebrow. "Oh. It's nothing, I was thinking of something else. Your Highness really trusts this person so much?"

He usually raised his brows when he was relaxed or teasing, but it didn't seem very natural right now.

Xie Lian nodded. "Mmm... Is there a problem?"

Hua Cheng bowed his head slightly and adjusted his silver vambraces. "Nothing major," he said, sounding nonchalant. "But, in my personal opinion, it'd be best if gege didn't trust others so easily."

"..."

Hearing him say that, Xie Lian wasn't sure whether Hua Cheng had figured out who he was talking about. But he didn't dare reveal any more, so he only gave a soft *oh*. Although he paused, in the end he still couldn't resist asking, "San Lang isn't going to ask who this person is?"

"Hmm? What?" Hua Cheng asked. "Since gege said he trusts this person and has determined that he has nothing to do with this affair, there's no need to ask."

Xie Lian rubbed his forehead.

Hua Cheng quickly added, "But if gege wants to tell, San Lang is happy to listen."

Although his words sounded gracious, it'd be awkward if Xie Lian told him now—it would be like he was begging Hua Cheng to ask who he trusted the most. Xie Lian couldn't tell whether Hua Cheng was just being polite or if he really didn't care.

Coincidentally, the wraith butterflies that engaged in bloody carnage against the corpse-eating rats had returned. After going through that strenuous battle, the silver butterflies were flying a little low, like they were drooping with fatigue. Xie Lian quickly went up to greet them, reaching out to catch a particularly tiny butterfly.

"Thanks for your hard work!" he said.

Now he'd done it. The butterflies paused in the air, and the next second, it was like they had smelled delicious pastry.[8] They all charged at him like mad. Xie Lian still had the little silver butterfly cupped in his hand and was almost struck dumb.

---

8   *"Delicious-smelling pastry" is Chinese slang for a highly desirable person or thing.*

Hua Cheng gave a calm, deliberate cough. The butterflies paused again, then backed off politely and calmly flew toward Hua Cheng to land on the silver vambraces on his arms, becoming one with the engraved butterfly patterns.

The two continued to search for Yin Yu. After they'd been walking for a while, Hua Cheng suddenly spoke up.

"It's not Feng Xin, is it?"

Xie Lian's mind had already moved on to something else, and when he heard him, he blinked. "Huh? What?"

"The person gege spoke of," Hua Cheng said.

Xie Lian instantly waved. "Of course not!"

Hua Cheng's brows twitched. "…It's not Mu Qing, is it?"

A drop of sweat rolled down Xie Lian's forehead, and his hand waved faster. "That's even more impossible. But why is San Lang asking about this again?"

Hua Cheng smiled. "I thought about it, and I think that this fourth person is the most suspicious. So to prevent any surprises, will gege please tell me? Who is this person you trust the most, and with whom you've shared many years of deep friendship?"

"…"

Xie Lian stared at the smile on his face. He had a gut feeling that this smile was very fake. But just as he inhaled deeply, preparing to speak, the faint silver light from the scout butterflies disappeared.

Darkness fell all around, and Hua Cheng swiftly seized Xie Lian's hand and dodged to the side of the street. Xie Lian could tell something was wrong.

"San Lang, is something coming?" he asked in a whisper.

Even though darkness had come unexpectedly and nothing could be seen, he followed Hua Cheng's steps closely and easily hopped into a house to hide.

Hua Cheng's voice sounded next to his ear. "It's here."

Within the darkness, they heard a very peculiar sound.

Thump thump, thump thump.

It was a strange dragging noise, and although it was still far away, each drag sounded extremely heavy. And each one also sounded much closer than the one before—the speed of its approach was astounding. Xie Lian thought this sound was oddly familiar and that he had definitely heard it somewhere before. When it sounded close by, he looked outside to see.

Sure enough, there was a woman dressed in wedding robes on the main street of the underground city.

Although she wore wedding robes, the robes themselves were in tatters; it was a chilling, haunting sight. Her face was beautiful yet held no sign of life. The glowing green ghost fire atop her head made her blanched complexion shine green. In her arms she cradled a small child whose face was also a ghastly pale shade, though he appeared more alive than her. He was obviously a living human.

"Bumping into old friends again," Hua Cheng said.

It was the ghost bride Xuan Ji—and Guzi!

88
Ghost Fire Top, the Unlocking Incantation

THEY'D COME to Mount Tonglu as well!

"Guzi is here. Does that mean Qi Rong has come too?" Xie Lian wondered.

"There's no doubt he has. Look at that ball of green light on top of her head," Hua Cheng said.

"..."

Guzi seemed a little afraid of Xuan Ji, staying very still while she carried him. But he did squirm subtly a few times—perhaps her cold body was uncomfortable.

"Don't move!" Xuan Ji admonished.

Beneath the glow of that ball of green ghost fire, the muscles of her face appeared even more twisted the moment she opened her mouth. Ghost fire was one of the telltale signs of a ghost, but wearing it on top of one's head was in exceedingly poor taste. Any lady ghost who valued her own image would refuse to wear such a garish thing over her head; Xie Lian suspected that Qi Rong must have forced her to wear it. The green flames and the red wedding robes formed a shocking contrast that assaulted the eyes. It was a more depressing sight than a sect leader forcing his disciples to wear extremely ugly uniforms.

"Jiejie, my tummy doesn't feel good after drinking that water," Guzi pleaded, his eyes brimming with tears.

Water? Xie Lian broke out in a cold sweat. Hordes of corpse-eating rats were swimming through the water here. While it might not be toxic, children had weaker constitutions and might suffer diarrhea after drinking it.

Xuan Ji was obviously the type who didn't like children, and she had very little patience for him. "Hang on for a bit. We'll be back soon."

Their backs disappeared, and they became one with the darkness ahead. No need to say another word—Xie Lian and Hua Cheng quietly trailed in their footsteps. After following Xuan Ji around a few turns, they came upon another large street, and at the end of that street was a particularly lavish house. There were voices coming from within—it was surely their destination. Under the cover of shadow, Xie Lian and Hua Cheng dashed ahead and hopped onto the roof of the house. They peered inside through the cracks.

Sure enough, Qi Rong was sloppily lounging in the center of the mansion's main hall. He had hauled in dozens of stone statues and positioned them so their heads were facing him. Because the stone people were all sprawled on the ground, they looked like they were in complete submission to him. He was basking in this fake prostration while munching on a bloody arm. He looked quite pleased with himself.

In the corner of the room sat several farmers. And there was someone else among them with his head bowed low and no presence to speak of. It was Yin Yu!

As they suspected, he had been captured by Qi Rong. No one was bound by rope, but there were balls of bright green ghost fire hovering over every captive's head. Upon closer inspection, these ghost fires were different from the ornamental one on top of Xuan Ji's head—these had grown *faces* with all five senses. Their narrowed eyes stared downward, and their expressions were treacherous and wicked. All were steadfastly watchful of the person below them.

"Those balls of fire must be doing something," Xie Lian whispered.

"It's Qi Rong's Ghost Fire Lock," Hua Cheng replied. "Once that fire sets its sights on you, if you dare try to escape, it will shriek at the top of its lungs. Then, the hostage will be burned to death in an instant when the spell is activated."

Qi Rong was munching on the severed arm with relish when Xuan Ji's voice rang from outside.

"My Lord, I've returned."

He immediately threw the arm away and wiped his blood-covered mouth. Xie Lian was somewhat amazed—what was *that* gesture? Did he not want someone to see? Had the day come when Qi Rong knew shame—could he actually be embarrassed by someone witnessing the way he ate?

Before Xuan Ji entered, she set Guzi down. Guzi scurried in with a *ta-ta-ta* and rushed straight to Qi Rong's side. But when he saw him, he pointed an accusing finger and shouted.

"Dad is secretly eating bad things again!"

"I'm not!" Qi Rong retaliated.

"I smell it! Your breath stinks when you eat bad stuff!" Guzi accused.

Qi Rong raised his hand and huffed a couple of breaths against his palm, and his expression showed that he could smell the blood reeking from his own mouth. Without any way to deny it, he grew annoyed.

"GODDAMMIT! Xuan Ji! Why did you bring him back so suddenly?! Didn't I say to walk him around a bit longer while I ate?!"

Xuan Ji walked in, visibly peeved. "He was making a fuss about a tummy ache after he drank water, so I brought him back early," she explained. "My Lord, please don't make me take care of children anymore. I don't know how to deal with him!"

Qi Rong glared. "What?! Aren't you a woman ghost?! How can a woman not like taking care of children?! You're disqualified!"

"But it's not even my own child!" Xuan Ji countered.

Guzi tugged at the hem of Qi Rong's sleeve. "Dad, don't eat those things anymore, they're not good for you…"

Qi Rong was growing annoyed by his nagging and scolded him. "Go outside. Go! Don't hang around here to annoy people. What is this, kids sticking their noses in grown-ups' business?! Go out and play by yourself!"

With that, Guzi could only drag his feet and go outside to play in the mud by himself, glancing at the group in the corner as he left.

Only when he was gone did Xuan Ji speak up. "My Lord, I really don't understand—why must you bring him along if you think he is annoying? He's been hungry, and thirsty, and weepy, and sickly the entire way. If we hadn't bumped into that mountain spirit and managed to ride it here, we would surely be lagging behind."

Qi Rong laughed wryly. "My cheap son is determined to call me dad, so just let him! *Pfft*, what rubbish—it's because I'm gonna eat that dumb little pecker, of course! A kid's meat is so tender; even without seasoning it'll be flavorful enough! Hee hee hee hee…"

"Then why hasn't My Lord eaten him yet?" Xuan Ji pressed.

Greedy green light flashed in Qi Rong's eyes. "You don't understand anything! I'll kill him after he's fattened up! I'm saving the best for last! Besides, we still have so many rations left—there's no rush!"

With the subject of rations raised, Xuan Ji peered at Yin Yu. "I think this new one you captured is suspicious. Very, very suspicious. My Lord, did you figure out where he came from?"

Knowing how much Qi Rong despised Hua Cheng, he would've eaten Yin Yu immediately if he'd known his new captive was Hua Cheng's subordinate.

"Yeah, I got it out of him. This bastard came with the Rain Master to help," Qi Rong replied.

A weak sense of presence and an unremarkable personality were sometimes a good thing—people wouldn't immediately link someone like Yin Yu with someone like Crimson Rain Sought Flower. It seemed Yin Yu had successfully deceived Qi Rong about his identity, and Xie Lian sighed a breath of relief. Xuan Ji's face, however, dropped.

"Yushi Huang has already chased us here?!"

"Nah," Qi Rong said. "This bastard found this underground city by accident, same as us. The Rain Master hasn't discovered us yet. God fucking DAMMIT!" He suddenly cussed. "Why is the Rain Master so hard to deal with? Chasing us and smacking us around all this way, forcing us to hide down here! We only nabbed a couple of those hicks to eat—WHY SO STINGY?! These heavenly officials—I just *knew* none of them were any good! SO NARROW-MINDED AND MISERLY!"

Qi Rong was always so self-righteous. Those farmers had been minding their own business when he snatched them all up with his wretched hands—and he had the gall to scorn their master for not being generous enough to provide him with a few more. His speech made Xie Lian's fists itch.

"Why don't we just release these people?" Xuan Ji said.

Qi Rong, however, seemed to think the very idea embarrassing. He glared. "No! I already ate half of them, so it won't matter even if I release the rest. The feud has begun. The only way to prevent it would be if I didn't snatch any farmers at the start—might as well eat them all now! But if anyone corners me, this ancestor will BURN THEM ALL TO THE GROUND! We can all be miserable together!"

"I didn't think it would go this way. Yushi Huang used to be so easy to bully; this never would have happened in the past. If we kidnapped people from Yushi Country, I thought it would be swept under the rug and the insult swallowed; that's the only reason I dared to make such a move. Who knew it would invite this much trouble and such relentless pursuit?!"

It seemed that Xuan Ji knew the Rain Master personally, but her opinion of the official was quite low. They likely knew each other when they were both still mortal.

Thinking back on all the legends, Xie Lian whispered, "Was Xuan Ji once a general of the Kingdom of Yushi?"

"Gege guessed right," Hua Cheng said. "That's exactly it."

Xie Lian was dubious. "But that's not right... Lord Rain Master is a descendant of Yushi royalty—quite high status. Xuan Ji was only a general, a subject. How can she look down on her monarch like that? She went as far as saying 'easily bullied'..."

Just then, Qi Rong started ranting, "Who cares about some Rain Master Dog Master? Just wait 'til this ghost king cultivates to supreme status in the Kiln! I'll be reborn so powerful that I'll rock the world, and everyone—from heavens above to earth below—will be forced to bow before me! To kneel and eat the mud at my feet! Then I'll tear down Ghost City, sink Black Water Island, and even Jun Wu will have to be careful where he treads. Ha ha ha ha ha ha..."

"..."

Listening to him rattle off so much bullshit, happily imagining his future glory... Other than an urge to laugh, Xie Lian felt nothing. Hua Cheng, on the other hand, didn't even bother with laughter.

Qi Rong then assured Xuan Ji, "When the time comes, I'll chop off Pei Ming's dick for you to play with and make him your slave."

Xuan Ji clenched her fists at the mention of that name, a trace of life flashing on her deathly pale face. "No need! As long as My Lord promises to give him to me and allows me to handle him myself, Xuan Ji will be infinitely grateful!"

When the matter didn't concern Pei Ming, Xuan Ji looked like a fairly normal ghost woman. But the moment General Pei was mentioned, Xie Lian could see a shadow of that mad, obsessed specter from Mount Yujun. She had actually placed such absurd hopes on Qi Rong—a choice that could only be described as "blinded by love."

Xie Lian looked up. "San Lang, Yin Yu and those farmers are in Qi Rong's clutches. What should we do?"

They could of course just saunter directly inside and beat Qi Rong and Xuan Ji to a pulp, but the farmers and Yin Yu were hostages. Qi Rong was a fiend, and they had more to lose—he could immolate a hostage with every punch they threw. Just as he said, he could burn it all to the ground if they cornered him.

Hua Cheng wasn't the least bit anxious. "There's an unlocking incantation for Qi Rong's Ghost Fire Locks. First, let's think of a way to wheedle it out of him."

"Who will do that, and how? We certainly can't," Xie Lian said.

As soon as he posed the question, their eyes simultaneously fell on Guzi, who was playing with mud outside the mansion.

After a momentary pause, Xie Lian said, "That won't do. It's too dangerous. Qi Rong is already thinking about eating Guzi—what if he suspects the boy is trying to trick him…?"

"Whether that brain of his can even detect trickery aside," Hua Cheng said, "if he tries to do anything to the child, we'll just rescue him. Maybe gege should be more worried about whether the child has been permanently damaged by this extended period of proximity to Qi Rong and whether his mental state is still normal."

"Judging by Guzi's reaction earlier, he probably isn't that bad off," Xie Lian said. "Let's give it a try, then."

Hua Cheng opened his palm flat and released a particularly tiny silver butterfly. It languidly fluttered down.

Qi Rong and Xuan Ji were still talking inside the house, and Guzi was outside drawing in the mud—a picture of a big person holding hands with a smaller person. Suddenly, he spotted a silver butterfly that was glowing slightly. He looked up at once, his eyes wide, and was just about to exclaim *"Wow!"* when a whisper came from the creature.

"Guzi, don't speak. The moment you speak, I'll disappear. It's me. Do you remember me?"

If Guzi had yelled anyway, Hua Cheng would've had the silver butterfly confound his mind. But Guzi covered his own mouth obediently.

"I remember Scrap-Collecting Gege's voice," he whispered back.

"...Ha ha ha, what a good memory you have." Xie Lian laughed awkwardly. "Yes, that's right, that's me, the scrap-collecting guy. Sneak over to the side of the house for a moment, and don't let Qi... Don't let your dad see you."

Guzi nodded. He rose to his feet and was about to sneak away, but Qi Rong immediately noticed.

"HEY! DON'T RUN AROUND RANDOMLY, YA HEAR ME?" he yelled from inside. "Run off around here and the big rats will eat ya! Get back here!"

The silver butterfly flew off at once and hid. Guzi's eyes widened.

"I... I'm going to pee!" he answered.

Qi Rong clicked his tongue. "Kids are so full of shit and piss!"

And then he stopped caring.

Guzi scampered to the side and whispered again, "Scrap gege, scrap gege!"

"...Just 'Daozhang' is fine," Xie Lian said from the roof. "'Scrap gege' sounds a little weird, ha ha ha... Guzi, those people your dad kidnapped are very pitiful. They're servants from someone else's household, and their master will keep chasing after your dad to beat him up. Will you help us set them free?"

"I know!" Guzi said. "They're from the house of the god riding the big black ox!" He scratched his head. "I want to let them go too... but my dad is sick. He said he has to eat human flesh to get better and that eating human flesh is normal. I'm still little and he'll teach me how to eat it when I'm bigger. But I don't think it's a very good idea..."

...It's more than just not a good idea! Xie Lian thought. *This is a close call.*

Having remained by Qi Rong's side for so long, Guzi's morals were beginning to go astray. If he was dragged down the wrong path for much longer, he might start believing that this kind of life is normal—and think nothing of eating human flesh.

"It's definitely *not* a good idea!" Xie Lian said quickly. "Eating human flesh will make you very sick. The ghosts of any people you eat will haunt you and your dad. Your dad isn't sick, he's just a glutton who refuses to give up something he likes. You have to figure out a way to stop him from ever eating that stuff again—otherwise, you won't have a dad anymore!"

"Then what should I do?" Guzi asked, clearly alarmed.

Hua Cheng turned to Xie Lian. "Gege, let me."

He said a few words to the silver butterfly, and Guzi listened on the other end, trying hard to remember everything. Once he was done, Hua Cheng looked up again.

"Let's lure Xuan Ji out of the way first," he told Xie Lian.

Inside the house, Xuan Ji said, "I still think this one is suspicious.

He says he's a servant of Yushi Huang, but he's covered with ghost qi. I think he's lying. I'll question him some more."

After seeing Guzi scurry away, Qi Rong took this opportunity to turn his back to the door and start munching on the arm again. "Sure," he vaguely replied.

Aside from the fact that Xuan Ji went mad whenever she ran into Pei Ming, she was otherwise much more detail-oriented and cautious than Qi Rong—she was a woman, after all. Besides, Guzi was a little scared of her, so the chance of him fumbling was higher with her around.

Xie Lian nodded. "How do we lure her away?"

The two exchanged a look and said in unison, "General Pei."

Xie Lian pressed his hands together in a prayer. "There's no other way. We'll need to temporarily sacrifice you, General Pei. Everyone will thank you once we're saved."

Hua Cheng laughed out loud. "They should thank gege instead."

Another silver butterfly materialized from the engravings on Hua Cheng's silver vambraces and flew next to Xie Lian's ear. A man's voice came floating through it—it was Pei Ming's voice. Hua Cheng had apparently left a few silver butterflies behind before they separated, and the voices on the other side were being broadcast to them.

Xie Lian listened closely for a bit, then he whispered, "Let's cut this up a little and use these lines..."

Xuan Ji's back was facing the window. She stared at Yin Yu like a hawk as she interrogated him.

"In Yushi Country, I'm responsible for attending to hungry ghosts who have nowhere to turn," Yin Yu answered, acting like an honest and dutiful soul. "When they wander to our doorstep, I give them a handful of rice and send them on their way, which is why I have ghost qi on me..."

The other hostages were the real farmers of Yushi Country. While there certainly were those who gave such relief to wandering ghosts, he was definitely not one of them. They knew he was making things up, but no one made a sound.

Qi Rong chortled. "Ho ho, I'm a hungry ghost too, why not give *me* some relief? I'm being hunted down over just a few farmers eaten. What's up with your boss? That cheapskate, pretending to be so generous..."

Xuan Ji, on the other hand, treated the comment with open disdain. "There are so many hungry ghosts in the world—how can you bring relief to them all? It's nothing but an act."

Just then, a silver butterfly with its light concealed flew soundlessly behind her. It flashed its light once before it hid. All the hostages saw, but they remained composed; with unspoken understanding, everyone pretended they didn't see anything. Xuan Ji was about to continue the interrogation when she seemed to hear the voice of a man.

"...If that's the case...these...first. Do you...any more...? Give... here..."

"*If that's the case, roast these rats first. Do you have any more snakes? Give them here.*" When Xie Lian had first heard Pei Ming say it, he was filled with both shock and pity. Some corpse-eating rats must have approached them, and Pei Ming must've thought they were normal rats and killed them to serve as a meal for Pei Xiu. Would eating such creatures cause problems? They had to hurry back soon.

However, the effect was fascinating after Hua Cheng muted some parts from the line—now, it sounded like the words meant *something*, but their meaning couldn't be understood. When Xuan Ji heard it, she shuddered violently and whipped her head around.

But the silver butterfly was cunningly agile; it emitted no light, and it had long since fluttered to the side and hidden by the time she turned around. Uncertain, Xuan Ji turned back to question the hostages.

"Did any of you hear something just now? Did you see anything?"

Yin Yu took the lead and shook his head, and the rest of the hostages did the same, all appearing honest and timid. Qi Rong looked over with his mouth covered in blood.

"What did you hear?"

Xuan Ji was slightly confused. "I...thought I heard Pei Ming's voice."

"Huh? You're probably delusional," Qi Rong said. "I haven't heard anything."

The silver butterfly pressed close to Xuan Ji so no one else could hear the voices it transmitted.

Xuan Ji was doubtful. "Really? But I keep feeling that...maybe he's close by." She was bewildered for a moment before she heaved a sigh. "Perhaps this is what they call lover's intuition...? My Lord, why don't I go out and take another look around?"

Xie Lian hadn't expected it to go this smoothly. He silently clenched his fists and looked up to flash Hua Cheng a smile. Hua Cheng smiled back. However, Qi Rong unexpectedly rained on his parade.

"*Pfft!* Didn't you go once already? Intuition, my ass—it's delusion for sure. You do nothing but think of him eight hundred times a day. Of course you're delusional."

It appeared Xuan Ji was slightly convinced by his assurance. Though still unsure, she seemed to relent on her plan to leave. Xie Lian wasn't discouraged by the failure of this attempt, though, because he had more lines where that came from. Xuan Ji was just about to continue her interrogation when she heard Pei Ming's voice once more.

"...You silly little thing! Come here, I'll teach you."

A moment later, a young girl's voice could be heard. "...Please, General Pei. I've done it once. I'm experienced now. Let me do it..."

That was, of course, Pei Ming instructing Banyue how to roast corpse-eating rats for Little Pei to eat...but it sounded like something completely different to Xuan Ji's ears. His disdainful dismay became tender resignation, and her gloomy rejection became bashful timidity. Xuan Ji screeched, and a red sheen crawled over her eyes. The ghost fire on top of her head erupted—just like the jealous flames blazing in her heart.

"*It's him!* It's him for sure! He must be here, I sensed it, my heart sensed him!" She pulled at her own hair and screamed. "*Pei Ming!* You're always like this! Which woman is it this time?! *I'm going to kill you!*"

She continued to shriek as she leapt outside, dragging her two broken legs. Qi Rong broke into curses.

"Hey! *Hey!* Xuan Ji! What the fuck! How can you run that fast on those fucked-up legs?! Is that manwhore really worth it?!"

Xie Lian watched as Xuan Ji's stumbling, wobbling back disappeared, feeling somewhat mournful. Hua Cheng probably thought he was concerned for the safety of those back at the temple.

"No need to worry," he said. "The wraith butterfly will lead her in the opposite direction. Even if she finds them, Ruoye is acting as a shield, and she won't be able to enter the protection circle. Let's end our business here quickly."

Now that Xuan Ji was gone, it was time for Guzi to enter the scene. He rose to his feet and wiped his muddy hands on his butt. Xie Lian was still a little worried.

"Will it really be all right?"

"Gege, trust me," Hua Cheng assured quietly. "If this doesn't work, we'll find another way. There are plenty of other options. If necessary, we can destroy Qi Rong's ability to speak forever, then take our time coming up with an idea."

"..."

By the time Guzi entered the house, Qi Rong had already licked his hands clean of blood. When he saw him, he called out, "Son, come here and massage-chop your daddy's legs!"

Guzi did as he was told. He chopped obediently for a while before he asked, "Dad, those people in the corner aren't bound by ropes... How come they still don't dare move?"

Qi Rong perked up at his question. "Heh heh! It's because they're so scared of your daddy that their legs are weak, of course!"

"..." Guzi's eyes and mouth opened wide and round. "You're that amazing?!"

Qi Rong's vanity was greatly satisfied, and he replied, "That's right! Look here, today I'll show you just how amazing your daddy is! You see that ball of fire? The moment I give the command, *WHOOSH!* They'll all burn to death, so of course they're afraid of me! And there are two more puny ghosts you need to remember."

Guzi was nodding enthusiastically throughout his father's rant like a little chick pecking at grain. Qi Rong continued.

"One is Hua Cheng, the other has the nickname Black Water. They're two weak-ass nobodies, two wretches pretending to be great. They got a little lucky, but in reality, their titles are hollow. Do you understand what a hollow title is? I'll teach you. It's a metaphor. It means they look like they're powerful on the surface, but when it comes to true strength, they're nowhere near my level!"

Guzi looked like he sort of understood, but not quite. "Oh..."

"They're just lucky! If I had their luck, I would be ten times greater than they ever were!" Qi Rong added. "Just you wait! This time, your daddy will break through this trial. I'll beat them black and blue and wipe the smiles off their faces! NO ONE WILL DARE LOOK DOWN ON ME AGAIN! ONLY I GET TO LOOK DOWN ON PEOPLE!"

He was full of fire, swinging his arms as he hollered. Guzi absolutely did not understand who or what he was talking about, but he still cheered.

"You can do it, Dad!"

"..."

On the roof, Xie Lian slapped a hand over his face. Qi Rong's great speech had rendered him utterly speechless. All too aware of—and quite embarrassed by—the fact that Qi Rong was his younger cousin, he turned to Hua Cheng.

"San Lang, this... He... I..."

Hua Cheng flashed a fake smile. "No need to worry about him, gege. He's full of memorable lines; this is just the tip of the iceberg."

Throughout history, men all over the world have loved to brag. A breeze could blow the handkerchief of a brothel girl into a man's hand, and he would turn around and say that the most beautiful and renowned of all courtesans had fallen madly in love with him. Holding shoes and wiping benches for the emperor's mistress's uncle's grandson's cousin's mistress would be twisted into an important administrator position at the residence of the royal family, raising his status. Men who didn't brag were a rare species.

Men who loved to brag primarily puffed themselves up to women, but bragging to their sons was a close second. Xie Lian recalled his youth, when his own father frequently spoke of his heroism and greatness in politics, both subtly and blatantly.

This was why, when Xie Lian was young, he deeply believed his father was a noble, valiant ruler whose great name would go down in history. When he eventually discovered that wasn't true, he'd been extremely disillusioned. The letdown was so great that it had sparked his teenage rebellion.

As he reflected on this, Xie Lian shook his head with wry humor. *Why would I compare Qi Rong with my father?*

Really, how baffling. Maybe they did both love to elevate themselves in front of their sons—but his father's boasting fell within normal parameters. Qi Rong, on the other hand, had reached a stage of absolute shamelessness and baseless self-righteousness. No wonder that even Black Water, who always tried to stay under everyone's radar, regarded him with such contempt that he'd find any excuse to beat him up whenever they crossed paths.

However, Xie Lian was still a little puzzled—why was Qi Rong cursing so many others right now but leaving Xie Lian out? Did he have a change of heart?

Xie Lian could also understand a bit better now why Qi Rong was dragging his feet on devouring Guzi. If he bragged to a normal person, or someone a bit older with more life experience, they might not buy into it. Even if they agreed with him on the surface, it still wouldn't feel sincere, or the response would be overly glib and exaggerated—like Qi Rong's little ghost minions in the past. But Guzi's praise was different. Every word came from the bottom of his heart; he genuinely believed that his "dad" was the most powerful guy in the world!

It had probably been a while since Qi Rong had bragged so heartily. Satisfied at last, he ended the rant. "You gotta be good, ya hear me? If you don't listen to me, I'll put a ghost fire on you too!" he threatened.

Sure enough, Guzi was scared and hastily covered his own head.

"No, I don't want to wear it... Oh yeah, Dad." He remembered what Hua Cheng and Xie Lian taught him, and said nervously, "O-once they have that green fire on their head, you won't be able to take it off them, right?"

If he had asked, *"Can you take it off them once they have it on?"* Qi Rong might not have told the truth, but instead, coached by Hua Cheng and Xie Lian, he phrased it as an expression of doubt: *"You won't be able to take it off them, right?"*

Qi Rong kicked out on the spot and sent the head of one of the stone people flying. "Bullshit! If Daddy wants to lock, he'll lock! If he wants to unlock, he'll unlock! Watch! Dad will unlock one to show you!"

Then he pointed at a farmer and yelled, "DOG-FUCKED XIE LIAN!"

Xie Lian had no comment. Neither did Hua Cheng.

The ghost fire on top of the farmer's head was extinguished, and he leapt to his feet. However, he didn't run very far before Qi Rong spat loudly. Another ball of bright green ghost fire spewed from his mouth, which landed and loomed over the top of the farmer's head. Qi Rong laughed boisterously and patted Guzi's head.

"What do ya think? Your daddy's powerful, right?"

On the roof, Xie Lian wiped sweat off his face. Hua Cheng looked cool and aloof, but the tone of his voice was chilling.

"I think that trash wants to be trashed harder."

He was cracking his knuckles, so Xie Lian said hurriedly, "It's fine, it's fine. He was tricked more easily than expected!"

They had originally taught Guzi many more ways to dig for information, but it seemed they wouldn't need any of them. And no wonder Qi Rong hadn't cursed Xie Lian earlier—it wasn't that he'd had a change of heart, but that cursing him had become the unlocking incantation. Qi Rong's feelings for Xie Lian clearly ran deep.

At that point, there was no more reason for the two of them to keep hiding. They immediately smashed through the roof and jumped down! The massive crash made Qi Rong fall off his chair in surprise.

"WHO'S THERE?! WHO'S THERE?!" And when he saw who it was, "DOG... DOG..."

Qi Rong probably wanted to curse at him, but he quickly covered his mouth, realizing that the phrase trying to burst out would free his prisoners.

From the corner, one of the farmers said, "I think he just yelled out the incantation... So let's see if we can unlock each other..."

"Yeah, it's just some cursing, right? While I kind of feel bad for that Xie Lian person, it's not like he's here. It should be fine!"

Hua Cheng raised an eyebrow and looked their way. A bead of cold sweat rolled down Yin Yu's forehead.

"Um... I suggest you don't say it, whether the person is here or not," Yin Yu said. "The consequences could be even worse than our present situation..."

Across the room, Qi Rong grabbed Guzi to shield himself and switched up his lines a bit. "DOG... DOG-MOUNTED XIE LIAN! You're shameless! You're spying! You're conniving!"

Xie Lian frowned glumly. "What the heck is 'dog-mounted'?"

Qi Rong grew smug again. "Heh, even if you know the incantation, it's useless! Would you curse yourselves? Hua Cheng, you can't say it either, can you?"

Hua Cheng scowled harder at this. His knuckles cracked a few more times, but Xie Lian didn't notice. Instead, he was baffled.

"Well, sure. It's nothing."

Then he recited the incantation several times with no hesitation, as each utterance could only release one person. The hostages now knew that *he* was the one being cursed at in the incantation, and they couldn't help but give him a thumbs-up in their hearts, thinking, *He's brave enough to humiliate himself—a real man!*

However, none of the Ghost Fire Locks atop their heads were unlocked by the attempt. Xie Lian's face changed slightly, and Qi Rong cackled.

"Ha ha ha ha ha! You fell for it! If I'm not the one who's doing the unlocking, the incantation is pointless! YOU CURSED YOURSELF FOR NOTHING! HA HA HA HA HA…"

A silver butterfly flew past Guzi's eyes. He blinked twice, his eyelids drooped, and he fell asleep in short order. Qi Rong was still cackling to himself when a forceful yank of his sleeve made him whirl around eighteen times before crashing into a wall.

"DOG-FUCKED XIE LIAN!" he blurted.

After he cursed, the ball of ghost fire atop Yin Yu's head disappeared. Yin Yu immediately leapt to his feet and dodged a good distance away. Qi Rong instantly covered his mouth, knowing he had slipped up.

"Come, come, come. Don't worry. Don't hold yourself back," Xie Lian said pleasantly. "Release your true self. Keep cursing."

He spoke with such serenity as he rolled up his sleeves and grabbed hold of Qi Rong. The ghost didn't fully understand what he meant by that, so he yelled with all he had.

"Go ahead! *Hit me!* Even if you beat me to death, I won't say that phrase again!"

Next to them, Hua Cheng said with an icy voice, "Perfect. Exactly the way I want it."

Qi Rong turned his head. He saw that Hua Cheng was smiling

at him with an incredibly fake smile, but it still disappeared in the blink of an eye.

Hua Cheng then slammed Qi Rong's head several centimeters into the ground.

"..."

Hua Cheng yanked his head out, and Qi Rong roared aloud.

"You dare treat me like this?! I've had it! I'll burn everyone! We can all die together! DOG HUA CHENG! BURN UP!"

It seemed that *"Dog Hua Cheng"* was the other half of the incantation, meant to initiate incineration. But after he yelled it, there were no cries nor wails from anyone. He opened his eyes in confusion.

The farmers were all fine, and they stood watching him from the other end of the room. Qi Rong was dumbfounded.

"What's going on? How come none of you died?! Go die! Who released you?!"

"You did," Xie Lian said.

He pointed at a silver butterfly on the side, which was broadcasting the exact same roar from earlier: *"YOU CURSED YOURSELF FOR NOTHING! HA HA HA HA..."*

That wraith butterfly had recorded everything. It had copied his voice, including the incantation. They could infinitely unlock with that one curse alone.

"Leave this plane," Hua Cheng said coldly. "Sorry, no one's coming with you."

With another violent strike, Qi Rong was bashed underground.

After the smoke finally cleared, the farmers all walked up and circled around to see. "Can... Can he still be fished up?"

Yin Yu hopped down into the deep crater that Hua Cheng had punched, and he jumped back out a moment later with a green budaoweng in his hand. "Chengzhu, Your Highness. The Green Ghost Qi Rong has been collected."

The vivid green budaoweng was baring its teeth and rolling its eyes back. A long tongue spat as it dangled from its mouth—it looked like it was laughing at someone, but also like it was blustering and ballyhooing with all its might. In any case, it was in extremely poor taste; even children would toss it aside in contempt if they saw it. Xie Lian couldn't tell if Qi Rong's character had influenced the design or if Hua Cheng purposely made him this way.

"Don't give that thing to us. You hang on to it, and keep it far, far away," Hua Cheng said.

"Yes, sir," Yin Yu acknowledged.

To be honest, Xie Lian didn't really want to hold the thing either. He picked up Guzi from the ground.

A few wraith butterflies came flying from a different direction and landed on the back of Hua Cheng's hand. He cast a glance down, then said, "We need to hurry back to the holy temple."

Xie Lian whirled around. "Did something happen there?"

89
Resentful Female Ghost, Flames of Jealousy Burn the Affection

HUA CHENG RAISED HIS HAND slightly and brought the silver butterfly perched there close to Xie Lian's ear. Along with the sound of the silver butterfly's fluttering wings, he heard Pei Ming's voice floating over.

"Silly thing, did you hear that strange noise?"

Even though Xie Lian knew that Pei Ming felt nothing for Banyue, the way he spoke would make anyone wonder. It was probably because Pei Ming had been chasing skirts for such a long time.

"I'm not silly..." Banyue muttered grimly. "And I heard. That noise was really weird. I don't think it's General Hua coming back."

Of course it wasn't—that was the thumping sound Xuan Ji made while hopping along on her broken legs!

The thumping didn't last long before the two on the other end fell silent. The next thing they heard was a woman's crazed laughter.

"Hee hee, heh heh, ha ha ha ha..."

That laughter echoed and resounded in the empty underground city, then carried over via the silver butterfly. Some white noise crackled over the transmission, and the result was even scarier than hearing it in person. Naturally, this was the laugh of the overjoyed and painfully hateful Xuan Ji, who had finally seen Pei Ming once more.

"Didn't the silver butterfly lead her in the opposite direction?" Xie Lian asked.

"She's smarter than expected," Hua Cheng replied.

Xuan Ji had been hot on the trail of that wraith butterfly, running with incredible speed all the way to the end of the main street in no time. However, she found no one there. She had once been a general on the battlefield, so she quickly realized that she had been led astray. She should've returned to Qi Rong the moment she figured it out, but she was dead set on finding Pei Ming. So she just turned around and ran in the opposite direction, throwing her boss completely out of her mind.

Xie Lian found it funny for some reason—it was a complicated sentiment. He quickly gathered the escaped hostages, and their group rushed to the Wuyong holy temple at the center of the city.

Xuan Ji had waited for Pei Ming for much, much too long; from the sound of her laughter alone, it was easy to imagine how crazed and twisted her face must look. Pei Ming was probably also stunned by the sight of her, and he was in shock for a long moment before he spoke.

"You are..."

Xuan Ji sneered coldly.

After a pause, however, Pei Ming unexpectedly asked, "Who are you?"

"..." Xuan Ji was so filled with hate that her voice turned sharp and trembling. "Are... Are you trying to anger me on purpose? You're actually asking who I am?!"

Xie Lian wiped away a drop of cold sweat. "No way, General Pei... Is he doing this on purpose, or does he really not recognize her?"

"Probably the latter," Hua Cheng said.

After all, if the rumors were true, Pei Ming had carried on affairs with over a thousand beauties over the course of many centuries. How could he remember each one? Especially an old one from so

RESENTFUL FEMALE GHOST

many hundreds of years ago. Furthermore, the Ghost Bride incident on Mount Yujun had been handed off to Pei Xiu to manage; Pei Ming didn't bother appearing in person at all, nor did he cast a single glance her way.

"Right. You're deliberately trying to anger me. I won't fall for it," Xuan Ji mumbled to herself. "Heh. You want to lie and say you don't remember me. You want to lie to me, hee hee hee." And then, she screeched again. "Who is this little whore?! Aren't your standards usually high?! What, trying a different flavor this time?!"

"...?" Banyue was confused.

"...?!" Pei Ming was even more confused.

Both made noises of confusion, but that resentful tone seemed to jog Pei Ming's memory. He slightly knitted his brows.

"Xuan Ji? What happened to you?"

Only then did Xie Lian remember that Xuan Ji must look quite disheveled. Her eyes were the red of a malicious ghost's, and the bottom hem of her bright crimson bridal robe was disgustingly filthy. She crawled like a crocodile on the ground, sluggish but dangerous. Presented with such a sight, it would genuinely be quite difficult to link her to the noble, composed general she once was.

Pei Ming's question infuriated Xuan Ji. "What happened to me? You *dare* ask how I've come to look like this?! It's *your* fault! I did all this for you!"

Hua Cheng was listening intently, so any subtle movements would not escape his ears. "She charged at the protection circle," he informed.

"Ruoye can hold her off," Xie Lian said.

Sure enough, a shriek was heard through the silver butterfly. Xuan Ji must've been bounced back and sent flying over thirty meters, dropping into the darkness once more.

Pei Ming spoke. "His Highness has an excellent spiritual device. I'll have to make one for myself sometime."

You wouldn't say that if you knew how it was forged... Xie Lian thought.

But before he could complete his thought, Pei Ming shouted, "What are you doing?! *Stop!*"

"Don't think you can keep hiding in there!" Xuan Ji yelled.

Rumble, rumble!

Xie Lian was dumbfounded as he hurried along. "What's that sound? Did something collapse? What did she do?"

"It appears she toppled the holy temple. The stone ceiling collapsed."

As it turned out, when Xuan Ji found out she couldn't enter Ruoye's protection circle, she knocked the entire building down in a fit.

"Are General Pei and the others all right? Little Pei and Banyue are both there too!" Xie Lian asked.

He was especially concerned for Pei Xiu, who was currently mortal—hopefully he didn't get crushed.

"They're fine. Pei Ming protected them," Hua Cheng said.

The moment the stone ceiling collapsed, Pei Ming became a meat shield and protected Pei Xiu and Banyue with his body. Xie Lian breathed a sigh of relief.

"Then it's fine. The protection circle won't break from that."

On the other end, Pei Ming was clearly furious. He smashed the stone slab on top of him with a punch and exclaimed, "Enough with the tantrum! Even if you topple the sky, you won't be able to get in!"

Xuan Ji only cackled wickedly in response.

"General Pei, watch out!" Banyue exclaimed.

"Wha..."

All their reactions happened at once. Amidst the chaos, Xie Lian heard the sound of a sharp sword piercing flesh. There was no question that Pei Ming was the one who was stabbed.

"What's happened?!" Xie Lian cried anxiously. "Who stabbed General Pei? Did the protection circle break? That's impossible... Wait, a sword?"

In that instant, he finally understood what Xuan Ji had been planning. So *that* was it!

After Xuan Ji had her fill of laughing, she said coolly, "Who said I wanted to get in?"

Another voice also started laughing. "Hey, Pei Ming, look who's here! It's your old sweetheart!"

Rong Guang!

As it turned out, Xuan Ji didn't topple the holy temple in a mad fit of rage, nor was she trying to enter the protection circle. Her goal was to crush the two ghost-sealing clay pots Banyue had with her in the circle. This would release the ghosts and allow them to attack from the inside!

As soon as Rong Guang escaped the pot, he quickly turned into his sword form and stabbed Pei Ming. Pei Ming seemed to be trying to pull him out, but Rong Guang wouldn't budge and kept himself firmly buried in Pei Ming's body.

"You wish! Time to die!"

Pei Ming gritted his teeth. "State Preceptor Banyue! Is the other pot okay?!"

Xuan Ji and Rong Guang were already attacking them from both sides. If Kemo joined the mix, it'd be over for them.

"Yes! Kemo is still sealed!" Banyue confirmed.

The situation was growing dire, and Xie Lian was worried. Just as he was about to quicken his pace, Hua Cheng stopped completely.

Perplexed, Xie Lian looked back.

"San Lang?"

On the back of Hua Cheng's hand perched another wraith butterfly, which seemed to be whispering to him about a new change in the situation. When the report was done, he looked up and smiled.

"Gege, no need to panic. Looks like it'll be fine even if we don't rush over."

Back at the temple, Mingguang had pierced Pei Ming's chest under Rong Guang's command. Xuan Ji gripped his boots before shimmying up his leg, looking like a red gecko. With the way she was dressed and that ghost fire looming over her head, she was the very picture of a crazed ghost woman.

"You—!" Pei Ming cried.

"Pei darling... Pei darling...!" Xuan Ji murmured.

She wrapped herself around Pei Ming, contorting her body and mangled legs in horrible shapes. In that position, it was difficult to tell whether she wanted to strangle him to death or embrace him tightly. At the edge of her vision, she suddenly spotted Pei Xiu, whom Pei Ming was shielding. She remembered that this cold and stoic martial god had sealed her under a mountain, and she gritted her teeth.

"You little *mutt*!"

Just as her claws were about to swipe, a hand seized her wrist. The skin of the hand that had halted hers was just as pale as her own. When she looked up, she realized it was Banyue who had stopped her.

Her heart burned whenever she saw another woman by Pei Ming's side, and she cried, "I haven't even come for *your* wretched life, but here you are, giving yourself up to me!"

And then she grabbed for Banyue's head. But Banyue wasn't one of those good, obedient little brides who would stand around waiting to be scratched to death. She deftly seized Xuan Ji's other wrist.

Xuan Ji was a general in life—she knew that her strength would put most men to shame, and typical human women and female ghosts could only submit to her beatings. But she never could have imagined that this little girl—who looked so thin and weak, like a simple breeze could knock her over—possessed such terrifying power in her arms, a strength that nearly dwarfed Xuan Ji's own! Not only were both her wrists cuffed and immobile, but Xuan Ji was even more stunned when their eyes met. This little girl's gaze was full of aggression and murderous intent, like the shimmer of a blade in combat; it reminded Xuan Ji of the battlefield. Her heart lurched, and she flung away her arms to break free of the hold.

Banyue picked up Pei Xiu and, borrowing the force of Xuan Ji's throw, hopped meters away, landing lightly on her feet.

"Let go of General Pei!"

The sword buried in Pei Ming taunted him. "Pei Ming, you're lucky with women as usual. Look at this—you've got two lady ghosts fighting over you! Ha ha ha…"

Xuan Ji clung to Pei Ming like a contorted scarlet python, and both her hands wrapped around his neck. "Your little lover seems to have some skill," she said coldly.

Pei Ming coughed out a mouthful of blood. "She's not my lover! I don't have one!"

"You're still trying to deny it?!" Xuan Ji cried. "If she's not your lover, why would she tell me to let you go?!"

"If my old ma was here, she'd tell you to let me go too! By your definition, would that make *her* my lover?" Pei Ming countered.

Only his frivolous character could be blamed at this point, since he went around calling women "silly thing" for no good reason. Xuan Ji was mad with jealousy and refused to believe a word he said.

"What? Afraid to admit it? You were so *intimate* when speaking to her before! Didn't you always admit it so frankly whenever you got your hands on a new flame? You'd always be honest with me, never caring for my feelings. Do you know how miserable I was? Why are you scared of admitting to anything now?! General Pei, have you started to fear death? Or do you love her so much that you can't bear to let me touch a single one of her fingers?!"

They were still a good distance from the holy temple, and Xie Lian watched this scene play out from afar. He couldn't bear to stand by anymore and looked back.

"San Lang, why don't we go rescue them?"

Hua Cheng laughed. "No need to worry, gege. Someone else will be showing up soon on our behalf. Besides, even if we headed over now, Xuan Ji wouldn't release her choke hold on Pei Ming."

That was true, and things would indeed be rather difficult with the hostages to look after. Yin Yu and the farmers were nervously spectating the action and providing commentary.

"Yeah, I can tell that lady ghost's love has warped into hatred. She's going nuts!"

"I don't think so. I'm sure she won't be able to bring herself to go through with it. Want some melon seeds?"

"Give me another handful, thanks."

"How can everyone be in the mood to snack on melon seeds?"[9] Xie Lian asked, frowning.

"Your Highness, didn't you eat a bunch too?" the people said.

"Huh?"

---

[9] "Snacking on melon seeds" is internet slang for spectating someone else's drama.

Only then did Xie Lian realize that while he was focused on the show, he had unconsciously accepted a handful of melon seeds that had been passed to him and eaten them all. He slapped his forehead.

"How... How rude of me..."

On the other end, Pei Ming was at the end of his rope. "Xuan Ji, do you have to be like this about everything? It's been so many years. Why can't we just bury the hatchet and walk away? Why must you be like this?"

Xuan Ji's hands squeezed his throat harder, her almond-shaped eyes bulging. "No! You messed with me first, and you want to bury the hatchet and walk away?! You wish!"

Pei Ming sighed. "You really...haven't changed at all. This is exactly why we didn't work out."

Xuan Ji thrust her face close to his. "*What* was that?! You think *I'm* the problem? What do you mean?!" she cried in rage. "Am I not beautiful enough? You told me I was gorgeous! Did I deny you Yushi's battle plans and army secrets? No, but you refused them! You said that you didn't like that I was strong-minded, so I threw away my own legs! Who could ever love you more than me?! But what about you? Over hundreds of years, you never even cast a single glance my way! When did you ever come to see me?!"

Pei Ming pushed away the face that was pressed so close to his. "I didn't visit because I knew you'd go crazy if I came to see you!" he shouted.

Xuan Ji seized the Mingguang sword in his chest and pushed it in deeper, then pulled it out. Pei Ming puked another few mouthfuls of blood.

"*Say it!*" Xuan Ji yelled. "Swear on your status as a heavenly official! Swear that from now on, I am the only one. Swear that you'll never look at another woman again—that your eyes will rot if you do!"

Rong Guang was clearly enjoying this. "Go on and say it, Pei Ming! Say it and you can salvage your pathetic life!"

Pei Ming cursed. "Shut *up*! Goddammit. I never could've guessed... I didn't die on the battlefield, I didn't die by the world's greatest sword... Instead, I'll die by the hand of a nutty ghost woman!"

Not receiving the answer she desired, Xuan Ji was absolutely furious, and her claws shot out to grip the crown of his head. Xie Lian really couldn't wait any longer.

"San Lang, I think things are getting out of hand," he said as he put his hand on Fangxin's hilt. "Will the person you spoke of make it in time? If not, then let me go first!"

"It's fine," Hua Cheng said. "Gege, look. Here they come."

Just as the words left his lips, the insane, furious Xuan Ji froze completely.

It was like someone had cast a petrification spell on her; her body and expression went rigid. Pei Ming had already been stabbed by her multiple times, and his vomited blood covered the floor. From within the darkness, they could hear the crisp sound of ox hooves.

Click clack, click clack.

Their pace was unhurried. Soon after, a person riding a black ox appeared before them.

The rider was a woman wearing robes of lush green. Her eyes were clear, and her expression was calm and quiet. As she languidly approached, she held her chin high, like she was gazing at something far away.

Pei Ming, with blood smeared around his lips, was momentarily stunned. "...Queen Yushi?"

The woman inclined her head to look at him, her demeanor unchanged. She then gave a slight smile and bowed her head to return the greeting.

Xie Lian was shocked as well. "...Queen Yushi?"

"That's right," Hua Cheng replied. "Heaven's current Rain Master, the sixteenth princess of the Kingdom of Yushi, Yushi Huang. She was also the last ruler of the Kingdom of Yushi."

90
The Last Princess, Throat Slit Before the Palace Gates

"I'VE NEVER HAD THE HONOR to meet the Rain Master in person, so I didn't know she was once a princess..." Xie Lian said.

On the other side, Xuan Ji gritted her teeth. "What...did you do...? Why...can't...I move?!"

The Rain Master moved her gaze away from Pei Ming and explained, "I have brought the Yulong[10] sword."

"The Yulong sword?" Xie Lian wondered.

"The sacred guardian sword of the Kingdom of Yushi, wielded by all of its rulers throughout history," Hua Cheng replied. "The Rain Master forged it into a spiritual device. It possesses a natural power of deterrence against the people of Yushi, and Xuan Ji was a traitor to her people. The fear and guilt still consume her heart—of course she can do naught but kneel and obey."

The Rain Master told her not to move, therefore she couldn't move.

"If you can't move, I'll do it myself!" Rong Guang exclaimed.

He prepared to stab Pei Ming again, but before his blade could sink even a centimeter deeper, there was an explosion of red smoke. *Clunk!* The sword piercing Pei Ming's chest disappeared, and a tiny blade no longer than a finger fell to the ground.

"What's going on? Why can't I move either?!" Rong Guang yelled furiously.

---

10 雨龍 / Yulong means "Rain Dragon."

Xie Lian and the others finally stopped spectating from afar and walked over. Hua Cheng glanced at the tiny, toy-like Mingguang sword on the ground and smirked.

"Much better."

"Let go, Xuan Ji," the Rain Master bid her temperately.

Xuan Ji's hands began to drop from Pei Ming's neck, but she refused to yield so easily. "I won't! I finally caught him; I won't let him go!"

"If you must cling to something in order to yield, why not pick up that which you have tossed away and hold it in your hands anew?" the Rain Master said.

Alas, the power of the sacred guardian sword was too strong, and Xuan Ji was forcibly torn away. She fell backward to the ground, looking unkempt and miserable, her hair disheveled.

"What right do you have to lecture me?! Do you really take yourself for the ruler of the kingdom?! Or have you forgotten how you became queen?! I won't acknowledge you! I won't!"

The Rain Master closed her eyes and softly shook her head. Banyue seized the opportunity to hurl a pot at Xuan Ji, which sucked her in, and then she swiftly sealed the ghost bride inside!

And so, the source of all this mess was finally subdued. Xie Lian went to Pei Ming's side and helped him up.

"General Pei's all right?"

"This won't kill me," Pei Ming said. Then he asked doubtfully, "I say, Your Highness, have you been here for a while already?"

"Ha ha... What do you mean?" Xie Lian replied.

Pei Ming picked up the tiny, shrunken Mingguang sword in his hand. "Crimson Rain Sought Flower, how tough is this seal? It won't break under pressure, will it?"

"Of course not," Hua Cheng replied. "To release it, you must hold the hilt, apply spiritual power, and mentally give permission. This seal can't be broken by accident or deception."

Only then did Pei Ming heave a long sigh. As for the farmers who had escaped Qi Rong's clutches, they all rushed forward like their parents had appeared before them.

"Lord Rain Master!"

The rest of the group turned around, and Xie Lian inclined his head in respect.

"Queen Yushi."

The Rain Master had dismounted the black ox, rope in hand, and she also bowed her head to return the courtesy. "Your Royal Highness."

As they greeted each other, Xie Lian inadvertently glimpsed her neck and was slightly taken aback, but he quickly replied, "During Xianle's drought, My Lord loaned me the Rain Master Hat and aided me in my time of need. I was never able to thank you in person, but my wish has come true today."

Then he bent forward and bowed deeply. The Rain Master stood still and waited until he had completed his respect before she replied, speaking very slowly.

"I imagine that Your Royal Highness might never have relaxed had I refused your one bow. Now that it is done, let us forget the whole affair."

The tone of her voice was clear and serene, slow and mild. She wore a soft smile, looking particularly tranquil.

Suddenly, a voice called out, "Hey, Pei Ming, isn't this embarrassing? Needing a woman to save you—and it's Yushi Huang, no less! Hee hee, ha ha ha ha..."

The Rain Master's demeanor remained unchanged, still very calm, but Pei Ming didn't look so comfortable anymore.

The black ox began snorting harsh breaths in Pei Ming's direction, shaking his head and swinging his tail. Although the aggression wasn't aimed at Hua Cheng, Xie Lian knew that bulls got angry when they saw red, and he recalled many painful experiences of being chased and struck. He quickly shifted in front of Hua Cheng, afraid the ox would be further provoked by the red of Hua Cheng's robes. At the same time, he slapped a talisman on the little sword to seal its mouth.

Pei Ming had to say something at this point. He scratched his nose and said politely, "My thanks to Queen Yushi for rescuing and helping Little Pei."

The Rain Master was also courteous, and she cupped her hands. "It was nothing."

Banyue came over and tugged on the Rain Master's sleeve. "Lord Rain Master, Pei Xiu-gege passed out from hunger…"

Hua Cheng glanced over. "Let's get to the surface first."

The question of provisions was solved very efficiently by the residents of Yushi Country. Since the Rain Master controlled agriculture, her people always carried food with them. By the time they got back above ground, night had passed and the sun had come out. The Rain Master retrieved seeds from a satchel on the ox, found a field, and planted them then and there. Before long, a small field of crops had sprouted and were ready for harvest.

Those who had been starving all cheered. Xie Lian realized that Guzi probably hadn't eaten well in the past few days either and woke him up. The moment he was awake, Guzi asked where his dad was, then concluded that he'd deserted him again. He cried up a storm, so Yin Yu had no choice but to give him that extremely ugly green budaoweng to hold. When Guzi heard this was his dad, it was like he had been given a treasure; he stopped crying and hugged it tightly as he ate a yam.

Meanwhile, Xie Lian, Hua Cheng, the Rain Master, and Pei Ming sat to one side to discuss serious business.

They could already see Mount Tonglu up ahead. Now that they were closer, they could tell that the lower half of the mountain was covered with large patches of crimson red, like splattered blood. The upper half was covered with harsh layers of snow.

"Not just General Pei Junior, but Banyue, Guzi, and the rest must all stay here," Xie Lian said. "They can't continue onward."

Pei Ming was pouring medicinal smoke from a small bottle over his wounds and shook his head as he sighed. "I've been unlucky this entire way. Hurdle after hurdle."

He'd had hellish bad luck—that really did describe his journey thus far, and he was feeling quite miserable.

The Rain Master sat with poise next to Xie Lian, and after some contemplation, she said, "Your Highness, your mission is to subdue all evil creatures who possess the potential to become a supreme. There is one that you may need to watch out for."

Xie Lian perked up. "Did Lord Rain Master run into something on the road?"

The Rain Master nodded lightly. "Yes. On the way here, I met a young man dressed in white."

Xie Lian let out a soft noise of acknowledgment. "We also heard rumors about the one My Lord speaks of while on the road. Many nefarious creatures were afraid of him; we almost ran into him as well. Has My Lord seen him in person? How did you manage to get away?"

"Much ashamed," the Rain Master said, "but if it wasn't for the Guardian Steed's astoundingly powerful legs and that young man's lack of interest, it is difficult to say how the meeting would have ended."

"What did he look like?" Xie Lian pressed.

"His appearance was not clear," the Rain Master said. "His head was wrapped in bandages."

Head wrapped in bandages?! Xie Lian was dumbfounded. "Was it Lang Ying?!"

Pei Ming frowned. "Your Highness knows him?"

"I'm not sure," Xie Lian replied, then immediately turned to Hua Cheng. "San Lang, Lang Ying is definitely in Ghost City, right?"

Hua Cheng also looked serious and only answered after a pause. "He *was*, but it's hard to say whether he still is. Gege, why don't you verify further?"

Xie Lian continued his questions. "Lord Rain Master, you said the white-clad young man's head was wrapped in bandages. Was he just over ten years of age, or maybe a bit older? Either way, a scrawny boy."

Yet unexpectedly, the Rain Master replied, "No. The young man was about sixteen or seventeen, and his body type was similar to that of Your Highness."

"Huh?" Now this was not what Xie Lian had expected to hear. "Sixteen or seventeen? Lang Ying isn't that old."

Was it really him? Based on the current information, he couldn't be certain.

Pei Ming tossed the little medicine bottle aside after he was done. "Either way, we'll all end up in the Kiln in the end. Let's just wait and see."

As a martial god, his recovery speed was exceptionally fast. With just one bottle of spiritual medicine, his severe chest wound was already mostly healed. The Rain Master inclined her head.

"Why doesn't General Pei have a sword?"

Pei Ming hadn't expected her to actively ask him anything and didn't know how to best respond. Pei Xiu, who was finally conscious, answered on his behalf while eating a roasted yam.

"General, Pei's, sword was, snapped."

"Eat your yam," Pei Ming said.

Pei Xiu shut his mouth. When the Rain Master heard this, she thought for a moment before removing her own sword and handing it to Pei Ming with both hands.

There was nothing off about her expression, and she acted with the utmost grace. It was instead Pei Ming whose face changed slightly, with an expression like she was giving him a poisonous snake.

After some hesitation, he said, "Thanks, but this is Yushi's sacred guardian sword. It's probably inappropriate for me to wield it."

"It has been centuries since the Kingdom of Yushi was destroyed. General Pei is a martial god, a skilled swordsman," the Rain Master said gently. "Since we are here to prevent the birth of a new ghost king, this sword will be more effective if you are the one to wield it, rather than I."

Pei Ming hesitated even longer, but in the end he still very politely declined. "Pei thanks Queen Yushi for her kindness. But there's no need."

The Rain Master didn't push further. They all chatted for a bit longer, and the Rain Master asked whether they had any news of the Wind Master. Only then did Xie Lian learn that the Rain and Wind Masters were on good terms. Shi Qingxuan had often visited Yushi Country to eat, drink, and be merry, but he hadn't been there in a long time—due to the Black Water incident, of course. The Lord Rain Master had sent out her own search party, but they had come back empty-handed. She couldn't help but sigh.

The group decided that they would rest for another two hours before continuing on their way. Xie Lian walked off, looking for a random tree to lean against and doze for a bit. However, Hua Cheng managed to produce some rope and cloth out of nowhere, and he set up two swinging hammock beds between two trees. Both of them climbed in and had a good time swinging, and the beds themselves were quite comfortable to recline in. After lying there for a bit, his arms pillowing the back of his head, Xie Lian wondered aloud in confusion.

"San Lang, why do you think General Pei won't take Lord Rain Master's sword?"

A martial god who lost his weapon should surely be anxious to find another one; was Pei Ming eager for a beating?

Hua Cheng also had his arms pillowing his head. "Someone like Pei Ming... While he loves women, he might not think highly of them," he replied leisurely. "Not only did he have to be rescued to begin with, it was by a woman—and one he knew in the past, no less. He must be quite frustrated and see the whole situation as embarrassing. Besides, the Rain Master once disciplined one of his descendants. He probably thinks she was trying to make fun of him. With all that rattling around in his head, how could he possibly take the sword?"

Their hammock beds squeaked as they swung. Xie Lian sighed. "What nonsensical pride. By the way, San Lang, did you notice? There's an old scar on Lord Rain Master's neck."

"I don't need to see it to know," Hua Cheng said. "She's the Princess Who Slit Her Throat, after all."

Xie Lian pulled himself up a bit. "I knew it."

"Did gege notice that the Rain Master speaks a little slowly? That's also caused by the old scar on her neck."

"Oh! I thought that was just her personality," Xie Lian said. "As a princess, why did she have to slit her own throat? Xuan Ji's comment also made me curious: *'Or have you forgotten how you became queen?!'* How *did* she become queen?"

"It's a long story, but I'll keep it short," Hua Cheng replied.

While Yushi Huang certainly was of royal descent in the Kingdom of Yushi, she lacked high status—she was a daughter born from a palace servant, so her rank was low. And her awkward, introverted personality did little to help. Each and every one of the fifteen older siblings above, as well as all the younger siblings below, were favored more highly than she.

The Temple of Yulong was the Kingdom of Yushi's royal cultivation hall. According to historical custom, in order to express their sincerity to the heavens, every ruler would select one descendant and send them there to cultivate and pray for prosperity and peace. It sounded like a grand assignment, but in truth, it was grueling work. The method of cultivation the Temple of Yulong practiced involved hard physical labor; no servants or any items of comfort were permitted, and those of royal descent were not exempt from harsh training. The position was traditionally pushed around; if one was unlucky enough to land it, they would often spend an impressive fortune to find a substitute. But when this generation came around, there was no selection process needed—Yushi Huang was sent off from the get-go.

Xie Lian shook his head at this point in the story. Although they both came from royalty and both entered their royal cultivation halls, the Rain Master's experience greatly differed from his own.

"No wonder Xuan Ji didn't sound like she thought highly of the Rain Master," Xie Lian remarked.

"Of course," Hua Cheng said. "Xuan Ji might not be a princess, but she came from an impressive background nonetheless and had many suitors. She was valued far higher in the eyes of royalty and nobility."

Now that Xuan Ji had ruined herself, it was no wonder she couldn't stand the sight of the Rain Master, who still planted fields so tranquilly. The Rain Master had urged her to let go, but from Xuan Ji's perspective, her words were probably seen as condescending and sarcastic.

In any case, the Rain Master spent her days at the Temple of Yulong cultivating in ascetic peace. Until one day, a few distinguished guests came from the Kingdom of Xuli.

Xuli and Yushi didn't immediately fall out; there was some forced civility and false courtesy at first. In order to maintain the bogus peace, the Kingdom of Xuli sent a few royals, generals, and civil officials to attend the national banquet of the Kingdom of Yushi, and they paid a visit to Yushi's royal cultivation hall while they were at it.

That day, Yushi Huang was cleaning the tiles on the roof of the temple. When she was ready to come down, she found that someone had taken the ladder away.

The people on the ground all found it funny to see someone stuck on the roof, unable to get down. Even the princesses and princes of Yushi were snickering behind their hands. It was a general of Xuli who, after chuckling, leapt onto the roof and helped her down.

That general was, of course, Pei Ming. Xie Lian was just thinking that General Pei was quite the Casanova when a new voice suddenly spoke up.

"That guy Pei Ming—he's like that everywhere he goes. Like a dog that always needs to piss and mark its territory."

THE LAST PRINCESS, THROAT SLIT

Xie Lian was instantly pulled back to the present by that malicious, vulgar comparison. He looked back and picked up the unbelievably shrunken sword.

"General Rong, when did you break free of the mouth-sealing talisman? Looks like you really want to talk, huh?"

"Don't seal me! Let me speak!" Rong Guang said. "I know every sordid affair Pei Ming has ever had like the back of my hand! Three days and three nights wouldn't be enough to list them all! He knew Xuli was going to invade Yushi soon, but he still went and seduced all the favored high-ranking princesses. They were all crazy for him and got in jealous fights. Don't you think that's a little immoral?"

It certainly wasn't nice—smile and laugh with me one day, then invade and trample my home the next. Xie Lian felt a little sorry.

"So did Queen Yushi and General Pei have a good relationship back then?"

"There was never any *relationship*," Rong Guang said. "That guy only met Yushi Huang twice. There were too many beauties in Yushi; he forgot her by the next day."

In this world, friendships between women fell out fast, but ones between men fell out even faster. The only difference was the end result. When women had a falling-out, it might be over after some slaps or scratching, but when men fell out, the end might very well be death—without an intact corpse. When Xuli no longer wished to maintain a false peace, they simply made up some excuse to invade. Pei Ming led their army and charged all the way to the palace gates, forcing the King of Yushi to hide deep within the palace and cling to it as his very last line of defense. However, Pei Ming only needed to apply a bit of pressure to crack the palace's delicate layer of protection like a snail's shell.

But he didn't crush them so simply; there were other considerations. At Rong Guang's suggestion, he did something else.

The Xuli troops took hundreds of felons from Yushi's death row, dressed them up as normal civilians, and dragged them before the palace gates. Pei Ming charged King Yushi with the crime of oppressing his people and stated that he must come outside, kowtow three times, and kill himself in atonement. Only then would they free the civilians, and only then would they promise to not harm the remaining members of the royal household. If the king refused, Pei Ming would behead the hostages. He gave the royals three days—and with each day that passed, a third of the group would be killed. After three days came and went, they would invade the palace to kill all the royals, then kill the rest of the civilians.

"General Rong, what a shrewd but beautiful move," Xie Lian remarked.

Rong Guang wasn't mad; he even seemed pleased. "I'll take that as a compliment."

It was a splendid excuse for Xuli to invade Yushi. *"The King of Yushi is negligent and oppressive in his rule, and for the sake of justice, Xuli shall rescue the suffering citizens of the kingdom."* The sheer righteousness—truly, a beautiful move.

If King Yushi refused to come out, then he was selfish, muddleheaded, and didn't care for his people—and he had always declared that he loved his people like his children. It would provoke resentment from the citizenry if his words and actions didn't match, and they would assume that they had been deceived. *"Didn't you say you loved your people like your children? Why would you turn around and let us be sacrificed for the sake of the royals?"* This would then destroy their loyalty to the Yushi royals.

After killing the last of those "civilians," the people of Yushi would be terrified that Xuli's next move would be to slaughter the whole city. Xuli would then announce that those who had been executed were felons on death row anyway, doomed to die—they had only been used to reveal the selfish lies of the Yushi royals. Seeing such an immense contrast would immediately calm the growing fears in the hearts of the Yushi people and turn them meek and obedient. That would make Xuli's subsequent takeover much easier, as the people would be suitably disheartened.

However, if King Yushi really did come out and kill himself to atone... Whatever, it'd make no difference, it would just save them the hassle of killing him themselves. Besides, Pei Ming and Rong Guang believed that King Yushi would never go through with it—or rather, that no monarch would be willing to end their life in a state of such humiliation. To bow before civilians and enemy troops alike, admit one's mistakes, and then die? Dream on!

But unexpectedly, the ruler of Yushi actually did emerge after only one day, just as Pei Ming was about to order the execution of the first group of "civilians."

The palace gates opened. With the sacred guardian sword Yulong hanging from the royal waist, the monarch walked out, kneeled before the people, and kowtowed three times. The sword was unsheathed, a throat was slashed, and the gates were splashed with blood.

Xie Lian could already guess what had happened. "Was it Lord Rain Master who came out?"

"Yes," Hua Cheng replied.

After the palace attendants and royal family had been thoroughly interrogated, the Xuli troops discovered what had happened.

The Xuli troops, which included Pei Ming and Rong Guang, had been loitering around outside the palace that day, laughing boisterously in an excessively arrogant display. On the other hand, the palace was utter chaos inside; crying and wailing filled the air. It was of course impossible that King Yushi would go out and kill himself. He sat upon his throne, his face grim and pale. Meanwhile, all the royal siblings, who usually fought each other bloody to curry favor with the king, had been howling and weeping for ages—but the king still hadn't moved a muscle. So each of them began to cautiously attempt to persuade him.

There were a variety of reasons and many types of arguments, such as: *"This is for the people!" "Even if you die, your name will go down in history!" "If you do nothing, your people are doomed!"*

Every excuse was trotted out, but nothing swayed the king, and soon a day had almost passed. Some of the sons were growing anxious, and they yelled at their father in agitation.

The king hadn't even died yet; he was outraged at their behavior and swung his staff out to beat them with it. The sons and grandsons would have never retaliated in the past, but no one cared now that they were in such dire straits. And so, one of the princes could no longer tolerate it and hit back. His punch was unexpectedly too powerful, and it knocked the king, who was in his sixties, to the floor. His head was drenched in blood, and he couldn't get back up.

The princes and princesses were petrified at first, but they soon relaxed when they realized he was still breathing. They began to discuss how they could drag the immobile king out of the gate, and then how they could manipulate his limbs into performing the difficult movements of kowtowing and atonement. Even ridiculous ideas were part of the heated discussion—such as stringing him up like a puppet to control him. The king was so furious he almost had a stroke right then and there. Finally, they decided that they would find two people to carry the old king outside to

THE LAST PRINCESS, THROAT SLIT

complete the process of atonement. However, now there was a new problem—who should those two people be? It was a dangerous position to be in; who knew whether General Pei Ming would simply shoot them dead with arrows if he wasn't pleased. Nobody was willing to do it.

The dispute and arguments went on and on and on. The whole time, the sixteenth princess stood there, silent and unnoticed, but she suddenly said something to the old king where he lay on the ground.

"Please allow me to succeed to the throne," Yushi Huang said.

King Yushi gazed at this daughter he had barely looked at over the course of her life, and a trifling tear finally rolled from the corner of his eye.

Only a single drop.

Normally, there would be endless fights over this position, but no one fought this time. Whoever gained the office was doomed to die. Thus, in less than an hour, after the crudest and most rushed succession ceremony in the history of the Kingdom of Yushi, the least likely monarch was born.

The new Queen of Yushi slit her own throat and blood poured forth like a fountain. She was no doubt beyond saving. Pei Ming had never thought things would go like this; when he glanced over between drinks and saw it play out, he was completely stunned. Rong Guang cursed loudly, upset that their luck had turned out this way. How could they do this?! The ruler had certainly atoned, but it wasn't the same ruler as the day before! The death of someone so insignificant wouldn't destroy the people's loyalty, and now they couldn't kill the old crook king.

Even today, Rong Guang still found it unbelievable. "We never thought they'd pull a move like that, passing the throne off at the last moment and finding a scapegoat. Absolutely outrageous!"

The soldiers of Xuli couldn't bear to watch this absurd succession farce anymore, and they made considerable noise about whether to save this so-called "queen." However, her injury was too great; the medical officers confirmed that she couldn't be saved. In the end, Pei Ming had to keep his promise not to touch the civilians outside the palace, nor lay a finger on the royal family. They dressed the injury on the neck of this "ruler," then sent her properly to the Temple of Yulong to allow her to breathe her last. They would find her a better place in the royal mausoleum, where she would be buried.

When Yushi Huang took her last breath that night beneath the divine statue of the former Rain Master, the statue sighed.

Thunder roared and lightning crackled. The new Rain Master had ascended.

As the tale drew to a close, Xie Lian mused, "No wonder General Pei wore that expression when he saw the sword."

91

Ride the Black Ox, Flying Hooves on Mount Tonglu

YULONG WAS THE SACRED GUARDIAN sword that Yushi Huang had used to slash her own throat, so of course Pei Ming couldn't take it! It was certainly a holy weapon, but it was also a murderous one.

"Yushi Huang sure is generous. Otherwise, I'd almost suspect she did that on purpose to scare him—or remind him," Rong Guang said. "I can't believe she'd actually bring out Yulong for him to use. You really think he'd dare? Ha ha ha ha…"

Xie Lian couldn't tolerate him anymore. "Why must you always think so negatively?"

And he slapped on another talisman to seal Rong Guang's mouth.

It just so happened that at that moment, Pei Ming called out to them from a distance.

"Your Highness, Crimson Rain Sought Flower, are you two rested? Time to put the beds away; let's get going."

There wasn't much time to rest in the first place, and it had flown by while they chatted.

Most of their group stayed behind while Xie Lian, Hua Cheng, and Pei Ming set off. The Rain Master had a steed and offered to give them a ride to the foot of Mount Tonglu. Xie Lian thanked her with delight. The black ox shook and transformed, becoming three times bigger than his previous size—there was room for six people on his back. He lowered his front legs to the ground, laying his body low for the Rain Master to mount him and ride at the very front. Pei Ming was next, but he left a large space between himself and the Rain Master. Last came Xie Lian and Hua Cheng. After Xie Lian mounted, the black ox rose to his feet, now incredibly tall. Xie Lian brushed his hands against the smooth, shiny black coat with amazement.

"Lord Rain Master's steed truly is magical. San Lang, I think you might've mentioned it before, but how did he come to be?"

Stretching out its legs, the black ox began to run. The scenery on either side quickly disappeared behind them, and the ride was as amazingly steady as it was amazingly fast.

Hua Cheng gently held on to Xie Lian's waist from behind, as if afraid he might fall. "He was once the door knocker on one of the side gates at the Temple of Yulong, the royal cultivation hall of Yushi."

There was a minor custom at the Temple of Yulong: visitors would rub the golden beasts carved on the door knockers to give them human qi and accumulate good karma. When devotees visited, they usually rubbed the dragons, tigers, herons, and other such holy beasts. People typically didn't rub the ox, so the carving was rather deserted and lonely. While Yushi Huang cultivated at the Temple of Yulong, every time she passed that door while seeking water, she would rub the ox's head. It absorbed her qi, and when the Rain Master ascended, the ox ascended with her. He was the only deputy she ever appointed.

The black ox ran quickly, and Xie Lian leaned back slightly from the force. It was almost like he was sitting in Hua Cheng's embrace. He chuckled at the story.

"There certainly isn't anything San Lang doesn't know. No tale or classic can trip you up."

Hua Cheng chuckled as well. "Is there anything else gege wants to know? If it's within my expertise, I'll tell you everything."

Pei Ming sat in front of them; since the Rain Master wasn't talking, he didn't make conversation either, and instead listened in on them. "Indeed, Lord Ghost King. Your Highness, why don't you ask about Crimson Rain Sought Flower's background? See if he'll answer you."

Xie Lian's smile immediately faltered. Inquiring after the background of a ghost king was not very polite; in Xie Lian's opinion, that sort of personal information was no different than asking about the size of a man's manhood. He instantly changed the subject, worried that Hua Cheng might get upset.

"General Pei," he called out nonchalantly.

"What?" Pei Ming asked.

"There are bumps up ahead, watch out," Xie Lian cautioned.

"What?"

As soon as he spoke, the black ox carrying the four of them lowed a long cry, deep as a bell. Pei Ming went flying off his back—and was completely dumbfounded.

"What the heck?"

Something like this had truly never been heard of nor seen before. Mistakes happened—if he fell off, then so be it. But how could only the person in the middle be thrown and not the ones in the front and back? Was that even possible?

The ox never paused in his step. Xie Lian looked back, his hollering trailing behind.

"Didn't I warn you to watch out for the bumps ahead, General Pei...?"

Over the course of their journey, Pei Ming was flung off seven or eight times. Finally, the four riding the Rain Master's Guardian Steed arrived at the foot of Mount Tonglu.

Much like Mount Taicang, Mount Tonglu used to be a lush green mountain sitting at the heart of the royal capital, its scenery elegant and beautiful. At its foot was the majestic imperial city, the most prosperous in the kingdom.

The city had once been buried deep underground, but it had probably resurfaced after many earthquakes and was now back above the earth. Xie Lian's eyes scanned their surroundings for a moment as he sat on the black ox. He was about to dismount when he saw Hua Cheng standing there, his hand outstretched toward him. Xie Lian's heart skipped a beat, and he gave him his hand before hopping down.

"There must be a holy temple here in the imperial city, right?"

"There certainly is," Hua Cheng replied.

Pei Ming had fallen many times during the ride, but he was very sturdy and didn't limp at all when he walked—as expected of a martial god. He even reached out to pat the ox's neck, failing to notice the ox baring his teeth at him dangerously.

"I'm guessing the tallest building in the city must either be the palace or the holy temple," he stated.

"No," Hua Cheng replied. "The imperial city's Wuyong Temple is on top of the mountain."

He pointed. Halfway up the crimson mountain, there was the corner of a roof peeking out. The majority of the building was hidden in a misty red shadow.

"Why is the mountain red...?" Xie Lian wondered.

He had barely finished his question before the ox roared and threw his head back. They'd already started walking away, but they looked back, startled. The ox was rolling on the ground, but the Rain Master never loosened her tight grip on the rope she used to lead him.

"What's going on?"

The ox let out a human scream. *"Aaaaaaaah!"*

As soon as she heard this scream, the Rain Master pulled out Yulong and struck down toward the black ox!

The blade flashed. Something black and furry was flung away and sent crashing into a wall on the street, staining it with a large bloody splash. It was a corpse-eating rat!

The scream hadn't been from the black ox but from a corpse-eating rat that had climbed onto the ox and bit him hard when no one was looking. Although the rat was on the brink of death, it still screamed and screamed.

"Your Royal Highness... Your Highness, Your Highness, Your Highness! Save me, save me, save me!"

BOOM!

Its shrill cries made Xie Lian seize up, and his head began to throb. Hua Cheng swiftly pulled him to stand behind him, then raised his hand. The corpse-eating rat was blown into a mist of blood, but the tiny eyes remained stuck to the wall and shimmered with madness.

"Lord Rain Master, I suggest you check over your steed," Hua Cheng said.

The Rain Master was already combing through and turning over the ox's black hair. "It's just a scratch."

However, more and more human voices rose in undulating whispers from all around.

"*Cough...cough, cough...* Take me away, take me away!"

"I should've fled a long time ago..."

"I can't get over it... We shouldn't have believed his nonsense! We face a wrongful death!"

"Gege... Gege? *Your Highness!*"

That last line was particularly clear—it was Hua Cheng's voice. Only then did Xie Lian snap out of it. "...I'm sorry!"

Hua Cheng looked grave. "Did you understand what they were saying again?"

Xie Lian nodded. Hua Cheng reached out and covered his ears.

"Stop listening to them. Those words weren't directed at you."

Xie Lian was still tense, his head tingling. "I know," he managed to say.

Thousands upon thousands of corpse-eating rats came swarming toward the four of them, pouring in like a black tide. This was the royal capital, and its population had been much denser than the previous city—which meant there were more dead and thus more abundant food for the rats. Their numbers were therefore quite large, and they were heavily surrounded. Pei Ming was getting serious; a thin sheen of protection aura had covered him.

"You all leave first. I'll lure them away—"

Before he could finish, the massive ocean of rats screeched and dashed toward him—but they brushed past him and continued running in one direction. He turned his head and saw that they were chasing after the Rain Master!

Without anyone noticing, the Rain Master had remounted her black ox and was running in the opposite direction to distract the rats. The ox had already put a distance of a few dozen meters between them, but he wasn't going too fast—just fast enough that the corpse-eating rats couldn't gain on them, but slow enough that they could keep him in sight. It was the perfect spacing to lead them away without letting them catch up.

The Rain Master called to them from the distance. "My Lords, please continue onward. I can lead them away."

As the Rain Master rode her ox, she scattered fat white grains of rice along the way. Rats loved rice by nature, and it had been countless years since they last saw such succulent grains, so they swarmed after her.

This was what Pei Ming had been planning to do, but the Rain Master had once again stepped forward and robbed Pei Ming of his heroics. His expression was extremely conflicted.

Hua Cheng dropped his hands. "Gege, let's go."

Xie Lian's head throbbed whenever he heard the voices of those corpse-eating rats, and he was able to let out a breath of relief as the voices receded into the distance. He nodded in agreement, but Pei Ming turned to address them.

"Hold on. You're going to leave, just like that?"

"Yeah?" Hua Cheng said.

Pei Ming frowned. "What about the Rain Master? She won't be able to handle this on her own. Isn't it reckless to run off?"

Xie Lian was perplexed. "How come General Pei doesn't think the Rain Master can take care of herself? Wasn't it obvious just now that Lord Rain Master is more than capable?"

Pei Ming didn't seem pleased by the point he made, and he came to a decision. "I don't think so. There's a martial god here, so there's no reason to make a woman official do this sort of work. Your Highness, you two go on ahead. If I can catch up with you later, we'll meet at the holy temple!"

With that, he set off on a chase. Xie Lian called after him a few times until Hua Cheng intervened.

"Let's go, gege. Don't bother with him. He just can't stand being protected by a woman and has to try to salvage his dignity."

Without wasting any more time, they ran through the imperial city and past the multitudes of empty-shelled stone people, toward the massive mountain.

An hour later, they finally set foot on Mount Tonglu's slopes.

The mountain looked like it was dyed the color of blood because all the trees on its slopes were red. They weren't maples, but they were the same fiery crimson color. It was indeed the color of blood, and Xie Lian could also faintly smell its thick stench. It seemed that, over the course of centuries, the plants here had feasted upon all the resentment and human blood that had soaked into the soil.

The fourth Wuyong Temple had been built on a stone outcropping halfway up Mount Tonglu's slopes. This was how it escaped the misfortune of being swallowed by lava. It was the largest of the four temples and also the best maintained. Within the halls there were many stone people, their poses and expressions all different. They had probably been temple attendants. The two ran straight for the grand hall—sure enough, they saw a mural as soon as they entered.

After only a single glance, Hua Cheng said, "It seems someone got here before us."

There was only one mural within the grand hall. While the other two walls themselves were intact, the murals on their surfaces had been slashed and destroyed.

This was the first time something like this had happened, and Xie Lian was dumbfounded.

"Who could've done this?"

They didn't even know who had painted the murals, and now they had to deal with the additional mystery of a mural destroyer. Still, they were short on time, so they studied the mural that remained. From his first cursory glance, not even a close examination, the hair on Xie Lian's neck stood on end.

What was this?!

This mural was completely different from those in the other three temples. There was only one person in the painting. The colors were dark, and the figure's lines and expression were extremely twisted. The person's appearance couldn't be discerned at all; one could only tell that it was a civilian in tattered clothing.

That, in itself, was nothing. What had made Xie Lian shrink back in terror was the fact that the person appeared to be in excruciating pain. He had torn apart his clothing and exposed his flesh.

And upon his body, there were three faces—each one as contorted as his own!

It was Human Face Disease!

Assaulted by such a shocking discovery, the black of this mural invaded Xie Lian's vision entirely. "…It's the same," he mumbled. "It's exactly the same!"

The people of Wuyong had also encountered the Human Face Disease!

Why were the experiences of the Crown Prince of Wuyong, someone from over two millennia ago, so eerily similar to Xie Lian's own?!

Hua Cheng saw how quickly things were going downhill and steadied him. "Your Highness, stop looking at it for now."

But the impact of that image was too great, and the trauma left in Xie Lian's heart by Human Face Disease was too severe. He stared at it like someone possessed. So Hua Cheng simply pulled Xie Lian over and pressed him into his embrace. The tone of his voice was firm but gentle.

"All right. Your Highness, listen to me. Listen to me…" He paused briefly, then continued in a low voice, "You see? The previous murals have told their story chronologically. There is cause and effect. The last one had the Crown Prince of Wuyong building a bridge to the skies, so the next one should depict an event that came right after. But this mural doesn't connect to the last one at all; the timeline doesn't make sense. Isn't that right?"

Xie Lian came back to himself quickly and began to think.

"…You're right, there must be something missing in between. Someone destroyed the previous two murals before we got here."

"If that person destroyed the other two murals, why didn't they destroy this one too?" Hua Cheng asked. "Why did they leave it?"

"There are two possibilities," Xie Lian said. "They might have thought that leaving this mural behind was inconsequential; that it didn't matter if it remained. They weren't concerned with us seeing it."

"And the second possibility?" Hua Cheng asked.

"The person actually did destroy all three murals, and this one was painted on afterward. Meaning that it's *fake*!" Xie Lian said slowly.

"Very right," Hua Cheng replied. "Why not think bigger—maybe *all* the murals we've seen along the way were lies. We're already very close to the answer, so before we get there, don't start overthinking things on your own, all right?"

After being buried in Hua Cheng's arms for so long, Xie Lian was able to finally, completely scrub the horrifying image of the mural from his brain. Only then did he realize the position the two of them were in. He quickly moved to pull himself away from the embrace.

"...How embarrassing, San Lang. I, um..."

However, Hua Cheng didn't let him break away. He instead pulled him in closer, smiling as he did so.

"Nothing to be embarrassed about, but..." He lowered his head. "There's actually a third possibility."

The bottom half of Xie Lian's face was still pressed to his shoulder, and Hua Cheng's voice was right next to his ear. It was extremely, extremely quiet, and no one could hear it except Xie Lian himself. His breath hitched slightly as he heard Hua Cheng whisper.

"The third possibility is that the person *wanted* to destroy all the murals, but they couldn't finish in time. We came in just as they were about to deal with the last one, which means they're hiding here, in the grand hall...right now."

RIDE THE BLACK OX

THE STORY CONTINUES IN
Heaven Official's Blessing
VOLUME 6

Characters

> The identity of certain characters may be a spoiler; use this guide with caution on your first read of the novel.
>
> Note on the given name translations: Chinese characters may have many different readings. Each reading here is just one out of several possible readings presented for your reference and should not be considered a definitive translation.

MAIN CHARACTERS

Xie Lian
谢怜   "THANK/WILT," "SYMPATHY/LOVE"

HEAVENLY TITLE: Xianle, "Heaven's Delight" (仙乐)
FOUR FAMOUS TALES TITLE: The Prince Who Pleased God

Once the crown prince of the Kingdom of Xianle and the darling of the heavens, now a very unlucky twice-fallen god who ekes out a meager living collecting scraps. As his bad luck tends to affect those around him for the worse, Xie Lian has spent his last eight hundred years wandering in solitude. Still, he's accepted his lonely lot in life, or at least seems to have a sense of humor about it. Even for the perpetually unlucky, there's always potential for a chance encounter that can turn eight hundred years of unhappiness around.

Xie Lian has seen and done many things over his very long life and originally ascended as a martial god. While it was his scrap-collecting that saw him ascend for the third time, Xie Lian's feats of physicality are hardly anything to scoff at…though he'd sooner use them as part of a busking performance than to win a fight.

His title Xianle is a multi-layered nickname. "Xianle" is Xie Lian's official heavenly title and also the name of his kingdom. "Xianle" itself can translate to "Heaven's Delight," which ties into Xie Lian's "Four Famous Tales" moniker, "The Prince Who Pleased God." Jun Wu referring to Xie Lian as "Xianle" sounds professional and businesslike on the surface (as Jun Wu generally refers to gods by their heavenly titles only), but it deliberately and not-so-subtly comes across as an affectionate term of endearment.

Hua Cheng
花城   "FLOWER," "CITY"

NICKNAME: San Lang, "third," "youth" (三郎)
FOUR CALAMITIES TITLE: Crimson Rain Sought Flower

The fearsome king of ghosts and terror of the heavens. Dressed in his signature red, he controls vicious swarms of silver butterflies and wields the cursed scimitar known as Eming. His power and wealth are unmatched in the Three Realms, and for this he has as many worshippers as he does enemies (with considerable crossover between categories). He rules over the dazzling and otherworldly Ghost City in the Ghost Realm and is known to drop in to spectate at its infamous Gambler's Den when he's in a good mood.

In spite of all this, when it comes to Xie Lian, the Ghost King shows a much kinder and more respectful side of himself. He does not hesitate for a moment to sleep on a single straw mat in Xie Lian's humble home, nor to get his hands dirty doing household chores at Puqi Shrine. That being said, it's impossible to deny that as he and Xie Lian grow closer, Hua Cheng seems to be growing more and more mischievous… From the very start, his secret identity as

San Lang seemed to be no secret at all to Xie Lian, but Xie Lian still calls him by this name at Hua Cheng's request.

Honghong-er
红红儿 "RED," "RED," FRIENDLY DIMINUTIVE

A young street urchin who Xie Lian saved from certain death long ago, when Xie Lian was a prince in Xianle. Honghong-er is tiny, emaciated, and hardly looks like the ten-year-old child that he is, nor does he act like it. He is constantly on guard and quick to attack, though he strangely seems to become tame—and quite bashful—when Xie Lian is around. He bears immense shame regarding his supposedly ugly appearance and refuses to remove the bandages he wears to cover half his face.

Honghong-er's life has clearly been one of immense suffering and hardship, and he clings to every one of Xie Lian's fleeting acts of kindness toward him as if he has never experienced anything like it before.

The name "Honghong-er" is obviously a nickname—it can be roughly translated to "Little Red."

Young Soldier

A nameless young soldier in the Xianle army. He keeps half of his face hidden beneath bandages at all times and seems determined to stick by Xie Lian's side in battle to protect him, even if it takes him to the most dangerous parts of the battlefield. His remarkable skill with the sword caught Xie Lian's attention and made the god-prince remember him fondly even during the difficult times leading up to Xianle's fall.

HEAVENLY OFFICIALS & HEAVENLY ASSOCIATES

Feng Xin
风信   "WIND," "TRUST/FAITH"

HEAVENLY TITLE: Nan Yang, "Southern Sun" (南陽)

The Martial God of the Southeast. He has a short fuse and foul mouth (especially when it comes to his longstanding nemesis, Mu Qing) but is known to be a dutiful, hardworking god. He has a complicated history with Xie Lian: long ago, in their days in the Kingdom of Xianle, he used to serve as Xie Lian's bodyguard and was a close friend until circumstances drove them apart.

Fu Yao
扶摇   "TAKE OFF/TAKE FLIGHT" (TO MEAN AMBITIOUS)

HEAVENLY TITLE: N/A

A junior official of the Middle Court, hailing from the Palace of Xuan Zhen (Mu Qing's palace). He is cold, quick to judge, and even quicker to roll his eyes. Followers of General Mu Qing do not tend to get on very well with followers of General Feng Xin, and Fu Yao is a proud follower of this trend, as seen through his constant fights with Nan Feng.

Jun Wu
君吾   "LORD," "I"

HEAVENLY TITLE: Shenwu, "Divine Might" (神武)

The Emperor of Heaven and strongest of the gods. He is composed and serene, and it is through his power and wisdom that the heavens remain aloft—quite literally. Although the heavens are full of schemers and gossipmongers, Jun Wu stands apart from such petty squabbles and is willing to listen to even the lowliest creatures to hear their pleas for justice. Despite this reputation for fairness, he does have his biases. In further contrast to the rest of the rabble in Heaven, he shows great patience and affection toward Xie Lian to the point that many grumble about favoritism.

Ling Wen
灵文   "INGENIOUS LITERATUS"

HEAVENLY TITLE: Ling Wen

The top civil god and also the most overworked. Unlike the majority of gods, she is addressed by her colleagues and most others by her heavenly title. She is one of the rare female civil gods and worked tirelessly (and thanklessly) for many years to earn her position. Ling Wen is exceedingly competent at all things bureaucratic, and her work keeps Heaven's business running (mostly) smoothly. She is the creator and head admin of Heaven's communication array.

These days, her name Nangong Jie [南宫杰, "South" 南 / "Palace" 宫 / "Hero" 杰] is only used by her close friend Pei Ming—though he usually calls her the friendly nickname "Noble Jie." She is also close to Shi Wudu, who is known in the heavens for his self-serving personality. Their friend group is dubbed the "Three Tumors."

Mu Qing
慕情   "YEARNING," "AFFECTION"

HEAVENLY TITLE: Xuan Zhen, "Enigmatic Truth" (玄真)

The Martial God of the Southwest. He has a short fuse and sharp tongue (especially when it comes to his longstanding nemesis, Feng Xin) and is known for being cold, spiteful, and petty. He has a complicated history with Xie Lian: long ago, in their days in the Kingdom of Xianle, he used to serve as Xie Lian's personal servant and was a close friend until circumstances drove them apart.

Pei Ming
裴茗　SURNAME PEI, "TENDER TEA LEAVES"

HEAVENLY TITLE: Ming Guang, "Bright Illumination" (明光)

FOUR FAMOUS TALES TITLE: The General Who Snapped His Sword

The Martial God of the North. General Pei is a powerful and popular god, and over the years he has gained a reputation as a womanizer. This reputation is deserved: Pei Ming's ex-lovers are innumerable and hail from all the Three Realms. He is close friends with Ling Wen and Shi Wudu, who are also known in the heavens for their self-serving personalities. This friend group is dubbed the "Three Tumors."

Pei Xiu is Pei Ming's indirect descendant, and Pei Ming took him under his wing to help advance his career in the heavens. He was very displeased when Pei Xiu ruined that career for Banyue's sake, but he seems to have accepted the situation and does not hold a grudge against Xie Lian for his involvement in uncovering the scandal.

Pei Xiu
裴宿　SURNAME PEI, "CONSTELLATION"

HEAVENLY TITLE: N/A

An exiled martial god and a distant (and indirect) descendant of Pei Ming. He's usually called "Little Pei" or "General Pei Junior" for this reason. He is often called in to clean up after his ancestor's messes, but regardless of the circumstances, he always maintains his composure with a polite yet detached air. His ascension to godhood occurred because he led the charge to slaughter the Kingdom of Banyue, and his exile from godhood occurred because of his morally dubious attempts to save his childhood friend Banyue from her fate of eternal punishment.

Quan Yizhen
权一真 "POWER/AUTHORITY," "ONE," "TRUTH/GENUINE"

HEAVENLY TITLE: Qi Ying, "Stupendous Hero" (奇英)

The (current) Martial God of the West. He previously shared this title with his shixiong, Yin Yu. After Yin Yu was banished from heaven, Quan Yizhen holds the title alone. He still yearns for his shixiong's companionship and is convinced that their falling-out was caused by a misunderstanding.

Quan Yizhen has a single-minded focus on martial arts and is considered a prodigy even among heaven's elite. He also has a reputation for beating up his own followers, though this somehow does not damage his popularity in the Mortal Realm. While his skill cannot be disparaged, he is widely disliked in the heavens for his lack of social etiquette. He cares not for the friendship or opinions of his fellow gods, though he has warmed up to Xie Lian.

Rain Master

HEAVENLY TITLE: Rain Master

The elemental master of rain, proper name Yushi Huang. Ascended to the heavens shortly before Xie Lian's own first ascension. The Rain Master is a reclusive heavenly official who is known to reside on a secluded mountain farm named Yushi Country (雨师乡) with many subordinates working in the fields. One of these subordinates is an intelligent talking ox, who is also capable of transforming into a human form that's equally as beefy as his bovine build.

While the Rain Master prefers a quiet and modest life of agriculture, any nefarious creature that's foolish enough to target the domain's farm hands is in for a very rude awakening indeed...

Shi Qingxuan

师青玄 "MASTER," "VERDANT GREEN/BLUE," "MYSTERIOUS/BLACK"

HEAVENLY TITLE: Wind Master

FOUR FAMOUS TALES TITLE: The Young Lord Who Poured Wine

The elemental master of wind and younger sibling of the Water Master, Shi Wudu. Shi Qingxuan ascended as a male god, but over the years, he began to be worshipped as a female version of himself. Shi Qingxuan eagerly embraced this, and she leaps at any opportunity to go out on the town in her female form...and will try to drag anyone she's traveling with into the fun.

Shi Qingxuan is as flighty and pushy as the element they command, and as wealthy as they are generous with their money. They possess a strong sense of justice and will not be dissuaded by notions of propriety. They appear to be close friends with the Earth Master Ming Yi, despite the latter's insistence to the contrary.

GHOST REALM & GHOST REALM ASSOCIATES

Bai Jing

白锦 "WHITE BROCADE"

The human spirit fused with the Brocade Immortal. He was once a young man with immense talent in martial arts who was destined for godhood. However, his life was gruesomely cut short when the girl he was in love with manipulated him into dismembering himself.

CHARACTER & NAME GUIDE

Banyue
半月 "HALF-MOON"

Former state preceptor of the Kingdom of Banyue, now a wrath ghost. She is a scrawny young woman who nonetheless possesses the power to call upon and control deadly scorpion-snakes. Despite her gloomy disposition, she earnestly wishes to save others from suffering, even if it means that she has to suffer in their stead.

Cuocuo
错错 "MISTAKE" (A CHILDISH TERM, LIKE "OOPSIE")

A malice-level ghost resembling a monstrous-looking human fetus. It targets pregnant women and seeks to usurp the place of the children in their wombs—killing both mother and unborn child in the process.

He Xuan
白无相 "CONGRATULATE," "BLACK," "MYSTERIOUS"

FOUR CALAMITIES TITLE: Ship-Sinking Black Water

One of the Four Calamities, Ship-Sinking Black Water. He is a mysterious and reclusive water ghost who rules the South Sea. Like Hua Cheng, he won the bloody gauntlet at Mount Tonglu and wields the power of a supreme ghost. He is consumed by ceaseless hunger and is driven by an equally consuming lust for revenge.

He Xuan disguised himself as the Earth Master Ming Yi for many centuries, and during this masquerade he cultivated a friendship with Shi Qingxuan. Although founded on falsehood, the feelings of friendship that "Ming-xiong" held for Shi Qingxuan seemed to be legitimate.

Jing Wen
敬文 "RESPECT," "LITERATURE"

A former heavenly official, now reduced to possessing a stone statue of a eunuch. He is a two-faced misogynist who used his position of power to abuse and demean his former errand girl, Ling Wen. He fell from his position as the top civil god many centuries ago and has since been entirely replaced and surpassed by Ling Wen.

Kemo
刻磨 "MILLSTONE"

A former general of the Kingdom of Banyue, now a wrath-level ghost. He bears great resentment against the State Preceptor of Banyue, even after his own death, and great hatred for the long-dead kingdom that destroyed his own.

Lan Chang
蘭菖 "GLADIOLUS [FLOWER]"

A malice-level ghost. Formerly a prostitute in Ghost City and now on the run with her monstrous child, the fetus spirit Cuocuo. She is hardly as delicate as her floral name implies—when it comes to throwing insults around on the streets of Ghost City, she can give as good as she gets. In Chinese flower language, the gladiolus flower means "tryst" (for romantic rendezvous) and also "absence." She was formerly known as Jian Lan (剑兰), which is another term for the same flower.

Lang Ying
郎萤 "YOUTH," "FIREFLY"

A mysterious ghost child afflicted with Human Face Disease. He has known nothing but abuse for hundreds of years due to his horrifying appearance, save for the fleeting kindness and warmth of the human girl Xiao-Ying. The combination of this trauma and his almost total lack of human interaction has left him mostly mute and constantly on high alert. Xie Lian was the one to give him this name: Lang being the national surname of Yong'an, and Ying to commemorate the girl who once took care of him.

Qi Rong
戚容　"FACE OF SORROW" OR "RELATIVE," "TOLERATE/FACE"

FOUR CALAMITIES TITLE: Night-Touring Green Lantern

One of the Four Calamities, also called the "Green Ghost." Unlike the other three Calamities, he's actually only a wrath ghost, not a supreme. Gods and ghosts alike agree that he was only included in the group to bump up the number to an even four. (Also, he's just that big a pest.) He is infamous for his crude behavior and ostentatious attempts to copy the style of the more successful Calamities, as well as for his ravenous appetite for human flesh.

More recently, his crimes have expanded to include kidnapping and body-snatching. In an attempt to hide from heaven's detection, he possessed the body of a human man and in doing so acquired a young son named Guzi.

Qi Rong is Xie Lian's younger cousin on his mother's side, much to Xie Lian's everlasting dismay. Surprising no one, Qi Rong has been a source of stress and trouble ever since their mortal childhoods in Xianle. His royal title in Xianle was Prince Xiao Jing.

Rong Guang
容广　"APPEARANCE/TOLERATE," "VAST/NUMEROUS"

A former military officer of the fallen Kingdom of Xuli. He was once Pei Ming's right-hand man and close friend; they were close enough for General Pei to name his sword "Mingguang," a portmanteau of their names. However, he now seeks revenge against Pei Ming as a malice-level ghost fused with that same broken sword.

White No-Face
白无相 "WHITE NO-FACE"

FOUR CALAMITIES TITLE: White-Clothed Calamity

One of the Four Calamities, White No-Face is mysterious, cruel, and powerful enough to battle with the Heavenly Emperor himself—truly, a supreme among supremes. He destroyed the Kingdom of Xianle with the Human Face Disease pandemic. His peculiar fixation on Xie Lian is unnerving, as are his equally peculiar displays of affection.

Xuan Ji
宣姬 "DECLARE," "PROCLAIM" / "CONCUBINE [ARCHAIC]"

A former general of the Kingdom of Yushi, now a wrath-level ghost. Also known as the Ghost Bride. She is obsessed with Pei Ming, who rejected her affections after she tried to take their physical-only relationship to the next level. Her fury at being scorned led to the gruesome deaths of many happy brides-to-be and her eventual imprisonment under heavenly law.

Yin Yu
引玉 "ATTRACT," "JADE"

Yin Yu, also known as the Waning Moon Officer (下弦月使), is Hua Cheng's right-hand man, subordinate, and all-around errand runner. He has been described by some as having a very weak sense of presence and a forgettable appearance. He bears a cursed shackle on his wrist, which marks him as a banished heavenly official. Yin Yu is the former Martial God of the West, who was cast out of Heaven after an incident where he endangered the life of his shidi, Quan Yizhen. He has mixed feelings toward his shidi, and even more mixed feelings over said shidi's dogged insistence on rekindling their former friendship.

Yin Yu's name is taken from the idiom 抛砖引玉 / "pao zhuan yin yu," or "throwing out a brick to attract a jade." It describes the act of making a rudimentary suggestion that is intended to prompt others to come forward with better ideas.

MORTAL REALM & MORTAL REALM ASSOCIATES

Guzi
谷子   "MILLET"

A young human child that Qi Rong kidnapped as a byproduct of stealing the body of the boy's father. Because Qi Rong is possessing Guzi's father, the poor little boy seems blissfully unaware that he's in any danger at all, though that hardly prevents him from enduring plenty of suffering at Qi Rong's hands.

Lang Ying
郎英   "YOUTH," "HERO"

A Yong'an man that Xie Lian made the acquaintance of in the Xianle era. He is a troubled man who has lost much—some might say everything—to the drought and famine that has struck his home region.

Heaven's Eye
天眼开 "HEAVEN'S EYE"

A wealthy, pompous human cultivator who leads a team of cultivators with a similar member profile. Despite his personality flaws, his powers are the real deal. His third eye can see the unseen, and in the process inadvertently reveal exactly how you've been "borrowing spiritual energy" recently.

State Preceptors of Xianle

A quartet of cultivators who serve as Xianle's state preceptors. They are also the religious leaders and head instructors at the Royal Holy Temple, Xianle's premiere cultivation school and largest place of worship for several gods. They are highly skilled cultivators and specialize in the art of divination, though they are very easily distracted by the allure of a game of cards.

The Chief State Preceptor, Mei Nianqing (梅念卿 "plum blossom," "to lecture/to long for," archaic word for minister/high official), is the most talkative of the bunch and has a close relationship with his most cherished student (and biggest headache), Xie Lian. While the names of the three deputy state preceptors are unknown, Xie Lian clearly respects their skill and wisdom.

The plum blossom in Mei Nianqing's name is a symbol of endurance in Chinese flower language, as it blooms in the depths of winter. The plum blossom is also one of the four flowers of the *junzi* (the ideal Confucian gentleman).

Xianle Royal Family

The king and queen of the Kingdom of Xianle, and Xie Lian's parents. Xie Lian's father is of the ruling Xie (谢 "to thank/to wilt") clan, and his mother is of the Min (悯 "to feel pity for/commiserate with") clan. Xie Lian is very close with his mother, who is a doting—if rather naive and sheltered—parent. Xie Lian has a more contentious relationship with his father and frequently squabbles with him.

When Xie Lian's given name (怜 / lian) and his mother's clan name (悯 / min) are written together, they form the word "compassion" (怜悯 / lianmin).

SENTIENT WEAPONS AND SPIRITUAL OBJECTS

Brocade Immortal
锦衣仙   "BROCADE," "IMMORTAL"

A semi-sentient brocade robe possessed by the ghost of a human man, Bai Jing. The name of this object is meant to be a play on the name of the spirit of the man who inhabits it. The Brocade Immortal is an immensely powerful and dangerous artifact—those who wear it can be controlled like puppets if they were given the robe by a person with nefarious intent, and even gods are not immune to its effect.

Eming
厄命   "TERRIBLE/WRETCHED," "FATE"

Hua Cheng's sentient scimitar. With a single blood-red eye that peers out from its silver hilt, it is a cursed blade that drinks the blood of its victims and is the bane of the heavens. It enjoys nothing more than receiving praise and hugs from Xie Lian, and its childish, forward personality is a great embarrassment to its ghostly master.

Fangxin

芳心   "AFFECTIONS OF A YOUNG WOMAN"

An ancient black sword with ties to Xie Lian. An antique, it easily tires when dealing with high-flying heavenly adventures. Xie Lian used the sword's name as an alias while serving as the State Preceptor of Yong'an.

Mingguang
明光

Pei Ming's famously broken sword named after a portmanteau of the sounds from Pei Ming and Rong Guang's names. Rong Guang fused with it to seek revenge.

Ruoye
若邪   "LIKE/AS IF," "EVIL" OR "SWORD"

Xie Lian's sentient strip of white silk. It is an earnest and energetic sort, if a bit nervous sometimes, and will go to great lengths to protect Xie Lian—quite literally, as it can stretch out to almost limitless dimensions.

Locations

HEAVENLY REALM

The Heavenly Capital is a divine city built upon the clouds. Amidst flowing streams and auspicious clouds, luxurious palaces dot the landscape, serving as the personal residences and offices of the gods. The Grand Avenue of Divine Might serves as the realm's main thoroughfare, and this road leads directly to the Palace of Divine Might—the Heavenly Emperor's residence where court is held.

The Heavenly Court consists of two sub-courts: the Upper Court and the Middle Court. The Upper Court consists entirely of ascended gods, while the Middle Court consists of officials who—while remarkable and skilled in their own right—have not yet ascended to godhood.

MORTAL REALM

The realm of living humans. Often receives visitors from the other two realms.

Kingdom of Xianle
仙乐   "HEAVEN'S DELIGHT" OR "HEAVENLY MUSIC"

A fallen kingdom, once glamorous and famed for its riches and its people's love for the finer things in life—such as art, music, gold, and the finest thing of all, their beloved crown prince, Xie Lian. Xianle's gilded exterior masked a declining kingdom plagued by corruption, and Xie Lian's meddling hastened its inevitable collapse in a most disastrous fashion.

Xianle's largest cultivation center, the Royal Holy Temple, sprawled across the peaks of the auspicious Mount Taicang. Its qi-rich landscape nurtures the blanketing forests of fruit trees and flame-red maples. The mountain hosted the kingdom's largest Palace of Xianle for worship of Xie Lian after his ascension, and the Xianle Imperial Mausoleum is located far underground.

Kingdom of Wuyong
雨师   "CROW/BLACK," "MEDIOCRE/ORDINARY/TO HIRE"

An ancient kingdom that was destroyed over two thousand years ago in a volcanic apocalypse and wiped from the annals of history. Mount Tonglu looms at the center of this once-prosperous realm, forever brewing chaos and destruction within its fiery womb. Wuyong is sealed within an evil domain that only opens when Mount Tonglu issues its call to slaughter. Its landscape and remaining wildlife have been distorted by the enormously evil power that periodically spews from the depths of the mountain. However, one just might be able to piece together the remaining fragments of its shattered civilization and learn the truth about what took place during its last days...

Kingdom of Xuli
仙乐   "NECESSARY MULTITUDE"

A fallen kingdom that was once widely known for its military might—and its lust for conquest. Led by the legendary general Pei Ming, it subjugated dozens of kingdoms. Its aspirations of further dominance were dashed after a violent internal insurrection, during which Pei Ming ascended. Missing their star general and torn by strife, Xuli went into rapid decline until it was finally ended for good through the efforts of another former-citizen-turned-heavenly-official, Ling Wen.

Kingdom of Yushi
雨师 "RAIN MASTER"

A fallen kingdom that is best known for being the birthplace of the current Rain Master, Yushi Huang. Yulong Hall was its royal cultivation center, and its disciples were trained through harsh asceticism—even highborn nobles and royalty were not exempt. Yushi Huang's diligent work ethic and humble nature took root here, in stark contrast to the rest of the spoiled Yushi ruling class.

Puqi Village
菩荠村 "WATER CHESTNUT"

A tiny village in the countryside, named for the water chestnuts *(puqi)* that grow in abundance nearby. While small and unsophisticated, its villagers are friendly and welcoming to weary travelers who wish to stay a while. The humble Puqi Shrine—under reconstruction and welcoming donations—can be found here, as well as its resident god, Xie Lian.

GHOST REALM

The Ghost Realm is the home of almost all dead humans, and far less organized and bureaucratic than the Heavenly Realm. Ghosts may leave or be trapped away from the Ghost Realm under some circumstances, which causes major problems for ordinary humans and gods alike.

Black Water Demon Lair

The domain of the reclusive Supreme Ghost King who rules the South Sea, Ship-Sinking Black Water. If one is unfortunate enough to wander into his territory, it will quickly become their final resting place. Should they avoid being eaten alive by the colossal skeletal fish that serve as threshold guardians, the sea itself will devour them instead. Nothing can float upon the waters of the Black Water Demon Lair—all intruders are forfeit to the abyss.

It is said that Ship-Sinking Black Water dwells on Black Water Island, located at the heart of his realm. His residence on the island is called the Nether Water Manor. In stark contrast to Hua Cheng's lively Ghost City, Black Water Island is a silent, gloomy place with few residents other than the master himself.

Ghost City
鬼市　　"GHOST CITY"

The largest city in the Ghost Realm, founded and ruled by Hua Cheng. It is a dazzling den of vice, sin, and all things wicked, which makes it the number-one spot for visitors from all three realms to shop for nefarious goods and cavort under the glow of the blood-red lanterns.

Hua Cheng is rarely present in the city and does not often make public appearances. On the occasion he is in the mood to do so, he is met with considerable adoration; clearly, Ghost City's citizens love their Chengzhu and respect him immensely. His residence within the city is the secluded Paradise Manor, which has never seen guests—at least until Xie Lian came to call, of course.

The city is also home to the beautiful, secluded Thousand Lights Temple, which Hua Cheng dedicated to Xie Lian for reasons the man seems reluctant to elaborate on. It serves double-duty as a place of worship and private school of calligraphy, though Xie Lian doesn't seem to be making much progress on teaching Hua Cheng to write legibly.

OTHER/UNKNOWN

Mount Tonglu
铜炉山   "COPPER KILN MOUNTAIN"

Mount Tonglu is a volcano within the domain of the fallen Kingdom of Wuyong, and the location of the Kiln, where new ghost kings are born. Every few hundred years, tens of thousands of ghosts descend upon the city for a massive battle royale. Only two ghosts have ever survived the slaughter and made it out—one of those two was Hua Cheng.

Name Guide

NAMES, HONORIFICS, & TITLES

Diminutives, Nicknames, and Name Tags

-ER: A word for "son" or "child." Added to a name, it expresses affection. Similar to calling someone "Little" or "Sonny."

A-: Friendly diminutive. Always a prefix. Usually for monosyllabic names, or one syllable out of a two-syllable name.

XIAO-: A diminutive meaning "little." Always a prefix.

Doubling a syllable of a person's name can be a nickname, and has childish or cutesy connotations.

FAMILY

DIDI: Younger brother or a younger male friend. Casual.

GE: Familiar way to refer to an older brother or older male friend, used by someone substantially younger or of lower status. Can be used alone or with the person's name.

GEGE: Familiar way to refer to an older brother or an older male friend, used by someone substantially younger or of lower status. Has a cutesier feel than "ge."

JIEJIE: Familiar way to refer to an older sister or an older female friend, used by someone substantially younger or of lower status. Has a cutesier feel than "jie," and rarely used by older males.

MEIMEI: Younger sister or an unrelated younger female friend. Casual.

XIONG: Older brother. Generally used as an honorific. Formal, but also used informally between male friends of equal status.

YIFU: Maternal uncle, respectful address.

YIMU: Maternal aunt, respectful address.

Character & Name Guide

Cultivation, Martial Arts, and Immortals

-JUN: A suffix meaning "lord."

-ZUN: A suffix meaning "esteemed, venerable." More respectful than "-jun."

DAOZHANG: A polite address for Daoist cultivators, equivalent to "Mr. Cultivator." Can be used alone as a title or attached to someone's family name—for example, one could refer to Xie Lian as "Daozhang" or "Xie Daozhang."

SHIDI: Younger martial brother. For junior male members of one's own sect.

SHIFU: Teacher/master. For one's master in one's own sect. Gender neutral. Mostly interchangeable with Shizun.

SHIXIONG: Older martial brother. For senior male members of one's own sect.

YUANJUN: Title for high-class female Daoist deity. Can be used alone as a title or as a suffix.

ZHENJUN: Title for average male Daoist deity. Can be used alone as a title or as a suffix.

Other

CHENGZHU: A title for the master/ruler of an independent city-state.

GONGZI: Young master of an affluent household.

Pronunciation Guide

Mandarin Chinese is the official state language of China. It is a tonal language, so correct pronunciation is vital to being understood! As many readers may not be familiar with the use and sound of tonal marks, below is a very simplified guide on the pronunciation of select character names and terms from MXTX's series to help get you started.

More resources are available at **sevenseasdanmei.com**

Series Names

SCUM VILLAIN'S SELF-SAVING SYSTEM (RÉN ZHĀ FǍN PÀI ZÌ JIÙ XÌ TǑNG):
ren jaa faan pie zzh zioh she tone

GRANDMASTER OF DEMONIC CULTIVATION (MÓ DÀO ZǓ SHĪ):
mwuh dow zoo shrr

HEAVEN OFFICIAL'S BLESSING (TIĀN GUĀN CÌ FÚ):
tee-yan gwen tsz fuu

Character Names

SHĚN QĪNGQIŪ: Shhen Ching-cheeoh
LUÒ BĪNGHÉ: Loo-uh Bing-huhh
WÈI WÚXIÀN: Way Woo-shee-ahn
LÁN WÀNGJĪ: Lahn Wong-gee
XIÈ LIÁN: Shee-yay Lee-yan
HUĀ CHÉNG: Hoo-wah Cch-yung

XIǍO-: shee-ow
-ER: ahrr
A-: ah
GŌNGZǏ: gong-zzh
DÀOZHǍNG: dow-jon
-JŪN: june
DÌDÌ: dee-dee
GĒGĒ: guh-guh
JIĚJIĚ: gee-ay-gee-ay
MÈIMEI: may-may
-XIÓNG: shong

Terms

DĀNMĚI: dann-may
WǓXIÁ: woo-sheeah
XIĀNXIÁ: sheeyan-sheeah
QÌ: chee

General Consonants & Vowels

X: similar to English sh (**sh**eep)
Q: similar to English ch (**ch**arm)
C: similar to English ts (pan**ts**)
IU: yoh
UO: wuh
ZHI: jrr
CHI: chrr
SHI: shrr
RI: rrr

ZI: zzz
CI: tsz
SI: ssz
U: When u follows a y, j, q, or x, the sound is actually ü, pronounced like eee with your lips rounded like ooo. This applies for yu, yuan, jun, etc.

Heaven Official's Blessing
TIAN GUAN CI FU

Glossary

Glossary

> While not required reading, this glossary is intended to offer further context to the many concepts and terms utilized throughout this novel and provide a starting point for learning more about the rich Chinese culture from which these stories were written.
>
> China is home to dozens of cultures, and its history spans thousands of years. The provided definitions are not strictly universal across all these cultural groups, and this simplified overview is meant for new readers unfamiliar with the concepts. This glossary should not be considered a definitive source, especially for more complex ideas.

GENRES

Danmei

Danmei (耽美 / "indulgence in beauty") is a Chinese fiction genre focused on romanticized tales of love and attraction between men. It is analogous to the BL (boys' love) genre in Japanese media. The majority of well-known danmei writers are women writing for women, although all genders produce and enjoy the genre.

Wuxia

Wuxia (武侠 / "martial heroes") is one of the oldest Chinese literary genres and consists of tales of noble heroes fighting evil and injustice. It often follows martial artists, monks, or rogues, who live apart from the ruling government, which is often seen as useless or corrupt. These societal outcasts—both voluntary and not—settle disputes among themselves, adhering to their own moral codes over the governing law.

Characters in wuxia focus primarily on human concerns, such as political strife between factions and advancing their own personal sense of justice. True wuxia is low on magical or supernatural elements. To Western moviegoers, a well-known example is *Crouching Tiger, Hidden Dragon*.

Xianxia

Xianxia (仙侠 / "immortal heroes") is a genre related to wuxia that places more emphasis on the supernatural. Its characters often strive to become stronger, with the end goal of extending their life span or achieving immortality.

Xianxia heavily features Daoist themes, while cultivation and the pursuit of immortality are both genre requirements. If these are not the story's central focus, it is not xianxia. *The Scum Villain's Self-Saving System*, *Grandmaster of Demonic Cultivation*, and *Heaven Official's Blessing* are all considered part of both the danmei and xianxia genres.

Webnovels

Webnovels are novels serialized by chapter online, and the websites that host them are considered spaces for indie and amateur writers. Many novels, dramas, comics, and animated shows produced in China are based on popular webnovels.

Heaven Official's Blessing was first serialized on the website *JJWXC*.

TERMINOLOGY

ARRAY: Area-of-effect magic circles. Anyone within the array falls under the effect of the array's associated spell(s).

ASCENSION: In typical xianxia tales, gods are conceived naturally and born divine. Immortals cannot attain godhood but can achieve great longevity. In *Heaven Official's Blessing*, however, both gods and immortals were born mortal and either cultivated deeply or committed great deeds and attained godhood after transcending the Heavenly Tribulation. Their bodies shed the troubles of a mortal form and are removed from the corporeal world.

AUSPICIOUS CLOUDS: A sign of good fortune and the divine, auspicious clouds are also often seen as methods of transport for gods and immortals in myth. The idea springs from the obvious association with clouds and the sky/heavens, and also because yun (云 / "cloud") and yun (运 / "luck") sound similar.

BOWING: Bowing is a social custom in many Asian nations. There are several varieties of bow in Chinese culture, which are distinguished by how low the bow goes as well as any associated hand gestures. A deeper bow indicates more respect, and those with high social status will always expect a deeper bow from those with low status. The kowtow (see associated glossary entry) is the most respectful level of bow. "Standing down in a bow" means holding a bowing position while leaving someone's presence.

BUDAOWENG: A budaoweng (不倒翁 / "wobbly old man") is an oblong doll, weighted so that it rolls back into an upright position whenever it is knocked down.

CHINESE CALENDAR: The Chinese calendar uses the *Tian Gan Di Zhi* (Heavenly Stems, Earthly Branches) system, rather than numbers, to mark the years. There are ten heavenly stems (original meanings lost) and twelve earthly branches (associated with the zodiac), each represented by a written character. Each stem and branch is associated with either yin or yang, and one of the elemental properties: wood, earth, fire, metal, and water. The stems and branches are combined in cyclical patterns to create a calendar where every unit of time is associated with certain attributes.

This is what a character is asking for when inquiring for the date/time of birth (生辰八字 / "eight characters of birth date/time"). Analyzing the stem/branch characters and their elemental associations was considered essential information in divination, fortune-telling, matchmaking, and even business deals.

Colors:

WHITE: Death, mourning, purity. Used in funerals for both the deceased and mourners.
BLACK: Represents the heavens and the dao.
RED: Happiness, good luck. Used for weddings.
YELLOW/GOLD: Wealth and prosperity, and often reserved for the emperor.
BLUE/GREEN (CYAN): Health, prosperity, and harmony.
PURPLE: Divinity and immortality, often associated with nobility.

CONFUCIANISM: Confucianism is a philosophy based on the teachings of Confucius. Its influence on all aspects of Chinese culture is incalculable. Confucius placed heavy importance on respect for one's elders and family, a concept broadly known as *xiao* (孝 / "filial piety"). The family structure is used in other contexts to urge similar behaviors, such as respect of a student toward a teacher, or people of a country toward their ruler.

COUGHING/SPITTING BLOOD: A way to show a character is ill, injured, or upset. Despite the very physical nature of the response, it does not necessarily mean that a character has been wounded; their body could simply be reacting to a very strong emotion. (See also Seven Apertures/Qiqiao.)

CULTIVATORS/CULTIVATION: Cultivators are practitioners of spirituality and martial arts who seek to gain understanding of the will of the universe while attaining personal strength and extending their life span. Cultivation is a long process marked by "stages." There are traditionally nine stages, but this is often simplified in fiction. Some common stages are noted below, though exact definitions of each stage may depend on the setting.

- Qi Condensation/Qi Refining (凝气/练气)
- Foundation Establishment (筑基)
- Core Formation/Golden Core (结丹/金丹)
- Nascent Soul (元婴)
- Deity Transformation (化神)
- Great Ascension (大乘)
- Heavenly Tribulation (渡劫)

CULTIVATION MANUAL: Cultivation manuals and sutras are common plot devices in xianxia/wuxia novels. They provide detailed instructions on a secret or advanced training technique and are sought out by those who wish to advance their cultivation levels.

CURRENCY: The currency system during most dynasties was based on the exchange of silver and gold coinage. Weight was also used to measure denominations of money. An example is something being marked with a price of "one liang of silver."

DAOISM: Daoism is the philosophy of the *dao* (道), known as "the way." Following the dao involves coming into harmony with the natural order of the universe, which makes someone a "true human," safe from external harm and who can affect the world without intentional action. Cultivation is a concept based on Daoist beliefs.

DEMONS: A race of immensely powerful and innately supernatural beings. They are almost always aligned with evil.

DISCIPLES: Cultivation sect members are known as disciples. Disciples live on sect grounds and have a strict hierarchy based on skill and seniority. They are divided into Core, Inner, and Outer rankings, with Core being the highest. Higher-ranked disciples get better lodging and other resources.

When formally joining a sect as a disciple or a student, the sect becomes like the disciple's new family: teachers are parents and peers are siblings. Because of this, a betrayal or abandonment of one's sect is considered a deep transgression of Confucian values of filial piety. This is also the origin of many of the honorifics and titles used for martial arts.

DRAGON: Great chimeric beasts who wield power over the weather. Chinese dragons differ from their Western counterparts as they are often benevolent, bestowing blessings and granting luck. They are associated with the heavens, the Emperor, and yang energy.

GLOSSARY

EIGHT TRIGRAMS MAP: Also known as the bagua or pakua, an eight trigrams map is a Daoist diagram containing eight symbols that represent the fundamentals of reality, including the five elements. They often feature a symbol for yin and yang in the center as a representation of perfect balance between opposing forces.

ENTRANCE COUPLETS: Written poetry verses that are posted outside the door of a building. The two lines of poetry on the sides of the door express the meaning/theme of the establishment, or are a wish for good luck. The horizontal verse on the top summarizes or is the subject of the couplets.

FACE: *Mianzi* (面子), generally translated as "face," is an important concept in Chinese society. It is a metaphor for a person's reputation and can be extended to further descriptive metaphors. For example, "having face" refers to having a good reputation, and "losing face" refers to having one's reputation hurt. Meanwhile, "giving face" means deferring to someone else to help improve their reputation, while "not wanting face" implies that a person is acting so poorly/shamelessly that they clearly don't care about their reputation at all. "Thin face" refers to someone easily embarrassed or prone to offense at perceived slights. Conversely, "thick face" refers to someone not easily embarrassed and immune to insults.

FENG SHUI: Literally translates to wind-water. Refers to the natural laws believed to govern the flow of qi in the arrangement of the natural environment and man-made structures. Favorable feng shui and good qi flow have various beneficial effects to everyday life and the practice of cultivation, while the opposite is true for unfavorable feng shui and bad qi flow.

THE FIVE ELEMENTS: Also known as the *wuxing* (五行 / "Five Phases"). Rather than Western concepts of elemental magic, Chinese phases are more commonly used to describe the interactions and relationships between things. The phases can both beget and overcome each other.

- Wood (木 / mu)
- Fire (火 / huo)
- Earth (土 / tu)
- Metal (金 / jin)
- Water (水 / shui)

Flowers:

LOTUS: Associated with Buddhism. It rises untainted from the muddy waters it grows in, and thus symbolizes ultimate purity of the heart and mind.

PINE (TREE): A symbol of evergreen sentiment / everlasting affection.

PLUM (BLOSSOMING TREE): A symbol of endurance, as it blooms in the depths of winter. The plum blossom is also one of the four flowers of the ideal Confucian gentleman.

WILLOW (TREE): A symbol of lasting affection and friendship. Also is a symbol of farewell and can mean "urging someone to stay." "Meeting under the willows" can connote a rendezvous.

FUNERALS: Daoist or Buddhist funerals generally last for forty-nine days. It is a common belief that souls of the dead return home on the night of the sixth day after their death. There are different rituals depending on the region regarding what is done when the spirit returns, but generally they are all intended to guide the spirit safely back to the family home without getting lost; these rituals are generally referred to by the umbrella term "Calling the Spirit on the Seventh Day."

During the funeral ceremony, mourners can present the deceased with offerings of food, incense, and joss paper. If deceased ancestors have no patrilineal descendants to give them offerings, they may starve in the afterlife and become hungry ghosts. Wiping out a whole family is punishment for more than just the living.

After the funeral, the coffin is nailed shut and sealed with paper talismans to protect the body from evil spirits. The deceased is transported in a procession to their final resting place, often accompanied by loud music to scare off evil spirits. Cemeteries are usually on hillsides; the higher a grave is located, the better the feng shui. The traditional mourning color is white.

GHOST: Ghosts (鬼) are the restless spirits of deceased sentient creatures. Ghosts produce yin energy and crave yang energy. They come in a variety of types: they can be malevolent or helpful, can retain their former personalities or be fully mindless, and can actively try to interact with the living world to achieve a goal or be little more than a remnant shadow of their former lives.

Water ghosts are a notable subset of ghosts. They are drowned humans that haunt the place of their death and seek to drag unsuspecting victims underwater to possess their bodies, steal their identities, and take their places in the world of the living. The victim then becomes a water ghost themselves and repeats the process by hunting new victims. This process is known as 替身 / *tishen* (lit. "substitution"). In *Heaven Official's Blessing*, there is a clear story parallel between the behavior of water ghosts and the birth and actions of Ship-Sinking Black Water.

GUQIN: A seven-stringed zither, played by plucking with the fingers. Sometimes called a qin. It is fairly large and is meant to be laid flat on a surface or on one's lap while playing.

GU SORCERY: The concept of gu (蛊 / "poison") is common in wuxia and xianxia stories. In more realistic settings, it may refer to crafting poisons that are extracted from venomous insects and creatures. Things like snakes, toads, and bugs are generally associated with the idea of gu, but it can also apply to monsters, demons, and ghosts. The effects of gu poison are bewitchment and manipulation. "Swayed by gu" has become a common phrase meaning "lost your mind/been led astray" in modern Chinese vocabulary.

HAND GESTURES: The baoquan (抱拳 / "hold fist") is a martial arts salute where one places their closed right fist against their open left palm. The gongshou (拱手 / "arch hand") is a more generic salute not specific to martial artists, where one drapes their open left palm over their closed right fist. The orientation of both of these salutes is reversed for women. During funerals, the closed hand in both salutes switches, where men will use their left fist and women their right.

HAND SEALS: Refers to various hand and finger gestures used by cultivators to cast spells, or used while meditating. A cultivator may be able to control their sword remotely with a hand seal.

HEAVENLY REALM: An imperial court of enlightened beings. Some hold administrative roles, while others watch over and protect a specific aspect of the celestial and mortal realm, such as love, marriage, a piece of land, etc. There are also carefree immortals who simply wander the world and help mortals as they go, or become hermits deep in the mountains.

HEAVENLY TRIBULATION: Before a Daoist cultivator can ascend to the heavens, they must go through a trial known as a Heavenly Tribulation. In stories where the heavens are depicted with a more traditional nine-level structure, even gods themselves must endure and overcome tribulations if they want to level up. The nature of these trials vary, but the most common version involves navigating a powerful lightning storm. To fail means losing one's attained divine stage and cultivation.

HUALIAN: Shortened name for the relationship between Hua Cheng and Xie Lian.

IMMORTALS AND IMMORTALITY: Immortals have transcended mortality through cultivation. They possess long lives, are immune to illness and aging, and have various magical powers. An immortal can progress to godhood if they pass a Heavenly Tribulation. The exact life span of immortals differs from story to story, and in some they only live for three or four hundred years.

IMMORTAL-BINDING ROPES: Ropes, nets, and other restraints enchanted to withstand the power of an immortal or god. They can only be cut by high-powered spiritual items or weapons and usually limit the abilities of those trapped by them.

INCENSE TIME: A common way to tell time in ancient China, referring to how long it takes for a single incense stick to burn. Standardized incense sticks were manufactured and calibrated for specific time measurements: a half hour, an hour, a day, etc. These were available to people of all social classes.

In *Heaven Official's Blessing*, the incense sticks being referenced are the small sticks one offers when praying at a shrine, so "one incense time" is roughly thirty minutes.

INEDIA: A common ability that allows an immortal to survive without mortal food or sleep by sustaining themselves on purer forms of energy based on Daoist fasting. Depending on the setting, immortals who have achieved inedia may be unable to tolerate mortal food, or they may be able to choose to eat when desired.

JADE: Jade is a culturally and spiritually important mineral in China. Its durability, beauty, and the ease with which it can be utilized for crafting both decorative and functional pieces alike has made it widely beloved since ancient times. The word might cause Westerners to think of green jade (the mineral jadeite), but Chinese texts are often referring to white jade (the mineral nephrite). This is the color referenced when a person's skin is described as "the color of jade." Other colors of jade will usually be specified in the text.

JADE EMPEROR: In Daoist cosmology, the Jade Emperor (玉皇大帝) is the Emperor of Heaven, the chief of the Heavenly Court, and one of the highest ranked gods in the Heavenly Realm, lower only to the three primordial emanations. When one says "Oh god/lord" or "My heavens," it is usually referring to the Jade Emperor. In *Heaven Official's Blessing*, Jun Wu's role replaces that of the Jade Emperor.

JOSS PAPER: Also referred to as ghost paper, joss paper is a form of paper crafting used to make offerings to the deceased. The paper can be folded into various shapes and is burned as an offering, allowing the deceased person to utilize the gift the paper represents in the realm of the dead. Common gifts include paper money, houses, clothing, toiletries, and dolls to act as the deceased's servants.

KOWTOW: The *kowtow* (叩头 / "knock head") is an act of prostration where one kneels and bows low enough that their forehead touches the ground. A show of deep respect and reverence that can also be used to beg, plead, or show sincerity.

MERIDIANS: The means by which qi travels through the body, like a magical bloodstream. Medical and combat techniques that focus on redirecting, manipulating, or halting qi circulation focus on targeting the meridians at specific points on the body, known as acupoints. Techniques that can manipulate or block qi prevent a cultivator from using magical techniques until the qi block is lifted.

MID-AUTUMN FESTIVAL: Zhongqiu Jie (中秋節), or the Mid-Autumn Festival, falls on the fifteenth day of the eighth month of the Lunar Calendar. It typically falls around September-October on the Western Calendar. This festival is heavily associated with reunions, both family and otherwise. Mooncakes—also known as reunion cakes, as they are meant to be shared—are a popular food item associated with this festival. Much like the Shangyuan Festival, the Mid-Autumn Festival involves the lighting of lanterns to worship the heavens. It is also commonly associated with courtship and matchmaking.

Numbers

TWO: Two (二 / "er") is considered a good number and is referenced in the common idiom "good things come in pairs." It is common practice to repeat characters in pairs for added effect.

THREE: Three (三 / "san") sounds like *sheng* (生 / "living") and also like *san* (散 / "separation").

FOUR: Four (四 / "si") sounds like *si* (死 / "death"). A very unlucky number.

SEVEN: Seven (七 / "qi") sounds like *qi* (齊 / "together"), making it a good number for love-related things. However, it also sounds like *qi* (欺 / "deception").

EIGHT: Eight (八 / "ba") sounds like *fa* (發 / "prosperity"), causing it to be considered a very lucky number.

NINE: Nine (九 / "jiu") is associated with matters surrounding the Emperor and Heaven, and is as such considered an auspicious number.

MXTX's work has subtle numerical theming around its love interests. In *Grandmaster of Demonic Cultivation*, her second book, Lan Wangji is frequently called Lan-er-gege ("second brother Lan") as a nickname by Wei Wuxian. In her third book, *Heaven Official's Blessing*, Hua Cheng is the third son of his family and gives the name San Lang ("third youth") when Xie Lian asks what to call him.

PHOENIX: *Fenghuang* (凤凰 / "phoenix"), a legendary chimeric bird said to only appear in times of peace and to flee when a ruler is corrupt. They are heavily associated with femininity, the Empress, and happy marriages.

PILLS AND ELIXIRS: Magic medicines that can heal wounds, improve cultivation, extend life, etc. In Chinese culture, these things are usually delivered in pill form. These pills are created in special kilns.

PLAGUES AND DISEASE: In ancient China, plagues and pandemics were considered to be the work of demons or other evil creatures, and were thought to be karmic punishment from the heavens for humanity's evil deeds. It was thought that the gods would protect the righteous and innocent from catching the disease, and mass repentance was the only way to "cure" or banish a plague for good. When the gods determined the punishment served to be sufficient, they would descend and drive out the plague-causing demons.

This outlook is why Human Face Disease is considered in-universe to be a mark against the Kingdom of Xianle's morality and a mark against Xie Lian as both a leader and a god—the plague only affecting Xianle is "proof" that they angered the heavens, and Xie Lian being unable to cure it by his own power is "proof" that he does not have heaven's blessing and is not a true god.

PRIMORDIAL SPIRIT: The essence of one's existence beyond the physical. The body perishes, the soul enters the karmic wheel, but the spirit that makes one unique is eternal.

QI: *Qi* (气) is the energy in all living things. There is both righteous qi and evil or poisonous qi.

Cultivators strive to cultivate qi by absorbing it from the natural world and refining it within themselves to improve their cultivation base. A cultivation base refers to the amount of qi a cultivator possesses or is able to possess. In xianxia, natural locations such as caves, mountains, or other secluded places with lush wildlife are often rich in qi, and practicing there can allow a cultivator to make rapid progress in their cultivation.

Cultivators and other qi manipulators can utilize their life force in a variety of ways, including imbuing objects with it to transform them into lethal weapons or sending out blasts of energy to do powerful damage. Cultivators also refine their senses beyond normal human levels. For instance, they may cast out their spiritual sense to gain total awareness of everything in a region around them or to feel for potential danger.

QI CIRCULATION: The metabolic cycle of qi in the body, where it flows from the dantian to the meridians and back. This cycle purifies and refines qi, and good circulation is essential to cultivation. In xianxia, qi can be transferred from one person to another through physical contact and can heal someone who is wounded if the donor is trained in the art.

QIANKUN: *Qiankun* can be translated to "universe." Qiankun pouches (乾坤袋) or Qiankun sleeves (乾坤袖) are containers that are bigger on the inside, used to easily carry cargo a person normally couldn't manage. Qiankun items are common in fantasy settings.

RED STRING OF FATE: Refers to the myth in many East Asian cultures that an invisible red string connects two individuals who are fated to be lovers. The string is tied at each lover's finger (usually the middle finger or pinky finger).

SECT: A cultivation sect is an organization of individuals united by their dedication to the practice of a particular method of cultivation or martial arts. A sect may have a signature style. Sects are led by a single leader, who is supported by senior sect members. They are not necessarily related by blood.

SEVEN APERTURES/QIQIAO: (七窍) The seven facial apertures: the two eyes, nose, mouth, tongue, and two ears. The essential qi of vital organs are said to connect to the seven apertures, and illness in the vital organs may cause symptoms there. People who are ill or seriously injured may be "bleeding from the seven apertures."

SHANGYUAN: Shangyuan Jie (上元節), or the Lantern Festival, marks the fifteenth and last day of the Lunar New Year (usually around February on the Solar Calendar). It is a day for worshipping and celebrating the celestial heavens by hanging lanterns, solving riddles, and performing Dragon Dances. Glutinous rice ball treats known as yuanxiao and tangyuan are highlights of this festival, so much so that the festival's alternate name is Yuanxiao Jie (元宵節).

SHRINES: Shrines are sites at which an individual can pray or make offerings to a god, spirit, or ancestor. They contain an object of worship to focus on such as a statue, a painting or mural, a relic, or a memorial tablet in the case of an ancestral shrine. The term also refers to small roadside shrines or personal shrines to deceased family members or loved ones kept on a mantle. Offerings like incense, food, and money can be left at a shrine as a show of respect.

SPIRIT BANNER: A banner or flag intended to guide spirits. Can be hung from a building or tree to mark a location or carried around on a staff.

STATE PRECEPTOR: State preceptors, or guoshi, are high-ranking government officials who also have significant religious duties. They serve as religious heads of state under the emperor and act as the tutors, chaplains, and confidants of the emperor and his direct heirs.

STEP-LITTER: [步輦] A "litter" is a type of wheelless vehicle. Palanquins and sedan chairs are in the same category of human-powered transport, but they often have boxed cabins. A step-litter is an open-air platform with a seat/throne atop it, often with a canopy of hanging silk curtains for privacy. Step-litters are usually reserved for those with high status.

SWORDS: A cultivator's sword is an important part of their cultivation practice. In many instances, swords are spiritually bound to their owner and may have been bestowed to them by their master or a family member, or obtained through a ritual. Cultivators in fiction are able to use their swords as transportation by standing atop the flat of the blade and riding it as it flies through the air. Skilled cultivators can summon their swords to fly into their hand, command the sword to fight on its own, or release energy attacks from the edge of the blade.

SWORD GLARE: Jianguang (剑光 / "sword light"), an energy attack released from a sword's edge.

SWORN BROTHERS/SISTERS/FAMILIES: In China, sworn brotherhood describes a binding social pact made by two or more unrelated individuals. Such a pact can be entered into for social, political, and/or personal reasons. It was most common among men but was not unheard of among women or between people of different genders.

The participants treat members of each other's families as their own and assist them in the ways an extended family would: providing mutual support and aid, support in political alliances, etc. Sworn siblings will refer to themselves as brother or sister, but this is not to be confused with familial relations like blood siblings or adoption. It is sometimes used in Chinese media, particularly danmei, to imply romantic relationships that could otherwise be prone to censorship.

TALISMANS: Strips of paper with spells written on them, often with cinnabar ink or blood. They can serve as seals or be used as one-time spells.

THE THREE REALMS: Traditionally, the universe is divided into Three Realms: the **Heavenly Realm**, the **Mortal Realm**, and the **Ghost Realm**. The Heavenly Realm refers to the Heavens and Celestial Court, where gods reside and rule, the Mortal Realm refers to the human world, and the Ghost Realm refers to the realm of the dead.

VINEGAR: To say someone is drinking vinegar or tasting vinegar means they're having jealous or bitter feelings. Generally used for a love interest growing jealous while watching the main character receive the attention of a rival suitor.

WEDDING TRADITIONS: Red is an important part of traditional Chinese weddings, as the color of prosperity, happiness, and good luck. It remains the standard color for bridal and bridegroom robes and wedding decorations even today. During the ceremony, the couple each cut off a lock of their own hair, then intertwine and tie the two locks together to symbolize their commitment.

WHISK: A whisk held by a cultivator is not a baking tool but a Daoist symbol and martial arts weapon. Usually made of horsehair bound to a wooden stick, the whisk is based off a tool used to brush away flies without killing them and is symbolically meant for wandering Daoist monks to brush away thoughts that would lure them back to secular life. Wudang Daoist Monks created a fighting style based on wielding it as a weapon.

YAO: Animals, plants, or objects that have gained spiritual consciousness due to prolonged absorption of qi. Especially high-level or long-lived yao are able to take on a human form. This concept is comparable to Japanese yokai, which is a loanword from the Chinese yao. Yao are not evil by nature but often come into conflict with humans for various reasons, one being that the cores they develop can be harvested by human cultivators to increase their own abilities.

YIN ENERGY AND YANG ENERGY: Yin and yang is a concept in Chinese philosophy that describes the complementary interdependence of opposite/contrary forces. It can be applied to all forms of change and differences. Yang represents the sun, masculinity, and the living, while yin represents the shadows, femininity, and the dead, including spirits and ghosts. In fiction, imbalances between yin and yang energy can do serious harm to the body or act as the driving force for malevolent spirits seeking to replenish themselves of whichever they lack.

ZHONGYUAN: Zhongyuan Jie (中元節), or the Ghost Festival / Hungry Ghost Festival, falls on the fifteenth day of the seventh month of the Lunar Calendar (this usually falls around August/

September on the Solar Calendar). The festival celebrates the underworld, and offerings are made to the dead to appease their spirits and help them move on.